*Praise for Pam Weaver*

'What a terrific read – Saga fans everywhere will love it and be asking for more from this talented author'
Annie Groves

'An engaging and gripping post-war saga . . . a hard-hitting story of female friendship tested against the odds'
*Take a Break*

'A heartrending story about mothers and daughters'
Kitty Neale

'Pam Weaver presents us with a real page-turner – with richly drawn characters and a clever plot'
*Caring 4 Sussex*

'The characters are so richly drawn and authentic that they pull the reader along through the story effortlessly. This book is a real page-turner, which I enjoyed very much'
Anne Bennett

'An uplifting memoir told with real honesty'    *Yours*

# Always in My Heart

Pam's saga novels, *There's Always Tomorrow*, *Better Days Will Come*, *Pack Up Your Troubles*, *For Better For Worse*, *Blue Moon* and *Love Walked Right In*, and her ebook novellas *Emily's Christmas Wish* and *Amy's Wartime Christmas*, are set in Worthing during the austerity years. Pam's inspiration comes from her love of people and their stories and her passion for the town of Worthing. With the sea on one side and the Downs on the other, Worthing has a scattering of small villages within its urban sprawl, and in some cases tight-knit communities, making it an ideal setting for the modern saga.

# Always in My Heart

## PAM WEAVER

PAN BOOKS

First published 2017 by Pan Books
an imprint of Pan Macmillan
20 New Wharf Road, London N1 9RR
Associated companies throughout the world
www.panmacmillan.com

ISBN  978-1-4472-7592-3

A CIP catalogue record for this book is available from the British Library.

Typeset by Palimpsest Book Production Ltd, Falkirk, Stirlingshire
Printed and bound by CPI Group (UK) Ltd, Croydon, CR0 4YY

Visit www.panmacmillan.com to read more about all our books
and to buy them. You will also find features, author interviews and
news of any author events, and you can sign up for e-newsletters
so that you're always first to hear about our new releases.

*For Barrie Arthur Stainer*

# PROLOGUE

## December 1938

The villagers huddled together round the graveside, struggling to keep their umbrellas from blowing inside out. The wind was so gusty it was hard to stay upright on the slippery grass between the gravestones. The vicar of St Margaret's, Angmering, Rev. Thomas Palmer, did his best to ignore the rain as he recited the prayer of the committal, but it wasn't easy with freezing water dripping down his neck and what little bit of hair he had in total disarray. Today was a day when he was glad that his retirement was imminent. Standing out in all weathers like this was for a much younger man. He had given fifteen years of his life to the people of this parish and it was time to hang up his cassock. Life was strange. Who would have thought that he would bury Elizabeth Oliver before her husband? Elizabeth, pretty, vivacious and still a young woman, had been a dutiful wife to Gilbert, even though he was so surly. Although not a church-goer, Elizabeth always had a cheery wave and a smile.

There weren't that many mourners – just a handful

of people, which was surprising because Elizabeth Oliver was only in her late twenties. She had been married for almost three years, and apart from meeting up with Marilyn now and again, she led a quiet life. She had died after falling into Patching Pond. It was a mystery why she was there so late in the afternoon, but Gilbert Oliver, her devoted husband, had tried desperately to save her. The police had ruled out foul play because she liked to collect holly in that area to make Christmas wreaths. She sold them door to door in the village and made them a nice little sum of money, something that a struggling farmer like Gilbert always welcomed. He was aware of the gossip. People said she had married him for his money and the farm, but he wept as he told anyone who cared to listen what a good wife she had been to him.

The pallbearers were preparing to lower the coffin as Rev. Palmer began the familiar words of committal.

'We have but a short time to live. Like a flower we blossom and then wither; like a shadow we flee and never stay. In the midst of life we are in death—'

He was halted by a strangulated cry from among the mourners and Elizabeth's husband pushed his way forward. Men lost their footing and women cried out in shocked surprise as he rushed past them, but before anyone could stop him, Gilbert Oliver staggered over the muddy mound of earth and threw himself across her coffin, sobbing loudly.

'For God's sake, put the soil over me as well. I can't live without her. Oh, Elizabeth, my Elizabeth . . .'

# CHAPTER 1

### August 1939

As the bell on the shop door jangled, Florrie Jenkins turned round. She stood as she always stood, behind the counter of her newsagent shop in the heart of the East End of London, sorting the papers ready for the newspaper boys to begin their rounds.

'Packet of Old Holborn, Florrie.' The early customer was Len Greene, a regular on his way to work. They exchanged a quiet smile, but as she reached up, a sharp pain under her right breast almost took her breath away.

'You all right, my lovely?'

'Bone in me corsets,' she quipped. 'Took me unawares.'

Anyone else would have countered her frankness with a lewd remark, but not Len. She took his money and handed him his tobacco. They had known each other for years and she looked forward to him coming, but she had learned the art of suppressing her feelings for him.

'Betty not in today?' he asked as he waited for change.

'She'll be here later,' said Florrie. 'Seven-thirty is her start time.'

Len took his watch out of his pocket and shook it. 'I must be early, then.'

'You off to the docks?' she asked as she closed the till. The question was superfluous. It was obvious to anyone that he was a dock worker. His work clothes, a cheap jacket with no buttons, were pulled together with a piece of string round his waist, and like all dockers, he had a big metal hook threaded through it. They used it to dig into the cargo sacks, which made it easier to move them around in the tight spaces on-board ship.

Up at five-thirty, like herself, Len was on his way to the wharf to join the other casual labourers waiting by the gates in the hope of being hired for the day. It was a precarious existence because there was no guarantee of work, and of course no work meant no money. They were hard men who lived a hard life, but Len Greene was better than most. Some, if they had nothing better to do, would spend all day drinking in the Huntingdon Arms or some other pub. Len would make his way up to the allotments on Freemason's Road and spend his time more productively. Occasionally if he had a glut of produce, he'd bring it to the shop and she would sell it at a small profit for them both.

'I heard there's a boat load of West African ground-nuts in the docks today,' he said, taking his change, 'and some Rhodesian tobacco.'

'Then you should have waited until you got to work for your baccy,' she joked.

'Should have done,' he chuckled, 'but that stuff is too raw for my liking.' He waved his Old Holborn in the air. 'I like mine matured.' Len touched the edge of his flat cap and turned to go. 'I'd best be off. See you on Tuesday.'

Florrie frowned. 'Tuesday?'

'Tuesday evening,' he said. 'We're getting the Anderson shelter, remember?'

'Oh yes, of course,' said Florrie. 'How could I forget that!'

'Tubby Wilcox and me have managed to borrow a coster barrow. We'll be round at about seven o'clock and I'll help you put it up next Saturday.'

'Thanks, Len,' she said, patting the back of her hair. 'I appreciate that.'

The shelters had been available since February, but she had never managed to get one until now. People earning less than five pounds a week got them for free, but those who had to pay for them were left waiting. Florrie had paid her seven pounds way back in April and here they were on the brink of war and her little back yard was still empty. Not having a man about the house created another problem, but happily, Len and Tubby had offered to help her put it up. 'See you Tuesday after work, then,' she said.

The door closed and Florrie allowed herself a small smile. Len was a man of few words. At one time, there had been a possibility that they might have been more

5

than friends, but as far as Florrie was concerned, it was impossible. She couldn't bear the shame again. How could she tell Len the truth? It would be like Sid all over again, and, she told herself firmly, you can't start a relationship on a lie. Even after all this time, she wished things could have been different, but there it was. She was still married and Len was still single.

Florrie could feel another cough coming on and did her best to suppress it. Damned thing. She'd had it for ages now. Once upon a time, if she caught a cold, she'd have a miserable couple of days and it would be over and done with, but not this time. This was harsh and dry and it left her breathless. When would she shake the flippin' thing off?

Florrie Jenkins was an attractive woman of thirty-eight, slim with light brown hair, which she curled along the nape of her neck and styled with a deep wave on the right side of her head. She wore little make-up – a dab of face powder and a light coating of rose-pink lipstick – but apart from her wedding ring, she wore no jewellery at all. A mother with fifteen-year-old twins, she made her living by running a newsagent-cum-tobacconist.

Alone again, she continued to pile the papers into their rounds. The piles weren't large because her little corner shop didn't have many customers who could afford to have their papers delivered. Most of the people who came into her shop were dock workers, labourers and gaffers, but because it was between Canning Town and the wharf, she had a steady passing trade. Florrie glanced at the front page of the *Daily Sketch*. She had little time to read anything more than the headlines, but it seemed that the papers were filled with the same old depressing stuff. She tutted to herself. After his trip to Munich last year, everybody had hoped that Prime Minister Neville Chamberlain had secured a lasting peace, but as her friend Betty said, 'That old bugger in Germany seems to be hell-bent on taking over the whole bloomin' world.'

Florrie had married Sid Jenkins in 1919. They began married life together living with her father. He had the downstairs rooms, while she and Sid lived upstairs. Her father was a sick man. He had never fully recovered from being gassed in the trenches and he had never really got over what happened to Florrie's mother, but when the twins, Shirley and Tom, were born in 1924, her father adored them. Things might have been all right, but when they'd discovered a few years later that Tom wasn't quite right, she'd been so upset she'd told her husband everything. He'd been appalled and after that, things were never the same.

By the time she'd moved here, in 1930, she was on her own with the twins, now six years old. By then, her father had died, but as luck would have it, during his final days on earth, he had inherited the shop and made a will leaving all his worldly goods to his only child, Florrie. It was the saving of them all.

She sighed. To go through one war was bad enough, but to face it for the second time in a lifetime seemed grossly unfair. According to the headlines, though, it looked as if Betty was right. Adolf Hitler was out to cause trouble, and even though it was a lovely warm August day, the gloomy threat of war hung like a black cloud over everybody's lives once again.

The jangle of the doorbell interrupted her thoughts and the Harper boys, Mick and Joseph, came into the shop.

'You're early today, boys.'

'We're going on the Sunday-school outing, Mrs Jenkins,' said Mick. 'Got to be at the school by eight fifteen.'

'We're going on a coach,' said Joseph in awed tones.

'Are you indeed,' said Florrie, heaving the bags full of papers off the counter. The effort made her start coughing again. She pressed her handkerchief to her mouth as the boys set out. Mick was already halfway towards the door with his bag of papers, but Joseph lingered. 'Is your Shirley coming, Mrs Jenkins?'

Florrie tucked her handkerchief back up her sleeve and rubbed her ribs. 'Are you going from Hallsville School?' Although she'd stopped coughing, she had a terrible stitch in her side. The boy nodded. 'Then yes, she is,' she said, turning her back so that he didn't see her wince with pain.

The boys hurried out of the shop and Florrie managed to pull herself together. The children were all going to Southend for the day and she was glad. Who knew what the poor little beggars faced if that damned Hitler had his way? She wasn't going with them. Shirley would be helping the Sunday-school teachers with the little ones, and Tom . . . well, Tom would be happy enough if his sister was with him. With a reasonable proportion of her customers off on a beano, which was what the people around here called a trip to the seaside for the day, Florrie was going to make the most of it. She couldn't afford to shut the shop – it was her only income – but Betty would be here before long, and Doreen was coming over later on for a natter and a cup of tea.

There was a short lull and then a few more customers came in. That's how it was in the shop: nobody for a while, then a mad rush. Some passed the time of day or chatted, while others only grunted. Nevertheless, by the time the next lull came, she'd heard that little Molly Smith had chickenpox, Mrs Payne's son, Charlie, had signed up for the merchant navy, and there was to be a jumble sale at St Luke's next Saturday. Florrie glanced up at the clock. Ten past seven. As soon as Betty Carr arrived, she'd have to make sure Shirley and Tom were ready or they would be late.

Standing at the door, she called up the stairs and was pleased to hear Shirley was already up. 'Get your breakfast and make some sandwiches for your lunch,' she instructed.

'Yes, Mum.'

About a quarter of an hour later, Betty bustled through the shop door. She was a well-built woman, homely, with her hair cut short and tightly permed. 'Hello, darlin',' she said cheerfully. 'Everything all right?'

Florrie nodded. 'Fine,' she said. 'I just need to make sure the kids get off all right.'

Betty hung up her coat and made her way to the counter. She had worked in the shop with Florrie ever since their children were small. As a married woman, it was unusual for someone like her to be out to work, especially doing the long hours she put in, but her husband, Raymond, was in the merchant navy and at sea most of the time, and Betty hated being on her own. Of course, in the beginning, she was busy bringing up their son, but he had joined the navy at sixteen. She hadn't liked the idea but compulsory conscription had started in April, so he would have had to have gone by now anyway.

Out in the kitchen, Shirley heard the murmur of voices and knew that Auntie Betty had arrived. Any minute now, her mother would take a break and come through, so she poured the boiling water into the teapot ready for her.

'Mick Harper tells me you have to be at the school by eight fifteen,' Florrie said as she walked through the door.

Shirley nodded as the two of them moved gingerly around each other to do what they needed to. Their property was small, but they had more room than most people in Canning Town. There were two bedrooms upstairs, and the one over the shop was quite spacious. She and her mother slept there, while her brother, Tom, had the back room, which was much smaller. Downstairs, there was a small stockroom at the rear of the shop and a passageway that led to the kitchen-cum-sitting room. In the scullery beyond, they had a copper, a single tap over the earthenware sink and a gas cooker. Outside, there was a lavvy and a rather dilapidated lean-to, where Florrie grew tomatoes in the summer months. The kitchen was heated by a range, which Shirley had to black-lead every Saturday morning. Studying her reflection in the mirror over the dresser, Shirley began taking the kirby grips out of her kiss curls.

'Is your brother up?' her mother asked. She was reaching for the teacups.

'Having his wash,' said Shirley.

Florrie sat in front of her steaming cup and took some money out of her purse. 'This is a little something for you both, but I want you to look after it,' she said, handing it to her daughter. 'Get Tom an ice cream and let him have a ride or two in the funfair, but don't give him the change. You know the bigger boys will only persuade him to give it to them.'

With a nod of her head, Shirley put the money into her pocket. 'Thanks, Mum.' She was grateful, and her mother had been generous, but she was tempted to have another go at her about doing a paper round. All she wanted was a bit of independence, and she could only have that if she had her own money. It was really galling that her mother wouldn't let her earn something for herself.

'Mum, I appreciate what you've given me, but if you

would let me do a paper round,' Shirley began, 'you wouldn't have to give me money.'

'Oh, Shirley, we've been over this before,' said Florrie with a sigh. 'It's not safe. They don't call round here "Draughtboard Alley" for nothing. You never know who's out there, and I dread to think what might happen to you, especially if there was paper-round money in your pocket.'

Shirley knew there was no malice in the nickname; after all, Canning Town was truly cosmopolitan. Being in such proximity to the docks meant that people from all over the world and every nationality roamed the streets: African, Asian, Chinese, French, Irish, West Indians . . . you name it, they were there. Most of them were fine, but of course there was always the risk of one bad apple in the barrel, and with whispered horror stories about white-slavers roaming the streets, her mother wasn't taking any chances.

'The boys have no problem,' Shirley retorted.

'The boys can take care of themselves.'

'I can take care of myself too,' Shirley insisted, but by the look on her mother's face she already knew her entreaty was falling on deaf ears. It was so unfair. Look at all the times she'd protected Tom from the bigger boys. She'd been ferocious and had even built up a bit of a reputation. Nobody took the mickey out of Tom Jenkins when she was around. Not any more they didn't.

Florrie coughed. Shirley turned to look at her, her

luscious curls bouncing on her shoulders. 'You really should go to the doctor again, Mum.'

'I'll be fine,' Florrie smiled.

'But you won't, will you?' said Shirley. 'You always make me and Tom go when we're not well, so why won't you go and see if he can't at least give you a cough mixture?'

'If I still have it on Monday,' said Florrie, 'I'll go.'

'Promise?'

Her mother nodded reluctantly, and her brother, Tom, came out of the scullery looking clean and tidy. Florrie stood up and straightened his tie, and then he sat down in front of the bowl of porridge Shirley had put on the table.

'Are we going to see any animals, Shirl?'

His sister scraped a little butter onto her toast. 'It's possible,' she said. 'There may be donkeys on the beach, or perhaps a photographer's monkey on the prom.'

Tom's eyes lit up.

'Don't get your hopes up, son,' Florrie cautioned. 'You'll have to wait and see.'

Tom glanced at Shirley and she motioned her head towards his spoon. If they let him talk too much, he'd forget to eat and that would make them late. Shirley had been looking forward to this outing for ages, so the last thing she wanted to do was miss the coach.

At eight o'clock, Florrie stood at the door of the corner shop to wave them off. Excited, the two of them ran up the street with hardly a backward glance. Florrie's emotions were mixed. She loved them equally, but she worried about Tom. At first glance, you would never believe that they were twins. Tom was as stocky and tough-looking as his sister seemed fragile. They were both wonderful kids and for fifteen years they had been model children. Whatever she asked of them, they both did their best, and they hadn't given her a day's trouble. Only ten minutes separated them and yet they were worlds apart. Shirley, the elder, was bubbly and vivacious, a pretty girl who was on the brink of becoming a lovely young woman. Her thick dark hair, so beautifully curled today, was the envy of all her friends. Her face was still slightly round, but once she lost her puppy fat, Florrie knew she'd be a real stunner. Before long, boys like Joseph Harper would be two a penny. Shirley was petite rather than small, but what she lacked in size she more than made up for in strength – both physical and mental. Shirley was gregarious. She made friends easily and she was fun to be around.

Tom, on the other hand, was different. He had been born the wrong way round and although the doctor had assured her that he was fine, Florrie knew right from the start that he'd been damaged in some way. At school, he was considered 'simple' and his teachers had low expectations of him. In fact, there was only one occasion when he wasn't bottom of the class, and that was only because the child at the bottom had missed almost a year of schooling while he battled polio. With less than a year to go before he went out to work, poor Tom still struggled. His marks were way down and in fact his name was synonymous with the words 'bottom' and 'last'. Usually the boys who couldn't do their lessons well were encouraged to do things like woodwork, but Tom was hopeless at that too. For that reason, he was teased mercilessly. She'd been up to the school a few times to complain, but the headmaster only promised to 'look into it'.

'You can't fight his battles all his life, Mrs Jenkins,' he'd said. 'The boy has to learn to stand up for himself.' The stupid man didn't seem to understand that Tom was incapable of fighting his own corner and that a child like him needed protecting.

Thankfully, Shirley had become his champion. It took a while, but after giving Tom's chief tormentor, a boy called Ivan Stokes, a bit of a bashing, much of the bullying stopped. Florrie wasn't sure if she should condone such behaviour, but boys like Ivan didn't want the reputation of being beaten up by a girl, and a little one at that, so she'd turned a blind eye and Tom seemed a lot happier.

Her son's appearance belied his temperament. He was a solid-looking boy with broad shoulders and the same dark hair as his sister, but if someone so much as raised his voice to him or put him down in any way, Tom found it impossible to retaliate. Florrie despaired of him. What did life hold in store for the likes of Tom Jenkins? How would he manage without someone there to look after him? He was kind and gentle with a passion for animals, but he had no friends at all.

As she watched her children disappear round the corner, Florrie spotted Doreen Kennedy coming up the street. She waved, and moving the large box she was carrying under one arm, Doreen waved back. Florrie felt a shiver of excitement. After waiting all this time, Doreen had brought it with her! Florrie could hardly wait.

Of the three of them, Doreen was the oldest. Forty-one and a spinster, Doreen had never found Mr Right, even though she had moved in far better circles than either Florrie or Betty. Betty always said she was too fussy, but Florrie was convinced it was more to do with Doreen's mother. Elsie Kennedy was a bitter woman who seemed to take great delight in spoiling things for her daughter. Florrie had never quite forgiven her for the time she'd faked an illness to stop Doreen going out with Bill Powers. At least the years had been kind to Doreen – she could easily pass for a much younger woman. Even if she married tomorrow, though, it would probably be too late for a family, which was such a shame. Doreen would have made a wonderful mother.

'The kids have got a lovely day for it,' said Doreen as she came up to her. She leaned forward and gave Florrie a peck on the cheek. 'And I've brought your order for you to try on.'

As soon as the driver stepped outside, there was a surge to be the first onto the coach. The boys wanted the back seats, and preferably without too much overbearing adult supervision. There were several adults on the coach, and because it was impossible for Florrie to close the shop for a whole day, Mrs Keene, one of the women workers from the local Boys' Club, had agreed to keep an eye on Tom and Shirley. Once everyone was seated, but before they left London, the curate of St Luke's, Rev. Goose, affectionately known by the parishioners as 'Father Goose', briefed everyone about the trip.

'We must all stick together as a group,' he told them. 'No sloping off on your own. Is that understood?'

There was a collective groan from the boys.

'We shall begin with a period of time on the beach, then after lunch, and I hope you've brought your sandwiches with you, we shall go to the Kursaal to enjoy the amusements.'

That brought a much happier response.

'And at the end of the afternoon,' Mrs Keene interrupted, 'we shall all line up and walk along the front to the Sunny Side Cafe, where we shall enjoy high tea.'

'What's "high tea"?' somebody whispered.

'You eat it on a stepladder,' someone else quipped, and there was a ripple of laughter.

Shirley was halfway down the coach, sitting next to Tom, who was looking out of the window. Her friends Ann Bidder and Helen Starling were across the aisle. There was a loud cheer as the driver started the engine and the coach moved off.

The journey was uneventful. They soon left the closely packed streets of East London and travelled on through main shopping thoroughfares, attractive leafy suburbs and finally the countryside itself.

Her brother turned to her. 'Can you tell me the story again, Shirl?'

17

Shirley looked around. She didn't like doing it with other people listening, but Tom was getting into a bit of a tizzy and it did help to calm him down. 'Only if I can do it quietly,' she said. Tom smiled and she leaned towards him.

'*The papers were saying that another girl had gone missing. Lucy Dacomb hadn't been seen since last week,*' she began.

'Do you think the children were scared?' asked Tom.

Shirley shrugged. 'I think so. I'd be scared if lots of my friends went missing, wouldn't you?'

Tom's eyes sparkled with anticipation. She'd told him the story of the Birthday Thief several times already, but he wanted to hear it again and again. It was hard to remember every little detail of the story because she'd made it up as she went along, but if she missed an important bit out, Tom was sure to tell her. She glanced over her shoulder. Helen and Ann said it was babyish to keep on repeating the same things, but if the truth were known, Shirley enjoyed telling the story, and every time seemed more exciting than the last.

'Go on,' said Tom eagerly. 'First of all, Billy's nan spots him sneaking out on his bike. What then?'

'"*Where do you think you are going?*"' said Shirley, acting out the voice.

'"*Nowhere," said Billy.*

'*Nan put her hand on her hip. "And where's nowhere?*"'

'Mum says it like that sometimes, doesn't she?' Tom interrupted.

18

'Are you going to let me tell you this story or not?' said Shirley crossly.

Tom became silent and his sister carried on. *'"I'm only going over to Dan's house," he said.'*

'But he's not, is he?' Tom chipped in.

Shirley ignored him. *'"Have you and your brother been fighting again?" said his nan.*

*'"No."*

*'"Then why not take him with you?"*

*'"I can't hang about, Nan," he said. "Danny's waiting." He put his leg over the saddle of his bike and pushed off down the path.*

*'"Don't go near the field, will you?"'*

Tom began chortling with excitement.

*'"I won't," said Billy. Billy hadn't been in the field since Megan disappeared.'*

Shirley had to speak up now. The further they were away from home, the louder the noise levels grew. After a while, Tom found it difficult to handle and ended up with his hands over his ears.

A little later, they had reached Basildon and the boys at the back were pelting him with screwed-up bits of paper. Shirley tried to stop them, but in the end, Rev. Goose, who was sitting at the front near the driver, came and told the boys on the back seats that if they didn't stop messing around, he would personally tan their hides. The rowdies quietened down after that.

They stopped at the toilets near the war memorial in South Benfleet and then boarded the coach for the last leg of the journey. Before long, someone spotted the sea and the excitement in the coach reached its peak.

'I wish we had time to go round the shops when we get there,' Helen whispered. 'I wanted to buy a lipstick.'

Ann's eyes grew wide. 'Will your mum let you wear lipstick?'

'Of course not,' said Helen. 'I'd only put it on when she's not around.'

'They're very expensive,' Shirley remarked.

'Well, I've seen them in Woolworths for one and eleven,' said Helen with a defiant shrug of her shoulder.

Shirley was suddenly tempted to buy one herself. Everybody said she looked more like seventeen than fifteen. If she wore lipstick, she might even get into the pictures to see an X-film on her own. They said Edward G. Robinson was very good. She'd always wanted to see him. 'Why don't we go to Woolworths?' she said, feeling deliciously naughty. 'If we get caught, we could always pretend we got lost trying to find the toilets.'

The three of them looked at each other with sparkling eyes as they savoured the idea of their own wickedness.

Ann took in a breath. 'Go on, then. Let's do it.'

'Can I come too?' Tom's voice boomed through the coach and several people turned round. Shirley jumped. He'd been so quiet since they'd all got back in the coach she'd almost forgotten he was there. Helen and Ann sat up straight and gazed out of their window, doing their best to pretend they didn't know what he was talking about.

'Shh,' Shirley said, elbowing him as she looked around nervously. 'And no, you can't.'

Tom was puzzled. 'Why not? I'd like to go to Woolworths. I could get a lipstick too. Mum said I should stay with you all the time.'

Listening to the stifled giggles all around her, Shirley felt her heart sink. Now she was torn. She desperately wanted to be with her friends, but it would be no fun at all with Tom tagging along, and besides, he was bound to give the game away.

'Let me come, Shirl. Please. I want to go to Woolworths.'

'All right, all right,' said Shirley. 'Just keep your voice down, will you?'

He stayed silent for about thirty seconds and then said in a voice just as loud as before, 'Why do I have to keep my voice down? Is it a secret, Shirl?'

'We're not taking him, Shirley,' Helen hissed when Shirley glanced at her, and rolled her eyes.

Shirley looked at them helplessly, but Helen and Ann just glared at her and she knew then that she wouldn't be going to buy lipsticks with them. Now she was annoyed with Tom. His crass behaviour had spoiled something that promised to be a little bit exciting, but at the same time, she knew she wouldn't be angry for long. Her brother couldn't help the way he was.

'I'm not going anywhere without you, Tom,' she said. 'All right?'

He nodded cheerfully. 'All right, Shirl.'

When she turned her attention back to her friends,

Helen and Ann had their heads together and were whispering. Shirley felt her stomach tighten with disappointment. She loved her brother, but because of him, she was often left out of things. Helen and Ann were busy planning, and once again Shirley wasn't included.

While Betty served in the shop, Doreen and Florrie were alone in the sitting room. Doreen placed the big box on the table and jerked her head towards it. 'You open it. Go on. I know you're dying to.'

Florrie tore the brown paper from the box and ran her hand lovingly along the beautiful copperplate letters on the lid, which were silver-embossed. *Spirella*. She glanced up at Doreen and smiled. 'I've waited a long time for these,' she said as she lifted the lid and pulled back the layers of soft tissue paper. A little air escaped her lips as her brand-new, made-to-measure corset first saw the light of day. It looked amazing. She fingered the ivory-coloured material and ran her fingers along the thick lacing.

Three months before, in her role as a Spirella representative, Doreen had come to the house to measure Florrie. For years Doreen had saved every penny she could so that she could afford to pay for her training as a corsetière and in 1935 she had finally made it. She'd spent several months at the Factory of Beauty in Letchworth Garden City learning her craft. For Doreen, it had been a magical time. Spirella were world-renowned for the way they looked after their staff. The factory girls themselves could have lessons in shorthand, book-keeping and typewriting if they wanted, all paid for by the company. She was expected to work hard, but the company also provided plenty of things to do in her leisure time. If she wasn't in the reading library, Doreen enjoyed folk dancing, outings and even taking part in the Spirella Olympics! At the end of her training, she bought herself a franchise and set to work building up a clientele. All her hard work paid off because last year Doreen was awarded a certificate for having the largest customer base in the country.

Florrie pulled her new corset out of the box and held it up to the light. 'It's beautiful.'

'Here, let me help you,' said Doreen.

'No,' said Florrie. 'You won't be here to do it for me every morning, so I'd better do it myself.'

'That's true,' smiled Doreen, 'but it will be easier if I show you the best way to get it on and make sure that the lacing at the back is really snug.'

They spent the next twenty minutes or so ensuring Florrie was fitted properly and that she felt comfortable. 'I never would have thought of lying on my back to do it up,' she said as Doreen helped her to her feet.

'Just make sure you remember to put a cushion under your bottom,' said Doreen. 'That way, when you're lying flat, all your internal organs are in the right place.'

'Will I have to get someone to undo the lacing at the back when I get undressed?'

'Oh no,' said Doreen. 'I suggest you leave that alone. All you need to do is do up the front and pull the straps here and here.'

Florrie patted her flat stomach. 'I can't believe how slim I look.'

'Get used to it,' said Doreen. 'A Spirella corset will last you for years.'

When she emerged into the shop, Betty was lavish with her praise. 'You've done an amazing job there, Dor,' she said. 'And I swear you look twenty-one again, Florrie.'

The three friends laughed together.

Florrie dragged three upright chairs onto the pavement outside the shop. 'We may as well enjoy a bit of the warm weather ourselves,' she said. 'There's little passing trade today and it wouldn't take much for one of us to get up and serve a customer, should one materialize.'

With a pot of tea on the card table, the three friends sat down to enjoy a decent natter. It was a strange time. In some respects, life went on as normal, although the streets were quieter than usual. A couple of weeks ago, several families left for Kent to enjoy a break from the overcrowding and pollution and do a bit of hop-picking. Canning Town was changing anyway. The long traffic queues to get into and out of the dock had been alleviated by a new approach road called Silvertown Way, and earlier in the decade, the council had embarked on a slum-clearance programme. Long-term residents relocated to new homes with indoor plumbing and, more importantly, space to move. The area boasted new clinics, children's nurseries and even a lido. That building programme had slowed down in the last two years as the sabre-rattling between Britain and Germany had increased. There was a lot of talk about working for peace, but already sandbags had been placed around important buildings, and public air-raid shelters were springing up everywhere.

'I can't stay too long,' Doreen cautioned. 'Mother will start to worry.'

'So how is your mother?' Florrie asked Doreen. She didn't really want to talk about Mrs Kennedy, but she was aware that she should at least show a little concern.

'Her feet are playing up again,' said Doreen. 'I have to do all the housework myself now. In fact, I was thinking of getting a cleaning lady in, but Mother says we can't afford it.'

'And can you?' Betty asked.

'I think so,' said Doreen, 'but Mother handles all the finances.'

Florrie looked away. Yes, and if you didn't have to do the housework, you might be out somewhere enjoying yourself, she thought acidly. Mother wouldn't like that!

'Surely you get a reasonable wage from your business, dear,' Betty remarked. 'You always seem to have plenty of customers.'

'I give it all to Mother,' said Doreen. 'She gives me pocket money. I don't need a lot, so I'm all right.'

Florrie pursed her lips but said nothing. Mrs Kennedy had a stranglehold over her daughter, which had only tightened as the years went by. In fact, Doreen's last little 'rebellion' must have been all those years ago when she'd gone to Letchworth to do her training with

Spirella. Mrs Kennedy had disapproved strongly, and made no secret of the fact, but for once in her life, Doreen had insisted. She wasn't an unattractive woman and had come close to marrying just the once, but it all fell through for some mysterious reason, and since then she had devoted her life to the care of her mother.

'What about you, Betty? How are you coping?'

'The house is a bit empty without Ken and Raymond,' she admitted, 'but apparently we may have people billeted on us before long.'

'I'm not sure Mother would take kindly to strangers in the house,' Doreen remarked.

'She may not have a choice,' Betty said sagely. 'What about you, Florrie? Are you sending the kids away to the country when the evacuation starts?'

'I don't think so,' said Florrie. 'I wouldn't worry about Shirley, but I can't imagine Tom settling down with someone he'd never met before. Besides, who would take him?'

'Vera's little girl, she's blind and she's going,' said Betty.

'Yes, but she's going with the whole school,' said Florrie. 'They'll all be in the same boat. Poor Tom is expected to be the same as everyone else, only he isn't.'

The other two nodded in agreement and a little chill settled over them.

'I heard a good joke the other day,' said Florrie, deliberately brightening up. 'There was this farmer who put a notice up in his field. "I will give this field to a contented man." A few days later, a man knocked on his door. "I am a very contented man," he said, "so I've come to claim the field." "Is that right?" said the farmer. "Well, if you're so contented, why do you want my field?"'

There was a second or two of silence; then Betty threw her head back and laughed, and Doreen joined in. Florrie smiled. 'Now, who wants an iced bun?' she said. 'I bought some from Mr Bolton especially.'

Southend was even more wonderful than Shirley could ever have imagined. Overlooked by boarding houses and hotels, the promenade led to a fairly small stretch of sand. They were disappointed until Rev. Goose explained that the tide was in and the beach would get progressively bigger as the day wore on. The beach itself was absolutely packed, but Mrs Keene managed to find a narrow area under the sea wall where she and the children could be together. Rev. Goose made it his business to collect a few deckchairs for the other adult helpers in the group, and the children sat on the sand either on an old army blanket, brought along for the purpose, or on their own towels. Somehow or other each person had a small area of sand to play on and before long they were making sand pies and building sandcastles.

Shirley and some of the bigger girls took some of the little ones down to the water's edge for a paddle. A few had brought swimsuits and they enjoyed splashing about. Tom wandered along with them, searching for shells, which he put into his pockets as he followed the ever-growing area of shingle along the water's edge. Shirley had no idea why he wanted them, but knowing her brother, he had a plan somewhere in that muddled head of his. Under Father Goose's expert eye, some of the older boys set about building an elaborate fort complete with moat and stream.

At twelve-thirty, everybody ate their lunch. Those who had sandwiches shared theirs with those who didn't. They watched one of the pleasure boats pull into the jetty to disgorge its passengers and take on a queue of people waiting for a trip along the shoreline. A toilet break came next and Shirley and the older girls took the smaller children. Telling their charges to stay with Shirley, Helen and Ann snuck off, and a second or two later, Shirley saw them running towards the town. They really had gone without her! Shirley's eyes stung with unshed tears. Oh, it wasn't fair! She felt a mixture of disappointment, envy and a little slither of fear, but amazingly, when they all congregated together again, nobody missed them. Not even when Rev. Goose bought every child and the adults an ice cream while they sat on the sand to watch the Punch-and-Judy show.

The trek to the Kursaal was a bit of a nightmare, but once they had arrived, Rev. Goose assigned a manageable ratio of children to adults or older girls, to make sure everyone was looked after. Tom, confused by all the noise, was content to stay close to Shirley and watch. No one managed to persuade him to go on a ride, but he did win a goldfish in a jam jar when he got a wooden hoop over a stand on the hoopla stall. He was delighted. It was only as they left the amusements that Helen and Ann were missed and a major panic ensued.

'Has anyone seen them?' Rev. Goose demanded, and when he was met with blank expressions, his face grew purple. 'Where on earth have they gone? If someone knows anything about this and I find out you've said nothing, I shall be extremely angry.'

Shirley busied herself with the little ones, bending low in case Father Goose saw her blushing. Eventually, the police were called and it looked as if the whole day was going to be ruined. Shirley didn't know what to do. Should she tell them that her friends had probably gone to Woolworths?

In the end, it was decided that Mrs Keene and one of the other Sunday-school teachers should go in a police car and be driven around the resort in the hope of spotting them. The rest of the party would go on to Sunny Side Cafe for high tea, as arranged. As the crocodile of excited children weaved its way slowly through the crowds, Shirley kept a lookout in case she spotted Helen and Ann first. She hoped to warn them of the pickle they were in so that they could get their stories straight. It was difficult to find them in the crowds, especially while she was holding the sweaty hands of two tired and hungry little ones. Tom trailed behind her with his goldfish in the jam jar.

The tea was amazing. They had more sandwiches, pork pies, sausage rolls and jelly and trifle, followed by chocolate cake. As the meal drew to a close, Ann came

into the cafe, escorted by a policeman. She was looking very red-eyed and upset, and it was obvious that
she'd been crying. Rev. Goose sat her at a table far away
from the others. He seemed fairly cross but anxious as
well. Shirley was conscious of the adults with their
heads together, whispering. It was bad enough that Ann
was in trouble, but where was Helen?

Back on the coach, Helen still hadn't materialized,
and Ann sat hunched up in her seat occasionally wiping
her tears away with a handkerchief. As Shirley and Tom
sat down, he put his jam jar on the floor and took a
cigarette packet out of his pocket. For a second, Shirley
panicked. Where had he got fags from? She hadn't
given him any money, just like Mum said. Tom pushed
the packet open to reveal not Player's Navy Cut cigarettes but a curled-up worm.

'Ugh,' said Shirley. 'Where did you get that from?'

'I found it,' said Tom. 'I'm going to look it up in my
book.'

The creature was about six inches long, pinkish-red
with a small head. It didn't seem to have any eyes, but
it was covered in something that looked like bristles.

Just at that moment, Father Goose came by counting
heads. 'What have you got there, Tom?'

'It's my pet,' said Tom, closing the cigarette packet.

'And do you know what it's called?'

'Walter,' said Tom seriously.

'Actually,' said Father Goose, 'it's a lugworm. I think
I'd better take it up to the front of the coach in case it

escapes, don't you? You can have it back when you get home.'

'Helen still isn't here, sir,' Shirley reminded him.

Father Goose nodded. 'I know where she is, thank you, Shirley.'

Reluctantly, Tom handed Walter and his goldfish over; then with everyone on board, except Helen, they set off, leaving behind the smell of the sea, the fresh air and the sunshine. Once they were well under way, Father Goose started a sing-song, and as the rest of the coach party burst forth with 'Ten Green Bottles', Shirley slid into the seat next to Ann's.

'What's happened to Helen? Has she been taken ill?'

Ann turned her tear-stained face towards her. 'Oh, Shirl, it was awful. She's still at the police station and she has to wait for her mum and dad.'

Shirley's mouth gaped. 'For buying a lipstick?'

Ann moved a little closer. 'Helen has been arrested for shoplifting.'

As she said her goodbyes to Betty and Doreen, Florrie started another coughing fit. This one was worse than ever. It was impossible to stop and it was gathering momentum. She was forced to lean forward and brace herself against the wall as she struggled to get her breath back. Her head felt as if it would explode and the blood pounded in her face. She brought up her tea before she could finally press her handkerchief to her mouth to stop it.

Betty, who had gone inside to fetch Doreen's coat,

came running out of the shop. 'You all right, love?' she said, concerned. 'Here, let's get you back inside.'

Florrie was aware of the two of them helping her through the door and plonking her onto the chair in front of the counter, which had been placed there for elderly customers. She was still trying to control herself when suddenly she realized she'd tiddled her pants. 'I'll be all right,' she said, anxious that her friends should never know. 'You go. You'll miss the bus.'

By now tears filled her eyes, and the stitch in her side was unbearable, but the minute she thought she'd stopped coughing, it would start all over again.

'Shut the door, Doreen,' said Betty, 'and turn the sign for a minute. I'm just going out the back.'

Florrie heard the bell jingle as Doreen closed the door, and a second or two later, Betty thrust a glass of water in front of her. 'That cough of yours is getting much worse, Florrie,' she said.

'I think we should get Dr Pringle to call,' said Doreen. 'If I run along now, he might come before evening surgery.'

'No need,' Florrie rasped.

'Don't listen to her, Dor,' said Betty. 'I've been telling her for weeks to get that cough seen to, but she won't go. I've never seen it as bad as this.'

Florrie waved her arm in protest, but inside her chest, her lungs were screaming. Once the spasm had died down, she held her throbbing head with one hand and did her best to breathe normally. When she took her handkerchief away from her mouth, she heard Betty gasp. Florrie looked down at it and reeled back in horror. Now there was no denying that something was very wrong. The pretty snow-white cotton was covered in blood.

# CHAPTER 2

Florrie was resting on the sofa when Doreen got back from the telephone box. She looked pale and exhausted, but at least she had stopped coughing.

'Dr Pringle says he'll be here within the hour.'

Betty came downstairs with a blanket and put it over her friend. The three of them avoided each other's eye. Nobody wanted to voice the fears they all shared, and each of them hoped against hope that she was wrong. Doreen made some tea and filled a hot-water bottle for Florrie to cuddle.

Dr Pringle was as good as his word. He arrived at the shop twenty minutes later. A robust-looking man with greying hair and a slight paunch, he had to knock on the kitchen window because Betty had put a *Closed due to illness* notice on the shop door. She and Doreen waited in the shop while he did his examination.

'She'll have to go away if it is what I think it is,' said Betty bleakly. 'And if that's the case, what's going to happen to Shirley and Tom?'

'I guess I'm the obvious one to take them in,' said

Doreen. They were talking in anxious whispers. 'But I know my mother would never agree.'

'And I can't manage the shop and the children,' said Betty, idly rearranging a couple of tins on the shelf so that the whole label showed. 'I have my own place to run as well, and besides, my Raymond will be home on leave next week.'

'There are plenty of people who will have Shirley,' Doreen observed.

'But not Tom,' said Betty, saying the unthinkable out loud for the first time. 'I know she wouldn't want it, but it looks like he might end up in a home.'

The two friends looked at each other helplessly. 'Is that why she didn't want them evacuated?' said Doreen.

Betty nodded. 'Florrie has always been afraid that if Tom went into a home, he'd never come out again.'

'Oh, what are we going to do, Betty?' Doreen said anxiously. 'She's in no fit state to make proper decisions, and they start moving everybody out on Saturday.'

'It's too late for them to be evacuated now,' said Betty. 'She told the woman from the WI in no uncertain terms to bugger off.'

Doreen couldn't resist a wry smile. 'That sounds like our Florrie.'

Dr Pringle came into the shop. 'I'll make arrangements for Mrs Jenkins to have an X-ray as quickly as possible,' he said in his usual businesslike fashion. 'Ideally she should be in bed, but I can't persuade her to go. One thing is absolutely certain: she can't work in the shop any more, and I've told her if I catch her serving customers, I shall shut the place down immediately.'

'Is it that bad, Doctor?' asked Betty.

'Coughing over the customers isn't a good idea,' said Dr Pringle, 'but more importantly, she needs to rest.'

Betty nodded sagely. 'I'll make sure she does, Doctor.'

He gathered his things and headed towards the exit. 'If my suspicions are correct,' he said, his hand on the door handle, 'Mrs Jenkins will have to go away for at least a year. You needn't tell anyone or they won't want to shop here any more, but something will have to be arranged for the children.' He unlocked and pulled open the shop door. 'Good afternoon, ladies.'

'Looks like you were right,' said Doreen, staring at the closed door. 'Do you think she realizes?'

'Only one way to find out,' said Betty with a sigh.

Back in the kitchen, Florrie had been crying. 'What am I going to do?' Her voice was choked with emotion. 'The shop is my livelihood. Without that income, my kids will starve.'

'Don't you worry about that, love,' said Betty, patting her hand. 'We'll soon sort something out. I'll still be here, and I'm sure some of the neighbours will help out.'

'For a day or two, perhaps,' said Florrie. 'Dr Pringle was talking about a whole year! I can't be away from home that long. And who's going to look after Shirley and Tom?' She gave them a fiercely independent look. 'Before you say anything, I won't send them to a children's home.' Then sucking in her lips, she added, 'No,

36

it's impossible. I can't go and there's an end to it. I just can't.'

Doreen perched on the edge of the sofa. 'Florrie, be sensible. If this is what we all think it is and you refuse to go for treatment, in a year's time you won't even be here for Shirley and Tom.'

Behind her, Betty took in her breath. 'Hang on a minute, Dor—'

'No, Betty, we all have to face facts. It's no good pretending everything is going to be fine. It won't. You need that treatment, Florrie, love. You have no choice.' Doreen's expression was firm.

Florrie covered her face with her hand. She made no sound, but they knew she was crying.

Doreen patted her shoulder. 'If the worst comes to the worst, I'll go and see someone from the Sally Army. They have some good contacts. I'm sure they can find someone to take them in.'

Florrie gulped back some of her tears. 'Maybe I could make some sort of private arrangement. I have got a bit of money put by – not a lot, but it might help to find the right person.'

'You'll need that money for yourself,' said Doreen. 'I don't know how much the X-ray will cost, but the cheapest sanatoriums are at least five guineas a week.'

'Five guineas!' Florrie gasped. Her friend nodded. 'Five guineas a week for a whole year . . .' She burst into tears.

Betty and Doreen looked at each other helplessly. If Florrie really did have to stay in a sanatorium for a year, it meant that she would have to find 260 guineas – an awful lot of money, and that was just for her own care. That didn't take into account the doctor's fees, and paying someone to look after Shirley and Tom would be on top of that.

'Don't forget you'll have the takings from the shop . . .' Betty added cautiously.

'You'll need to take your wages,' said Florrie. She tried to dry her eyes with her already sodden handkerchief. 'You must take it.'

'I will, don't you worry,' said Betty.

Florrie wasn't convinced. 'I mean it, Betty. If I let you do this, promise me you will. Promise.' Her anxious entreaty started another fit of coughing, but fortunately, she didn't bring up any more blood. They heard the shop door open and Shirley calling, 'Mum, we're home.'

Florrie half sat up. 'I don't want the kids to know about this just yet,' she said earnestly. 'If they ask what's wrong with me, just say I'm a bit under the weather, that's all.'

'Mum?'

'In the kitchen, love.'

Betty reached for her coat and hat. 'Try and rest as much as possible. I'll pop round again tomorrow.'

The children bounded into the room. 'Mum? There's a note on the shop door. Are you ill?'

'I'm just a bit tired, that's all,' said Florrie with a chuckle. 'Auntie Betty and Auntie Doreen and I have been nattering all day and it's worn me out. Nothing to worry about. I'll be as right as ninepence in the morning.'

'I lost Walter,' said Tom, coming over to his mother, 'but I've still got my shells.'

'Who's Walter?' asked Doreen.

'His lugworm,' said Shirley.

Doreen looked away quickly lest he saw her half-grin. He might be taller than her but he was still only a kid.

'Did you have a nice time?' said Florrie, and spotting the goldfish in the jam jar, she added, 'What's that?'

Tom beamed. 'I won it.'

Everybody admired it, and after he'd told them about winning it on the hoopla stall, Betty said, 'I think you need a bit more water in that jam jar. Looks like you've spilled some. Goldfish like cold water and I reckon you've been cuddling it so hard that the water has got a bit too warm as well.' She took him to the sink and they put the jar under the cold-water tap. As the water cascaded in, the goldfish swam around dizzily.

Doreen stuffed five bob into Shirley's hand. 'To save your mum cooking tonight, why don't you pop down to the chip shop and get your tea? I'm sure you'd like a nice bit of cod, wouldn't you, Florrie?'

'Can I have some cherryade?' Tom called over his shoulder.

'Course you can,' said Doreen, shooing Shirley back out of the door. 'Come on. I'm going that way to the bus stop. We'll walk together.'

Florrie mouthed, 'Thank you,' and leaned back on

39

the sofa, while Tom put his goldfish in the jam jar on the table and got all his shells out of his pockets to show her. He'd been a bit upset when Walter in the fag packet had mysteriously disappeared. He only found out when he got off the coach. 'I can't think what happened to him,' said Father Goose with an apologetic shake of his head. 'One thing I do know. Lugworms like to burrow in the sand. He probably got off the coach and wandered back to Southend.'

School didn't start for another week, but Florrie had had a letter from the head at the end of the summer term, asking for all pupils to come to the school hall for compulsory gas-mask practices, which were to be overseen by a member of the local newly formed Air Raid Precaution Unit, the ARP they called them for short. With Shirley and Tom gone, Florrie took the opportunity to go for her X-ray.

She had to go to the Mildmay Medical Mission Hospital in Hackney Road, Shoreditch. It was a fair step, especially when she wasn't feeling too well, and although she had gone armed with her cheque book, to her great delight, there was no charge because the fee was being taken out of a charitable fund. Florrie felt a mixture of relief and embarrassment.

'I am able to pay,' she began, but the nurse behind the desk waved her hand. 'Dr Pringle has it all arranged,' she said, speaking in a discreetly quiet manner. 'If you have a problem with that, perhaps you would like to take it up with him.'

For the X-ray, she was required to remove her stays and brassiere. Clad only in a hospital gown, she walked into the X-ray department, where she was positioned in front of a large black plate. The room was rather cold. Having told her to put her arms down by her sides and stand up straight, the technician slotted a large black piece of metal behind the plate and instructed her to take a deep breath. It wasn't easy, because that always set off her coughing again, but eventually the man was satisfied and asked her to change her position so that he could view her from the side. To him, it was just a job, but Florrie was very self-conscious. It had been years since a man had seen her in a state of undress. When it was over, she dressed quickly and was glad to get out into the warm sunshine.

She told herself it really was nothing to worry about, but at the same time, she knew she had to be realistic. A few weeks ago, when the woman from the WI had come round to take down the particulars of her children, Florrie had told her what she'd told the school. She didn't want Shirley and Tom sent away. They had argued, but Florrie was adamant. When the WI lady, a rather rotund middle-class, middle-aged woman who had probably had it cushy all her life, said she was an absolute fool, Florrie lost her rag. 'Don't you come in here telling me what to do,' she'd snapped. 'Just bugger off, will you!'

She regretted her rudeness now. Supposing old Hitler really did send all those bombers over like they were saying. Being so near the docks was just about the worst place they could be. She'd been an utter fool. Her kids would be like sitting ducks and she wouldn't be there to protect them.

Of course, Florrie had a perfectly good reason to hold back. Her biggest fear was for Tom. Shirley was quite a resilient child and she would adapt to any situation, but Tom always found change devastating. She and Shirley understood him and could handle his foibles, but people who didn't know him all too easily resorted to shouting at him or hitting him to get him to do what they wanted. How could she put him at the mercy of strangers miles away from home? Yet if she was as ill as Dr Pringle had hinted, it was highly likely that she'd have no choice.

At the end of another bus journey, Florrie found herself in a leafy suburb. A few yards down, she came to a detached house set back from the road. Florrie stood in the road for a while looking up at the windows. It must be all of twenty-two years since she'd last stood here. Florrie had wracked her brains half the night for some other way, but she kept coming back to this. She had always been a fiercely independent woman and hated asking favours, but needs must . . . She wouldn't, she told herself, be doing this for herself. This was for her kids. This was for Shirley and Tom. Mustering all her courage, she walked up to the door and knocked. When a maid wearing a black dress and a white apron opened the door, Florrie asked to speak to Mrs Andrews.

'Do you have an appointment?' the girl said coldly.

Florrie shook her head. 'But if you wouldn't mind—'

'I'm sorry,' said the girl, looking down her nose. 'Madam doesn't see anyone without an appointment.'

'Yes, but—' Florrie began again.

'I'm sorry,' the girl repeated as she began closing the door.

Florrie was appalled, but just before the door finally closed, she heard a voice behind the maid saying, 'Who is it, Sally?'

'She didn't give her name, madam,' said Sally, 'but it was nobody important. Just one of the women from the docks.'

Deeply offended, Florrie called out, 'It's Florence Jenkins, madam. Mrs Andrews, I need to speak to you. I need your help.' But by now she was talking to the wood.

As Florrie turned to leave, the door flew open and Mrs Andrews, facing towards the house, came out onto the step. 'That's no way to treat anyone who comes to my door,' she was saying to the maid. She turned towards Florrie. 'Florence, I do apologize, my dear,' she said. 'Please come inside.'

The maid gave her an insolent stare as Florrie walked past. Florrie avoided her eye. She felt angry and humiliated. How dare she? A woman from the docks indeed.

Florrie followed her into a bright sitting room with a small Axminster rug in the middle of several comfortable-looking chairs. 'Please sit down,' said Mrs Andrews, and turning to the maid, she said, 'Bring us some tea, will you, Sally?' The maid left the room with a surly expression.

43

'I must apologize again, Florence. She's new to the post and not used to our ways.'

'Please . . .' said Florrie, shaking her hand to dismiss the need for an apology.

'So,' said Mrs Andrews, 'to what do we owe this pleasure? Are you well? And the children?'

'Oh, madam, I desperately want to speak to you,' said Florrie. She lowered her head and stared at her own hands. 'I've come to ask for your help.'

Mrs Andrews pushed the cushion back and relaxed into her chair. 'Fire away.'

But Florrie didn't know where to start. Asking for anything was alien to her. She was the type of woman who just got on with it. She'd never asked for help, not even when her husband left. She glanced up at Mrs Andrews's kindly face, remembering the past and all that had happened. Back then, Mrs Andrews had said if ever she needed help, she was to go to her at once. Florrie had dismissed the offer with a wave of her hand, but here she was again. And desperate too. She'd never wanted to bother the woman again, but what could she do? Florrie knew Mrs Andrews was a busy person. Her nephew, Rev. Goose, who lived near Canning Town, had already gained quite a reputation in the area, and St Luke's was the best-attended church for miles. A whizz with a table-tennis bat and a keen footballer, Father Goose, as the kids nicknamed him, was a popular, fun-loving man. When he had arrived in 1933, unlike some of his rather aloof counterparts, he'd knocked on doors and made himself known in the pubs and clubs of

44

the East End. He'd made himself one of them. His aunt, a spritely woman still, despite her advancing years, was just as popular. Married to Dr Andrews, she played an active part in the community. She was a member of the Townswomen's Guild and several other organizations as well. Florrie guessed that Sally was probably some silly girl who, like herself, had found herself in a spot of trouble and Mrs Andrews was giving her a fresh start.

Mrs Andrews was sitting on the edge of her seat, giving Florrie her full attention. Florrie took a breath and sucked in her lips, but as she was about to begin, the door burst open and the maid came in with a tray of tea. They waited until she had clattered it down on the occasional table and left the room.

Mrs Andrews smiled. 'Let's begin again, dear.'

It took every ounce of courage she had, but finally Florrie explained everything. She had been hasty. She'd said no to evacuation and now it looked as if she might be too ill to care for her children. The WI lady had said that if she refused to let her put Shirley and Tom on her list, their places would be given to other children. What was even worse, she'd become irritated by the woman's insistence and she'd been rude. In fact, she'd used a swear word, and for that she was truly sorry, but instead of looking shocked or telling her off, Mrs Andrews threw her head back and laughed. 'You swore at her? Oh dear, poor Cynthia, but don't worry, I suspect she'll dine out on that tale for several weeks.'

Florrie's eyes filled with tears when she talked about Tom. She didn't say it, but in her heart she'd always felt that the way Tom was had been her punishment for giving away the baby. How would she have coped without Mrs Andrews back then? When she'd told her about the pregnancy, Mrs Andrews hadn't taken the moral high ground as so many others had done. She'd offered to arrange everything. Right now, the ache in Florrie's chest wasn't just from the cough, it was the ache of loss. The loss of that pretty little girl she'd last seen when she was only a week old. She swallowed hard. Now she was making a fool of herself. She was losing control. The words just gushed from her like a waterfall. She was saying far too much.

Mrs Andrews left her own chair and came to sit on the sofa next to Florrie. Taking her hands in hers, she said, 'There's no shame in asking for help, my dear. I shall be pleased to do what I can.'

Florrie looked up at her. 'Do you ever hear anything about—'

'You know better than to ask me that,' said Mrs Andrews firmly. 'Best to leave the past where it is. Right now, we have to concentrate on you. I'm sorry to hear about your health, but let's hope you'll soon be on the mend.'

They smiled at each other even though they both knew the words were hollow and that Florrie's recovery, if there was to be one, would take an awfully long time.

'Now,' said Mrs Andrews, giving Florrie's hands a final squeeze, 'here's what we'll do.'

\* \* \*

'You must keep your mask with you at all times,' Miss Lloyd, Shirley's teacher, reminded everybody, 'and be ready to put it on at a moment's notice.' Several children were already yawning. They'd all heard the instruction so many times before. The school had been holding gas-mask drill for many months. 'What do we look for if there is a gas attack?'

Several hands shot up. Miss Lloyd pointed at Tom.

'The pillar boxes change colour,' he said without looking directly at her.

'That's right. Well done, Tom. The postboxes have been coated in special paint.' She glanced over at the ARP warden. 'Who can tell me what we listen for?'

One of the younger children got her hand up first.

'Yes, Pat?'

'The warden will turn the rattle,' said Pat, and as if on cue, the warden lifted a heavy wooden rattle and gave it three or four turns. It was very loud. Tom put his hands over his ears and rocked himself gently.

'Good,' said Miss Lloyd, ignoring him, or perhaps not even noticing. 'Now, put on your respirators. Chin in first and then pull the straps over your head.'

They all spent the next few minutes putting their own gas masks on, the older children helping the younger ones. They had to sit for five minutes with the gas mask on before they were allowed to take it off. It wasn't a pleasant experience. The masks were made of rubber, which was hot and smelly, and sometimes the see-through window got steamed up. The filter in the snout was quite heavy, but the rest of the mask was sucked in

47

and pushed out as you breathed. Then one of the older boys discovered that by blowing hard with the mask on, the rubber made a rude noise rather like a loud fart. The idea soon caught on and before long the whole room had erupted into a cacophony of loud giggles and more rude noises.

'That's enough!' snapped Miss Lloyd. 'The next person who does that will be sent straight to the head-master.'

It was tempting to lift the mask by pulling up the heavy snout, but they had to learn to pull the straps back over their heads and then take it down from the face. This was tricky because sometimes a few hairs got caught in the straps and were torn from the roots as the mask came off, which could be quite painful. As Shirley took her mask off, she noticed Ann was in the room. She was too far away to speak to, and there was still no sign of Helen, but she was pleased to see that her friend had returned to school. Shirley gave her a shy smile, but Ann averted her gaze.

'Who can tell me what I should do if I've got a blister burn after taking my mask off?' said Miss Lloyd.

Several hands shot up. 'Don't rub it,' said Victor when she pointed to him. 'And put some number-two cream on it.'

'Good. But what if I've run out of number-two ointment?'

'Use soap and water,' Tom boomed, and everybody laughed.

'Quite right, Tom,' said Miss Lloyd. 'Well done.' She

dismissed the assembly and Shirley hurried over to the place where Ann was sitting, but even though she called out her name, by the time she got there, her friend was gone. Shirley felt hugely disappointed. She wandered along with the others towards the playground but decided to pop into the toilet on the way there. As she walked through the cloakroom door, Ann came out of a cubicle and the room was filled with the sound of flushing water.

'Ann!' cried Shirley. 'It's so nice to see you. How are you? Can you come back to mine to play?'

Ann looked very uncomfortable. 'I'm not supposed to talk to anyone.'

'Why ever not?' cried Shirley.

'I have to go,' said Ann as she washed her hands. 'The Welfare lady is waiting for me outside.'

'Why have you got a Welfare lady? And where's Helen?'

'I never should have gone with her to Woolworths,' said Ann confidentially. 'It's been awful. She told them it was all my idea and that I put the stuff in her pocket.'

Shirley was confused. 'Stuff? What stuff?'

'She stole six lipsticks,' said Ann. 'I've got to go to court next week and tell the judge.' Ann finished washing her hands and reached for the roller towel. 'Helen's not my friend any more. My mum says she'll end up in an approved school.'

Shirley was stricken. 'Oh, Ann.'

'And if the judge doesn't believe me,' she said, wiping away an angry tear with the palm of her hand, 'I'll have to go there too.'

The door burst open, making both girls jump. A big woman in a brown dress and matching jacket came into the toilets. 'Hurry up, Bidder,' she said sharply. 'And I thought I told you not to talk to anybody.'

Ann hung her head. 'Yes, Mrs Harris. Sorry, Mrs Harris.'

'She only asked me to pass her the soap,' said Shirley, trying to be helpful.

Mrs Harris glared at her and Shirley felt tears in her own eyes as they closed the door, leaving her alone.

# CHAPTER 3

Len Greene and Tubby Wilcox knew it would be a bit of a struggle getting the Anderson shelter onto the coster barrow. Both men were tired. It had been a long day at the docks unloading Rhodesian tobacco. A true East Ender, and in his early thirties, Tubby acted as if it was his sole purpose in life to avoid anything physical unless there was a financial reward. For that reason, Len had slipped him ten bob to enlist his help.

Florrie wasn't the only single woman Len and his mates had helped out in these increasingly difficult times. He still liked Florrie a lot. There was a time when they'd gone for walks together, although she would never let it get more serious. He would have liked it to, but he'd got all tongue-tied and missed his chance. Len had served his time in the Great War. He used to tell everybody he'd gone in as a boy and came out a changed man. It took years for the nightmares to stop. Florrie was an independent woman and a real looker. He'd never known her husband, but apparently he'd turned out to be a rotter and a feckless father as well. Rumour had it that as soon as it became clear that Tom was a bit different, Sid had run off with a publican's wife, leaving Florrie to cope on her own. Given a decent length of time, Len would have made a play for her, but she was haunted by something in her past, so he made the fact that she owned the shop his excuse for not being more assertive. He didn't want people saying he was only after her for her money.

The Anderson shelter was in bits and the barrow much smaller than they'd envisaged.

'I'm bloody cream-crackered,' said Tubby. 'I hope this ain't going to take long.'

'Don't worry, pal,' said Len. 'I've got some extra help.'

Len had encouraged Tom to come along as well. It would do the boy good to feel useful.

'Bloody 'ell,' said Tubby when he saw Tom. 'What's 'e doing here? He's not going to be much use, is he? He's as thick as a bloody brick.'

'He'll be fine,' said Len.

The shelter, which was supposed to accommodate six people, consisted of six curved panels made of galvanized steel. There were also six straight sheets, which had to be bolted on either side, and finally two panels for either end, all of which needed to be loaded onto the barrow. It was hot and sweaty work. Unfortunately, they hadn't gone very far when Tubby noticed a wheel flying down the road just ahead of them.

'Look at that,' he laughed. 'Some poor bugger's lost his wheel.' It wasn't so funny when he realized that he was the 'poor bugger' because the barrow suddenly developed a severe list to port and one by one the sheets of corrugated steel clattered onto the road.

'What the . . . !' cried Tubby, standing in the road holding on to the handles of the empty barrow.

Tom looked slightly confused, but Len was laughing like a drain. 'It's not funny,' Tubby grumbled, but it took several minutes for Len to control himself again.

'Right,' he said eventually, 'if you lift it, I'll shove the wheel back on.'

'I've got a bad back,' said Tubby, suddenly remembering. He turned to Tom. 'Come on, twerp, you lift it up so that we can get the bugger back on.'

Tom lifted the barrow effortlessly and then began picking up the sheets of corrugated iron as if they were pieces of cardboard. With a lot of heaving and swearing on Tubby's part, the job was done in no time.

'I had him down as two sandwiches short of a picnic,' Tubby whispered in Len's ear, 'but that boy is a ruddy marvel.' He turned to Tom. 'You'd make a great boxer.'

'Tom doesn't like fighting, do you, Tom?' said Len, giving Tom an affectionate nudge with his elbow.

Tom made no eye contact, but he shook his head.

Tubby lit up a woodbine. 'You should think about it, sonny,' he said. 'I know a good gym where you could train. You could be bloody world champion before you're twenty.'

'Come on, then,' said Len. 'Let's get going.' But the barrow only managed a few yards before the wheel came off again and they were forced to watch the whole lot clatter onto the pavement once more.

Tom began manoeuvring the barrow so that he could lift it up enough for Len to put the wheel back on, but Tubby had had enough. 'Florrie's place is a mile away,' he cried. 'If you fink I'm doing this every few yards, you can bloody well fink again.'

'We can't let her down,' said Len as Tom brought the wheel back, but Tubby was all for giving up and going home. 'Do it one more time,' Len coaxed, 'and I'll buy you a pint at the Taverners.' This was costing him a fortune.

By now, a crowd of Tom's schoolmates had joined them in the street. Tom lifted the barrow and Len pushed the wheel into place. It only remained for them to get all the sheets back on top, but this time it was a lot easier with half the street lending a hand. The wheel stayed in place until they were thirty yards from the Taverners; by then, Tubby's thirst had got the better of him, so they went inside. Tom waited on the doorstep, and a second or two later, Len came out with a cherry-ade and a packet of crisps. Inside the Taverners, Tubby had his pint and the regulars had quite a laugh when they heard the story.

The rest of the journey was just as fraught with problems but far more manageable and a lot more fun. They had three more stops to put the wheel back on before they reached Florrie's shop. Although the men were all a bit the worse for wear, with help from the schoolboys, the shelter had arrived safe and sound. Len and Tom trundled the parts into Florrie's small back yard, and the rest of the men set off for the pub down the road for more refreshments.

'I'll be back on Saturday, my lovely,' Len called out as he left, 'to help you put it up.'

When they'd gone, Florrie sighed. She hadn't the heart to tell them she might not be around by Saturday.

Dr Pringle knocked on the door the next morning. Florrie had been trying to do what he said and rest, but it was hard when she was worrying about Shirley and Tom getting enough to eat. So far, she'd spent her day baking pies, not to mention making sure the washing and ironing were up-to-date. She took her time, but every little thing seemed to leave her breathless and exhausted. The cough was as bad as ever.

'Where are the children?' Dr Pringle asked as he came in through the back door. He always looked the same: tweed jacket in winter, linen in summer, white shirt, bow tie and waistcoat. He'd been the family doctor for years. When he'd learned Sid had gone, he'd advised her what to do about Tom and had become almost a family friend.

'At school,' said Florrie. 'They're not having lessons this week, but the headmaster wants everybody there.'

Dr Pringle nodded. 'And the shop?'

'I haven't been in there,' said Florrie. 'Mrs Carr has taken over for as long as it takes me to be well again.' Dr Pringle looked around, so she added, 'There's no one to disturb us, if that's what you're thinking.'

It was only now that Florrie could see that he had

brought another man with him. The first thing that Florrie noticed was his exceptionally long neck. It supported an egg-shaped head with a receding hairline. He had brown-rimmed glasses, and he was dressed in a suit and tie.

'Dr Scott is the tuberculosis medical officer for the East End,' Dr Pringle said, introducing them. 'Mrs Jenkins, I'm afraid it is as I feared. Your X-rays show that you have tuberculosis in your right lung.'

Florrie sat down, her heart suddenly pounding. She opened her mouth, but there was no sound and it felt as if she already had a lump in her throat the size of an orange. She looked away to avoid his eye. TB. How awful. Whenever someone round here got it, it caused a stir. People would say it was in the family. She had honestly thought that once she'd reached the age of thirty, she'd be safe. Well, that was an old wives' tale, wasn't it? What was going to happen to her? Now that it was confirmed, she knew she faced weeks, if not months, of treatment. How was she going to afford it? A kind of panic gripped her throat.

'We are here to discuss your treatment, Mrs Jenkins,' Dr Scott said gently. 'We suggest' – and here he looked to Dr Pringle for confirmation – 'that you have at least six to nine months in a sanatorium with complete bed rest.'

'Six to nine months?' Florrie squeaked, even though it was no great surprise. She'd imagined it for ages, but to hear it actually spelled out as fact made her whole body tremble. Six to nine months away from the chil-

56

dren. They would have left school by the time she saw them again. They'd be all grown up – at least, Shirley would, but what would happen to poor Tom?

'You mustn't worry about the cost, Mrs Jenkins,' said Dr Pringle.

The cost . . . the cost. Dear Lord, for a moment she'd forgotten all about the cost. Six to nine months away from home. That would cost a fortune. Her eyes were smarting and she desperately wanted to run away.

'Mrs Jenkins. Mrs Jenkins, look at me.' Dr Scott was trying to gain her attention. She reluctantly raised her gaze to meet his grey eyes behind the glasses. 'I know this is a lot to take in, but I'm glad to tell you that we can offer you a place in a sanatorium for the first two to three months.' Florrie stared at him, trying to take in what he was saying. 'It's under a government scheme and it's free.'

'Free?' Florrie said faintly.

'Yes, and after that,' Dr Scott went on, 'we'll do another X-ray and see where we go from there. You may have to stay a bit longer, but we'll wait until then to discuss your contribution towards any future costs. Or if there is a marked improvement, we could move you on to a convalescent home. There is every possibility that with complete bed rest, you could make a really good recovery.'

Florrie blinked back her tears. 'What if I don't get better?'

'Best not to look on the black side, Mrs Jenkins,' said Dr Pringle.

'Then we shall go for another treatment,' said Dr Scott at the same time.

Florrie struggled to grasp what he was saying. 'What sort of treatment?'

Dr Scott looked directly at her. 'We may want to collapse your lung for a period of time,' he said. 'We believe that by doing that, we would be giving the organ time to heal itself.'

Florrie's eyes grew wide. It sounded absolutely terrifying.

'But it may not come to that, Mrs Jenkins,' Dr Pringle said quickly. 'One step at a time, eh? All you need to know is that you will be in safe hands. I have it on good authority that Dr Scott is the best in his field.'

Florrie's brain was galloping at a hundred miles an hour. The children, the shop, Betty Carr – could she manage the shop all those months? – a collapsed lung, complete bed rest . . . She fished for her handkerchief. 'When do I have to go?'

'As soon as possible,' said Dr Pringle.

'I can't just up and leave my children,' said Florrie. She could feel herself giving way to tears, so she sat up straight and cleared her throat. 'Can I get you both some tea?'

'No, thank you, Mrs Jenkins,' said Dr Pringle, 'and there's no need to worry about Shirley and Tom. Mrs Andrews came to see me last night. It's all in hand.'

'Oh?' said Florrie.

'I believe she's coming round to see you later this afternoon,' Dr Pringle went on. 'We realized that at first you were not keen for them to be evacuated, but two girls in Shirley's class won't be going, so Shirley and Tom have been offered their places. Most providential, if you ask me. It's by far the best option, Mrs Jenkins. Anyway, I'm sure that Mrs Andrews will discuss it with you more fully.'

Florrie clapped her hand over her mouth. 'When will they have to go?'

'They are booked on a coach on Saturday.'

A little gasp escaped Florrie's lips. 'But Tom . . .' she began.

'He will be given due consideration,' said Dr Pringle. 'He will be well looked after.'

'And I shall arrange for someone to bring you to the sanatorium on the same day,' said Dr Scott.

So that was it. Her little family was to be separated. She said a short prayer under her breath – 'Please God, let them be all right' – but there was nothing more she could do. Everybody had done the best they could. All she had to do was get better. Florrie rose to her feet. 'You've both been very kind. I can't thank you enough,' she said, her voice thick with emotion.

She stood at the door with dignity as they left; then she closed it and went upstairs to her bedroom. She stood in front of the mirror for a long while, staring at her reflection as if truly seeing herself for the first time. Her hair was dull and untidy, and her eyes had dark circles underneath. Her skin was sallow and her breathing laboured. She leaned forward. Her youth was gone. She looked ten, maybe fifteen years older than she really was. She was an old hag and she wasn't even forty. Turning round, she lay down on the bed, and pressing her face into her pillow, Florrie sobbed as if her heart would break.

# CHAPTER 4

The next few days were very difficult. Shirley already knew that whatever was going on was serious, even though her mother still insisted she was only suffering from a touch of flu. Shirley tackled the subject when she came home from school on Thursday. Her mother was in the kitchen making pastry for meat-and-potato pies and Tom was in the yard playing with next-door's cat when Shirley pressed Florrie to tell her what was wrong.

'I'm not a baby, Mum,' she said. 'You can tell me.'

'There's nothing to tell,' said Florrie, rubbing her fingers together to get rid of the fat and flour. 'I've changed my mind about the evacuation, that's all. I was wrong to try and keep you and Tom here with me. If that ol' Hitler declares war, the docks will be the first place he'll bomb.'

'I thought you said there were no more places on the coach,' said Shirley.

'As luck would have it, two girls have dropped out,' said Florrie, reaching for the jug of cold water. 'They're going somewhere else.'

Shirley felt her face colour. 'Not Helen Starling and Ann Bidder?'

'Yes,' said Florrie, slightly surprised. 'What do you know about them?'

Shirley shrugged. How could she tell her mother they were being sent away for stealing from Woolworths? She'd been so jealous when the girls set out on their big adventure, but now she was relieved she wasn't with them when they got caught. She felt sure she would never have taken anything that didn't belong to her, but if she had been there, she would have been deemed just as guilty as them. Isn't that what had happened to poor Ann?

Shirley jumped as her mother suddenly said, 'You are both very lucky. Mrs Andrews put in a good word for you and Mrs Ashley from the WI agreed to take you on the coach.'

Shirley was still thinking over what had happened to Helen and Ann. 'Mum,' she began cautiously, 'what's an "approved school"?'

The question, right out of the blue, took Florrie by surprise. She had kneaded the dough and was getting it ready to roll on the drop-down shelf of the kitchen cupboard. Brushing away a stray curl that had escaped from her turban, she said, 'It's a special school where they put very naughty girls. Why do you ask?'

'Nothing,' said Shirley.

'They won't send you to one of those, love,' said Florrie, pushing the rolling pin over the pastry dough. 'You'll be a long way away, but you'll be close by people you know, and you'll still go to school with all your old friends. It won't be for long.'

'How long?'

'Not long,' said Florrie brightly.

'Mum, Tom and I could leave school,' said Shirley. 'I know you wanted us to stay on, but maybe now is the time we should look around for a good job.'

'Don't be daft, Shirley,' said Florrie. 'You won't be able to earn enough to support yourselves. Everybody has to start at the bottom. Anyway, even if we do go to war, they say it'll all be over by Christmas. You'll be back home in no time.'

'What about you?' said Shirley. 'You mustn't stay here if Hitler is going to bomb the docks.'

'And I won't be, will I?' said Florrie, cutting the pie shapes. 'I'm going to live in the country for a while too.'

'Then why can't we go with you?' Shirley cried.

'I'm not well enough to look after you,' said Florrie. She snatched a renegade tear away with the back of her hand, leaving floury marks on her face.

'Then let me look after you, Mum,' said Shirley. 'I can do it.'

'No, you can't,' said Florrie. This was almost too much to bear. She felt as if her heart was breaking.

'I still don't see why we can't be together.'

'Because we can't,' Florrie snapped. 'For God's sake, Shirley, stop asking me questions. My head is thumping.'

'Sorry, Mum,' said Shirley, giving her mother a wounded look.

'If you want to be useful,' said Florrie, anxious that her daughter wouldn't see her tears, 'wash up that bowl and put the kitchen scales away.'

As she worked miserably at the sink, Shirley felt very frustrated. If her mother didn't want her around, there had to be something seriously wrong. She wasn't stupid. She knew when she was being fobbed off.

As she came through the shop on Friday, Shirley had an idea. There had been times in the past when she was a little girl when Auntie Betty had been an ally. If Shirley had eaten a few too many sweets, Auntie Betty would shake her head disapprovingly, but she never told her mother, and once when Shirley had torn her best dress, Auntie Betty did what she called an 'invisible mend' on the tear. Her mother had never even noticed. Maybe Auntie Betty would be honest about Mum.

'Can I ask you something?' she began.

'Course you can, darlin'.'

'Is my mother going to die?'

Auntie Betty was shelf-filling and had her back to Shirley. Shirley saw her stiffen, but when she turned to look at her, Auntie Betty had altogether too bright a smile. 'Good Lord alive, child,' she cried. 'Your mother's going away to get better, not to die. You know what this place is like in the winter. When that fog comes down the river and everybody's got a fire in the grate, it's like breathing in Bird's custard powder. She can't get well here, now, can she? Not on your nelly. A bit of fresh country air will do her the world of good.'

Shirley could understand the logic of that, but she was still none the wiser as to the nature of her mother's illness. There was nothing for it but to ask a direct question. 'What's wrong with Mum?'

Auntie Betty took a deep breath. Shirley waited. 'You'll have to ask your mother that,' Auntie Betty said gravely.

'But—'

The shop door opened and the bell rang.

'Run along now, Shirley, there's a good girl. I've got a customer.'

Shirley wasn't the only one who sensed something was very wrong with Florrie. Who wouldn't? She lay around on the sofa and she didn't go into the shop any more. Tom didn't know how to express his feelings, but when he came into the house, he brought her gifts. On Wednesday, he'd picked some wayside flowers for her, some pinkish-blue borage, a few sprigs of yellow kidney vetch, a bladder campion and a piece of purple wild basil. Florrie had no idea where he'd found them – most likely on that piece of waste ground just up the road, or maybe by the water's edge – but she'd been moved to tears and had to turn her back as she put them on a saucer, next to the goldfish. The stems were far too short for a jam jar. On Thursday, Tom had saved her one of his sandwiches from his school lunch. His mother had cupped his face in her hands and given him a quick kiss before he could pull away.

They packed their cases on Friday evening. They

weren't allowed to take much; two changes of clothes and a toy was about it. Tom was very clear about what he wanted, but his mother drew the line at taking the goldfish. 'It'll get too hot in the coach,' she said. 'And what happens if you drop the jam jar? With no water, he'll die.' Tom understood that, so he took his animal book instead.

Florrie gave Shirley four postcards, each with a stamp on the corner. 'I want you to post these when you get there,' she'd said. 'Don't send them all at once – space them out – and don't forget to put your new address on them. I want to know where you are so I'll know where to come and fetch you to bring you back home.'

'Oh, Mum,' Shirley scolded. 'I'm old enough to make my own way home.'

Florrie nodded. 'Course you are.'

'What if we don't like where we are?' said Shirley. Her stomach was already in knots and she felt a bit like crying. How long would it be before she could see her mother again?

'If we go to war,' said Florrie, 'we may all have to put up with a lot of things we don't like until it's over.' She saw her daughter's face fall, so she added, 'But if it's really, really unbearable, write and let me know, and somehow or other, I'll get someone to come for you.'

'But how can I?' said Shirley. 'I don't know where you're going.'

'Write to the shop,' said Florrie. 'As soon as I have my address, I'll let Auntie Betty know.' She had a second thought. 'But you'd better not write on the post-card if you're unhappy. The people you're staying with might read it.'

'How can I let you know, then?'

It was a conundrum until Tom, who had been watching his goldfish, said, 'Can I put a kiss on Shirley's card for you, Mum?'

'That's it!' cried Florrie. 'Put one kiss each on the card if everything is all right, but add a few more if you are being badly treated. If you're unhappy, I shall know by the number of kisses.'

And so it was agreed.

Shirley didn't take a toy. 'I'm too old for baby things,' she insisted, so Florrie gave her a pretty writing set from the shop.

'You can write down everything that happens,' Florrie told her. 'When we get together again, I shall want to know all about it.' Her daughter looked less than enthusiastic, so she added, 'Or you could write one of those stories you're always telling Tom.'

'I like the one about the Birthday Thief,' he said. 'That one has rats and things in it.'

Saturday came all too soon. Tom was in his school clothes and short trousers. Shirley wore her Sunday-best clothes, a blue and white polka-dot dress with three buttons down the front and a gathered skirt. She didn't like it much because it had a tie belt round the waist and she thought it looked babyish, but there was no persuading her mother. 'You look really sweet,' said Florrie, so Shirley had no choice.

They said their goodbyes at home. 'Be a good lad,' Florrie told Tom. 'Try and do what you're told and listen to Shirley.'

'Yes, Mum.' Just for a split second, although he didn't look at her, Tom returned her hug. It was a precious moment for Florrie. Her son had never been one for hugs and kisses.

'Look after your brother,' Florrie told Shirley, her voice cracking with emotion. 'Be a good girl and don't do anything to make me ashamed.'

Shirley frowned. 'Why would I do that?'

Florrie patted her face. 'You're a pretty girl. Don't believe everything the boys tell you.'

The road leading to the school was choked with children of all ages. They weren't all from Hallsville School. Some wore smart gaberdine mackintoshes, some had school blazers, while others were dressed either in their Sunday best or ordinary clothes that were patched and worn. The only thing they had in common was that they all carried the dreaded gas masks in cardboard boxes slung over their shoulders and a small suitcase with everything they owned inside. As they approached the school gates and the fleet of waiting coaches, some ladies from the WI checked the luggage label threaded through their buttonhole against the names on a long list they held on a clipboard.

'You two, bus five,' a woman told Shirley and Tom.

Everyone was putting on a jolly face, but some of the much smaller children were already crying. Mothers waiting in silence on the other side of the school railings dabbed their eyes and waved their handkerchiefs as the children boarded the coaches.

Tom and Shirley sat together, and their teacher, Miss Lloyd, checked their names against her register. Shirley felt a bit miserable without their mother there to wave them off, but all at once she spotted Auntie Doreen waving and calling their names. As the coach moved off, she blew them kisses and walked briskly beside it until she could no longer keep up. By the time they'd reached the end of the road, everyone was lost to view, and for a few moments the coach fell silent.

Then Miss Lloyd stood up at the front of the coach. 'I want you all to enjoy your trip,' she said. 'It won't be the same as the trip to Southend you had last week, but I'm pleased to tell you this coach is going to a place right near the sea.' An excited murmur ran along the coach as she added, 'We're off to a place called Worthing.'

'Where's that?' Penny Forge whispered across the aisle to Shirley.

Shirley shrugged. 'Never heard of it.'

'We shall stop on the way for a toilet break,' Miss Lloyd went on, 'and we shall arrive in Worthing at around one o'clock.'

It's a long way, then, Shirley thought to herself.

Gradually the noise level in the coach grew louder and before long they were singing songs. Tom didn't join in, of course, but unlike the day they'd gone to Southend, he didn't seem upset by the racket. He wasn't even bothered about having a story. He was enjoying the view from the coach window. Shirley pressed her head against the back of her seat. Worthing. It had a nice ring to it. She sighed. If only Mum was coming too.

'They looked fine,' Doreen reassured Florrie. 'They were both smiling and waving – well, Shirley was, but Tom looked happy enough.'

They were sitting in Florrie's little sitting room having a cup of tea while they waited for the car to come. Betty had one ear on the shop door, in case of a customer, and disappeared every time the bell rang.

Florrie felt terrible. Her chest hurt, and she'd been coughing a lot this morning. Doreen said it was because she was upset about the children going, and she was probably right. It might be true that every other mother in Canning Town was going through the same thing, but that didn't help. They didn't have TB to cope with as well. They didn't have to leave everything familiar behind and go to Lord knows where . . . Florrie checked herself. She mustn't do this. Whatever happened, she must not allow herself to give in to self-pity. No good would come of it. That was a downward path that led nowhere. No, she had to think of the more positive things. She had a lot to be grateful for. Good friends like Doreen and Betty, for a start. Plenty of people with the disease were ostracized by their nearest and dearest. Even though the treatments were much better nowadays, there was still a bit of stigma attached to getting TB. No. Florrie had a lot to be thankful for. She had a lovely shop that would bring in an income to take care of the expenses. Even being part of the government scheme was a blessing. All she had to do was get well again and keep as cheerful as possible. Nobody liked someone who never stopped complaining, she told herself crossly, so no more tears.

She was wearing a pink and blue striped dress with short sleeves. There were little buttons down the front, and the dress had a small belt at the waist. Under a white lace Peter Pan collar, the stripes went in the opposite direction, straight across the shoulders rather than vertically like the rest of it.

The person Dr Scott had asked to take her to the sanatorium arrived at around eleven o'clock and then it was a mad dash to get her into the car. He was a very nice man, thoughtful and kind. He made her lie down on the back seat, and put her suitcase in the boot. There was hardly time to say goodbye to Doreen and Betty before she was on her way. Probably just as well, Florrie thought as they headed away from the docks and out of London. Long-drawn-out goodbyes were always painful.

'My name's Neil,' said the driver. 'Neil Woodfield.'

'Florrie Jenkins,' said Florrie. She didn't feel like talking. Her chest felt tight and she was close to the dreaded tears.

It was only when they'd been travelling for about twenty minutes that it occurred to her she didn't even know where the sanatorium was. 'Where are we going exactly?'

The traffic was slow going because the roads were choked with coaches full of children. Every time they had passed one, Florrie had leaned up on her elbow to see if she could spot Tom and Shirley.

'To the sanatorium at Godalming,' said Mr Woodfield. 'They say it's the best in the country. You're lucky to be going there.' He paused for a second, and she knew he'd embarrassed himself. 'Well, you're not lucky because you're ill, but you know what I mean.'

Florrie smiled.

'They've got everything there,' the driver went on. 'Iron lungs and all.'

Florrie felt her heart sink. Iron lungs . . . Don't say she was going to need one of those as well. The thought had never crossed her mind before. Dear God, this was a living nightmare.

# CHAPTER 5

When the coaches pulled into Worthing almost an hour later than expected, they found themselves in Christchurch Road outside the Baptist church. They were ushered into the hall on the side of the building, where the local WI ladies and members of the church had laid on a feast of sandwiches and cakes.

By this time, everyone was starving, but they behaved in an orderly fashion, first lining up for the toilets and then sitting patiently at the trestle tables. Before coming to the table herself, Shirley had helped some of the smaller children to pull up their knickers and wash their hands. She was happy to do it. It kept her mind off things. Surprisingly, nobody cried for his or her mummy, probably because what awaited them on the white tablecloths looked so inviting. Miss Lloyd managed to keep everyone at bay until the minister had said grace and then they all tucked in. The ladies went round with a choice of Corona fruit squashes in a jug, lemonade or dandelion and burdock. The adults drank tea poured from an enormous teapot.

Just as the last of the home-made cakes were being

passed round, people started coming into the hall to collect the children. One by one and occasionally in twos, they were peeled away from the main group. Shirley couldn't help noticing that the younger children, in particular the prettier ones, went first. A couple of times someone asked her to go with them, but when she insisted that Tom be allowed to come with her, they shook their heads and asked someone else. By four o'clock, there were only about eight children left.

'Now, I don't want any of you to be upset,' said Miss Lloyd with a bright smile. 'We knew this was going to happen so we are off to a lovely village called Angmering, which is not very far from here, and I have arranged for the rest of you to be billeted there.'

Having thanked the tea ladies, she bustled them back onto one of the coaches and they set off once again. Nobody spoke. There was an air of despondency in the coach, especially as there had been no sign of the sea so far. Two disappointments in one day was almost too much to bear. Once they'd left the suburbs, they motored past what seemed like miles and miles of glasshouses until eventually they turned right and found themselves in a pretty little village. Once again they were met by a reception committee at the village hall, and several people who were going to take the children in were already waiting. Adults and children were quickly paired off, until only Shirley and Tom were left. Tom seemed confused and agitated. Shirley felt tearful, but she had to keep strong for the sake of her brother. It was beginning to look as if nobody wanted them.

What would happen if they had nowhere to go? Would the coach driver take them back to London, and if he did, who would look after them? There was nobody living at the shop. Mum had gone to the country.

Tom was getting agitated, so as they sat close together Shirley picked up the thread of his favourite story and told him the next instalment.

'You remember I told you there was a fair on the field,' she began.

Tom's eyes lit up. 'With a magician.'

'That's right,' said Shirley. *The magician did a few tricks with cards, but he dropped most of them on the table. Then he held up a red tube so that everyone could see it was empty, and a chicken stuck its head out of the end of his coat sleeve.*'

Tom laughed. 'Then Elsie told him it was her birthday.'

'That's right,' said Shirley. She was distracted by the woman in charge of the village hall as she drew Miss Lloyd to one side with an animated whisper.

'But she mustn't tell him her name,' said Tom, 'or he'll steal it.'

The door banged and Miss Lloyd jumped as a man came into the hall. He was wearing patched-up clothes and holding a battered hat with a greasy headband in his hands. Two buttons were missing from his jacket, but he had made some sort of an effort: his hair was slicked down with Brylcreem, although his weather-beaten face was badly in need of a shave.

Tom snatched at Shirley's arm. 'Is that him?' he said anxiously. 'Is that the Birthday Thief?'

'The Birthday Thief is only a story,' said Shirley. 'I made it up.'

All the same, it was a little disconcerting. As he walked into the hall, the man's gumboots deposited bits of straw and mud on the swept floor, much to the disapproval of the lady from the village.

'Mr Oliver,' she said, looking down her nose at him. 'To what do we owe this pleasure?'

'Only two left?' said Mr Oliver, looking Shirley and Tom up and down. 'I'll take 'em.'

The lady shook her head. 'Oh no, you won't, Mr Oliver. If you had wanted evacuees, you should have told me before. You have to be vetted.'

'You know me well enough, Mrs Dyer,' he said, giving her a brown-toothed smile. 'We've been neighbours long enough.'

'I'm supposed to inspect the rooms,' she said haughtily. 'I have no idea if your rooms will be suitable.'

'Then come and have a look,' he challenged. 'Them looks hale and hearty, and I could do with some help around the farm.'

'These children have to be in school,' said Miss Lloyd stiffly. 'They're not unpaid workers.'

'I knows that,' said Mr Oliver, 'but round 'ere, on the farm, everybody mucks in together.'

'Like I said,' Mrs Dyer repeated, 'I haven't checked—'

'Who else is goin' to take 'em?' said Mr Oliver, looking around. 'I don't see nobody. If you don't like it, tough. It seems to me beggars can't be choosers.'

Shirley could hardly believe her ears. They were being bartered like the cargo on one of the ships in the docks. She glanced at Tom, but he seemed impassive. Perhaps he didn't understand what was going on.

Mrs Dyer opened the main doors of the hall and looked helplessly up the street. It was deserted. 'He's right,' she whispered to Miss Lloyd. 'Nobody else is coming.' She drew a little closer. 'What about your aunt?'

'I'm afraid not,' said Miss Lloyd, shaking her head vigorously. 'She's old. She couldn't cope with boisterous youngsters.'

'The girl looks capable,' said Mrs Dyer. 'Perhaps your aunt would like to train her as a maid.'

'No,' Miss Lloyd said stonily. 'I can't take them. I just can't.'

'Then it looks as if we have no choice,' Mrs Dyer said stiffly.

The two women looked behind them to where Mr Oliver waited. He was cleaning his ear with his finger.

'Is he married?' Miss Lloyd whispered. 'I wouldn't want Shirley . . .'

'He got married quite recently, I believe,' said Mrs Dyer confidentially. 'I hear his wife is pregnant.'

Miss Lloyd wrinkled her nose. 'Then I suppose you're right. We have no choice.'

They separated.

'Very well, Mr Oliver,' said Mrs Dyer. 'But before we

leave the children in your care, Miss Lloyd and I shall come to your farm to inspect the room right now.'

'Suit yourself,' he said. 'You got a car? Only I's on foot.'

'No, I haven't, Mr Oliver,' said Mrs Dyer.

'What about the coach?'

'The driver has gone back to Worthing,' said Miss Lloyd. 'I'm staying in Angmering with my aunt tonight.'

'Then us shall have to walk.'

'Walk?' said Miss Lloyd faintly. 'How far is it?'

'A mile, give or take,' said Mr Oliver. 'Nice evening like this, it'll do you good, lady.'

Miss Lloyd gave him a withering stare.

Mrs Dyer locked up the hall and they set off. When they reached the centre of the village, they went up the hill past the Lamb Inn. Although they were all tired, it didn't take long to go along Dappers Lane and reach a small cluster of houses on Swillage Lane; from there, they turned right. It was very quiet. Apart from the occasional birdsong, the only sound was their own footsteps on the rough path. Before long, they came to a gate, and beyond it, a rather run-down farmhouse.

A plethora of chickens ran around the yard, and at the side of the house, a mangy-looking dog came out of its kennel and ran towards them barking furiously. For one ghastly second it looked as if it was going to attack them, but fortunately it was attached to a lead, which in turn was looped onto a chain. As they came through the gate, the dog flung itself at them. Mrs Dyer cried out in shocked surprise, but before the dog could make any physical contact with her, its whole body was wrenched backwards as it reached the end of the chain. The dog quickly regained its footing and continued to snarl and bark angrily from a safe distance.

'What a vicious animal,' cried Mrs Dyer as she recovered her composure.

'A good watchdog, that,' said Mr Oliver, rolling up his sleeve to reveal some old bite-mark scars. 'Don't touch 'e and you'll be fine.'

'But with children . . .' Mrs Dyer began.

Mr Oliver turned to Shirley and Tom. 'You'm old enough to understand, ench you? He's only doing his job.'

Miss Lloyd whispered, 'I'm really not sure about this.'

'Perhaps just for tonight?' said Mrs Dyer faintly.

Shirley glanced at Tom. It seemed that they didn't get a say in the matter.

'Come on in, then,' said Mr Oliver. 'I'll show 'e the room.'

The women went inside, but Shirley stopped in her tracks and looked around. Surely they weren't going to make her stay in this awful place? The dog was a danger, one of the scrawny chickens had almost all of the feathers missing from its bottom, a cat with its leg in the air washed itself by a dilapidated shed, and beyond the yard, she could see some cows grazing in a muddy field. The farm could have been idyllic but for the fact that the whole place was mucky and unpleasant and showing signs of prolonged neglect. Even the yard had a peculiar smell about it. Perhaps that was normal on a farm, but Shirley wasn't sure. Mr Oliver hadn't been rude or anything, but she, for one, didn't want to stay here. What should she do? What *could* she do? She turned to her brother, and to her surprise, he was smiling.

'They've got lots of animals here, Shirl.'

It was only as the car came to a halt that Florrie realized that she must have drifted off to sleep in the back seat. The door opened and a nurse manoeuvred a wooden chair on wheels next to her.

'I can walk,' Florrie said defiantly as she stepped out of the car.

'I'm sure you can,' said the nurse crisply, 'but you're not to.'

Florrie sat down and her suitcase was placed on her lap. She turned to thank Mr Woodfield, but he was already preparing to drive away. Florrie waved her hand, but he didn't see her. What a pity. He was such a nice man. He'd been chatty and kind until she'd nodded off. She suddenly felt orphaned and alone. The nurse took her along a covered walkway lined with flower beds. The air was heavy with the scent of roses, but Florrie felt tears close by.

She found herself in a small ward some distance from the entrance. A few women were reclining on their beds as she came in. Florrie's bed was right at the far end of the ward, behind a set of portable screens. The room itself was full of light, and a gentle breeze from the open veranda wafted inside. The whole side of the building was made up of doors, and every one was wide open. At the nurse's insistence, Florrie undressed and got under the covers. The same nurse then took her temperature, using a thermometer kept in a little vase-shaped container on the wall behind her bed. It had been soaking in a pink solution that tasted a bit like aniseed. She took Florrie's pulse and recorded it on a chart that hung on a clipboard at the foot of the bed.

'It's best for you to lie down,' said the nurse. 'If you do sit up, you must be propped by pillows, and whatever you do, don't take deep breaths.'

'I brought some knitting,' said Florrie, pointing to her case.

'Absolutely not,' said the nurse. 'From now on, you have to live like a log. Rest is the only cure. I'll leave the screens. The doctor will be with you in a minute.'

Florrie was left staring at the floral pattern on the screens. By the time the doctor arrived, she had noticed that whoever had sewn it had mismatched the pattern in a most irritating way.

The hospital doctor was a fresh-faced young man who looked as if he'd only just left school, but he was a lot more friendly and relaxed than the nurse. He pulled up a chair and unscrewed his fountain pen. First, he took down her particulars: where she lived, her age, her marital status and what her living conditions were like. After that, he asked questions about her health. When did she first develop the cough? How long before she coughed blood?

'Can you tell me what your symptoms are?'

'I have a pain in my right side,' said Florrie, 'and when I start coughing, it's very hard to stop.'

He probed even further and Florrie did her best to be truthful. No, she wasn't on any medication. She had no other problems. She didn't smoke. She only had the occasional drink.

'Are you more tired than usual? Have you lost weight? Do you suffer from sudden chills?' The answer in each case was yes. 'Do you have children?'

The sudden reminder of Shirley and Tom was like a knife in her heart.

'It must be hard bringing them up on your own,' the doctor sympathized. 'Are they being looked after by a relative?'

'They've just been evacuated,' said Florrie, conscious of the catch in her voice.

'Then I'm sure they'll be well looked after,' he said with a sympathy that was surprising in one apparently so young. 'Is there anything you would like to ask me?'

She had answered all his questions as honestly as she could, but there was only one real cause for concern. Florrie chewed her bottom lip anxiously. 'Could I have passed it on to them?' There, she'd asked the one thing to which she dreaded the answer. If she had given Shirley or Tom this terrible disease, she'd never forgive herself. And what about Betty and Doreen? She'd been an utter fool trying to keep going and ignoring what was happening to her body.

'It is possible to pass it on if you've been living in very close quarters with somebody,' he said gently.

Florrie felt her heart sink. Oh no, please God, no . . .

'But you mustn't worry about that now,' he went on. 'You are here to get better, and the more relaxed you are, the quicker that will happen.'

He finished his examination by listening to her chest, and then he folded the screens back. 'I'm afraid this is going to be a bit difficult for you,' he said. 'From now on, you must have complete rest. You can read, but you cannot sit up. Is that clear?'

Florrie nodded miserably. As she watched him walk down the ward and out through the door, his white coat flapping behind him, she sighed. Months on end of doing nothing . . . How on earth was she going to survive without going loopy?

Shirley and Tom followed Miss Lloyd and Mrs Dyer into the farmhouse. They went through a narrow porch and found themselves in a large, open kitchen, which although impressive, was also very dark. It didn't help that the window over the sink was extremely small, or that the paintwork was dark brown and the floor dark-grey flagstone. Even the ceiling was a pale shade of tan, probably caused by smoke from the open range. Being still summer, the fire was small – just enough to keep the saucepan on the rest simmering. On the other side of the range, a kettle sang, and beneath it was a small tank with a tap in the front and a bucket underneath. Above the mantelpiece hung a rusted piece of metalwork. It looked very old and was square with a central plate; a long chain was looped over it. It seemed rather an odd thing to have as an ornament. Across the mantelpiece over the range was an iron bar with several pieces of intimate clothing airing on it: a vest, a pair of ladies' pants and a nightdress.

A woman sitting at the large scrubbed wooden table in the middle of the room leapt to her feet and snatched the clothing down; screwing it into a ball, she threw it into a washing basket in the corner of the room. She had obviously been washing and setting her hair. She had a towel round her shoulders and several kirby grips and steel grippers in place. She turned with an embarrassed expression, but the farmer walked past.

'Excuse my wife,' he said, ignoring her completely. 'This way.'

The inspection party trailed behind him, nodding a greeting to Mrs Oliver as they went. She seemed to Shirley to be a lot younger than her husband, not much older than she was, in fact.

Mr Oliver took them through a door and up the stairs. The farmhouse had an odd layout. There was obviously another room downstairs to the side of the stairs, but he didn't open the door. Upstairs, there was a door to the left, which Mr Oliver closed as they walked by. Immediately in front of them, there was a bed under the eaves.

'The boy can sleep there,' he said dismissively.

Shirley saw a pair of women's slippers peeping out

from under the bed and wondered vaguely to whom they belonged.

At the end of the corridor was another room. Mr Oliver swung back the door to reveal a very pretty bedroom. It was much brighter than the corridor and decorated mainly in pinks and rose reds. The bed had a delightful floral satin counterpane, which reached to the floor. The curtains were pink with a frilly pelmet in the same material. On the washstand stood a jug and bowl with red and white roses all over them, and beside a wooden chair there was a large mahogany wardrobe. Shirley held her breath. It was the most beautiful room she had ever seen in her life, and this was to be hers for as long as they stayed?

Mrs Dyer and Miss Lloyd seemed pleasantly surprised. 'Very nice, Mr Oliver,' said Mrs Dyer. 'Shall we go back downstairs to discuss the details?'

Everybody traipsed back downstairs. Mrs Oliver had covered her head with a scarf, tied turban-style. The kitchen table had been cleared of hair-washing paraphernalia, and six cups and saucers stood in their place.

'Oh, thank you, Mrs Oliver,' said Mrs Dyer, 'but I'm afraid we won't be stopping. Miss Lloyd is anxious to get back to her aged aunt.'

The adults sat at the table while Shirley and Tom looked on.

'There's your government permit,' said Mrs Dyer, pushing a piece of paper across the table to Mr Oliver. 'Take that to the post office and they will issue you with your payment book. You get eight and six per child.

Any medical problems, show them this' – she handed him two cards – 'and all medical expenses appertaining to the child in question will be met.'

Mr Oliver stuffed them both in his wallet.

'We begin school at nine o'clock on Monday,' said Miss Lloyd. 'Please make sure the children are on time. We finish at four.' She turned to glance at Mrs Oliver. 'Any problems, please see me.'

They stood to shake hands. 'The children should have a packed lunch with them for a few days until we can sort out a hot meal at lunchtime,' said Miss Lloyd.

'Which comes out of my pocket, I suppose,' Mr Oliver mumbled.

'Your government grant begins from this moment, Mr Oliver,' Mrs Dyer said stiffly.

Miss Lloyd turned to Shirley. 'I hope you will make the most of this opportunity,' she said, 'but make sure Tom doesn't wander off into any danger.'

'I will,' said Shirley. She was already imagining herself in that beautiful room.

With the adults gone, Mrs Oliver motioned for them to sit at the table and she dished up a plate of stew. Shirley and Tom didn't like to say but they weren't all that hungry. However, they made a valiant attempt at the meal out of politeness.

'Where do you come from?' Mrs Oliver asked.

'Canning Town,' said Shirley. 'It's right by the docks.'

Mrs Oliver nodded. It seemed odd that she was married to such an old man. Mr Oliver must be at least forty, but his wife only looked about nineteen or twenty, just a few years older than Shirley herself. Mr Oliver wasn't even nice-looking. As she stood over them to take their plates, Shirley noticed that under her wrap-over apron, Mrs Oliver's tummy was very rounded. She was having a baby.

As they cleared up, Mr Oliver came back. His wife ladled a huge portion of stew onto a deep plate and he sat down without a word. Hunched over the plate with a spoon, he steadily demolished the lot, while Mrs Oliver did the washing-up in the sink. Remembering her manners, Shirley helped herself to a tea towel and began to dry. Afterwards, Mrs Oliver made a pot of tea and they all sat down again. Tom remained motionless in his chair until quite unexpectedly, Mr Oliver gave a loud, rumbling belch and then he looked up at Shirley. She looked away quickly, hoping and praying that Tom wouldn't make some inappropriate remark that would get him into trouble. Their mother disapproved strongly of belching and any other bodily noises, especially at the table or in company.

Mr Oliver looked at his watch. 'Time you young 'uns was in bed,' he announced.

They all got to their feet, and picking up her case, Shirley headed for the stairs.

'Not that way,' Mr Oliver barked. 'You'm sleeping out here.'

'Oh, Gil, you can't,' his wife said quietly.

He turned sharply. 'You hush your mouth, woman. I does what I likes in my own home.'

'But you showed Mrs Dyer upstairs,' she said.

'Nobody sleeps in Elizabeth's room.'

'What if they report you?'

Mr Oliver banged his fist on the table, making the cups rattle. 'I told you to hush up, Janet,' and giving Shirley and Tom a long stare, he added coldly, 'They'll keep quiet if they knows what's good for them.'

Shirley's heart was thumping, and Tom began to sway from side to side, the way he always did when he was confused or frightened.

Mr Oliver walked towards the porch. 'Come on.'

Shirley and Tom followed him out of the kitchen and into a scullery at the other end of the porch. The temperature had dropped considerably. They walked past a copper boiler and a large mangle. He took them to another door and pushed it open. Inside a small oblong room were two low wooden beds complete with army-issue blankets. The walls were bare brick, and there were huge cobwebs on the single bare lightbulb hanging from the high ceiling.

'You want us to sleep here?' Shirley squeaked.

'You got a problem with that?' Mr Oliver challenged.

Shirley did some quick thinking. He was the adult; she was the child. She was miles from home and in a strange place. If she stalked out, which was what she wanted to do, where would she go? And what about her brother? With animals all around him, he'd most likely refuse to come with her. 'I'm not allowed to undress in front of my brother,' she said haughtily.

The farmer disappeared.

Tom sat on one of the beds. 'I bags this bed, Shirl,' he said.

Shirley looked around. This was awful. The room was completely bare. It seemed to have been some sort of storeroom at one time. There was something smeared on one of the walls. If Shirley didn't know better, she would have sworn it was blood. High on the ceiling, there was a large meat hook. Mr Oliver must have hung carcasses or something in here, and now he was proposing that it become their bedroom! The wooden door didn't even come all the way down to the floor. There was a gap of a foot or more at the bottom. It wasn't too bad now, but if they were still here at Christmas, they might as well be out in the fields for all the shelter it would give them from the cold.

Five minutes later, Mr Oliver came back with a piece of rope and two more blankets. Shirley watched in horror as he rigged up a blanket wall between the two beds.

'There you are, Miss Fussy-Pants,' he said, leaving the room. 'The lav is outside. Sleep well.'

Shirley sat staring at the blanket wall for some time. She could hear Tom on the other side getting ready for bed and climbing in.

'I like being here, Shirl,' he said. 'I like all the animals.'

Eventually, Shirley got ready for bed and after a trip to the outside lavatory, climbed in. Her mood shifted from misery to anger. How dare Mr Oliver do this? He had no right. Tomorrow, she would tell Miss Lloyd exactly what had happened. With the light switched off, she fantasized about Mr Oliver's arrest. 'The worst case of child cruelty since the time of Charles Dickens,' the judge would say at his trial. Yes, she would go first thing in the morning . . . It was only as she drifted off to sleep that Shirley realized that she didn't have the faintest clue where Miss Lloyd was staying.

# CHAPTER 6

The ward was quite large. After a troubled night, Florrie was woken up at six forty-five by the sound of the nurses bringing round the tea trolley. That was quickly followed by another nurse pulling the screens round every bed and giving each woman a bowl of water for washing.

'Here we are, Edna,' she heard the nurse say to the woman in the bed next to her. 'Rise and shine.'

The nurse poked her head round the screen and smiled at Florrie. 'I'll be along a bit later to give you a blanket bath, Mrs Jenkins.'

'I'm perfectly capable—' Florrie began.

'I'm sure you are, but you mustn't. I'll be back in a minute.'

'Can't I do anything, then?' Florrie protested.

The nurse came closer. 'I know it's hard, but I promise you it will get better,' she said gently. 'These ladies have been through it and survived. You just have to tell yourself it's only for a while.'

'Yes, months and months,' she said brokenly, and ridiculous as it was, Florrie felt her eyes filling with tears. For goodness' sake, she told herself crossly, she was behaving like a child.

'You'll soon be well enough to live to be an old lady,' said the nurse, 'so what's a few months in the grand scheme of things?'

Florrie nodded miserably. When she'd gone, Edna called through the curtains, 'Chin up, love. You'll get there.'

The weekend dragged by, but Florrie began to get used to the routine. After her blanket bath, she had breakfast leaning against the back rest with several pillows to support her. The meals were hearty and nourishing. She was used to grabbing a slice of toast and a cup of tea, but here she had porridge followed by scrambled egg, and then toast and marmalade. She read, dozed and roused herself for a mid-morning cup of tea, lunch, afternoon tea and, finally, supper. The only little light relief came from her excursions to the toilet, but even then the nurses kept an eye on her to ensure she didn't stay up too long.

By Sunday, Florrie had discovered that Edna had been living there for eighteen months. 'I remember what it was like when I first came in,' she told Florrie. 'You think you'll go mad, but you don't.'

'I see you're allowed up now,' said Florrie. 'How long did it take?'

'Try not to think like that,' Edna advised. 'Counting the days and weeks is a mug's game.'

Florrie nodded. She was right. It was best not to get her hopes up.

'Anyway, I'm going home at the end of the month,' Edna told her. 'I can't wait to be with my Frank again.'

'Lucky you,' called the woman across the ward. 'I've just had another bloody setback. My sputum test came back positive.'

'Oh, I'm sorry,' said Edna.

'Can't be helped,' said the woman. 'By the way, my name is Tina. Tina Cook.'

'And I'm Edna Poole.'

'Florrie Jenkins,' said Florrie.

'You sound like a Londoner,' said Tina.

'Canning Town,' said Florrie.

The first Sunday in the month was visiting day. Consequently, a noisy gaggle of people began to assemble outside the ward doors from two-thirty. At two forty-five on the dot, the nurse opened the doors and the crowds surged in. Only two people were allowed to be at the bedside at any one time, so they took it in turns to sit beside friends and relatives they hadn't seen for a whole month. Children cried, and husbands kissed their wives' hands over and over again, because kissing on the mouth was forbidden. Florrie took refuge in her book. No one was coming to visit her, and besides, she'd only just got here.

As time went on, she caught snippets of the same conversation happening around the ward. 'Looks like it's really happening.' 'It'll be finished by Christmas.' 'They say the call-up papers are already in the post.' The nurses hadn't said a word, but it looked as if the prophets of doom and gloom could be right. At three, someone put the ward radio on. After a few pips and squeaks, Neville Chamberlain's voice filled the air with a repeat of the message he'd given the nation at eleven fifteen that morning.

'This morning, the British ambassador in Berlin handed the German Government a final note stating that, unless we heard from them by eleven o'clock that they were prepared at once to withdraw their troops from Poland, a state of war would exist between us . . .'

He said more, but the room had already fallen silent, each person lost in his or her thoughts. Thank God, Florrie told herself; thank God that Shirley and Tom were safe in the country. She offered up a prayer that whoever they were with would look after them. Tom wouldn't understand, of course, but Shirley was a bright girl. She wished she could put her arms around them and tell them everything would be fine, but she couldn't. Damn this disease, and damn Hitler and his cronies. At times like these, life seemed bloody unfair.

On the first day of the weekend, Shirley and Tom had woken to the sound of the cock crowing. It was only just getting light, and Tom's watch, lying on the chair between their beds, said it was only five fifteen.

'Can we see the animals now, Shirl?'

'Presently,' Shirley said grudgingly. 'It's very early.' Her heart was already sinking at the thought of staying in this awful place for a whole weekend before she could tell Miss Lloyd how they had all been taken in.

Once again her brother's voice came from the other side of the blanket wall. 'Tell me the story, Shirl.'

'Not now.' She was in no mood for stories. As well as feeling cross, she was upset and homesick. A thought crossed her mind. What if she did complain? What would happen? She already knew there was no one else to take them in. They couldn't send her back home, and Auntie Betty had already said she couldn't manage the shop and looking after them. Auntie Doreen's mother wouldn't take them in, that was for sure. Mind you, she wouldn't want to be with Mrs Kennedy. She was a mean-spirited old bag who made everybody's life a misery, especially poor Auntie Doreen's. Tom wouldn't last five minutes with her.

She heard footfall on the other side of the door and Mr Oliver called out, 'Look lively in there. You can help us with the milking.'

The blanket wall moved vigorously as Tom scrambled out of bed and into his clothes.

'You need a wash first,' said Shirley petulantly, but her brother was already leaving the room.

It took Shirley a bit longer to get dressed. She used the scullery to wash. At least she was alone and undisturbed, but she only had freezing-cold water in the tap. By the time she found everybody, the job of milking was well under way. Mrs Oliver was showing Tom how to sponge the cow's udders, and especially the teats, ready to milk.

'Give the end of her tail a wash too, Tom,' she said. 'You don't want her swishing it in your face.'

Once the teats were clean, Mrs Oliver dried them with a towel, and with a clean bucket underneath, showed Tom how to get milk. Shirley was convinced he wouldn't want to do it, but once he got going, Tom was a natural.

'Come on, girl,' said Mr Oliver suddenly at Shirley's elbow. 'Don't stand there gawping at it. Get yourself an apron. You can do Buttercup.' Shirley's jaw dropped. The cow was huge, and frightening. Mr Oliver grabbed her by the arm and propelled her forward. 'We ain't got all day,' he snapped.

Reluctantly, Shirley put on a white apron and stood close to the waiting cow. Her rear and flanks were caked in dried-on poo, and her underparts looked as if she'd been wallowing in mud. Shirley was revolted. A rag was thrust into her hand and she was forced to wash the offending parts. Every now and then, Shirley retched and Buttercup turned her head to look at her.

'We got another five to do after her,' said Mr Oliver, settling down beside another cow. 'Better get used to it, girl. We milks the cows twice a day.'

Trying not to cry, Shirley did her best, but she already hated every disgusting, smelly minute of it.

There were two rows of cows back to back. The space between them was narrow, and the straw was already sodden with excrement. Shirley had to be careful to avoid a cow relieving itself as she walked by. It took her a while to master the firm hold on the teat, and the fact that she had to keep going until the udder was flabby, so she only managed one and a half cows to Tom's three. The milk was strained over muslin and then taken to a clean room, where it was poured into churns. When all the churns were ready, Mr Oliver took Tom to the stables. A few minutes later, the two of them were loading churns onto a cart to take down to the Arundel Road, where the Milk Marketing Board lorry would collect them and take them to the dairy.

While they were doing that, Mrs Oliver showed Shirley how to make butter. By the time they'd finished, Shirley was starving. They ate a hearty breakfast and then Mr Oliver wanted them to do more chores. Tom was quite happy, but Shirley was getting crosser and crosser.

'I could do with some help in the house,' said Mrs Oliver.

Her husband harrumphed but left them to it.

'You didn't enjoy that, did you?' said Mrs Oliver when they'd gone.

'No, I didn't,' said Shirley indignantly. 'And he has no right to demand that we work our socks off. We may be fifteen, but we're still schoolchildren.'

Mrs Oliver smiled and said nothing. Shirley suddenly felt ashamed of her rudeness. Her mother wouldn't have wanted her to be so cheeky to an adult, even if she was only a couple of years older than herself. It beggared belief that an attractive young woman like her was married to such a surly old man.

'I could say you'll get used to it,' said Mrs Oliver, 'but I get the feeling you won't. Perhaps you'd prefer the cleaner chores. Making the butter wasn't so bad, was it?'

'No,' Shirley agreed, but she was cautious. What was being cooked up for her now? They were cleaning and dusting in the sitting room. Everywhere smelled of 'farm', and the room was cluttered up with old newspapers and beer bottles. Shirley wondered how long it had been since Mrs Oliver had tidied.

'I think we could be friends,' said Mrs Oliver. 'My name is Janet.' She held out her hand and Shirley shook it. 'I have to say I'm glad you're here. It can be a lonely life on a farm.'

The day wore on. Shirley helped in the house for a bit, but then she told Janet she wanted to walk to the village. She had it in mind that she might bump into Miss Lloyd, and if she did, she might persuade her to find other accommodation.

'You'd better be back by four,' Janet cautioned. 'He'll want you here for the milking.'

Shirley shuddered. Mrs Oliver gave her some packs of butter for the village shop and asked her to buy a few much-needed groceries.

She found the shop quite easily, and the people were very friendly, but Shirley was out of luck as far as bumping into Miss Lloyd, or anyone else for that matter. There were a few children about, but no sign of Miss Lloyd. She posted a card to her mother, resisting the desire to put masses of kisses all over it. Her mother would only worry, and that might slow down her recovery.

*Dear Mum,*

*We are on a farm. Mr Oliver made us do the milking today. Tom enjoyed it very much. I didn't, but Mrs Oliver is quite nice. Hope you are feeling better.*

*Love,*
*Shirley and Tom xx*

Shirley had made up her mind to stick it out for a bit if she had to, but she couldn't bear the thought of being here any longer than was absolutely necessary.

Sunday was much the same as Saturday had been, except that Mrs Oliver gave her the butter pat and left her to it. She spent the rest of morning in the small orchard at the back of the farmhouse picking plums with Janet.

'I shall bottle them,' Janet told her.

'I've never done that,' Shirley admitted.

'I've never done it before either,' said Janet. 'It'll be a voyage of discovery for both of us.'

Shirley frowned to herself. Janet made it sound as if she wasn't a country girl either.

Mid-morning, they took their plums back to the house, and Janet put the kettle on for a cup of tea. Tom was out on the field with Mr Oliver and the horse and cart.

'They're lifting the spuds,' said Janet, switching on the wireless on the dresser. 'Gil won't bother to come back until lunchtime. I'll take a flask out to them.'

Shirley sat at the kitchen table with an old *Picture*

*Post* magazine belonging to Janet. She lingered over the beautiful dresses worn by Joan Greenwood and Margaret Lockwood. She felt another sensation too. Her heart gave a little flutter when she saw Hugh Sinclair dressed in his Musketeer costume for his latest film. What she wouldn't give for someone like him to come and rescue her.

At eleven fifteen, Prime Minister Neville Chamberlain came on the radio. Shirley would have preferred to enjoy the music that had been on before. With a bored sigh, she resigned herself to wait until he'd finished. She was only half listening as she turned the pages of the magazine. Mr Chamberlain droned on and on, but all at once she heard him say, 'I have to tell you now that no such undertaking has been received, and that consequently this country is at war with Germany.'

War. Everybody had talked about it for ages, but what exactly did it mean? She knew her parents and their friends had lived through the Great War, but nobody talked about it much. Was Hitler going to come here? She could almost hear the German troops marching up to the farmhouse door. She didn't want to die. Her heart was beginning to thump. What was she going to do? Supposing she never saw her mother again? The prime minister was still speaking. Shirley forced herself to concentrate on what he was saying.

'Now may God bless you all. May He defend the right. It is the evil things we shall be fighting against: brute force, bad faith, injustice, oppression and persecution.' Shirley's hand was shaking so much her tea spilled into her saucer. All that gas-mask practice and talk of air-raid shelters was a reality now. 'And against them,' Mr Chamberlain continued, 'I am certain that the right will prevail.'

As the wireless programme of music continued, she thought of her mother and remembered something she had said. 'If we go to war, we may all have to put up with a lot of things we don't like until it's over.'

Shirley took a deep breath. It was time to grow up. She'd been saying all week that she wasn't a child any more. What had happened to her and Tom was unfair, and it wasn't right, but she had a roof over her head and a full stomach. It dawned on her that some of the lads she'd grown up with, especially the older ones, would be signing up before long. They'd be marching off to battlefields and God knows what, risking their lives for king and country. It was time to stop feeling sorry for herself. The country was at war.

# CHAPTER 7

Florrie was taken in the wooden wheelchair to the treatment room, where Dr Scott, the man who had come to her house, was waiting for her. She had been examined several times that week, and she'd had another X-ray. Each morning, she'd spat into a small container, which was taken for testing. As she came into the room, Dr Scott was holding an X-ray film up to the light and studying it carefully. It didn't mean a whole lot to Florrie, but she could see that whereas the majority of her lungs were dark, there was a light area at the top of her right lung.

'Right, Florrie,' he said, turning his attention to her, 'here's what we'll do.'

Over the past week, the formality of being called 'Mrs Jenkins' every time she had treatments had slowly been dropped. She was still treated with respect, and everyone was kind, but she was being made to feel more at home. She had made friends with quite a few of the women in the ward, who were all at different stages of recovery. Pauline had only just come out of an iron lung, while Florrie's nearest neighbour, Edna, was about to be discharged.

'I think it best if we perform an artificial pneumo-thorax of your right lung.'

Florrie stared unblinking at the doctor. Artificial pneumo . . . What on earth was that?

'Don't be alarmed,' he said. 'I already explained it to you, remember? We collapse the lung for a period of time so that it can rest. It gives the organ a chance to heal a lot more quickly if it doesn't have to work at the same time.'

Oh yes, now she understood. 'Will it hurt?' Florrie asked. She was aware that her voice had become very small.

'Surprisingly,' said Dr Scott, 'my patients tell me they hardly notice the difference. You will have to continue with complete bed rest, of course, but once we've done it, we shall wait to see what happens.'

'How will you know if it's worked?'

'We'll give you another X-ray in two or three months' time.'

Florrie was beginning to get used to the idea of long timescales. The thought of two or three months of in-activity didn't appal her as much as it had done when she'd first arrived. 'When do you want to do it?'

Dr Scott pushed his glasses back up the bridge of his nose. 'There's no time like the present,' he smiled.

The nurse wheeled Florrie next door into a small treatment room and she took off her nightdress. She was asked to lie on the bed. 'Lie on your left side with your right arm draped over the top of your head and dangling over the edge,' said the nurse.

While she was doing this, the doctor and the nurse were washing their hands. The nurse laid a white cloth over Florrie's side, and the doctor painted her skin using a piece of white muslin soaked in something so cold it made Florrie shiver.

'I must ask you to keep very still,' he said. 'This is a local anaesthetic. I am going to put a needle into your chest and then we shall push some air into the area between your chest wall and your lung.'

It sounded terrifying, but Florrie was surprised that she only felt a slight tugging sensation. The procedure didn't take very long, and once it was done, apart from a 'heavy' sensation in her chest, it didn't bother her at all. She dressed herself and sat back in the wooden chair.

'Florrie,' said Dr Scott, 'are you good at writing?'

Florrie raised an eyebrow. 'Writing? Well, I can write, if that's what you mean.'

'Would you be amenable to keeping a journal of your experiences? We are looking for patients who will express their feelings on the page,' he went on. 'It doesn't have to be brilliant, but we would like a week-by-week account of how it feels to be a TB patient.'

'May I ask why you need it?'

'We treat the symptoms,' he said, 'but you are the one having the experience. We think if we understand a patient's struggles, we will be better able to help them.'

Florrie smiled. 'In that case, I'd be honoured.'

'I must be honest,' said Dr Scott. 'We are not looking for romance, but for you to tell it as it is.'

'I understand,' said Florrie. 'Yes, I'll do it.'

He gave her a little leather-bound book and a pencil. 'I shall look forward to reading your account,' he said.

Back on the ward, her fellow patients greeted her like a conquering hero. 'Here she comes!'

'Hello, soldier. Had your wings clipped, then?'

'No blowing your own trumpet, now, Florrie.'

Resting in her bed, although she knew she faced two or three months before she went back to see Dr Scott, she felt strangely encouraged. At last she was taking positive steps to battle this dreadful disease.

There was a postcard on her dresser. She recognized the picture on the front straight away. It was one of the postcards she'd given Shirley. She ran her finger lovingly over the handwriting and looked for kisses. Two. Shirley and Tom must be all right, then. Her daughter hadn't said much, and foolishly she'd forgotten to put her address on the card, so Florrie couldn't reply, but surely that had to mean she was happy. What a relief.

As usual, the school week began on a Monday. Shirley and Tom set off in good time to walk into the village. Tom had already been up for ages. He'd done the milking, while Janet left Shirley to set the table, prepare breakfast and get the vegetables ready for tea. Mr Oliver grumbled quite a lot when the suggestion was mooted, but she heard Janet whisper, 'You like the boy, don't you? If she complains, the authorities might come and take them both away,' and so Shirley was allowed to stay out of the milking parlour.

It took half an hour to do the walk on that first day but only twenty minutes once they'd got used to it. Janet had drawn a map for Shirley, which turned out to be easy to follow. They began by walking through the little hamlet of Swillage and down Dappers Lane. There were only a few dwellings scattered along the route. Most of the surrounding area was farmland. After passing some allotments on Water Lane, they came to the village itself. It had two public houses – the Lamb Inn on the right and the smaller Red Lion at the bottom of the hill to the left – two grocery shops, a fish-and-chip shop, a baker's and the war memorial in a triangle of grass in the middle. They turned right and found themselves with St Margaret's Church to the left and Older's School, their new school, on the right. On their first day, several children were already in the playground and Shirley recognized three girls from Hallsville.

'What's your place like?' Hazel Freeman asked. 'I'm staying in that shop across the road. It's lovely. I've got a bed to meself, and yesterday we went to the seaside.'

'Lucky you,' Gwen Knox said dismally. 'I'm staying with two old fogeys. They must be a hundred years old and all they want to do are jigsaw puzzles and singing round the piano.'

'Sounds all right to me,' said Bobbi Mackenzie. Her proper name was Roberta, but everybody called her Bobbi.

'I suppose,' said Gwen grudgingly. 'They say I've got a nice voice. What about you, Shirley?'

'Tom and I are on a farm,' said Shirley, grateful to hear the teacher ringing the school bell so that she didn't have to elaborate.

Miss Lloyd wasn't there to introduce them to the other teachers. Shirley was horrified to learn that she was back in Worthing teaching the rest of the school in some hall or other. How was she going to let Miss Lloyd know what had happened to them? If she couldn't contact her, they'd be forced to sleep in that awful room with no proper door all winter! According to their new head teacher, the few Londoners who were left in Angmering were to be integrated with the pupils of Older's School. It was obvious that everybody was thinking they were almost school leavers anyway, so what did it matter?

They began their lessons with an air-raid drill. When the school bell rang, everybody had to get under their desks as quickly as possible and stay very still until the bell was rung a second time.

'You won't hear a bell when the real one comes,' said the headmaster. 'There will be an air-raid siren.'

For most of the younger children, it was a little frightening, but for the pupils of Shirley's age, it seemed a bit stupid. They didn't really fit under the desks either.

To start with, Shirley and Tom were together in the upper class, but it didn't take long for Tom to be sent down a class or two. He was a bit upset at being in what he called the 'babbies' class', but Shirley didn't make a fuss because it did make life a little easier for him.

On their way home on their first day, an old woman in one of the cottages in Swillage stood in her doorway and waved to them. Tom waved back, but Shirley stuck her nose in the air. She didn't mean to be snooty, but she didn't know anything about the woman and she might be drawn into telling her something she shouldn't. Her mother always drummed into her to keep away from gossips. Although she and Tom never stopped to talk, the woman was there every day and funnily enough Shirley found herself looking forward to seeing her.

Shirley's new teacher was called Miss Smith and she took to her straight away. She wasn't very old, probably in her early twenties. She had blonde hair, which she wore pinned back from her face with combs, and she had some nice clothes. There was an air of sadness about her and some of the girls said she looked like that because she'd been jilted by her boyfriend.

Their very first assignment was to write an essay about their experiences during the holidays. For the local children, it meant writing about harvest time, when friends and neighbours gathered in the fields to bring in the crops. Others wrote about holidays with distant relatives or camping in the woods with their brothers and sisters. One girl had a week-long coach trip, and another boy had gone to a place called York to see his grandmother, perhaps for the last time. For the children of Hallsville School, it meant writing about their evacuation and the alien environment in which they were now living. Shirley wrote a vivid account of a boy who had a hard time understanding what was going on around him. Of course, she didn't disclose that the boy she was writing about was her own brother (that would have been a sort of betrayal), but in thinking deeply about it, she began to appreciate how confusing and upsetting life could be for him. She'd reflected on how frustrating it must be to reach out and never be able to grasp the meaning of things, and yet paradoxically be so brilliantly clever at things that other people didn't appreciate or understand. In doing so, everything that Tom struggled with suddenly came into sharp focus in her own mind. At the end of the exercise, Shirley had written twice as much as anyone else, but more importantly, not only had she enjoyed doing it but in a funny sort of way, it made her feel a lot better.

Tom was never one for showing affection, but that afternoon as they walked back to the farm, he'd let her slip her arm though his and hug him for a couple of seconds.

Gilbert Oliver stared out over the water. He hated being here and yet there was something within him that drew him back again and again. Patching Pond, which fed a tributary of the River Arun, was quite large and was famed for its multitude of fish. People swam in the water, and in his grandfather's day, they had even held duck races on what they called Pond Days. Just down the road was the Horse & Groom, a popular local inn, where the men would have a couple of jars of beer before making their way home to the villages of Patching, Clapham and Angmering. The whole experience made it a day to remember. Pond Days were long gone, but the pond itself still entertained fishermen, and the locals enjoyed walking round it as they watched the ducks. It was an oasis in the middle of miles of farmland where moorhens and coots scratched around the muddy banks. It was an idyll, but for Gilbert it held a dark secret.

Every time he came here, he was taken back in time to the day Elizabeth died. He would go over and over the event in his head and the things they said to each other. He remembered the cold, the water swirling round his thighs as he waded in. He remembered her screams and the way her arms flailed in a frantic attempt to stop herself from sinking. He remembered the heaviness of her poor dead body as he carried her out of the water and the sound of running feet as the people from down the hill came to the rescue. He remembered the prayers he'd said as they tried to revive her and gave an involuntary shudder. He'd been so angry. Perhaps he should never have married her. He knew farming was hard work and that she wasn't cut out for the life right from the start. That Shirley reminded him of her: headstrong and digging her heels in to get her own way. He thrust his hands into his pockets. He'd been a damned fool. He had hoped he could persuade Elizabeth that everything would be all right, but she didn't believe him. All he'd ever wanted was to keep the farm, and he would have moved heaven and earth to make her stay here. He stared out over the water for one last time.

'I will make it work this time,' he said under his breath. 'You wait and see. I'm not beaten yet, girl. It'll all come to me in the end.'

# CHAPTER 8

*Dear Florrie,*

*Just a line or two to let you know that everything is going well with the shop. We still have just as many customers, even though it's very quiet around here. I really miss the sound of children's voices, especially the little gaggle of girls who used to play hopscotch on the corner of Forty-Acre Lane and Roscoe Street. St Luke's has stopped the Sunday school for the time being in case of bombing. No sign of the Germans, but we have been busy putting brown-paper strips over all the windows.*

*You probably don't know that Len Greene signed up under the National Service Act. He read in the paper that men up to the age of forty-one are allowed to go and he said he didn't want to leave it too late and miss the chance of doing his bit.*

*They're saying petrol is to be rationed by the end of the month.*

*Soon after you left, they closed all the cinemas. It said in the paper that they were worried that if a bomb fell, it would mean a lot of people getting killed. They stopped all the football matches too. It was a miserable time. I really missed going to* the Odeon. *It was my only treat with my Raymond away. I wasn't the only one. People complained and by the middle of September, they'd changed their minds. A good job too, if you ask me. We have to have a bit of fun in life, and so long as we know where the air-raid shelters are, where's the harm?*

*Shall I send you your ID card when it comes? My Raymond has gone back to sea. I try not to think about it, but they are saying that once it gets going, the merchant ships will be targeted as well. Ken is somewhere at sea in the Royal Navy. He writes, but he's not allowed to say where he is. We have to be so careful not to say anything that might be somehow passed on to the enemy. I don't know what the world is coming to.*

*Still, it's not all doom and gloom. Rhona Parry had a little baby boy. He's a dear little chap with pretty blond hair just like his daddy. Chas is hoping to come home on leave soon to see him, but so that he doesn't miss out, Rhona has taken the baby to the photographer's. She's got some lovely photographs. Of course, it's not the same as seeing the baby in the flesh, but at least Chas knows what his son looks like.*

*Doreen sends her love. Her mother wants to get out of London, so she's going to stay with her sister in Coventry. It'll be much safer than being in the capital. Doreen is refusing to go with her. She says her livelihood is here. Just between you and me, with Mrs Kennedy out of the way, I think she will join the WVS, and good luck to her, I say.*

*The takings are about the same. I've put them in the bank, less my wages, like you said.*

*Keep your pecker up.*
*All my love,*
*Betty*
*PS I hope you got the postcard Shirley sent. So*
*far that's the only one she's posted. Still, I suppose*
*no news is good news.*

* * *

When Shirley and Tom arrived in Angmering, the boys in the village found a new target for their bullying. It didn't take long for them to realize that for all his size and strength, Tom Jenkins was a bit of a pussy cat. They did all the usual things, like snatching his lunchbox, 'accidentally' bumping into him and calling him names, but after a while that became boring. Of course, they had to pick on Tom when Shirley wasn't around. Petite as she was, she was a firebrand when it came to protecting her brother. A couple of times, one of his tormentors left it a bit late to run and came face to face with her. She didn't have to do much – just a look was enough to send them scurrying.

As it turned out, being in the lower class was good for Tom. Because everything was at a slower pace and he'd been this way before, he made steady progress with his reading. They had been in Angmering just about two months when he managed to read a whole book for the first time in his life. Called *The Beacon Infant Readers Book Five*, it had a few illustrations, and the key words were at the front of each story. They were shortened versions of fables and fairy tales like the stories of King

Midas, Rumpelstiltskin and David and Goliath, but his favourite was 'The Bell of Atri'. In it, a wise king placed a bell within reach of every man, woman and child in his kingdom. To get justice, they just had to ring the bell. When a poor abandoned and starving horse pulled the rope, thinking it was food, and rang the bell, the villagers came running. The king gave the faithful old horse justice by making his owner give him fresh hay and a warm stable. Tom hated the thought of any living creature being ill treated, so he read that one over and over again.

Of course, he still wanted to hear Shirley's stories and so occasionally she would retell 'The Birthday Thief'.

'The children in the story are a bit like us,' he said one day. 'They want to go back home, but they are trapped by the Birthday Thief, aren't they?'

'I suppose they are,' said Shirley, 'but it's not quite the same. You and I still have our birthdays.'

'Tell me about when they found the cake,' said Tom.

'*It was like a big white tower,*' said Shirley. '*It stood about sixty feet high and had ladders propped against it. Down below, the children were pushing trucks full of white stuff.*'

'That's the icing,' said Tom, his eyes glistening with excitement.

Shirley nodded. '*Next to the cake,*' she went on, '*he saw some crystal medallions hanging on hooks. Each one had a name on it. Billy ran up to the platform, but as soon as he put his foot on it, an ear-piercing alarm went off. Weee-o, weee-o.*'

Tom would have her tell the story over and over again, but now that he could read for himself, she wanted him to practise his newly found skill. She remembered that there were some books upstairs in that lovely room they'd been shown when they'd first come to the farm. She knew it was forbidden, but if she was careful not to get caught, and they looked after whatever they took, no one need ever know. Shirley planned to borrow a book at the earliest opportunity.

'Shirley,' Miss Smith said one day as everybody was leaving for home, 'would you mind staying behind for a minute or two?'

As she waited for everyone to go, Shirley wondered what it was all about. She knew she wasn't in trouble. She hadn't done anything wrong, but her teacher looked very serious. While she waited, Shirley admired her striking navy and white striped blouse. She was sure she'd seen it a couple of weeks before as a dress, but it had been cut down and put with a navy skirt. Miss Smith had real flare because she had added a red silk scarf, which she'd tied as an artist's bow at the neck under the wide white collar. Once the classroom was empty, Miss Smith opened her drawer and took out Shirley's essay.

'This is very good, Shirley,' she said, indicating that she should sit down, 'and I should like you to think about something.'

Shirley lowered herself into a chair.

'Every year,' Miss Smith went on, 'the Duke of

Northumberland sponsors an essay competition for the under-sixteens. It brings in funds for the RNLI – that's the lifeboats, you know. I think your story would be a worthy entry.'

Shirley blinked. How exciting. Nobody had ever said anything like that about her work before.

'Would you agree to my sending it in?'

Shirley didn't have to think about it. 'Yes, please.'

Miss Smith nodded and put the essay back into her drawer. 'Have you given any thought as to what you would like to do when you leave school?'

The answer was no. Shirley knew Mum wanted them both to stay on at school for as long as possible. If she could have her way, she would have left the previous July, but Mum wanted them to stay until they were both sixteen. Some of her friends had left school as early as fourteen, and most of the others left in the summer. They had found jobs, one as a waitress in a small cafe just round the corner from the shop back home, and the other worked in the local greengrocer's. Their wages were a pittance, but at least they had their own money. That's why it galled Shirley so much that her mother wouldn't even let her do a paper round. She shrugged her shoulders. 'Shop work, I suppose.'

Miss Smith sighed. 'There's nothing wrong with shop work,' she said, 'but I think you are perfectly capable of greater things.'

Shirley blinked.

'You are good with the little ones,' her teacher went

on. 'They relate to you.' She leaned forward. 'Shirley, I want you to think about training to be a teacher.'

It sounded wonderful, but Shirley knew Mum didn't have that kind of money. Florrie hadn't exactly told her the details about her illness, so Shirley had no idea how much her mother's treatment might cost, but she'd already been away for just about six weeks, and even that wouldn't be cheap. She really couldn't imagine Mum paying for teacher-training college as well. But she didn't mention the money. Mum had drummed it into her that she should never talk about a lack of money or that she couldn't afford something. 'We're not a charity case,' Florrie would say. 'We pay our own way.' (Even if they couldn't.) Which was why Shirley was pretty sure that teacher-training college would be out of the question.

Shirley shook her head. 'I don't—' she began.

Miss Smith put up her hand to silence her. 'Before you make up your mind, I'm suggesting that we put you up for a scholarship. You would take an exam, which is not easy, so you will have to work hard, but if you pass, all your expenses would be taken care of.'

Shirley's mouth fell open. She tried to say something, but Miss Smith interrupted her again. 'Don't tell me now, Shirley. Go away and think about it. Write and ask your mother what she thinks.'

Shirley was rooted to the spot. Miss Smith began to collect her things together. 'That's all, Shirley. You can go now.'

She walked out of the classroom in a dream. Could

she really be a teacher one day? Outside in the playground, she looked around for Tom. He was usually sitting on the wall near Church Lane that ran adjacent to the school, waiting for her, but today the wall was empty. She called his name a couple of times. Where was he? Surely he wouldn't have decided to walk home alone? It wasn't that he would get lost, but he knew Mum had said he had to stay with her at all times.

'Down the hole, down the hole . . .' she could hear the boys chanting somewhere. She followed the sound until she reached the centre of the village. Across the triangle beyond the war memorial, she could see a group of boys gathered in the road. One boy was holding her brother's coat. Shirley sprinted across the road to see what they were doing.

'Where's Tom?' she demanded. 'What have you done with my brother?'

The boys pulled back. 'Go away,' said one. 'Girls aren't allowed.'

She could see now that they had the cover off some sort of large drain in the road. She supposed it was to funnel excess water coming down the hill and keep it away from the centre of the village. One of the boys, bent right over, was inside the drain egging someone on.

'Is my brother in there?' Shirley demanded.

'Anyone who wants to be in our gang has to walk to the end of the culvert,' said another boy. 'It's fairly easy, although it makes your back ache.' He demonstrated how they had to walk. Shirley was horrified.

119

'It comes out by the village hall, dunnit, Kev,' said another boy.

'My brother is much taller than you lot,' Shirley said angrily. 'If you have to bend over, he'll be bent double.'

It was clear from the expressions on their faces that they hadn't thought of that.

'He can always go on his hands and knees,' said Kev.

'It's all slimy and dirty down there,' Shirley protested. She pulled the boy away from the mouth of the drain and went inside a little way. 'Tom, you don't have to do this. Come out of there.'

Some of the boys began to drift away. 'Sissy,' Kev muttered, and that's when Shirley saw red. She spun round and glared at him, pushing her face really close to his. 'No, I'll tell you what this is,' she spat. 'You're a load of bullies. You can see he doesn't understand, so you pick on him. You haven't got the guts to stand up to someone who is your equal.'

The landlord and another man came out of the Red Lion. He was a big man with a bald head and tattoos on his arms. The other man was nice-looking, but he wore a grubby shirt, and the braces on his trousers were frayed.

'What are you lot doing here?' the landlord roared. 'Put that cover back on and clear off, the lot of you.' The boys scattered. 'You heard me,' he said to Shirley.

'Leave off, Cyril,' said the other man. 'Can't you see you're scaring the poor girl half to death?'

Shirley took a deep breath, and although she was

120

trembling inside, she squared up to him and said, 'I'm not leaving here until my brother comes back out.'

The landlord grinned. 'I take that back, Vince. This little lassie has some real pluck.' He turned to Shirley. 'You're one of them 'vacuees, ench you? Where do you live? I shall have a word with whoever's looking after you, cheeking your elders and betters like this.' He looked at Vince and winked.

'Oliver's Farm,' said Shirley, her face burning. 'And I'm sure Mr Oliver won't care tuppence.'

The landlord threw back his head and laughed.

'Oh,' said Vince, 'you're the girl with the simpleton brother.'

Shirley put her hands on her hips, her eyes blazing. 'No, he's not,' she said angrily. 'Just because he's a bit different doesn't mean he's stupid.'

'Feisty little madam, isn't she?' the landlord said good-naturedly. 'I think you met your match there, Vince.'

A couple of seconds later, Tom backed out of the drain. His jacket was filthy from touching the walls, and his shoes were caked in mud and slime. He straightened himself up painfully. 'I didn't really want to go down there, Shirl,' he said. 'And when you get near the middle, it smells awful.'

Vince kicked the cover back into place. 'If you'll take my advice, you'll stay away from there.' His tone was a lot more conciliatory.

Shirley and Tom stared after him as he headed up the hill towards the Avenals.

'Look, sonny,' said the landlord, 'you don't have to do everything those boys tell you. If you get any more trouble from them, you come straight to me, all right?'

Tom nodded. Shirley began brushing his clothes with her hand. 'You should have asked me first. Don't let them talk you into these things.'

The landlord turned to go. 'And don't take any notice of Vince Carter either. He didn't mean to be offensive. He's got a lot on his mind, that's all.'

'Thank you, mister,' said Shirley and, grabbing Tom's arm, they headed back to Oliver's Farm.

# CHAPTER 9

Shirley watched for the post for nearly three weeks until the reason why her mother hadn't written suddenly dawned on her. It was the address! She hadn't sent her mother her address. How daft she'd been. Shirley had been imagining the worst – that Florrie was too ill to write, or even that she was dead. She'd withdrawn into herself with her dark thoughts, but she hadn't said anything to anyone. She told herself her mother would never forget her, and of course she hadn't. She simply didn't know where Shirley and Tom were! Tom was in the stable grooming the horses, which gave her a golden opportunity to write to Mum in private. Shirley closed the door of their bedroom and sat herself down with the second of her four postcards.

To be truly honest, she was feeling a little better about being here. Janet was friendly and chatty, and a couple of days ago they had spent a lovely time together. They both talked about their past lives, but not in depth. Shirley wasn't ready to share everything with her just yet. Janet knew Shirley and Tom lived over a shop and that her father had run off with another woman.

123

Shirley told her how hard her mother worked and that the strain of it had made her ill. She'd even found herself telling Janet what it felt like having a twin like Tom.

'I feel really lucky that I was born normal,' she confided. They were getting apples ready to store in the loft of the barn for winter. 'But sometimes I feel a bit guilty about it too.'

'Don't be,' said Janet. 'He's happy enough.'

'Mr Oliver shouts at him all the time,' Shirley remarked.

'But Tom loves being with the animals,' said Janet. 'For him, that more than makes up for it.'

Shirley nodded. Janet was right. Tom did seem to have a gift with animals. The percherons responded to him, and he enjoyed mucking out the stables and grooming them. They were called Darby and Joan, and from the very first week they were here, he'd mastered the skill of harnessing them as if he'd been doing it all his life. Tom's strength meant that he could handle the heavy milk churns and bales of straw as if they were no trouble at all, and he couldn't wait to get home from school to throw himself into his chores.

As for her past, Janet told Shirley that she had been brought up by her father and her father's new wife after her own mother had died when she was six.

'My stepmother never liked me,' Janet said. 'We rowed all the time, until she kicked me out.'

The small orchard had several apple trees, but they weren't in very good condition. They were all varieties of Sussex apples, and Janet seemed to know a bit about them.

'That's because one day when Gil was out, I asked one of the old boys in the village to come and identify the varieties,' she told Shirley. 'This one is the Egremont Russet. They say this apple was first grown at Petworth and they named it after the earl. It's an eating apple. Lovely, very crisp and they will last until Christmas.' Janet saw Shirley's look of confusion and chuckled. 'Petworth is one of the big country houses around here,' and putting on a posh accent, she added, 'Country seat and all that.'

Shirley laughed. This was a totally different world from Canning Town.

The Alfriston apple was slightly larger. Janet explained that it was a cooking apple and was sometimes a bit sharp to the taste. 'If we can keep it away from the rats and mice, this one will keep until the spring.' The final apple was the Forge, another cooking apple. It was pale green with a tendency to turn slightly orange-coloured. Each totally unblemished apple was put into a newspaper twist and placed side by side, but not touching, in a straw-lined crate. Shirley quite enjoyed 'laying the apples down', as Janet called it. When Janet began to talk about her days in service and her marriage to Mr Oliver, Shirley, an incurable romantic, wanted to hear all about their courtship, but Janet wasn't very forthcoming about that.

It was an odd relationship. Although they were man and wife, the pair of them seemed to live very separate lives. They skirted around each other all the time. They never kissed or held hands. They never went out together or had friends over for a meal. Even when they were working in the same place, like the milking parlour, they were oblivious of each other.

Now that she was alone in her bedroom, Shirley pulled the postcard towards her and wrote the address of the farm on the correspondence side. It didn't leave a lot of space for her news, so what should she say? Should she tell her mother about the terrible room with the blanket wall that she and Tom shared? Should she mention all the hard work they had to do? Thanks to Janet, she had been spared having to work in that horrible, smelly milking shed ever since that first weekend, but she was still expected to be a virtual skivvy in the house. She was sometimes asked to do the washing, and the ironing. Then there was the dusting and sweeping, the apple-picking and storing, and lifting spuds in the field . . . No, she'd better not tell her mother all that. It would only worry her.

First, she asked how her mother was; then she told her that Tom was loving the farm and that she, Shirley, had come top in the essay-writing competition at school. As a result, her new teacher wanted her to take an entrance exam for teacher-training college. When it came to putting their code on the card, two kisses seemed about right. Shirley wrote the address of the shop on the right-hand side of the postcard and slipped it into her school bag. She would post it on the way to school tomorrow.

The dog was barking and Shirley heard raised voices. When she looked out of the window, she saw Mr Oliver yelling at a man in a smart blue suit. The man didn't look very old, but he did look important because he carried a leather case. He had brown curly hair and was every bit as good-looking as the film star Gilbert Roland. Tom was still in the stables, and Janet was somewhere in the house. Shirley opened the door and peered outside.

'If you think I'm going to be dictated to by some wet-behind-the-ears, snotty little toad like you,' Mr Oliver was shouting, 'you've got another think coming. Now, get off my land.'

By this time, the dog was nearly demented. As she saw its slavering jaws and bared teeth, Shirley couldn't help thinking that it was a good job it was held back by the chain.

'There's no need to be abusive, Mr Oliver,' the man said patiently. 'And turning me away won't change anything. There's a war on and the Ministry of Agriculture is encouraging all farmers to grow more. According to this inspection' – he held up a piece of paper – 'you've already been informed that your farm is underproductive.'

'What happens on my land is my business,' Mr Oliver snapped. 'I run my farm the way I want to.'

The newcomer stood his ground. 'I also believe the Milk Marketing Board are not satisfied with the level of your milk production or your milk-parlour hygiene.

Quite frankly, Mr Oliver, your farm needs a thorough overhaul.'

Mr Oliver looked as if he was about to burst a blood vessel. 'I don't have to stand here and listen to this,' he yelled. 'People have been working this land the same way for six generations.'

'That's just the point,' said the man. 'What was good enough for the Victorians isn't good enough for today.'

'How dare you!' Mr Oliver spluttered. He advanced towards the man in a menacing way.

The man put his hand up defensively. 'But we can change all that, Mr Oliver,' he said. 'We want to come alongside you. By working together, we can help you to make this farm more productive.'

By this time, the barking dog was hysterical with rage, and Mr Oliver was standing so close to its quarry that the two of them were almost nose to nose. 'I remember what the government did in the 1920s to people like my father,' he snarled. 'Ever heard of the Great Betrayal? No, I don't suppose you have. That was when jumped-up city types like you took away the subsidies given to farmers during the Great War and the wheat and corn markets collapsed.'

'Mr Oliver—' the man began again. He was still backing away, until he tripped over a raised stone on the path and stumbled. Fortunately, the gate saved him from an actual fall. Conceding defeat, the man went through the gate and closed it behind himself.

As if to prove a point, Mr Oliver took up a position leaning on the bars.

'You haven't heard the last of this, Mr Oliver,' the man called out. He walked to his car and opened the back passenger door. Throwing his brown case inside, he said defiantly, 'I shall be back.'

'And the next time, I shall set the bloody dog on you,' Mr Oliver growled.

As the man drove off, Mr Oliver shook his fist in the air and shouted after him, 'Remember that old saying "A Sussex man will not be druv"? Nobody tells me what to do. Nobody.'

He turned and saw Shirley watching him through the crack in the door. 'What are you staring at?' he demanded.

Shirley panicked and slammed the door shut.

Boredom was the worst part of being ill. Quite early on, Florrie realized that she had to find something to do during the long hours, but the question was, what? The nurses weren't very keen for her to knit, and neither was she, especially when she discovered that the wool fibres made her snuffly. She tried a little beadwork but didn't enjoy it very much. She enjoyed doing crosswords, but Florrie was the sort of woman who liked to be productive, and crosswords were only an indulgence. What she wanted was a new skill – with something to show for it at the end. The patients sometimes helped each other. There was an opportunity to learn another language when it was revealed that Mary Dolman spoke French, but Florrie quickly discovered that she didn't have an aptitude for learning languages. Another patient offered her lessons in watercolours and tatting, but she found it easier to paint the sheets than the canvas, and she had no patience at all for tatting.

The biggest setback with learning a new skill was that everything had to be done in bed lying down and with as little effort as possible. She was still only allowed up for a couple of trips to the toilet each day. The one thing she did have was plenty of fresh air. The windows were wide open no matter the weather, and as the winter months drew on, Florrie only wanted to snuggle down under the covers all the time.

The thing she enjoyed doing the most came about quite by accident. Someone had given her a newspaper. It was pretty dog-eared by the time she got it, because just about everybody else had already read it. As it lay on the bedcovers waiting to be put in the bin, she remembered how when she was a child, her father used to fold paper into shapes. He was clever enough to make birds and flowers of all shapes and sizes. She struggled to remember how it was done, but three or four afternoons later, Florrie had managed to fold a half-decent paper rose. It took several more days to perfect it, and when she showed it to the girls and the nurses, they were very excited. It seemed like everybody wanted one.

'You should do them in pretty paper,' said Tina.

So Florrie wrote to Betty asking her to send some from the stockroom in the shop, but it was a long time coming, so a couple of the nurses brought in some old present-wrapping paper and Florrie tackled her new project with great gusto.

She had made some new friends. Edna had left in September, but Tina was still on the ward. She had left two small children behind. Because there was no one to look after her children, they had been sent to Dr Barnardo's. Florrie really felt for her. If her own problems were hard, life seemed to have dealt Tina a particularly bitter blow. Her husband had been killed in a car accident during the first few days of the blackout, and as her babies were only small (a year old and two and a half years old), she was terrified that they would forget her.

'You don't think they'll put my kids up for adoption while I'm in here, do you?' she'd asked Florrie one day.

Florrie had said, 'No, of course not,' but when Tina turned her head away, she and Edna had shared a look of concern. It was a terrible thought, but in these troubled times, it was quite possible. Some children, like her own, had been evacuated to the country, but the papers were full of children being sent to Crown dominions in far-flung places such as Canada, South Africa, Australia and even New Zealand! Newspaper pictures of these little waifs with their luggage labels on their coats, waving goodbye from the railings of some huge ocean liner, were enough to tug at anyone's heart-strings. They might be safe from bombs and bullets, but popping over for a weekend to see them was impossible, and how on earth would their parents manage to afford to get them back again once the war was over?

A woman called Jill came to occupy Edna's bed. During the first few days, she spent a lot of time crying. She didn't do it openly, but everyone recognized the glassy-looking, puffy red eyes and the wobbly chin firmly set in one position so that she wouldn't lose control. Florrie knew exactly how she was feeling; in fact, they'd all been there. Jill's husband had been called up and was part of the British Expeditionary Force in France. She wouldn't have known that except that one of his mates let it slip. He'd ended up on a charge and was in the glasshouse at Colchester for giving away information that might be useful to the enemy.

The first air attack on the country came in October, when German war planes fired on ships in the Firth of Forth in Scotland. Now that it was really happening, they put the wireless on each evening and listened with a mixture of dread and horrible fascination for news of the outside world. Once the news programmes were over, the BBC went back to its usual deadly-dull diet of light music, gramophone records and Sandy Mac-Pherson playing the organ, with the occasional bit of first-aid instruction thrown in for good measure.

When the monthly visiting time came round again, Florrie was surprised and delighted to see a familiar face walking down the ward towards her.

'Doreen! I never expected to see you,' she cried. To Florrie's amazement, she was dressed in a WVS uniform. 'Fancy you coming all this way. You look fantastic.'

'My pleasure,' said Doreen, twirling round for her

friend to admire her from all angles. She put her hand to her mouth in a confidential manner. 'I only wore it to get a seat on the train,' she whispered. 'It's amazing what a uniform will do for a girl.'

They both laughed.

Her friend was carrying a small holdall, and to Florrie's great delight, she opened it to reveal lots of brightly coloured paper – everything from tissue paper to patterned wrapping paper to wallpaper. 'The tissue is from me,' Doreen said. 'The factory is closing down for the duration.'

Florrie was horrified. 'But what will people do for corsets?'

'As it turns out, people have stopped buying corsets,' said Doreen, 'and anyway, the government have requisitioned the factory to make parachutes.'

'Does that mean you'll be going to join your mother in Coventry?'

'Absolutely not,' said Doreen emphatically. 'I'm staying to do my bit. I've joined the WVS and am being trained in first aid and fire-watching. If the war goes on for some time, I'm thinking of getting another job, or I might even join the WAAF.'

Florrie's eyebrows shot up. She'd never heard Doreen be so decisive before. 'Why the WAAF?'

Doreen looked thoughtful, as if considering the question. 'Because they've got an even nicer uniform,' she said, and they both giggled.

Doreen fished around in her handbag. 'Betty gave me

something else for you.' She held up another postcard. 'It came yesterday.'

Florrie took in a breath. While she read it, Doreen pulled up a chair and made herself comfortable. When she looked up at her friend, Florrie was a bit teary. 'Sorry,' she said.

'No, no, it's quite all right.'

'I wish I could be sure she and Tom are happy,' said Florrie, holding the precious card to her chest.

Doreen looked thoughtful. 'Listen,' she said. 'With Mother gone, I've discovered that I have quite a bit of money coming in. It seems she was keeping an awful lot of it for herself and I never knew.' Florrie went to say something, but Doreen waved her hand. 'I know, I know. She's a mean old cow, but she's still my mother. Anyway, while I still can, why don't I go to Worthing to see Shirley and Tom for myself, and then it'll put your mind at rest?'

Florrie clamped her hand across her mouth. 'Oh, Doreen, would you?'

'Why not?' said Doreen. 'I could do with a few more days out, and a little excursion to the seaside would be just the thing.'

Florrie asked her to reach for her handbag in the locker beside the bed. She handed Doreen a pound note. 'Would you give this to Shirley? Tell her to treat herself to something and to give Tom some too.'

'Of course,' said Doreen. They both relaxed. 'Why do you want all this paper, anyway?' she added as her foot

134

accidentally knocked against the holdall she'd shoved under the bed.

Florrie showed her a paper rose.

'That's amazing,' said Doreen, admiring it from all sides.

'You can have that one,' said Florrie.

'Are you sure?' Doreen put it carefully in her bag. 'Anyway, how are you doing, Florrie? Are you getting any better?'

'I had my lung collapsed when I came here,' said Florrie. 'They say if they rest it, it gets better more quickly. That was just over two months ago. The doctor is going to see how I am next week and then I'll have another X-ray.'

Doreen nodded sagely. 'What then?'

Florrie shrugged. She wasn't sure herself. She'd never really asked. 'If it's healed, I suppose I can get up.'

'That'll be nice,' said Doreen. 'You'll be able to get out for some fresh air.'

'Oh, believe you me,' Florrie chuckled, 'I have plenty of that!'

Nobody at the farm spoke of the incident concerning the man from the Ministry of Agriculture, but his visit seemed to have changed Mr Oliver's attitude. He became more morose and moody. Nothing pleased him any more. If he had been difficult before, he was even more so now.

Each morning, Mr Oliver would walk to the gate to collect the post from the postman, rather than let him leave it in the covered enamel pail that was left on the other side of the gate for the purpose. Some time ago, the postman had made it clear that he wouldn't come to the house so long as the dog was there. Mr Oliver often teased the animal or lashed out a kick when he wasn't looking. That sort of treatment and the fact that he kept it short of food contributed to the dog's vicious behaviour. Both Shirley and Tom hated to see what was happening to it, and Tom often snuck it extra food.

While she was doing the washing-up, Shirley could see Mr Oliver searching through the envelopes the postman had given him. Sometimes he would shout out loud and rip one to shreds without even opening it, before coming back to the house. When they ate their meals together, he would release a tirade of abuse towards government officials using language Shirley and Tom had never heard before.

'What gives them the right to come here and tell me how to run my farm?' he'd rant. 'Me, what's done it all me life. They're all bloody communists, I tell you.'

'What's a communist?' Shirley asked Janet when Mr Oliver had gone out to the fields.

Janet shrugged. 'I don't know, but he's terrified they'll take the farm off him.'

'Why would anyone want to do that?'

'We're at war, Shirley,' said Janet. 'The country needs to be fed. Just look around you. Even you and I can see where improvements can be made, but will he do it? Will he heck.'

Shirley was slightly surprised. Janet's outburst was

mild enough, but it was the first time she'd ever heard her voice an opinion on anything, let alone express her disapproval of her husband's decisions. Janet was right, of course. Mr Oliver was pig-headed. 'Can't you say something?'

Janet gave her a withering glance. 'Do you really think he'd listen to me?'

The answer, of course, was no. Mr Oliver only did what Mr Oliver wanted.

# CHAPTER 10

The fact that it was nearly Christmas brought a little light relief to everybody in the country. The First Lord of the Admiralty, Mr Winston Churchill, had promised that if they survived the winter without any serious blow, Britain would have gained the first campaign. Husbands, fathers, brothers, nephews and grandsons might be abroad, but thus far there had been little in the way of skirmishes. Half the civilized world had mobilized when Hitler had overrun Poland and instigated war, and he was now on the back foot and talking of peace, but Churchill refused to back down and the whole of the British Empire was rallying to the cause with even greater conviction.

In Angmering, the war hadn't made a great deal of difference to everyday life, and preparations were well under way for a Christmas pageant in the village hall. Called *Kings and Queens of England*, it was a celebration of Christmas through history. Rehearsals had been taking place since the beginning of November, and Shirley was very excited to have been offered the leading role as Good Queen Bess. It meant learning a lot of lines and she soon found that she was stretched to the limit. Miss Smith had already given her extra work in preparation for the scholarship examination, which she would take next Easter, and of course there was no let-up in the chores she had to do on the farm. Tom took on a few extra things for her, like mucking out the hen house and collecting the eggs, but Mr Oliver still grumbled and complained if he saw her studying. When he'd heard that the pageant was going to take up two days – Thursday for the dress rehearsal and then Saturday evening for the performance – Mr Oliver was furious and stomped off in a huff.

Finding a place to work became a problem as well. Shirley couldn't possibly do it in her bedroom. There was no table and no heating either, so Janet cleared a place on the kitchen table. Mr Oliver would put the radio on just to annoy her, but before long Shirley learned how to shut out distracting noises. Occasionally, although deep in thought, she would look up.

'What is that thing?' she asked Janet one evening when they were alone. Mr Oliver had gone to the pub, and Tom was with his beloved horses, Darby and Joan. Shirley pointed to the large metal square with the chain wrapped round it that was over the mantelpiece.

Janet shuddered. 'It's a mantrap.'

'A mantrap!'

'You put it on the ground and cover it with leaves,' said Janet. 'Then when a poacher comes along and puts his foot on the plate, it snaps shut. It's self-locking and you can't get out until someone gets the key.'

'That's horrible,' cried Shirley.

'They never use them now,' said Janet. 'It's illegal. That one dates from early Victorian times apparently.'

'Not my choice of ornament,' Shirley remarked stoutly.

Janet would often sit by the hearth knitting or sewing for the baby while Shirley did her homework. She was 'as big as a house' now (her own joke), so Shirley teasingly asked her if she had the pram in there as well. They'd both enjoyed the laugh, but it reminded Shirley that Janet was ill prepared for her baby. Where was the pram? Where was the cot? Come to that, where exactly was Janet going to have her baby? Shirley didn't like to ask such personal questions directly, but all her hints were ignored.

Then one day, the old woman in Swillage who had waved to them since they'd first arrived at the farm stopped her and asked Shirley and Tom to come inside her cottage. Shirley wasn't too keen. The woman and her husband looked a little dishevelled, and, Shirley thought, she'd probably go on and on for hours when Shirley had other things she'd rather be doing. She made an excuse that they couldn't stop, but the old woman insisted that she only wanted them to take something back to the farm for Janet. Shirley waited impatiently by the gate while Tom went inside. When he came out, he was carrying an old-fashioned rocking crib and some neatly folded bed linen.

'Is she a relative of yours?' Shirley asked Janet when Tom had put the crib by the fireside.

Janet shook her head. 'Everybody calls her "Granny Roberts",' she said. 'Sometimes when you're at school, I go and sit with them.'

Shirley raised a disparaging eyebrow.

'They are old and they are lonely,' said Janet irritably. 'One day, you might be like that yourself.'

Shirley felt ashamed. Janet was being kind, and by contrast, she was behaving like a selfish little madam. Granny Roberts's cottage was humble and run-down probably because she and Mr Roberts were old and infirm and not able to do things the way they used to. Janet hadn't said so in so many words, but she was right. Shirley had no right to look down her nose at them.

'Sorry,' she said, and resolved to be a bit more friendly in the future.

In November, the senselessness of war had been brought into sharp focus. A lieutenant commander called Gerald Molsom, who had lived in the village, was killed in action. Shirley didn't know him, but apparently he had lived in the Pigeon House, a two-storey seventeenth-century timber-framed house on the north side of The Street in Angmering. Second-in-command and a gunnery officer, he was on HMS *Rawalpindi*, an armed merchant ship, when she was sunk by the German battleships *Scharnhorst* and *Gneisenau* while on patrol in the area around Iceland. The whole village was deeply affected. He was one of their own and the villagers felt a mixture of anger, tragic loss and pride.

A special service was to be held in St Margaret's and the whole school was required to attend. Tom took it in his stride, but for Shirley, it was a sobering occasion. Up until now, war had been just a word, something that had separated them from their mother and all that was familiar. Now she knew it took lives as well.

Things on the farm quietened down from the beginning of December, but because of the unchanging routine, the days seemed to merge into one another. Mr Oliver still went to meet the postman at the gate, but no one took much notice now. Shirley was a bit surprised that she still hadn't had a letter from her mother. She had definitely put the address on that last card, but nothing had appeared on the kitchen table. It distressed her, but she made up her mind to send another postcard in time for Christmas. She wouldn't complain. Perhaps her mother was too ill to write.

Life for Shirley was doing her homework and her work. She had no money to go to the pictures, even though Bobbi, Gwen and Hazel had asked her time and again. She even had the embarrassment of having to ask Janet for some more bunnies when her period came. Her mother had given her a couple of packets of sanitary towels, but they were quickly used up. Shirley's only relaxation was reading. By now, she had borrowed several books from Elizabeth's room and devoured them. She treated them as if they were priceless heirlooms, never turning down the corners of the page as a bookmark, or leaving them in a place where they might get damaged. Judging by the selection in the bookcase,

142

Elizabeth had a wide and varied taste in books, and Shirley loved every single one of them.

One day in December, Gilbert Oliver watched Shirley and Tom setting off for school. He'd wait a little longer; then Janet would head off for Granny Roberts's place. She thought he didn't know she went there, but he'd seen her sneaking off to their house weeks ago. Not much got past him. Still, mustn't grumble. She'd been a good investment. She'd kept house for him, and she'd worked hard in the beginning. She still did as much as her condition allowed. He wasn't sure how things would work out once the nipper came, but if she knew what was good for her, Janet would do everything she could to keep a roof over both of their heads.

The weather was getting a lot colder. He had a feeling in his bones that they were in for a hard winter. They'd already had a few snow flurries; nothing much – it didn't settle – but it wasn't even Christmas yet. This side of the Downs, they didn't usually get much snow. In places beyond Brighton and Crawley, the snow was often feet-deep, and as coal was to be limited to two tons a year per household this year, they'd have to be a bit more careful. The kitchen range was hungry for fuel, but if the worst came to the worst, there was plenty of dead wood lying around the farm.

As soon as he saw Janet waddling down the hill, Gilbert took two envelopes out of his pocket; then he went into the kitchen and put the kettle on the range.

He wanted some privacy with this post. Turning the first envelope over in his hands, he studied the handwriting on the front. It was addressed to Mr and Mrs Oliver. He'd leave that one for a minute. First, he'd steam the other one open, the one addressed to Miss S. Jenkins and Master T. Jenkins.

*My dearest Shirley and Tom*, he read.

> *It was lovely to get your card. I am doing well and the doctor is pleased with my progress. I am so glad you are enjoying life on a farm, Tom. You always did love animals. How wonderful that your teacher is giving you a chance for a scholarship, Shirley. Make the most of this opportunity, won't you, dear? Do your best.*
>
> *I have enclosed a postal order for you to buy Mr and Mrs Oliver something for Christmas. Tell them I am very grateful for their kindness.*
>
> *All my love,*
> *Mum*

Gilbert snorted. A scholarship indeed. Who did the silly mare think she was? And what a waste of money. All that education for a girl who would be a married woman before she was twenty. Gilbert slipped the postal order into his pocket. Very nice too, he thought. He lifted the lid of the range and threw the letter into the fire. He would have given it to them if their mother hadn't mentioned the postal order. It was only three pounds, but he wasn't about to share it with anyone.

He didn't bother to steam open the other one; after all, it was addressed to him.

> *Dear Mr and Mrs Oliver,*
> *I am a friend of Mrs Florrie Jenkins, Shirley and Tom's mother. Mrs Jenkins is indisposed in hospital at the moment, so she has asked me to come and see the children before Christmas. I intend to travel from London on the train and would be grateful if you would tell me which station to come to and what day would be the most convenient.*
> *I'm afraid I can't stay long, two hours at the most, but it would be so good to see the children again. Please contact me at the above address.*
> *Yours sincerely,*
> *Doreen Kennedy (Miss)*

Gilbert scowled. Damn and blast it. Visitors from London were the last thing he wanted.

Florrie felt more than a little nervous. She'd waited for this day for so long, and now at long last Nurse Baxter came trundling down the ward with the wooden wheelchair. Florrie pulled her dressing gown tightly round her body and sat down. Swathed in blankets to keep the cold at bay as she was wheeled from one end of the complex to the other, she set off from the ward with a chorus of 'Good luck, love' and 'All the best, Florrie' from her fellow patients, so just for a lark, she waved and nodded like the king on one of his royal processions.

The ground outside was frosty, but Nurse Baxter walked confidently on the paths strewn with sand. The flower beds were empty now. The riot of colour that had greeted Florrie when she first arrived at the sanatorium was long gone. A few dried-up old brown leaves poked out of the soil, but that was it. Winter was tightening its grip.

Nurse Baxter wheeled her to the treatment room, where Dr Scott was waiting. First, she had to stand on the scales. She had lost more than two stone. How ironic. She had always wanted to be slimmer, but faced with her own stick-like limbs and skinny body reflected on the stainless-steel strip on the door, she was not a pretty sight. There were no mirrors on the ward. The hospital staff knew only too well how depressing it could be to see yourself, but when Florrie looked at the gaunt faces of those around her, she supposed she didn't look much better.

'Well, Florrie,' said Dr Scott as she was wheeled back into the treatment room, 'today I am going to examine your lung and then we'll take another X-ray. I'm hoping that there will be a significant change and then we can move on to the next stage of your recovery. That would be a nice Christmas present, wouldn't it?'

Florrie smiled cheerfully. She felt encouraged. Dr Scott was a cautious man. He wouldn't say something unless he was reasonably confident she would be all right. Wrapped up in blankets again, she was wheeled by Nurse Baxter to the X-ray department. Not so far this time, and they didn't have to go outside, but Florrie began to shiver and started to feel a bit peculiar as she waited her turn. Feeling so grotty, it was hard to keep still for the X-ray, but about an hour later, she was back with the doctor again.

His expression said it all. Florrie's heart sank.

'I'm sorry, Florrie. The shadow has decreased but not nearly as much as I had hoped.'

She stared at him hopelessly. What did that mean? Was he going to give up on the treatment? Was she going to be left to die?

'I think it best if we deflate the lung again and bring you back in the spring.'

She felt a mixture of abject misery – spring was months away – and relief. At least he hadn't given up on her. She was trembling now. Dr Scott looked up at the nurse. 'I'm not going to do it right away. She's had enough. She looks exhausted. Bring her back in a day or so for the treatment.'

How she stayed upright in the chair Florrie never knew. Her head was spinning, and every time she coughed her chest felt like it was on fire. Never had she been more grateful to see her bed and to crawl between the sheets.

The full dress rehearsal was on Thursday. Shirley was up early to get all her chores done, and then she and Tom raced to school. She had lessons in the morning, but in the afternoon she was in the village hall. Her costume was amazing. Fashioned using material from some old damask curtains and decorated with glass

147

beads, Shirley looked every inch the queen. The dress smelled musty, but that was only because the curtains were ages old. She still looked regal and important. Shirley had folded several sheets of fairly stiff paper into fans, which the wardrobe mistress had sewn together to make a ruff. Sir Walter Raleigh (a boy who had tried to terrorize Tom when they'd first arrived in the village) bowed low, and as he stood up, she knew he wouldn't fail to notice the smirk on her lips. If this was for real, she would have gladly sent him to the Tower for life for the way he'd treated her brother.

The dress rehearsal went well. They were a bit late getting back home, but surprisingly Mr Oliver was all right about it. Shirley vaguely wondered why he wasn't ranting and raving, but in truth, her mind was on the days ahead, when they would be doing the play in front of an audience. If the dress rehearsal was nerve-wracking, what would it be like to perform in front of the whole village?

'Did you see them? How were they?' The words tumbled out of her mouth as Betty welcomed Doreen into the cosy warmth of her sitting room. 'Here, let me take your coat. You make yourself at home and I'll get the tea. I want to hear all about it.'

She bustled out of the room. Doreen lifted the snoozing cat from the chair and sat down. As she warmed her hands by the fire, she could hear the clink of teacups coming from the kitchen and the kettle whistling. A few minutes later, Betty came back with a tea tray and some home-made scones. 'You must be famished,' she said. 'Have one of these for now and then I'll go to the fish-and-chip shop a bit later on.'

She poured the tea into their cups and handed one to Doreen. 'Help yourself to sugar.' There was a minuscule silence. Then she said, 'So how are they? Has Tom grown any taller? I reckon that boy will be over six foot by the time he's a man. Has Shirley still got her lovely dark curls?'

Doreen shifted awkwardly in her seat. Betty stopped prattling and stared at her with a startled expression. 'What is it? What's happened?'

'I didn't see them,' said Doreen.

'Didn't see them?' Betty squeaked. 'What do you mean, you didn't see them? He wrote and told you to come, didn't he?'

'Yes, but . . .'

'But what?'

'Mr Oliver told me to meet him at Goring-by-Sea Station,' said Doreen. 'I thought it was a bit odd because the next station is called Angmering and that's their address, isn't it? But in his letter, he said Goring-by-Sea was nearer the farm.'

'So? Didn't he bring the children with him?'

Doreen shook her head.

'But he took you to the farm?'

Again Doreen shook her head. 'He met me off the train and we sat in the waiting room. There was a lovely fire in there, and for the most part, we were quite alone.'

Betty frowned. 'That's a bit odd, isn't it?'

Doreen met her gaze. 'I suppose it is, but it didn't seem like it at the time.'

'What did he look like?'

'He was utterly charming,' said Doreen. 'Smartly dressed, although his suit and tie had seen better days. Oh, and he wore a hat. I remember that because he took it off and kept turning it round in his hands.'

'So what explanation did he give . . . for the children not being there?'

'He said their teacher had taken the whole class on an outing because it's Christmas. He said he was sorry and that he should have insisted that they came with him, but he hadn't told them I was coming.'

'Why ever not?'

'He said he'd wanted to surprise them,' said Doreen, 'but when he saw how excited they were about the outing and how much they were looking forward to being with their friends, he hadn't the heart to disappoint them.'

Betty and Doreen looked at each other. 'I suppose when you put it that way,' said Betty, 'it was nice of him to think like that.'

Doreen nodded. 'He did seem very sincere, and he spoke very highly of them both.'

'Did you give him the suitcase?'

Doreen nodded. 'He even asked me if I would like him to post it back when they'd emptied it, but I said not to bother. After all, it is Florrie's case.'

Betty handed her a scone. 'Did he say anything else?'

'Only that Tom loves being with the animals and that Shirley has become very close to his wife,' said Doreen. 'He says his family have been working that farm for over two hundred years.'

They bit into their scones. 'These are lovely,' said Doreen, and Betty glowed.

'I suppose I could have stayed the night in Worthing or something,' said Doreen. 'That would have given me a chance to see the children in the morning, but I didn't even think about it until I was on the way back here.'

Betty leaned forward to stoke the fire. 'Maybe you could have stayed,' she said, 'but from what you've told me, he seems a nice man, and we wouldn't want Mr Oliver to think we didn't trust him, would we?'

# CHAPTER 11

When the post arrived the next morning, Shirley and Tom were delighted to see Mr Oliver walk into the kitchen with a brown-paper parcel addressed to them. Shirley ripped off the paper to find a neat pile of their old winter clothes. It was a slight disappointment, but it was a welcome sight as well. The few things they had brought with them were becoming very shabby. Her dresses were only thin cotton material, and Tom's shirts were all frayed at the collar. Shirley's knickers were far too tight, and she was in desperate need of a different bra. It was good to have them, but as she looked over the pile, Shirley wondered if any of Tom's old winter clothes would even fit any more. He had grown so much bigger since he'd been doing all that physical work on the farm.

Her mother was still in hospital as far as she knew, so the parcel must have come from Auntie Betty. Shirley hoped to find a letter but was disappointed. Her heart sank a little. The pair of them went to their bedroom to put everything away.

'They don't need old stuff,' said Janet when they'd gone. 'They need new clothes.'

Gilbert, who was stuffing the brown-paper wrapping from the parcel into the fire, looked up sharply. 'Don't look at me.'

'There's a jumble sale in the village hall on Saturday,' Janet said pointedly. 'That boy needs long trousers for a start.'

'If they needs clothes,' said Gilbert, 'they must ask their mother.'

'Didn't their mother send any money?'

Gilbert shook his head.

'You get money from the government for keeping them,' said Janet, glaring. 'Use some of that.'

'Eight and six a week,' Gilbert spat. 'It costs more than that to feed that boy. I'm the one who's out of pocket.'

'You can spare five bob each for some new things.'

Gilbert jumped to his feet, his face black with rage, but Janet was unmoved. 'You can call it their wages for that unpaid work they do.'

He stomped out of the kitchen, slamming the door behind him, and took himself off to the stables, taking his temper out on the dog as he walked by. The dog yelped in pain and snarled helplessly at his receding back. Alone in the stables, he leaned against the door to calm himself down. How dare she put him on the spot like that? Of course, she didn't know it, but the family had sent money. In total, he had six pounds in postal orders waiting to be cashed, but he needed it more than they did. He had enough kale to feed the cows for a while, but then he'd have to start buying animal food before long. He'd never make it through the winter with what he had in the barn, especially now that the rats were coming in from the cold. That money would come in handy for animal feed. Janet just didn't understand. He hadn't done anything wrong. The kids' mother had told them to use the first postal order to buy something for him and Janet, but if he gave it to Shirley, what would she do with it? Most likely buy something daft, like a box of chocolates or some flowers. No, he needed that money for the farm, not frivolous fripperies.

When he'd brought the suitcase home, the kids were still at school and Janet was out, so he'd opened it himself and found another three-pound postal order on the top. There was a note saying that it was from Auntie Betty, Auntie Doreen and Mum, and that Shirley was to buy herself and Tom something for Christmas. He'd pocketed that with the other one and burned the note.

The stuff inside the suitcase was a bit of a problem, until he remembered some old brown paper Elizabeth had kept in the cupboard. She always preserved things like wrapping paper and string, in case they became unavailable. It had been a while since he'd been in Elizabeth's room and he felt uncomfortable being there. It made him jumpy and a couple of times he was spooked by a sound. Nothing had changed except perhaps the bookcase. He counted them. One was missing and he felt the hackles on his neck rise. Someone had been touching her things. Then he remembered Shirley. She always had her nose in a book, didn't she? She had no money to buy books, so where did she get them from? His nostrils flared slightly and he clenched his fists. The little madam had been in here, hadn't she? He looked around, but as far as he could see, she hadn't touched anything else. Well, she wouldn't come in here again.

He found the brown paper. It had come from a Christmas parcel her mother had sent a few years before. The address was still on it, so he went downstairs and piled the clothes onto the paper and folded it with the address still showing. He tied it with string and then added, 'To Miss S. Jenkins and Master T. Jenkins, c/o,' over the top of the place where it said, 'Mr and Mrs Oliver.' When it was done, he felt quite pleased with himself. The only thing that might give him away was the ancient postmark, but who would look closely at that? Shirley, Janet and Tom were none the wiser than the aunt who had come to see them, and he'd made another three quid for himself, and he had no intention of sharing it. If they needed clothes, that was nothing to do with him.

He put the parcel in the postman's pail outside the gate. It was a bit of a squeeze, but it went in. The suitcase was upstairs in his room, hidden from view. Nobody ever went up there anyway. All he needed to do was produce the parcel after the postman came the next morning. He'd timed it very well, and the plan worked perfectly. He began harnessing the horse. It was time to start the ploughing in the bottom field. He would spend the day turning over the top layer of ground to bring the goodness to the surface and at the same time bury the weeds and allow any of the previous crop to break down. There was always something to do on the farm. Now that Tom was capable of using the threshing machine, he could start slicing turnips for cattle feed. Once the ploughing was done, that left Gilbert free to cart the manure and mould away from the sides of his hedges; at the same time, he could take a look at his fences. He might even manage to do some quick repairs.

But as he worked, he began to feel uneasy. If the evacuees looked half naked, someone might complain to the authorities. That being the case, they might even be taken away. He couldn't afford that. They were a useful pair of hands to have around. By the end of the morning, Gilbert had grudgingly decided to give Shirley ten bob to spend at the jumble sale, but he'd see to it that she didn't go into Elizabeth's room again.

Florrie spent a miserable couple of days with the screens round her bed. Tears came easily, and despite her resolve not to, she had begun to feel sorry for herself. The trip to the treatment room had been a bitter disappointment. She had been feeling so much better and was utterly convinced that her lung was healed. It came as a shock to discover that she would have to endure weeks, if not months, more bed rest. If that wasn't bad enough, she began to worry about the expense. Betty was doing well in the shop, and her savings were steadily mounting, but how long would the money last? Being part of the government scheme had saved her a ton of money, but when Dr Scott had accepted her on to it, he'd said they would

156

have to discuss it again in a couple of months. She had been here for three and a half months already and so far her treatment was a failure, so what would happen now? She had an insurance policy, of course: everyone in the country had something. Her policy paid out for twelve weeks' hospitalization. When she'd taken it out, twelve weeks seemed ridiculously long. Who would have to be in hospital for twelve weeks? Now, of course, it was no time at all. Should she cash it in or leave it a bit longer? What if one of the children had to go to hospital? What would she do then? She wished she had someone to talk to – someone like Len. If only she could have brought herself to tell him why she held him at arm's length, but she couldn't, could she? Florrie sighed. She missed her little chats with Len.

The more she thought of it, the worse it seemed. It would cost at least four guineas a week for the cheapest nursing home, but that didn't cover the cost of X-rays and other treatments. It probably didn't include the cost of the doctor's visits either.

After two days on her own, the nurse pulled back the screens and Florrie was able to see the other girls on the ward. Jill, who was still in the bed next to her, turned her head. 'Hello, stranger,' she said cheerfully. 'Glad you've joined us again. How are you feeling?'

Florrie managed a wan smile. 'I don't think I want to go to the Palais with you tonight if you don't mind.'

'Don't blame you,' said Tina, walking towards them. 'I've heard that the band is bloody awful and the singer's got laryngitis.'

'The blokes aren't up to much either,' Jill quipped. 'Either fifteen or fifty-five. Everybody else has gone to France.'

Florrie chuckled. Tina sat on the chair between them and they talked of other things. 'I've had a letter from the children's home,' Tina said eventually.

Florrie was suddenly anxious for her, but Tina reached into her pocket and pulled out a small photograph. It was of two little girls sitting on the floor, the bigger one cuddling the smaller one. It had been taken with a Box Brownie, so the quality wasn't that good, and it was quite dark because it had been taken indoors only with available light. However, the children looked happy. They were both clean and tidy, the older girl with a huge bow in her hair, and the baby, clearly distracted by someone off camera, was smiling broadly.

'Oh, Tina,' cried Florrie, 'they look lovely. What did you say they were called?'

'Vera and Ann,' said Tina. 'The nurse who took it says they're both happy and healthy, which is the main thing.' There were tears in her eyes as Jill passed the photograph back, and Tina kissed it before putting it in her pocket.

'That should put your mind at rest again,' said Florrie. 'I shouldn't think they would send you a picture if they were going to take the girls from you.'

Tina nodded. 'That's what the nurse said. All I have to do is get well again.'

You and me both, thought Florrie.

'I never showed you, but I've started on a present for

each of them,' she said. She went to her bedside and rummaged in her locker. 'What do you think?' She held up two partially made rag dolls.

'Oooh, I think they're lovely,' said Jill. The dolls were well on the way. Tina had made the body and was working on the features. One doll had dark hair (wool, sewn onto the head and plaited at each side), and the other had yellow.

'I've got some pink flowery stuff for this one and some blue striped material for that one,' said Tina.

'They're fantastic,' said Florrie. 'They'll love them.'

Tina coughed.

'Don't overdo it, Mrs Cook,' said a passing nurse. 'I think you'd better get back into bed again.'

'I'll be fine,' said Tina in between coughs.

'Bed,' insisted the nurse.

As she went, Tina pointed out that Florrie had two unopened letters on her locker. Florrie opened them eagerly. Betty had written to say that all was well in London, and Doreen had written to tell her about her visit to Worthing. While Florrie was disappointed that she hadn't actually seen Shirley and Tom, it comforted her to know that Mr Oliver was such a kind and considerate man.

'Did you hear the news?' Tina called out as Florrie looked up from her letters. 'Nurse Baxter is getting married.'

'Really?' Florrie was delighted.

'It's all very quick because her fiancé is being posted

to North Africa,' said Tina, 'but everybody's been thinking about what we can give her.'

'Gladys is making some chair-back covers,' said Jill, 'and Madge down the far end has almost finished that latch-hook rug she's been making. I think she's going to give it to her as a wedding present.'

'They're getting married three days before Christmas,' said Tina, sinking wearily back onto her pillows.

Florrie leaned back and smiled. A wedding – how lovely. A wedding made everybody feel good. She didn't feel like it right now, but as soon as she was able, she'd get them to sort out some paper for her. She'd make Nurse Baxter a rose or two, and if she was well enough, she might even manage a whole bouquet.

The show went well. The village hall was packed to the gunnels, with standing room only. The undoubted star of the show was Gwen Knox, who, it turned out, had the most exquisite singing voice. Shirley got an extra round of applause, and Tom managed to sit through most of the performance, but the music in the finale got a bit much for him and he went outside. Nobody minded because by then he'd already seen his sister's performance.

To Shirley's great delight, Janet and Granny Roberts came to see the show. Granny was in her element, meeting up with old friends and catching up with the news. Some of the villagers greeted Janet like a long-lost friend, but Shirley noticed that a few looked a little po-faced or preferred to stand in little huddles whispering behind their hands.

'You must be near your time,' said a robust-looking woman in a heavy tweed suit. Shirley stared fascinated as a ribbon of spittle gathered at the top of her lip and attached itself like a piece of elastic to her bottom lip. Her bright red lipstick only served to draw attention to it. The woman was totally unaware of it, because she never once licked her lips to get rid of it. In her reply, Janet was polite but not very forthcoming.

'Is everything working out well?' said the woman.

'I have no regrets,' Janet said rather pointedly, and the woman seemed satisfied.

Shirley went to get Granny Roberts a cup of tea. When she came back to her, the old lady motioned her to sit down beside her.

'Leave Janet to enjoy herself,' she whispered. 'Young girl like that needs to get out more.'

Shirley nodded. Granny Roberts was right. Janet was only young and yet she seldom left the farm. Shirley still couldn't help wondering why on earth she had married a middle-aged man like Mr Oliver. 'Did you know Mr Oliver's first wife?' she blurted out.

'Oh yes,' said Granny Roberts. 'A lovely girl. He led her a dog's life and yet,' she added, looking thoughtful, 'he was very upset when she died, throwing hisself over the coffin like a man demented.'

Shirley was surprised. Mr Oliver didn't seem the sort of man who was given to emotion.

'What happened to her?'

'She drowned,' said Granny Roberts with a sigh. 'In Patching Pond.'

Shirley was shocked.

'At the time, everyone felt for him,' Granny Roberts went on. 'He looked like a broken man at her funeral, but then he up and marries Janet less than six months later.'

'I noticed some of the villagers haven't been very nice to her,' Shirley remarked.

'It was all too quick for some,' said Granny Roberts, 'but it suited them both. She needed a home, and he wanted a skivvy. Course, if they that gossip knew the truth of the matter, they wouldn't be so hard on her.'

'So why don't you tell them?' cried Shirley. 'Explain . . .'

Granny Roberts frowned. 'That's up to Janet. It's nothing to do with me, and I've never been one to talk about folks behind their backs.'

Someone called her name and Shirley was surprised to see Miss Lloyd had been in the audience. Her former teacher was very complimentary about her performance and enquired about Tom. Shirley introduced her to Janet and they shook hands. Now was Shirley's chance to complain about their living conditions, but somehow the words stuck in her throat and the moment was lost as soon as Gwen Knox appeared from the back of the stage. Miss Lloyd was lavish in her praise of Gwen's singing.

'Who would have thought it?' she cried. 'You were absolutely wonderful.'

'I've been asked to sing in a dance band,' said Gwen. 'I'm learning that new song Vera Lynn sings, "We'll Meet Again". Have you heard it? It's lovely.'

'Make sure you have a grown-up with you when you sing with the dance band,' Miss Lloyd cautioned.

Gwen looked slightly crestfallen at the suggestion, but promised that she would and Miss Lloyd moved on.

Granny Roberts decided to go home, saying she didn't want to leave her husband, Seth, for too long on his own, but everybody else stayed for cups of tea and mince pies before setting off for home. The night was cold, but the air was clear and there was a bright moon. Janet had a torch, anyway. She and Shirley linked arms and they sang as they went, with Tom tagging along behind. Their choice of song was anything from the Christmas carol 'In the Bleak Midwinter' to the most popular song of the moment, 'Run, Rabbit, Run'. As they came to Swillage, Granny Roberts's cottage was shrouded in darkness, but Janet called, 'Night, Granny,' and a thin, wavery voice from inside called, 'Goodnight, dear.'

Shirley hugged Janet's arm tighter. She felt happier than she had done in a long time. All the hardship of living with an irascible old man like Mr Oliver melted away. Shirley still missed Mum, but she'd had a wonderful evening, and being with Janet felt almost as good as being with family. Her brother was happy too. She glanced behind to see him peering into the hedgerow at something that had obviously caught his eye. He loved the peace and quiet of the countryside, and he loved being with the livestock. Funny how things turn out. If the nation hadn't gone to war, most likely Tom would never have had that experience.

The farmhouse was in darkness. Everyone had to observe the blackout, and it was especially important in this area. There were RAF bases being set up all around: Tangmere, Westhampnett, Shoreham and Ford were only a few miles away in either direction. As they walked in, Mr Oliver was sitting by the fire. He looked up as they took off their coats, and Janet put the kettle on the range.

'So you decided to come back, then,' he said sourly. It was obvious that he'd been drinking. His eyes were glazed, and every now and then he hiccupped. A half-empty bottle of Vat 69 whisky stood on the table beside his chair, and he had an empty glass in his hand.

Janet ignored him. Turning to Shirley, she said, 'Would you two like a hot-water bottle?'

Shirley nodded and went to fetch them.

'I'm talking to you, you ignorant bitch,' said Mr Oliver.

Shirley was already halfway down the corridor, but she heard Janet say, 'You're drunk.'

Shirley snatched up the stone hot-water bottles and made her way back to the kitchen. When she got there, Mr Oliver was on his feet and swaying. 'You should have been home hours ago.'

Janet, defiant, stood with her chin jutted out slightly. 'Don't you tell me what to do,' she challenged him.

'I bloody well will,' he retorted. 'You're my wife.' He

swung at her, but Janet ducked out of the way. Unfortunately, she was caught off balance and toppled backwards. Mr Oliver lunged towards her again, but Tom pushed himself between them. 'Leave her alone!'

Mr Oliver's blow landed on the top of Tom's arm. Tom squeezed his eyes shut and winced. 'You girt ninny,' Mr Oliver sneered. 'Look at you cowering away. You wants to stand up and be a man for once.'

Janet had fallen against the arm of the chair and was struggling to right herself. Shirley put the water bottles on the table and ran to her aid.

'He's more of a man than you'll ever be, Gilbert Oliver,' said Janet as Shirley helped her upright. 'What sort of man hits a pregnant woman?'

Mr Oliver wobbled unsteadily for a few seconds and then punched her full in the face. Shirley cried out in alarm as Janet was propelled backwards and fell heavily in the chair. Tom was rooted to the spot, but Shirley was at her friend's side in an instant, trying to assess the damage.

'You two, get to bed,' Mr Oliver roared. 'Go on – get out of here.'

Tom scurried away, but Shirley chose to stay. There was blood coming from Janet's nose. She had put her handkerchief against it to stem the flow, but Shirley remembered that once, when she had a nosebleed, her mother had put cold water on the bridge of her nose to stop it. She hurried to wet the end of the tea towel under the cold-water tap and handed it to Janet. All at once, Mr Oliver was looming over her and grabbing her arm. 'I told you to get to bed!'

Shirley was torn. She was terrified of him, but she didn't want to leave her heavily pregnant friend to his drunken rage.

'Go on, Shirley,' Janet said quietly. 'I'll be fine.'

Still holding her arm, Mr Oliver propelled Shirley towards the door. 'And keep out of Elizabeth's room,' he snarled.

'Elizabeth's room?' Shirley said indignantly.

'Don't tell me you haven't been in there,' Mr Oliver cried. 'I don't want nobody touching her things, d'you hear me? Not her books nor anything!' Then pushing her out of the kitchen, he slammed the door behind her.

Shirley waited in the cold corridor listening, but apart from the clink of bottle against glass, there was no other sound. Eventually, she heard low voices.

'I never should have done this,' Mr Oliver said.

'I know you think you can do what you like with me,' said Janet, 'but lay a hand on me once more and I promise you I shan't be here in the morning.'

Shirley heard Mr Oliver scoff. 'You've got too much to lose, my girl.'

Shirley heard the sound of her footsteps on the stairs. 'And you've got a lot more,' said Janet defiantly.

Miserably Shirley made her way back to her bedroom, where Tom was already in his bed.

'He shouldn't have hit her like that, should he, Shirl?' he said.

'No,' she said. She undressed behind the blanket wall and switched off the light.

'Tell me the story, Shirl.' Tom hadn't asked for the story for weeks, but now he sounded like a frightened child again. 'Tell me about the Birthday Thief.'

# CHAPTER 12

Shirley woke as someone shook her arm. She turned, half expecting to see Tom wanting her to give him the torch because he needed to go to the toilet. Instead, she was surprised to see Janet, her hair dishevelled and her face contorted, standing beside her.

'Are you all right?' said Shirley, sitting up.

Janet was squeezing her eyes shut and blowing out her cheeks, and it was a couple of seconds before she could speak. 'The baby,' she said breathlessly. 'It's coming.'

Shirley was horrified. The baby! What was Janet expecting her to do? She'd never seen anyone having a baby before. In fact, the smallest baby she'd ever seen was little Thelma Wilson, and she had been two weeks old! Shirley pulled on her coat, which was at the bottom of the bed covering her freezing feet. Tom was awake now as well. Janet held her belly and moaned.

'Shouldn't you be lying down?' Shirley asked.

Janet nodded. 'I'll go back to bed in a minute. Can you get Granny Roberts for me?'

'What about a midwife?' said Shirley.

'He wouldn't let me have one,' said Janet. 'Get Granny Roberts.'

'Tom will go, won't you, Tom?' said Shirley. 'I'll stay with you.'

Tom was already putting his clothes on as Shirley led Janet back into the house. The warmth of the kitchen was most welcome. Mr Oliver was sprawled across the chair next to the range. He had one leg over the arm and the other stretched out in front of him. His head was back and his mouth wide open. The bottle of Vat 69 was empty on its side on the floor beside him. Clearly he was no use at all. He was sleeping off a drunken stupor.

Janet and Shirley went up the stairs as quietly as they could, even though it would have taken nothing less than an invading army of Nazis to wake him. The bedding on the bed under the eaves was in disarray and Shirley was taken aback when Janet heaved herself onto it. Was this where she slept? Shirley remembered seeing a pair of slippers under the bed when Mrs Dyer and Miss Lloyd came to inspect the lovely room at the end of the corridor. Those slippers must have belonged to Janet. But why was Mr Oliver so horrible to her, especially when she was about to give birth to their baby?

'Can I get you anything?' Shirley asked. She was feeling way out of her depth and pretty useless. She had to wait for an answer while Janet went through another pain. Shirley had no idea that giving birth could hurt so much.

'Get plenty of towels from the linen cupboard,' said Janet. 'This will be a bit messy, I'm afraid.'

Shirley did as she was bidden. In between pains, they laid the towels across the bed, and Janet positioned herself with her bottom in the middle. It didn't take Shirley long to realize that the pains were coming closer together. All she could do was hold Janet's hand and pray that the baby wouldn't come before Granny Roberts arrived. Some while later, her voice called upstairs. Shirley had never been more pleased to hear it.

Tom had gone back to bed and the old woman needed a little help to get upstairs. There was no banister rail, only a rope slung between four stout rings fixed to the wall. Once she was up under the eaves, Shirley was happy to let Granny Roberts take over and wasted no time in taking the opportunity to go downstairs to make a pot of tea. Mr Oliver remained exactly as he had been until she had one foot on the stairs with the tray of cups. He opened one bloodshot eye and sat up straight.

'What the 'ell are you doing in 'ere?' He snatched his head in his hands and groaned. 'I told you before to keep out of Elizabeth's room.'

Shirley didn't stop to give an explanation. Let him find out for himself. He didn't deserve a girl like Janet, and he certainly didn't deserve to be a father. She suddenly thought about her own father. She didn't remember him, of course. She'd been very young when he'd run off with another woman, but sometimes her mother talked about him. She never said anything bad, but Shirley knew her mother had been deeply hurt.

The moment his head had cleared, Mr Oliver came to the stairs and shouted at Shirley.

'Stay where you are, Gilbert Oliver,' said Granny Roberts. 'This is no place for a man.'

'What's going on?' he said. 'What are you doing in my house, you interfering old bid—' Having reached the landing, he could see the three of them: Janet panting slightly, Granny Roberts mopping her brow with a piece of muslin and Shirley putting down the tea tray.

'The girl's having her baby,' Granny said coldly.

Mr Oliver seemed slightly flummoxed, but then he said, 'Tell her to hurry up, then. I need a hand with the milking in the morning.' He pointed a finger at Shirley. 'And you – get back downstairs.'

'I need her here,' said Granny Roberts. She seemed totally unfazed by Mr Oliver's belligerent attitude. 'I'm not so young as I used to be. I need the girl with me.'

Mr Oliver opened his mouth to say something, but at the same time Janet cried out as another pain came. He didn't stay. They heard him clattering his way downstairs, and shortly after that, the back door slammed.

Janet's little girl was born at eight forty-five. Mr Oliver had been back a couple of times to demand help in the milking parlour, but each time Granny Roberts sent him packing. When she told him the baby had been born, he made no attempt to come up and see her. Shirley washed the baby, as Granny Roberts said her hands weren't so good because of the arthritis. If seeing the baby emerge into the world wasn't amazing enough, giving her a bath in a bowl of warm water was the most fantastic thing Shirley had ever experienced. She felt an instant link with the child, and the fact that it was

171

December 17th and so close to Christmas made it feel all the more special.

At around ten o'clock, Shirley went back downstairs. Mother and baby were sleeping and Granny Roberts was anxious to get back home to her husband. They put the afterbirth on the fire, and the towels went into the scullery sink to soak for a while in Drummer Boy Blue until Shirley could light the copper and give them a good boil. It had been a long night for all of them, but they felt contented. Granny Roberts said it was good to feel useful again, and even Tom was happy. He'd been working flat out in the milking parlour. Lucky it was Sunday and there was no school. Trudging to the village after the night they'd all had would have been a hard task. Shirley prepared breakfast for everybody. They were all ravenous.

'Aren't you going upstairs to see the baby?' Granny Roberts asked Mr Oliver as Shirley offered to walk her home.

'What fer?' he said, pulling on his jacket. 'One baby is much the same as another.'

Florrie had been working as fast as she could. It was the Wednesday before Christmas and Nurse Baxter was getting married today. Florrie had hoped to make a whole bouquet of roses, but it had taken her a couple of days to recover from having her lung deflated for a second time. She constantly felt tired and it was hard to keep cheerful. Her friends on the ward did their best, but everyone was feeling a bit down at the thought of spending Christmas away from friends and family. It didn't help that they were also concerned about husbands and brothers away in France. Florrie didn't tell anyone, but even though they weren't that close, Len was on her mind all the time. Where was he? Was he safe? Dear Lord, supposing he was actually fighting? He could be lying injured somewhere. Concentrating on her paper-folding, Florrie worked hard to keep her dark thoughts at bay.

In the end, Florrie managed to make four roses, but floristry superstition dictated that all arrangements should be done in odd numbers. Three definitely wasn't enough, so she had to do a fifth rose. She had worked until lights out the night before. As soon as the morning tea trolley came round, Florrie sat up to do the finishing touches. For some reason, it was taking her twice as long to be completely happy with what she'd done. She'd managed to get hold of some glitter, so she added just a touch – not too much or it would look tacky – and then the roses were fastened to a ribbon to form a headdress fit for a princess.

The day nurses gathered round the ward sister's desk for morning prayers. They bowed their heads as Sister read the morning collect from the Book of Common Prayer and then they recited the Lord's Prayer. Florrie closed her eyes and mouthed the words along with them.

'*Our Father in heaven . . .*' Please take care of Shirley and Tom. It's been over a month since I heard from them. '*Give us today our daily bread . . .*' Thank you that Dr Scott has kept me on the government scheme. It's such a godsend. I will write up the journal every day just like I promised. Help me to do it even on the days when I don't feel like it, and please let my observations help somebody else with this terrible disease in the future. '*Deliver us from evil . . .*' Look after Len and bring him back safely. Protect Betty's boy and her husband at sea and keep them from harm. '*For thine is the power . . .*' Bless Doreen and don't let that old dragon of a mother persuade her to join her in Coventry. '*Amen.*'

The nurses raised their heads and began their duties. Thank God for every one of them, thought Florrie. They put so much into everything they did. With Christmas only five days away, the ward was already looking festive, with paper chains and a tree in the far corner. There was talk of a visit from Father Christmas, Christmas carols and a Christmas meal. Despite the bleakness they all felt inside, everyone was determined to make the most of the season as they clung to the hope that they would be with their families in 1940. It was Florrie's constant prayer that Shirley and Tom would enjoy themselves without her.

Nurse Cook, who was on night duty, was one of the bridesmaids, so she took the headband with her when she went off duty. 'Wish Nurse Baxter all the best,' said Florrie as she saw her go.

'Show us a photograph if you can,' Tina called across the room, and Nurse Cook gave them the thumbs-up.

The postman had brought another postcard from

Shirley. When Florrie looked at the postmark, she saw it had taken a bit longer to get here, probably because of the Christmas rush. Florrie savoured every word.

> *Happy Christmas, Mum. I am in a show in the village hall. Tom is helping behind the scenes. Thanks for posting our winter things. Mrs Oliver's baby is coming soon. I can hardly wait. Please write if you can. We miss you.*
> *Love,*
> *Shirley and Tom xx*

Florrie frowned. Shirley didn't mention the postal order. She knew Betty and Doreen had added to the pound she'd given Doreen when she came, but Shirley hadn't bothered to say thank you. Florrie excused her a little because there wasn't much space on the card, but she should have said something. Shirley had been brought up to know better than that. Ah well, at least they'd got their warm things.

The day passed by uneventfully until teatime, when there was a bit of a commotion around the ward sister's desk. Florrie, who had had her eyes closed, looked up to see Nurse Baxter with her bridegroom. Everyone was very excited. He looked so handsome in his uniform, but he hardly looked old enough to be in the RAF! His new wife was wearing a blue suit with a crisp white blouse. She carried a Bernhardt bouquet on her arm, which was made up of Christmas foliage with a scattering of snow-white chrysanthemums intertwined with white ribbon. On her head, she had a jaunty little hat, which was pulled over to the right side of her forehead. Her hair was swept back and pinned in a roll on the neckline. When she turned her head, Florrie could see that her paper roses lay along the top of the roll. Nurse Baxter, now Mrs Antell, did a twirl at the end of Florrie's bed and everybody clapped. They all agreed that she looked every inch the beautiful bride. Florrie was pleased too. That bit of glitter had made all the difference.

When she had gone, Florrie leaned back against her pillows. She would write to Betty tomorrow and ask about the postal order. Maybe they forgot to send it to Shirley. Or perhaps they'd sent it in a separate envelope and it hadn't arrived when she'd sent the postcard. Florrie sighed. She longed with every fibre of her being to see her children again . . . to hold them . . . to tell them she loved them . . . She pulled herself up short. Stop this, she told herself sternly. No good ever came of self-pity. She pulled the postcard towards her and read it again. *Thanks for posting our winter things.* That was funny. Doreen had taken them to Angmering in a suitcase, hadn't she? And according to her letter, she'd given them to the farmer personally. How odd. Come to think of it, Shirley hadn't mentioned the special little surprise she'd asked Betty to put in the inside pocket of the suitcase either. Now Florrie knew something was wrong. What sort of girl would forget to thank her mother for her first lipstick?

# CHAPTER 13

Christmas at the farm had been a small affair. Mr Oliver was still moody, so apart from eating a meal with them, he spent the day working outside. Shirley, Tom and Janet enjoyed having the day virtually to themselves and they made the most of it.

When Mr Oliver had given Shirley the money to buy warmer clothes at the jumble sale, she'd also bought a small teddy for the baby and a bottle of scent for Janet. The scent wasn't up to much, which was probably why it had ended up in the jumble sale in the first place, but Janet was very appreciative of the thought. Shirley had hung around until the very end of the sale and picked up a picture book for Tom. Called *The Observer's Guide to British Birds*, it had been published in 1937 by Frederick Warne & Co. The dust jacket was a little buffed, but she knew he would enjoy looking up the species of bird he'd seen on the farm. Although she didn't like him much, Shirley didn't forget Mr Oliver either. She'd bargained for a pack of playing cards and got them for a farthing. It was a complete set, including two jokers. Shirley was careful to have enough money left over to buy two postage stamps when she'd finished shopping. Now at last she could write her mother and Auntie Betty and Auntie Doreen a proper letter. Without stamps, there had been little point in putting pen to paper.

Janet had no money either, but she'd made Shirley and Tom a pair of gloves each. It came as a complete surprise to Shirley because she'd never even noticed Janet knitting them. They were made out of old scraps of wool, but that only made them all the more colourful.

Tom hadn't been idle either. To Shirley's surprise and delight, he'd found some hedgerow edibles for them. Janet got a few wild mushrooms layered on some watercress (where on earth had he managed to find that in this frosty weather?) in an old blackbird's nest, while Shirley got some cobnuts tossed into an abandoned robin's nest.

Mr Oliver had poured scorn on the giving and receiving of presents. He had bought nothing and left the playing cards where Shirley put them down. He pointed out sourly that although Janet was excused, the farm jobs still had to be done. Shirley and Tom went into the milking shed and on to the parlour and did everything together to make light work of it. When they finally came back into the house, they were greeted by a wonderful smell.

Sometime before, Janet had selected a chicken for the meal. It showed no sign of illness, but it wasn't a good layer and it picked on the other hens in a very aggressive way. It wasn't a young bird, so she had killed it a week before and hung it up in the cold pantry before slow-cooking it for about eight hours with some onions, celery and herbs from the garden. By that time, the meat was falling off the bones, but she wasn't finished yet. She used the carcass to make a delicious-looking chicken stock. On Christmas morning, she had put the meat back into the juices and added carrots and parsnips before simmering. By the time she had served it with roast potatoes and cabbage, they had a meal to remember. Shirley made an apple pie using some of the Alfriston apples they'd stored a month or two earlier, and they ate it with a hot sauce a bit like custard, made with cornflour and milk. It was delicious.

Later in the afternoon, they listened to the king's speech from Sandringham. It seemed incredible that they were actually hearing as he spoke the words. When it was over, Shirley couldn't remember much of what he said, except that he had talked of the nation fighting against wickedness and that waiting was a trial of nerve and discipline. He ended the speech with a poem. They cleared the table and used Mr Oliver's playing cards to play whist, snap and sevens. Each time the baby was fed, Tom and Shirley gazed in wonder. By the time bedtime came, they all agreed that, although it was quiet, they'd had a wonderful day.

Florrie's Christmas had been better than expected. She'd had to rest a lot of the time, of course, but the nurses had done their best to make the day memorable.

Father Christmas came and gave everyone a present from the nurses. Florrie received a small tin of Imperial Leather talc. She felt strangely touched, even more so when someone told her that the nurses had bought their presents out of their own money.

The nurses themselves were inundated with boxes of chocolates, but the ward sister refused to let them open them. Florrie heard a bit of muttering about it from one or two of the younger nurses. Nurse Fletcher was particularly annoyed. 'I've given up my family Christmas,' she complained, as she tidied away the chairs after visiting hour, 'but we haven't even had a sniff of anything Christmassy on this ward. My friend works on Larch Ward. Sister has set aside a whole room for her nurses. They've got sweets and biscuits and even a little sherry.'

'The nurses aren't the only ones on the ward who work hard and give up their Christmas,' said Nurse Cook. 'There's the cleaners, the ward orderly and the laundry lady, not to mention all the night staff. If we open a box of chocolates now, I guarantee they'll all be gone by teatime.'

Nurse Fletcher was unimpressed. 'So if we don't get them, what happens to them?'

'Sister saves them all up until we have enough to go round,' said Nurse Cook, lowering her voice. 'She gets one of the nurses to put everybody's name on bags and then we all get to take some home.' She glanced at Florrie, who was leaning back against her pillows. Florrie pretended to be preoccupied with her book. She knew

Sister didn't like her nurses talking about each other within earshot of the patients.

The two nurses walked away. Florrie watched them go. Having no chocolates might be a little disappointing today, but it seemed a much fairer way of doing things.

It looked as if it was going to be a bad winter. The weather outside was awful, but it was lovely and snug in her sitting room. Augusta Andrews liked times like this. She and Bertram were tired but not yet ready to go to bed. He was catching up with the newspapers, and she was knitting some thick woollen socks on four needles. She'd read an article that said deep-sea fishermen in the North Atlantic needed warm clothing and so she'd persuaded the Townswomen's Guild to begin an initiative to send them a hundred pairs of long socks as part of the war effort. As a woman who led by example, Augusta enjoyed 'doing her bit'.

She had always taken her position as a doctor's wife very seriously. She had no children of her own. Sadly, they'd never been blessed that way, but helping the people around here more than made up for her lack. She belonged to a number of organizations. She was chairman of the local Townswomen's Guild, an active Guider, a member of the board of governors at the local hospital and a member of the Church Missions Board. And if all that wasn't enough, she was thinking of becoming a member of the Inner Wheel, a women's organization that was closely linked to the Rotary Club. Of course, all these activities could be seriously curtailed if this part of

London was bombed in the way everybody thought, but so far, despite all the preparations for war, it seemed a long way off.

Augusta's cat, Marmaduke, leapt up beside her and sought the warmth of her lap. She lifted her knitting to accommodate him and then stroked his fur. She was so glad she hadn't acted as hastily as some of her friends. The day after war was declared, Millicent Tucker had had her dogs put down. Colonel Watson had his cat put to sleep a week later, but Augusta couldn't bear the thought of losing Marmaduke and so she had kept putting it off. That was months ago and she still had him. The cat wriggled and purred. He was such a delightful animal.

A sharp rap on the door knocker made them both look up. 'Oh no,' said Augusta, 'not tonight, surely?'

'Absolutely not, my dear,' said her husband. 'Harris is the duty doctor tonight. Send whoever it is to him. I'm determined not to give up my fireside even if it's Mr Churchill himself.'

Augusta rose to her feet. When she opened the door, a young woman stood on the step. 'Mrs Andrews?'

'Yes,' she said uncertainly.

'You don't know me,' the woman went on, 'or at least you did know me a long time ago when I was a babe in arms, but we've not met since then.'

Augusta looked at her steadily.

'You organized my adoption,' the woman said. 'My name is Hannah now, but back then it was Ruth. May I come in?'

Augusta, too polite to say, 'Come back tomorrow,' stepped aside. 'I'm rather busy at the moment, so I'm afraid you can't stay. Is there a complaint?' It seemed a bit ridiculous, but why else would the girl be here?

The girl shivered in the hallway. 'Oh no. I had a wonderful life with my parents. Sadly, they've both passed away now.'

'I'm sorry for your loss,' said Augusta.

'My father died in 1937, and my mother died last month,' said Hannah. 'Before she went, she told me all about the part you played in my adoption.'

'I see,' said Augusta, wishing she would get to the point.

'I want to meet my birth family.'

Augusta stared at her, startled. No one had ever come back and asked that before. 'I'm not sure—' she began.

'Oh, please don't say no, Mrs Andrews,' the girl interrupted. 'Please try. Ask them if I could meet them. If they say no, I won't make a fuss, but please try.'

'What is your name?'

'Ruth Mitchell,' said Hannah.

Some distant and not-so-distant memories tumbled into place. 'You're Florrie's daughter,' she murmured.

'So you do remember me!' Hannah cried. 'Oh, please say you'll help.'

Augusta did some quick thinking. Florence was ill. Perhaps far too ill to cope with such a shock, and she didn't want to tell the girl what was wrong with her. She'd have to see how Florence felt about meeting Hannah, as she was known now. 'I'll tell you what I'll do,' she said. 'I cannot discuss anything with you until I have spoken to all the relevant parties. When I took on this role as mediator, I took a solemn promise not to divulge any information without prior consent.'

Hannah was clearly disappointed. 'I understand.'

'If you'd like to leave your details, I shall write a letter as soon as you've gone.'

'Oh, that would be wonderful!' cried Hannah.

Augusta raised her hand. 'I urge you not to get your hopes up. Your relative made a decision in what she thought were your best interests and she has got on with her life since then. She may not want to be disturbed.' Augusta still felt the need to protect the child, and it was easier to put it that way rather than say, 'She's got tuberculosis of the lung and is desperately ill.'

Back in the sitting room, Bertram glanced up from his evening paper. 'You were gone a long time.'

'The most extraordinary thing . . .' Augusta began. 'Only a month or two ago, Florence Jenkins asked me if I knew what happened to the baby she gave up for adoption, and would you believe it, that was her, twenty-two years old now, knocking on the door to ask me about her birth family.'

'Well, I'll be damned,' said her husband.

A couple of weeks later, when the morning milking was finished, Shirley asked if she could change the baby's nappy. Janet was back at work and tidying up the milking parlour. It was a bitterly cold day. 'Why not?' she said. They could both hear a plaintive, reedy cry coming

from inside the house. 'I think she's ready for her breakfast.'

Shirley went inside, glad to be in the warm at last.
She washed her hands at the kitchen sink and headed
for the stairs. It was wonderful to be able to play with
the baby. Janet still hadn't decided on a name for her,
which was a bit frustrating, and being so young, the
baby wasn't very responsive as yet, but she was a sturdy
little thing and Shirley loved her to bits. Funny but
Shirley never minded changing the baby's nappy. The
smell of cow dung still turned her stomach, but even
though the nappy could be awful, it didn't worry her.

As she mounted the stairs, the baby's lusty cry
became a little muffled. Shirley reached the top of the
stairs and saw Mr Oliver leaning over the crib. She
smiled. This was the first time the baby's father had
shown any interest in her. Maybe she should go away
and leave them together for a while. The baby's cry
wasn't nearly as loud as it had been when she'd first
mounted the stair. They must be getting to know each
other. Shirley had a sudden thought. It was a bit
cramped and draughty up here on the landing. Maybe
Mr Oliver would prefer to sit down with his daughter
and give her a cuddle.

'Shall I change her nappy for you, and then you can
give her a cuddle?'

She saw him visibly jump and then straighten up. The
baby bellowed at the top of her lungs, twice as loud as
before.

Mr Oliver turned round and glared at her. To Shirley's

dismay, he pushed past her and almost ran down the stairs. Guiltily, she watched him go. Perhaps she should have crept away and said nothing. She'd obviously embarrassed him by the interruption. She bent to look down into the crib. The baby was hot and sweaty and clearly very upset. The pillow that Janet put at the back to protect her daughter's head from the wooden back was lying across her head and shoulders. Shirley spoke gently and took it away from her face. There was a pool of saliva and sick in the centre of the pillow and crease marks going towards the edge. Shirley's blood ran cold. What had Mr Oliver been doing? She picked up the distraught baby and did her best to soothe her and gradually she calmed down.

Shirley changed her nappy, remembering to put her fingers between the towelling nappy and the baby's skin. That way, if the pin went in too quickly, she would prick her own fingers rather than Janet's little girl. Still eyeing the pillow, she wrapped the baby in her shawl and took her downstairs.

# CHAPTER 14

Janet had washed her hands and was waiting for her in the chair by the fireside. 'What do you think of the name Lucy?' she asked.

'It's lovely,' said Shirley. She handed the baby to her mother. They'd been over a thousand names. Barbara, Sally, Patricia, Alice . . . Janet suggested them and then grew tired of them. A couple of days ago, Granny Roberts had told her that the baby had to be registered within forty-two days of the birth. With only another fortnight to go, the search for a name was deadly serious now.

'Ooh,' said Janet, as she took the baby into her arms, 'she's very hot.'

Shirley chewed her bottom lip anxiously. 'The pillow at the end of her crib had fallen onto her face,' she said. Should she tell Janet about her suspicions?

'I'd better take that out, then,' said Janet. 'Good job you were there. Poor little Lucy.' The baby latched on to her breast and before long Shirley could hear little gurgling sounds as she swallowed her milk. 'What's wrong, Shirley?'

Janet's question took Shirley by surprise. She had been doing her best to hide her feelings, and Janet had appeared to be totally preoccupied with her daughter. 'Nothing,' she said brightly.

'Yes, there is,' said Janet. 'Tell me.'

Shirley sucked in her lips. If she told Janet and she confronted her husband, he'd only call her a liar, but it really did look as if Mr Oliver had been trying to smother the baby. Shirley tried to make sense of it, but she couldn't. Why would he do that? What sort of a father would want to harm his own child? Perhaps it was best not to say anything; after all, she had no proof. On the other hand, what if it happened again?

They heard the sound of a car drawing up outside and the dog started to bark.

'Shirley?'

'When I walked upstairs,' she began reluctantly, 'Mr Oliver was there.'

Janet searched her face. 'And?' She continued to look at Shirley while she fumbled for the right words; then all at once the realization dawned on her face. Janet took in her breath. 'For God's sake, Shirley, what are you saying?'

'I may be wrong,' Shirley protested quickly. 'In fact, I probably am. My mother always says I have an over-active imagination.'

They could hear angry voices outside and the dog was going crazy. Distracted, Shirley glanced towards the window.

'Just tell me,' Janet insisted. 'What was he doing?'

'I made a mistake,' said Shirley. 'Yes, that's what happened. He was probably just looking into her crib, that's all.'

'But you think he was doing something he shouldn't have been doing, don't you?'

'I couldn't really see,' said Shirley, 'but when I picked her up, she was all sweaty and upset.'

'And the pillow?'

This was making her feel very uncomfortable, but Shirley held her gaze. 'It was on her face.'

Janet's face went pale.

'It could have been an accident,' Shirley flustered. 'I mean, he could have found it like that and have been getting it out of the way. I mean, he wouldn't do anything to harm his own baby, would he?'

Janet began stroking the top of her daughter's head with her thumb. 'There's something I haven't told you, Shirley,' she said. She looked up. 'The baby isn't his.'

The shock of what she'd just been told made Shirley feel weak at the knees, and even though it was just as loud, the sound of Mr Oliver's angry voice outside seemed to fade. She lowered herself onto the chair opposite. 'What?'

'She belongs to another man,' said Janet. There was no shame in her voice. It was strong and defiant. 'I fell in love with a lad from the village, but he and his family emigrated to Canada. After he'd gone, I found out that I was pregnant.' She kissed her daughter's head. 'Lucy isn't Gil's baby.'

Outside, they could hear Mr Oliver yelling, 'Get off my land!'

Janet sighed angrily. 'Oh no, not again.'

Mr Oliver had obviously moved closer to the house because now they could hear the more measured tone of another man's voice. 'Mr Oliver, this isn't helping. I really must insist that you talk to me.'

'Come any closer and I'll set the bloody dog on you.' They heard the dog yelp as he goaded it.

'Are you shocked, Shirley?' Janet was saying. 'About the baby?'

Shirley shook her head. 'A bit surprised, that's all. So how come you . . . ?'

'He wanted help in the milking parlour,' said Janet. 'I came here to work, and when he found out I was in the family way, he turned on that charm of his and offered to make an honest woman of me.'

'So you and Mr Oliver aren't . . . ?'

'Good Lord, no,' said Janet. She laughed sardonically. 'And it didn't take me long to work out that he'd only married me to save money.'

Shirley was puzzled.

'As his wife, he doesn't have to pay me,' said Janet. 'Tight-fisted old git. I hate him.'

Shirley blinked. This had been quite a revelation, but a lot of things fell into place now: the bed under the eaves, the people in the village preferring to whisper behind their hands rather than talk to Janet, the fact that Mr Oliver treated her more like a servant than a wife.

The racket outside continued. 'Janet!' Mr Oliver shouted. 'Janet!'

Ignoring him, Janet looked up at Shirley. 'Do you really think he was trying to smother my baby?'

Shirley nodded miserably. 'I do now.'

Mr Oliver was shouting, 'Janet, get out here, woman!'

'Then I can't stay here,' said Janet urgently. 'I can't risk it.'

Shirley's heart sank. If Janet went, she'd be on her own and at the mercy of that awful man. Tom wouldn't be able to cope if things got much worse. He responded to encouragement, but if people got frustrated and angry with him, he clammed up. She could just imagine her brother cowering in a corner while Mr Oliver yelled at him or hit him with a stick. What was she going to do?

'Where will you go?' Shirley's voice was edged with tension.

'I don't know,' said Janet. 'I've no money.' She gazed lovingly at her daughter and sighed. 'I suppose Granny Roberts might take me in, until I can work something out.'

'But what about Tom and me?' said Shirley. She was desperately trying to stay calm, but this was beginning to feel very scary indeed.

'Janet, where are you, woman?' Mr Oliver shouted again. 'Will you get out here now!'

Janet made no attempt to move. She had more important things on her mind. Lucy was feeding nicely and she didn't want her disturbed. 'Don't you worry about that,' she said, leaning forward to grip Shirley's hand. 'I'll make sure the authorities resettle you both somewhere else.'

'But they might put Tom in a home,' said Shirley, her eyes burning with unshed tears. 'That is my mother's one dread.'

They both fell silent for a second or two.

'Maybe she'll be better soon,' said Janet sympathetically. 'Then you can go back home. Things don't always work out the way we think. Everybody was convinced that Hitler would be over here by now. Bombing in the streets, they said, but nothing's happened. It's probably as safe in London as it is down here.' She sat Lucy up and rubbed her back gently.

The door burst open, bringing with it a blast of cold air, and Mr Oliver came rushing in. Shirley leapt to her feet and Janet jumped. The baby's face crumpled. 'Didn't you hear me calling, you lazy mare? That man from the Ministry of Agriculture is back here again.'

They stared at each other for a second, but Janet didn't move. 'I know what you did,' she said coldly. 'Touch my baby again and I'll see you hang.'

Mr Oliver looked taken aback but quickly recovered. 'I haven't got time for all that now. Didn't you hear what I said? That bloke from the ministry is back. Where's me gun? Get me gun, girl!' Shirley was fixed to the spot, so he rushed over and snatched his shotgun from the corner of the kitchen where he always left it and then headed back towards the door.

'Don't be such a damned fool, Gil,' Janet shouted after him, but he took no notice.

As he went back outside, they heard a voice say, 'There's no need for that, Mr Oliver. Put the gun down.'

'Oh, my stars,' cried Janet. 'The silly old fool is going to blow somebody's head off.'

'He didn't take any shot,' said Shirley. She pointed to the box of cartridges on the dresser.

'Quick, Shirley,' cried Janet. 'Hide them somewhere.'

Shirley grabbed the box and headed for the stairs. Where could she put it? When she reached the top, she looked around desperately. Apart from Janet's single bed, the landing was bare, and there was little point in putting it in Mr Oliver's room. It had to be hidden somewhere he wouldn't think of looking. She was facing the door to Elizabeth's room and remembered his threat about if she ever went in there again. Surprisingly, it wasn't locked. Shirley burst into the room and looked around. Pulling open the bottom drawer of the dresser, she stuffed the box of cartridges inside. There was hardly anything in there to cover it, but she shoved it as far back as she could. Grabbing the baby's shawl from the crib on the way past, she raced back downstairs. As she handed the shawl to Janet, they heard a high-pitched creaking sound behind them. Shirley took in her breath and the two of them gripped each other as the outside door slowly opened.

It was Tom. Shirley clutched at her chest. 'Tom! You scared the life out of me.'

'Mr Oliver is very angry, Shirl.'

'I know, love,' she said, soothing him like a small child. 'He'll be all right in a minute. You'll see.'

'Is it time for breakfast?'

She pulled out a chair and her brother sat down. Shirley cut him a piece of bread. 'Have this for now. I'll cook something in a minute.' Tom smeared the bread with jam.

The standoff outside continued, with Mr Oliver now threatening to shoot the man from the ministry.

'If he calls Gil's bluff,' Janet remarked, 'he's just as likely to set the dog on him.'

'Is he going to shoot his gun?' Tom said suddenly.

'Mr Oliver doesn't know it,' said Shirley, reaching for the frying pan and putting it on the range, 'but the gun isn't loaded.'

Tom relaxed and carried on eating his bread.

Janet put Lucy onto her shoulder and began rubbing her back gently. 'Shirley,' she said in a whisper designed for her ears only, 'we're going to have to watch him like a hawk. Lucy mustn't be left alone for one second.'

Shirley nodded. 'Tom, could you bring Lucy's crib downstairs for us? It feels a bit too cold for her upstairs.'

Her brother, his mouth stuffed with jammy bread, pushed back his chair and headed for the stairs.

'I'll go and see Granny Roberts as soon as I can,' Janet said hurriedly. The dog had stopped barking and they heard the sound of a car engine running. 'Sounds like he's given up.'

'For now,' said Shirley.

Tom was halfway downstairs when they heard Mr

Oliver scream. That was followed almost instantaneously by a loud bang as the gun went off. Janet froze, Shirley nearly jumped out of her skin, and the baby began to cry. Tom stared at his sister with a look of horror on his face and, putting down the crib, hurried to the window.

'Careful,' Janet cautioned.

Tom ducked, and using the curtain as a shield, tried to see what was happening.

'Can you see anything?' Shirley asked.

There was another loud bang and then they heard the car reversing backwards down the lane at high speed. The three of them ducked and dived by the window, but in a few minutes everything was quiet. Judging by the speed of the man from the ministry's car, he was clearly terrified. Even the dog had gone quiet.

'Oh Lord, he hasn't hit that man, has he?' said Janet. 'I thought you said that shotgun was empty?'

'I thought it was!' cried Shirley. 'He must have a secret stash of cartridges somewhere.'

'Or maybe that bloody thing was loaded all the time,' said Janet crossly. 'Where did you put the box?'

'In Elizabeth's room,' said Shirley.

'I dread to think what sort of a mood he'll be in now,' said Janet, 'and if he thinks that will stop them, he's got another think coming.'

They heard a moan outside the back door.

'Quick,' Shirley said to Tom, 'get away from the window – he's coming back.'

# CHAPTER 15

The streets in London had almost returned to normal. Most of the children who had been evacuated were back, and on Saturday, even though it was cold and snowy outside, their mothers had wrapped them up warm and sent them out to play. It was the type of morning when any kid with a penny to spare bought sweet cigarettes. The cold, frosty air made it look as if they were actually smoking as they sucked one end and blew out their breath. In Florrie's corner shop, Betty had almost run out of them, but then she remembered she had a box right at the back of the storeroom. When it had been delivered, she'd had a shop full of customers and no time to put it in its proper place. Supplies were still fairly good, but they didn't always come on time. She hazarded a guess it was to get her customers used to doing without, so that when rationing started, there would be fewer complaints.

During a lull, she popped out to get the new stock. She was just heaving the box onto the front of the counter when someone came up behind her and said, 'Here, let me help you, my lovely.'

Betty swung round. 'Len! Oh, how nice to see you.'

Len Greene picked up the large tin as if it were a child's building block. 'In here?'

Betty nodded. 'Thanks.' He looked very smart in his uniform. It was unusual to see British soldiers around. She was more used to seeing the Canadians. They were everywhere, even guarding Buckingham Palace, so they said. 'Home on leave?'

He nodded. 'Forty-eight hours,' he said, 'before I get shipped out.'

'Do you know where you're going?'

'Now, Betty,' he said teasingly, 'you know better than to ask me that.'

'You're right,' she said, laughing and slapping her own wrist. 'Now, what can I do for you?'

'Is Florrie around?'

Betty looked surprised. 'Oh, Len, I'm sorry. You don't know.'

'Know what?' said Len. His expression changed. 'Dear God, she hasn't sold up and gone back to Sid, has she?'

'No, no,' Betty smiled. 'Nothing like that.' She leaned forward confidentially, even though there was no one else in the shop. 'Florrie's got TB. She's in a sanatorium in Surrey. She's been there since the autumn of last year.'

Len looked shocked and surprised. 'I thought she'd gone with Shirley and Tom to get them settled in,' he said. 'That's what I heard.'

'She didn't want everybody knowing,' said Betty.

'People might stop coming to the shop if they thought there was something bad here.'

Len nodded. 'So where are Shirley and Tom?'

'They were evacuated,' said Betty. 'Living on a farm, and Tom loves it, by all accounts.'

'Well, I never,' Len remarked. 'It's an ill wind . . .'

Betty glanced around at the still-empty shop. 'Fancy a cuppa?'

'Don't mind if I do,' said Len. 'It's perishing cold out there.'

'Turn the sign on the door,' said Betty, 'and come out the back.'

Since day one, Betty had made herself at home in Florrie's kitchen, but she never took advantage. She treated her things with respect, and she'd kept everything clean and dusted throughout the whole place in case Florrie came home unexpectedly. She heard a footfall and Len came up behind her. 'So how have you been keeping, Len?'

'Mustn't grumble,' he said. 'We're not seeing much action at the moment.'

'We all thought it would be over by Christmas,' she added with a wry smile. 'Just like we did last time.'

Len sat down with a small sigh.

'Are you still living at your old place?'

Len nodded. 'I've got a couple of lodgers living there while I'm away. They don't keep it very clean, but at least someone's getting the use of it.'

'Did I tell you I'm doing a first-aid course with the St John in the evening?' Betty told him just for something to say. 'It's for six weeks. The local council want all shopkeepers to do it, and I suppose with things being the way they are, you never know when it might come in handy.'

Len nodded. They drank their tea.

'Tell you what,' said Betty eventually. 'Why don't I put a card in the shop window for a cleaning woman? I'm sure there's plenty around here who would jump at the chance to make a few bob with an honest job.' She handed him a plain postcard. 'I could keep an eye on things if you like?'

'Good idea,' said Len. 'What's the going rate?'

Betty shrugged. 'Half a crown an hour sounds about right.'

'Half a crown it is, then,' said Len. He paused. 'Have you got an address for Florrie? I might drop her a line if I can.'

Betty wrote it on a piece of paper and handed it to him. 'I never understood why you didn't ask her to marry you all those years ago,' she remarked. Then, seeing his startled expression, she immediately regretted her forthrightness. 'I'm sorry. I didn't mean to sound rude. It's none of my business.'

He gave her a shy smile and stood to his feet.

'Take care of yourself, Len,' said Betty stiffly.

Len put his cap back on. 'Thanks for your help, my lovely.'

As he headed for the door, he paused, and still with his back to her, he said, 'And as for Florrie, I guess I could never find the right time.' He hesitated before adding in a barely audible mumble, 'More fool me.'

Betty didn't move. She heard him walking through the shop. Then the door opened and closed again, and just for a second or two she felt unbelievably sad.

There wasn't a lot to do on the ward. Several patients had gone home, and although she was still on bed rest, Florrie didn't need much nursing. She watched the nurses cleaning out cupboards and rolling bandages – anything to make it look as if they were working hard.

After lunch, Sister sent two nurses into the big linen cupboard, but before they went, Nurse Cook came over. 'Have you got any more paper bags, Florrie?'

Florrie pointed to her bedside locker, where she kept the small suitcase of paper and tissue Doreen had brought. Her supply was nearly used up now, but she hadn't asked for any more. If truth be told, she was getting a bit bored with making paper flowers. What she wanted was a new challenge. She might be low on paper, but she still had plenty of paper bags.

'Are you sure you don't mind us having these?' said Nurse Cook.

'Not at all,' said Florrie.

Nurse Cook took a handful and put the case back in the locker.

'If you need any more,' said Florrie, 'just help yourself.'

She guessed they were going to sort out the choc-olates – one bag for every person who worked on the ward, but the two nurses were only in the linen cupboard for a short while before they came back out again. Most of the patients were asleep, and as they looked around the ward, Florrie closed her eyes quickly.

When she opened them again, the two nurses were talking with the ward sister. They spoke in low tones, but it was so quiet Florrie could just about hear them. Her lungs might be shot, but her hearing was excellent.

'She's even put the wrapping paper back over the boxes,' said Nurse Cook.

'How many chocolates are left?' asked Sister.

Nurse Davies slid the box from its wrapping paper and opened the lid. 'Four.'

'Only four!' exclaimed Sister in hushed tones. 'I can hardly believe it.'

The three of them stared down at the nearly empty box. Florrie could see that they were dealing with mixed emotions: anger, disappointment and disgust. They were angry because someone had obviously been helping herself to the chocolates, chocolates meant for everybody to share; disappointed because it was one of their number; and disgusted that the thief could be so devious. With so many chocolates gone, it was clear that the theft had been going on for some time.

'What are we going to do?' said Nurse Davies.

Sister looked thoughtful. 'Gentian violet,' she said. 'Leave the box with me and say nothing.'

'I don't understand,' said Nurse Cook.

'The less you know, the better,' said Sister. The two nurses began to walk away. 'Perhaps you would get us some more lint from the pharmacy, Nurse Davies, and, Nurse Cook, you can tidy the patients' dayroom. There are magazines all over the place.'

When they had gone, Sister went into the small treatment room. She closed the door, but Florrie could see her reflection on the glass. She was injecting something into one of the chocolates. When she came out, Florrie snapped her eyes shut. The next thing she knew, she was waking up as someone pushed the tea trolley onto the ward.

The kitchen door opened and Gilbert Oliver almost fell into the room. Everybody stared at him in shocked surprise, and then they saw the blood. Shirley and Tom rushed to help him. Janet put Lucy back into her crib first.

His trouser leg was soaked in blood, and it was all over his hands. As Shirley and Tom helped him into a chair, it was hard to see exactly where the blood was coming from, but with every move he made, he winced and moaned in pain.

'What happened?' Janet gasped.

'That bloody dog,' he said. 'Oh, me leg, me leg . . .'

Shirley tried to lift his trouser leg to get a better look, but he cried out and pushed her away roughly. 'Get off me, you stupid cow.'

'Tom, hand me my workbox,' said Janet.

The workbox was on the end of the dresser, but as soon as Tom handed it to her, her husband said, 'Keep away from me. You're not cutting my clothes.'

Janet stepped back and put her hand on her hip. 'Now look here, Gil,' she said. 'You've lost a lot of blood and it's still coming. A dog bite can easily become infected, but if you don't want help, that's fine by me.'

They glared at each other for a second. Mr Oliver's face was ashen and he was beginning to sway. All at once, he leaned over the side of the chair and was sick on the flagstone floor. Shirley grabbed the bucket from under the sink to put it beside him, but Janet grabbed her arm. 'What's it to be, Gil? Do you want help or not?'

He looked as if he was going to pass out at any minute, but she still made them wait. At last, he managed to nod and Shirley put the bucket down. Janet sliced through the trouser leg with her scissors. The wound was on his calf. It was fairly obvious that he'd stepped backwards and the dog he'd teased, goaded and beaten for so long had seized its opportunity. It had sunk its teeth into the back of Mr Oliver's leg and done a lot of damage. The flesh was virtually hanging from the bone, and blood pulsed from the wound. Shirley felt so queasy she had to sit down.

'Give me your belt, will you, Tom?' Janet put the belt round Mr Oliver's upper thigh and pulled it as tight as she could. With Tom's help, she made another hole in the belt and did it up. The flow of blood slowed.

'Shirley,' said Janet, 'I want you to get yourself a drink of water and then run down to the village for help.'

'No,' Mr Oliver moaned. 'No help.'

'Don't be daft,' said Janet. 'It's still bleeding, and I can't patch this up on my own. You need a doctor. It needs stitches.'

It was obvious that although he didn't want strangers in his house, Mr Oliver had no choice and was in no position to stop them. With the onset of shock, he'd started to tremble.

Shirley steadied herself with a drink of water and grabbed her coat, hat, scarf and gloves. The weather was very cold and there had been flurries of snow since early morning. The ground was icy and it would be hard to keep her footing, but she was determined to do her best. She didn't like the man, but she didn't want to feel in any way responsible for the hastening of his death.

'Be careful,' said Janet. 'If you don't think you can make it to the doctor's, there's a farm in Water Lane just as you come into the village. You'll have to go back a yard or two, but they'll most likely have a telephone. His number is Goring 952. Got that?'

Shirley nodded.

'If you can carry on, go to the bottom of Water Lane,' Janet went on. 'His house is up the hill by the Red Lion. You'll see a brass plate by the door.'

'I know where it is,' said Shirley.

Janet glanced behind her at Mr Oliver. 'Be as quick as you can,' she said, and giving Shirley's hand a squeeze, she closed the door behind her.

Janet and Tom pulled the other fireside chair towards the one Gilbert was sitting in and raised his leg onto it.

Janet had put towels down to cushion the leg, but he cried out in agony as she lowered it. She wanted to bandage the wound, but it was far too big. The bandages in the first-aid tin were only suitable for a finger wound, so she laid a clean tea towel over it instead. Her husband was almost unconscious, but she sat with him, talking gently to keep him calm.

Tom made it his business to clean up the mess. Janet watched him with admiration. He made such a good job of it, she complimented him. Taking a bucket of clean water into the porchway, he methodically began mopping up the trail of blood right up to the back door. Janet sat in the quiet of the kitchen, watching Gilbert's breathing. It seemed to be getting more shallow. She glanced at the clock. Shirley had been gone for nearly an hour. Normally the walk into Angmering would take twenty minutes, but at this time of year, it wasn't so easy. The rough lanes were slippery, and if the ditches had overflowed, she would have to watch out for black ice. She heard Tom open the back door to throw the contents of the bucket outside into the yard, and then he let out a loud wail. Janet leapt to her feet and ran to him. The door was wide open, but he wasn't there.

'Tom? What's the matter? Where are you, Tom?'

When she saw him, she slapped her hand across her mouth to keep the scream at bay. Tom was on his knees in the yard and sobbing like a baby. In front of him lay the dog, bloodied and still.

'He's dead,' Tom sobbed. 'Mr Oliver shot the dog.'

# CHAPTER 16

The cold air had pierced through Shirley's coat in no time. She hurried as quickly as she could, but the slippery ground made it almost impossible to run. It was also very difficult to stay warm. She had plenty of layers on the top half of her body – vest, blouse, jumper, coat and scarf – but her socks only went up as far as her knees, and where they met her skirt, her thighs were bare. After a while, she was so cold she began to feel slightly detached and shivery.

When she reached the farm at the top end of Water Lane, the pond was completely frozen over. As she approached the gate, six or eight noisy geese ran to meet her. They looked so threatening with their necks jutted out like javelins that she decided not to risk it and went back onto the lane. She was so cold she couldn't remember the doctor's number, anyway. Was it Goring 592 or 925?

Then just past the allotments, she fell over. She recovered herself quite quickly, but now she felt light-headed and her teeth were chattering. There was nobody about in the village. The weather was so bad that most people had decided to stay indoors, and no wonder. The paths were very slippery. People had been grumbling for some time that the culvert wasn't taking the surface water away like it used to. The council had promised to do something about it, but in this terrible weather, the workmen were a long time coming. As a result, there was a sheet of black ice right across the middle of the triangle, and already there were reports of villagers falling. So far between them, they'd clocked up two broken arms, a fractured wrist and a badly bruised back.

Turning left, she walked up the steep hill; where the road fell away and the pavement rose above it, Shirley had to hold on to the icy railings to steady herself. She heard someone coming up the hill behind her. Her frozen legs felt like lead, and she had a dull ache in the middle of her body. At last she spotted the brass nameplate, but it took all her strength to lift the heavy iron knocker on the door. It seemed like an age before someone came to answer it.

The woman who finally opened the door seemed vaguely familiar. She was also a little put out. 'The surgery is on the side of the house,' she said curtly. Shirley stepped away from the door with a mumbled apology. 'Just a minute,' said the woman. 'Sheila, isn't it?'

Without the rail to hang on to, Shirley staggered.

'Quick,' the woman cried, and Shirley felt a pair of strong arms around her. 'You'd better bring her inside,' the woman said. 'The poor girl looks frozen to death.'

When the warmth of the room hit her, Shirley almost

fainted. Now the pain started. She was hardly aware of what was happening to her, except that she was crying. Before she knew it, her damp coat and scarf were removed and she was swathed in a warm blanket. She could see now that she had been saved from falling by the postman delivering letters. She recognized his navy uniform with red piping on the sleeves and his peaked cap.

A cup of warm tea was put in front of her, and a man came into the room.

'She's one of the evacuees,' the woman told him. 'I thought they'd all gone home, but it looks like this one stayed. I settled her myself. Sheila something.'

'Shirley,' said Shirley. She recognized the woman now. It was Mrs Dyer.

'That's right. Shirley,' said Mrs Dyer. 'Well, Shirley, my husband is here now and he's going to look you over.'

'Move over, my dear,' said the newcomer good-naturedly, 'and let me get to my patient.'

Shirley blinked in surprise. When they'd met in the village hall all those months ago, Shirley had had no idea that Mrs Dyer was the doctor's wife.

'Before you drink that tea,' said the doctor, 'I need to take your temperature.' He stuffed a thermometer in her mouth and held her wrist while he looked at his watch. 'What on earth were you doing running around outside dressed like that? You should have put on much warmer clothes, young lady. Your temperature is only

88.6 Fahrenheit. You've got a case of moderate hypo-thermia.'

Shirley willed her befuddled brain to function. 'It's Mr Oliver, sir,' she said as she suddenly stopped shivering. 'There's been an accident.'

'Now I remember you,' cried Mrs Dyer. 'Miss Lloyd and I took you and your brother to Oliver's Farm.'

Shirley nodded.

'An accident, you say?' said Dr Dyer. 'What sort of an accident?'

Shirley's head was spinning. The ache in her middle was still there, and her legs wouldn't stop shaking. 'The dog.' Her speech was slurred. 'Dog bite. Big bite. Lost lots of blood.'

'I'd better get over there, then,' said Dr Dyer. 'Muriel, put her to bed and keep her warm. I'll get the car out.'

'You can't possibly drive up there in this weather,' his wife protested. 'That road will be lethal.'

'What choice do I have?' said the doctor. 'And besides, if this young lady has risked her life to get help, I can't very well refuse to go, now, can I?'

At the farm, the waiting seemed endless. Janet kept an eagle eye on the tourniquet on Gilbert's leg, loosening it every now and then to make sure the blood was still flowing. She rubbed his foot a couple of times to help his circulation, but he didn't like it and became aggressive.

The weather was deteriorating all the time. The sky was battleship grey with snow clouds, and it was very cold. Once he had got over his initial shock at finding the dead dog, Tom had become subdued but calm. They ate their breakfast, two hours late, and then he went outside to see to the chickens. Janet had persuaded him to leave the dog where it was for the time being. The ground was far too hard to dig a hole to bury it, and she didn't want Tom wandering around the farm on his own in this awful weather. After all, she was worried enough about Shirley. Of course, she knew they'd have to dispose of the dog's body fairly quickly. The smell of decay would attract scavengers and she certainly didn't want foxes near the chickens.

They'd covered the dog with a piece of sacking. She felt wretched about it, but at least the poor animal was out of its suffering. Gilbert couldn't torment it any more, and even though the dog had paid a high price for it, to finally get its revenge must have felt sweet, even if it did only last for a few seconds. From what they could gather during Gilbert's lucid moments, the gun had gone off accidentally when the dog had attacked his leg. The second shot, the one that killed it, was deliberate.

Being on a farm meant that they always had something to do. The cows were under cover, so she and Tom fed them hay and pulped turnips. For the afternoon milking, they prepared a mixture of wheat straw, cow cake and bran. If the cows were feeding as they were being milked, it flowed more easily.

Back in the kitchen, Gilbert appeared to be sleeping. The baby was in her crib, which Janet had put well out of his reach. Lucy was beginning to whimper. Janet had just washed her hands and was preparing herself to feed the baby when she heard the sound of tyres on the lane outside. A few minutes later, a voice hailed them from the gate. 'Dr Dyer.'

Tom opened the kitchen door. 'The dog is dead,' he called. 'It's safe now.'

Janet again heard the sound of car tyres and took Lucy off the breast. She didn't mind Dr Dyer seeing her feeding the baby, and she could hide herself from Tom, but if they had visitors, Lucy would have to wait a bit. Lucy pouted a little and stretched herself as she came off the breast, but she didn't cry. The door opened and Dr Dyer came into the room. 'Thank you for coming,' said Janet. 'He's over there.'

'A dog bite, you say,' said the doctor, putting his bag on the table. He lifted the tea towel and examined the leg. 'Nasty. He'll have to go to hospital.'

Gilbert stirred and winced with pain. 'No hospital,' he croaked.

'You've got two choices,' Dr Dyer said drily. 'Go to hospital or stay here and die.'

Janet was watching the door. 'Where's Shirley?'

'She's at my house,' said the doctor. 'She's got hypothermia. My wife has put her to bed.' He turned his attention back to his patient. 'This is going to hurt a bit, old man.' With that, he poured iodine onto the wound and Gilbert's roar went through the roof.

At the same time, several policemen burst into the

kitchen, two of them brandishing revolvers and shouting, 'Police! Stay where you are.'

Lucy jumped in her mother's arms and began to cry. Janet froze. The doctor instinctively stepped back, his arm across his face as if to protect his head. Tom pressed himself against the wall, his face pale and his eyes wide with fright. It was a surreal moment.

'Oh, sorry, Doc,' said the police sergeant as he recognized the village doctor. 'We were informed that an armed and dangerous man was here.'

'Well,' said Dr Dyer, looking down at his patient, who was still grimacing with pain, 'he's no danger to anyone now.'

'He fired his gun at me,' the man from the ministry insisted as he came into the room. 'I had to run for my life.'

Gilbert raised himself slightly and pushed the doctor's arm. 'Get off my land,' he croaked angrily. 'Go on. Clear off!' He was so beside himself with rage that he jerked his leg and shouted out with pain.

'The gun went off when the dog bit him,' said Janet, but her voice was lost in the general mayhem that followed. Everyone was talking at once. Gilbert had recovered slightly and was again demanding that everyone leave. The doctor wanted peace and quiet for his patient, and the policemen were having to restrain the man from the ministry, who had, at last and after much provocation, finally lost his temper.

'Gilbert Oliver,' the sergeant was saying, 'I am arresting you for threatening a ministry official with a firearm, namely a double-barrelled shotgun, contrary to the Firearms Act 1937. You are not obliged to say anything unless you wish to do so, but what you say may be put into writing and given in evidence. Do you understand?'

Gilbert attempted to lash out with his arm and hit him but fainted instead.

When Shirley came back to the farm a day later, Dr Dyer brought her in his car and dropped her at the gate. Janet was overjoyed to see her. 'Are you sure you're all right?'

'Once I'd got warm again,' said Shirley, 'I was fine. Mrs Dyer kept me in bed most of the time and I had some really long sleeps.'

'Lucky you,' Janet grinned.

'Where's Mr Oliver?' said Shirley, looking around.

'He's in hospital,' said Janet, 'and after that he'll be spending some time in the police cells.'

Shirley raised an eyebrow. 'Police cells?'

'They've arrested him,' said Janet. 'The sergeant said he'd be locked up straight away because he'd threatened a government official with a firearm. They are going to send him for trial.'

Shirley had to turn her back in case Janet saw her smile of relief. How marvellous. Life would be so much better now. Tom came in and touched her arm awkwardly. 'Are you all right?' she asked. She didn't attempt to hug him. Even though she was his twin, Tom found showing affection difficult and she respected that. She could see how pleased he was to see her from the smile on his face, although he didn't make eye contact.

'He killed the dog,' said Tom.

'I know,' she said. 'Mrs Dyer told me.'

'Mr Roberts helped me bury him,' said Tom. 'In the orchard.'

'That's good,' said Shirley. Mrs Dyer had sent her back with a suitcase. She put it on the table and opened it. The case was full of warm second-hand clothes. 'Look, I've got you a lovely corduroy jacket.'

They could tell at once that Tom loved it. It was light tan with dark patches on the elbows, and it had woven leather buttons. He put it on immediately.

Shirley turned her attention to Janet. 'How have you been managing?'

Janet sighed. 'Mr Roberts came to help with the milking. I never realized but he used to work here years ago, so he knows what's what.'

'He's quite old,' Shirley observed.

'And he's a bit slow, which is why Gil got rid of him,' Janet said, 'but he gets the job done. Anyway, he says he'll help out for as long as we want.'

'Did you ask Granny Roberts about staying there?' Shirley could hardly bring herself to ask the question. She dreaded the answer, although she knew it was by far the best option for her friend and her daughter.

'I did,' said Janet, 'and she says I can.'

Shirley smiled grimly.

'Do you want to put that suitcase away?' said Janet.

'We've got the man from the ministry coming back this afternoon.'

'He's very persistent,' Shirley remarked.

'If they want to take over the farm,' said Janet, 'this is probably the best opportunity to do it, with Gil out of the way.'

Shirley's heart sank. So this was it. What was going to happen to her and Tom now? He was a good worker, but would anyone give him a chance? It was more likely that the minute they challenged him, he'd clam up and go back into his shell. It was a great pity, because he was so good with animals, and if he had to leave the farm, he'd be devastated. Where would he go? Who would look after him? His future seemed bleak. Her future wasn't so hard to predict: she'd have to go out to work, of course – a live-in post, which would give her a roof over her head. Perhaps she could find a job in Worthing. They said that the big stores even had a hostel for their staff. Of course, that would put paid to her dreams of going to teacher-training college, scholarship or no scholarship. And if they all parted, would she ever see Janet and Lucy again?

As she stuffed the suitcase under her bed, Shirley bit back her tears. Should she write to Auntie Doreen and Auntie Betty? She couldn't imagine Auntie Doreen's mum taking them in, and even if she did, Tom would hate it. 'Pull up your socks, boy. Can't you find something to do? Stand still! I can't bear it when you sway like that.' Mrs Kennedy's bark really was ten times worse than her bite. Auntie Betty had enough to do

215

running the shop, and she'd never allow Shirley and Tom to be at home on their own. They couldn't stay with Auntie Betty either. Her place was very small. Besides, if she told Auntie Doreen and Auntie Betty what was going on, they'd be duty-bound to tell Mum. Oh dear, what a pickle she was in. Sometimes life was so unfair. With Easter only a few weeks away, what she needed was a proper plan.

# CHAPTER 17

'And how are we today?' Nurse Fletcher smiled down at Florrie as she drew the blackout curtains and let the chilly morning air flood the room. Even in the depths of winter, the windows were left open. Florrie pulled the bedclothes up over her shoulders and snuggled back into the warmth of her bed. She yawned. She'd slept well. Today she was going for another treatment. Whenever she had the procedure, she always felt pretty awful for a couple of days afterwards, despite the fact they'd give her a local anaesthetic. The doctor would pump air between the chest wall and her lung to make it collapse. Once it was done, her chest was so tight that it was hard to find a comfortable position in bed. Gradually the air dispelled and her lung would begin to function again. The trouble was, almost as soon as it felt a little easier, she'd have to have another 'refill' and she'd be back to feeling lousy again. There was no getting out of it. This was the standard treatment for TB and it was repeated again and again. How many times had it been now? Four? Five? She'd lost count. The days merged one into another and everything became a grey blur.

Nurse Fletcher put a cup of tea on the bedside locker. 'Rise and shine,' she said cheerfully.

Florrie blinked at her in disbelief. She looked most peculiar. Her teeth and lips were a bright shade of violet.

Florrie's expression must have told her something because Nurse Fletcher became concerned. 'Are you all right?' she asked.

Florrie pulled herself together. 'Fine.'

'Good,' said Nurse Fletcher.

Florrie watched her go with a mixture of sadness and amusement. So Nurse Cook, Nurse Davies and Sister had caught the thief. Nurse Fletcher must have eaten the doctored chocolate. There was no other way she could have ended up getting teeth that colour. Oh dear. How embarrassing.

Shirley and Janet were together in the kitchen when they heard a car drawing up outside. Shirley was washing up at the sink. 'The man from the ministry is here,' she said. It seemed strange to have visitors without the dog barking. Janet took Lucy off the breast, tidied herself and then put the baby onto her shoulder to burp her while Shirley opened the door and let him in.

'Philip Telford,' he said, offering her his hand. Now that he was close up, she could see that he wasn't the same man as she'd seen before. Mr Telford was younger, and he had an honest, open face. Shirley shook his hand and introduced Janet as the head of the house in Mr Oliver's absence. He turned towards Tom, but he slipped out of the door and headed towards the big barn.

'Don't mind my brother,' said Shirley. 'He doesn't mean to be rude. He just doesn't understand some things.'

Mr Telford gave her a knowing nod and sat at the kitchen table in the chair she had indicated. Janet had put Lucy back into her crib, and Shirley was making some tea.

'Mrs Oliver,' he began, 'as you know, the country is at war. At this moment, we import seventy per cent of our food and the War Agricultural Committee is tasked with making sure that every farm is as productive as possible.'

Janet poured from the teapot. 'Biscuit?'

Mr Telford shook his head. 'It is rumoured that later on this year, every farm in the country will have been surveyed. The Ministry of Agriculture will have the power to requisition any farm that is inefficient and place it under their control. The farmer himself may even be replaced by a tenant farmer of the ministry's choice.'

Shirley and Janet exchanged a glance.

'I understand,' said Janet, 'and it doesn't surprise me that Oliver's Farm is one of them. When do you plan to take us over?'

'Not yet, Mrs Oliver,' said Mr Telford.

Janet gave him a puzzled look. 'But Gil . . . my husband believes that—'

'I'm afraid that your husband has rather jumped the

gun,' said Mr Telford, 'if you'll forgive the pun. We merely wanted to make him aware of what was coming so that we could advise him of a suitable course of action, but I'm afraid he refused to discuss anything with my colleague.'

Janet blinked. 'Silly old fool,' she muttered. 'All this for nothing.'

Mr Telford looked slightly embarrassed. 'Perhaps if I could take a look around—' he began.

Janet put up her hand. 'If you want to explain it to me, you're wasting your time,' she said. 'You see, I'm planning to—'

'Janet,' Shirley interrupted sharply. 'Before you say anything else, could I have a word?'

Janet looked nonplussed. 'Shirley, I've already explained how I feel . . .'

'Please,' Shirley said earnestly. She turned to Mr Telford. 'Mr Telford, would it be all right if you started your look-around on your own? I want to talk to Mrs Oliver for a second or two and then we'll join you.'

Mr Telford followed her lead and rose to his feet. Taking his clipboard in his hand, he looked at Janet rather uncertainly. 'I'll start with the milking shed, if that's all right, Mrs Oliver?'

Janet nodded and he left the room. As soon as the kitchen door closed, she looked at Shirley with a frown. 'Now, what's this all about?'

This was turning out to be a good day. Florrie had gone for what she thought would be another screening and

220

refill, but this time it was different. Dr Scott had a smile on his face when he walked back into the treatment room with her X-ray.

'You'll be pleased to hear that the shadow on your lung is a lot smaller, Florrie,' he said. 'I think we can move on to the next stage of your treatment.'

Florrie's eyes lit up. Progress. Progress at last. After six months of stagnation, she was beginning to improve.

'We still have a long way to go,' he cautioned, 'but everything is heading in the right direction.'

'So what happens now?' Her voice cracked with emotion.

'I think you can begin with a little light exercise,' he said. 'Nothing strenuous, of course, but you can get out of bed for an hour in the morning and an hour in the afternoon.'

Florrie beamed.

'You can also go to the bathroom to wash,' he went on, 'and you can sit up in bed for the rest of the day.'

Now that all that awful treatment was behind her Florrie could scarcely take it in. It sounded wonderful. She had been on bed rest for so long. It wasn't easy eating and drinking while lying down, and even doing her flowers had to be done leaning back on two or three pillows. She'd managed to keep up her journal, and every now and then, Dr Scott read it. He'd asked her to bring it today.

'This is really helpful,' he told her.

The nurse began to wheel her from the room. 'One other thing,' Florrie said.

Dr Scott was leafing through her journal, but he looked up again.

'Am I still on the government scheme, or do I have to pay for myself now?' She'd toyed with the idea of saying nothing, as perhaps she'd get another few more weeks of free treatment before they even noticed, but then she remembered how grateful she'd been to have been given two bites of the cherry already. She mustn't be greedy. There were others in the queue, perhaps far more deserving of financial support. She dreaded what he would say, but she felt obligated to raise the subject.

Dr Scott scanned her notes. 'I'll see what I can do, Florrie,' he said.

Florrie could hardly believe her ears. Part of her wanted to protest that she didn't deserve special treatment, but if she did that, she'd be a fool. She knew for a fact that it cost five guineas a week to stay here, and that didn't include Dr Scott's fees. Edna had told her it cost her twenty guineas every time she saw her doctor. Florrie had some savings, but they would run out very quickly if she faced doctor's bills on that scale.

Back on the ward, there was an air of excitement.

'You'll never guess,' said Belinda, a new girl who had been on the ward for about ten days.

'Nurse Fletcher has been dismissed?' said Florrie.

'Whatever made you say that?' said Tina, surprised. 'Actually, she's gone off in a huff to see Matron. She says everyone on the ward has been accusing her of stealing.'

Florrie made a small sound. 'That's not really true. I

bet nobody accused her of anything. She condemned herself by her own actions.'

When she explained what she had seen, everybody began to grin.

'So that's why she kept her hand over her mouth when she was talking to Ward Sister,' said Tina.

'It is stealing really,' Belinda observed. 'Those chocolates were meant for all the nurses.'

'I almost feel sorry for the girl,' said Florrie. 'She must have been very embarrassed.'

'Rightly so,' said Tina. 'After all, she was caught red-handed.'

'Or was it purple-mouthed?' Belinda asked, and they all giggled.

There were three letters waiting for Florrie on her bedside locker. She took in her breath excitedly. For someone who was only used to the occasional postcard, this was almost a deluge of mail. Which should she open first? When she looked more closely, there was no contest. She recognized Shirley's handwriting on one envelope and tore it open. It had been written over a period of several days, the first part dated a week ago.

*Dear Mum, I hope this finds you well and getting better.*

Oh yes. Today, I was told I am improving.

*I miss you. We both miss you.*

And I miss you too, my darlings.

*We don't have a lot to do on the farm at the moment. The ground is too hard for digging and we can't use the plough. Mr Oliver is cleaning out the ditches and repairing fences, but we can't help him with that. Tom is really good with milking. The cows seem to like it when he does them. He's learned how to harness the horses and he enjoys grooming them.*

*Did I tell you I can make butter? First, I have to separate the cream. Then I churn it in a special thingy. When it goes really thick, I drain off the buttermilk and then pat it into a butter roll. It's not hard at all. I quite like working in the milk parlour.*

*I am doing extra work for the exam. It's at the end of March. Think of me then, won't you? Miss Smith says if I work hard, I should pass. I don't know what I shall do when I leave school, but there are plenty of shops in the village. Perhaps I can get a job in one of them until I know if I have won the scholarship.*

*Better go now.*

*Love you, Mum.*

*Shirley and Tom xx*

Florrie pressed the precious letter to her chest and closed her eyes as she whispered a little prayer that they would all be together soon. 'Please God let it be sometime this year.'

The second letter came from the army. It was marked 'BFPO' and had an official stamp on the front. She wasn't sure but it looked as if the envelope had been opened and stuck down again. Florrie was puzzled. Who did she know in the army?

When she opened it, she looked for the signature first. *Yours, Len.* Good heavens, Len Greene! She would never have expected to get a letter from him, not in a million years!

> *Dear Florrie,*
> *I was home on leave and came to the shop. Betty told me that you weren't well, so I got your address. I am sorry to hear you are poorly and hope you will soon be well. If I get any more leave, I'll try and come to see you.*
> *That's all for now.*
> *Yours,*
> *Len*

Florrie smiled to herself. How kind, and knowing him, short and sweet as it was, it probably took hours to compose. She sighed. Funny how life works out. When Shirley and Tom's dad had cleared off, Len had done some repairs on the house and helped to give the shop a lick of paint. She'd felt comfortable with him around. He was good-looking, steady and reliable. She had hoped they might be together, but she was still married to Sid and she couldn't afford a divorce. Even if Len had asked her, she couldn't have just lived with him. What would people think? She'd tried to put him off, but it was really hard. He never overstepped the mark, but she knew the feelings he had for her were the same as the feelings she had for him. But she couldn't tell him, could she? She wasn't free. So she let him go and hoped that he'd find someone else. Of course, she would have hated it if he had, but she convinced herself that for his sake, it was the right thing to do. As it turned out, Len had never married. He didn't even seem to have a lady friend.

Florrie turned her attention to the third envelope. She didn't recognize the handwriting ... or did she? It looked vaguely familiar. It was signed Augusta Andrews. Florrie smiled. How nice of her to write and enquire after her health. Mrs Andrews always had been a considerate woman.

*Dear Florence* ... Mrs Andrews always called her Florence. Her mother had the same name and so it helped to distinguish them one from the other.

*I do hope this finds you well on the way to recovery by now. We are all well and as busy as ever. The German bombs we all expected haven't materialized, so life has returned to normal.*

*I expect you are wondering why I am sending this letter. I'll get straight to the point. I have had a visit from Ruth. It seems that after all this time, her adoptive mother has passed away and Hannah, as she's now called, would very much like to meet you. How do you feel about that? You don't have to decide immediately. Perhaps you would rather wait until you have fully recovered.*

*It seems almost providential that you asked after her the last time we met and now here she is, wanting to be put in touch with her birth*

226

*family. Let me know what you would like me to*
*do.*
    *Yours faithfully,*
    *Augusta Andrews*

Florrie stared blankly ahead. Her brain had gone numb. She felt as if a bomb had been dropped into her lap and was about to go off. She wasn't sure how to react. She had never stopped thinking about Ruth, and now after all this time . . . How often she had longed to see her and explain why she'd had to give her up. Heavens above, she had only been sixteen when Ruth was born. Ruth would be twenty-three soon. She must know something of the ways of the world by now, but would she understand? What did she look like? Would there be a family resemblance? The thought of seeing her was wonderful, but then another thought crossed her mind. What on earth would she tell Shirley and Tom? The years rolled back and she saw herself, only a young slip of a girl, standing outside the doctor's house. Mrs Andrews had been very understanding. The baby had only been a week old when she'd handed her over for adoption.

'You mustn't blame yourself, Florence,' she'd said. 'I can assure you that you are doing the right thing.'

But had it been the right thing? Florrie had worried about it for years. After all, Ruth was her own flesh and blood, and no matter how difficult things are, you don't give up on your own flesh and blood, do you?

# CHAPTER 18

Shirley chewed her bottom lip anxiously. She knew it was now or never. This was her one and only chance.

'Well, come on,' said Janet irritably. 'What do you want to tell me?'

'I don't really want to tell you anything,' she said, 'but I have a suggestion. One that might serve us both.'

Janet spread her hands impatiently and raised her eyebrows.

'It looks as if Mr Oliver may not be back for quite a while,' Shirley said.

'I think that's pretty obvious, don't you?' said Janet. 'He's having treatment on his leg. Even if he's lucky enough for it not to get infected, he'll probably be in hospital for a week at least.'

'And then he's got to go to court,' said Shirley.

Janet nodded. 'And the police tell me there's no chance of him coming home before the trial. They don't take kindly to government officials being threatened with a shotgun.'

'And we're looking at a month or six weeks before he goes to trial?' said Shirley.

'I guess so,' said Janet. 'What's your point?'

'And if he's found guilty,' said Shirley, 'what sentence will he get?'

Janet shrugged. 'I dunno. Six months? A year?'

'I think it could be a lot longer,' said Shirley.

'Who cares?' said Janet dismissively. 'I'll be long gone.'

'That's just it,' said Shirley. 'You don't have to be.'

Janet's expression soured. 'I have to keep my daughter safe.'

'So long as he's not here,' said Shirley, 'she's perfectly safe, and so are you.'

Janet looked taken aback.

'You could bring this farm back from the brink,' said Shirley.

'Why would I want to do anything to help that pig?' Janet said angrily.

'The person you'll be helping is yourself,' said Shirley. 'There's money to be made in this farm, and by the time Mr Oliver comes out, you and Lucy could have enough to make a real start somewhere else.'

Her friend still wasn't listening. 'But why should he reap all the benefits of my hard work?' she said indignantly. 'What if he comes after us?'

'He won't,' said Shirley. 'Yes, the farm will be a going concern, but we both know he'd want to go back to the way things were. It'll be heading downhill before you know it, but why should we care? And as for chasing after you, he'll be far too busy trying to keep the officials at bay.'

Janet lowered herself back down into her chair and looked thoughtful. 'Why should you care?' she said. 'You don't even like farming.'

'But Tom does,' said Shirley. 'I reckon if he got a reputation for being a good worker, there's a real possibility that he'd be taken on by somebody else. I want him to have that chance.'

Janet's expression broke into a slow smile. 'You've got an old head on those young shoulders of yours, Shirley Jenkins. How on earth did you come by all this?'

'I mulled it over and tried to think what my mother would say,' said Shirley. 'I have to leave school at Easter. If I join the Land Army, I could stay on too.'

'You're too young,' said Janet. 'You have to be eighteen.'

'I can look eighteen,' said Shirley. 'And Tom already does. That's half his problem. People think he's much older than he is.'

Janet pulled a face. 'They'd check your papers.'

'I asked Miss Smith about it and she told me the farmer checks the paperwork,' said Shirley. 'Do you think you could make a mistake about my age? People lied about their age in the First World War. Why not now?'

'And here's me thinking you were a sweet little innocent schoolgirl,' Janet teased, 'when all the time you're nothing more than a scheming little madam.' She laid her hand over Shirley's. 'All right. You're on. Let's do it.'

\* \* \*

230

A week later, Shirley threw herself down in the kitchen chair and pulled off her headscarf. 'Well, at least we got a few things right.'

The three of them were exhausted. They had spent most of the afternoon with Mr Telford walking around the farm. He had been unequivocal in his criticism of what they were doing, but he had been encouraging rather than condemning. In every case they could see that he was absolutely right, and once he'd gone, they'd still had to finish off the outside jobs.

Janet took the casserole out of the oven. Knowing that they'd be tired at the end of the day, while Janet fed Lucy that morning, Shirley had put tinned corned beef with haricot beans, cabbage, a leek, vegetable stock and herbs into a large dish. All they had to do was place it in the range oven for forty-five minutes before they needed it. By the time Shirley had finished in the milk parlour and laid the table, Lucy had been fed again. Everybody had a wash and the meal was ready.

It had been an eventful couple of days. Before Mr Telford's visit, some men from the dairy had turned up. Shirley could tell straight away that they were in some kind of trouble. The man in charge, Mr Swan, was rather curt in his manner.

'Who is responsible for the milk churns?'

'I am at the moment,' said Janet. 'Usually my husband does them, but he's in hospital. Why?'

Mr Swan consulted his paperwork. 'How long have you been doing them?'

'Since last Wednesday.'

He tapped a page with his fountain pen and his colleague looked over his shoulder, nodded.

Janet frowned. 'Would you mind telling me what this is all about?'

'You've only got eight cows,' said Mr Swan, 'and yet our records tell us that for some time your churns had an average of twenty-seven gallons of milk in them. There is no way you could get that much milk from eight cows.'

'There must be some mistake,' Janet said faintly.

'We did a routine test,' said the second man. 'The milk was diluted.'

Shirley was aghast. 'What? How?'

'One sample had fifty-seven per cent added water and the other twenty-six per cent,' Mr Swan went on. Janet opened her mouth to say something, but he stopped her with a wave of his hand. 'However, since last week your returns have dropped considerably.'

'That's what put us on to you,' said the other man.

'Since then you've been sending approximately seven and a half gallons to the dairy,' said Mr Swan, 'a figure far more consistent with the yield of eight cows.'

'In other words,' Shirley piped up, 'you know we have nothing to do with watered-down milk.'

'If you were involved,' said Mr Swan, 'the dairy would have refused to deal with you and you would have been blacklisted. Nobody in this area would take your milk.'

Janet looked anxious. 'I'll make sure it doesn't happen again.'

'Now,' said Mr Swan, 'if you tell me where Mr Oliver is, I shall issue him with a summons.'

Janet and Shirley had watched them go with a sense of relief. 'Thank goodness they could see we were the innocent party,' said Janet. 'If they'd stopped taking the churns, we'd have been jiggered.'

Since Mr Telford had told them he'd help, the three of them concentrated on making the farm look as efficient as possible before his visit. It was added pressure for Shirley. She had less than a week before her exams and she wanted to spend as much time as she could swatting up. She did her fair share of work, but Mr Telford still found plenty of things that needed changing.

'It's better if you have all the cows facing the same way when you milk them,' he said. 'Empty pails and those full of milk left in that narrow passageway between their backsides risk contamination.'

Shirley could see the sense of that at once. If a cow defecated, the buckets could easily be splashed.

'And keep those cats out of the milking parlour,' said Mr Telford. 'I saw one balancing on the edge of a pail to drink. Just remember the last thing it may have done,' he added with a grin. 'Perhaps killed a rat or had a nice lick of its pussy bottom.'

Shirley shuddered at the thought.

Having all the cows facing the same way meant rearranging the milking shed. That took time, and clutter that had been simply piled up because Mr Oliver couldn't be bothered to put it in its proper place had to be moved. Once they'd created eight empty stalls down one side of the shed, Tom promised to sweep it out more thoroughly the next day.

Mr Telford complimented them on their method of milking and singled Tom out for a special commendation. He also suggested that when the milk was taken to the cooler, the weight of each pail should be recorded against the name of the cow. 'That way,' he explained, 'you'll know how productive each one is.'

Although it would take a little longer, it sounded like good sense to Janet. Gilbert never knew what a cow's yield was. He'd just say, 'She gives a good pail full' or, 'She only gave half a pail today.'

Before it got dark, they walked the fields with Seth Roberts. The winter had been harsh, but already the days were getting slightly warmer. Mr Telford advised them to begin drilling oats and barley.

'If Tom puts on the 'arness,' said Seth, 'I can manage to walk behind the 'orse.' Just the thought of being active again made him look years younger.

'If you mend the fences round the orchard,' said Mr Telford, 'you might consider keeping a few pigs. You'll need a permit, of course, but it would mean fresh meat for yourselves. The government will want half. I know it seems unfair, but as a country, we have to make ourselves self-sufficient.'

When they got back to the farmhouse, their heads were reeling with facts and suggestions, but they were still enthusiastic.

'Did your husband always manage this farm on his own?' Mr Telford asked.

Janet shook her head. 'He used to have a labourer. Reuben Fletcher, he was called, but he was before my time.'

'So what happened to him?'

Janet shrugged. 'Moved on to pastures new, I suppose.'

'I shall recommend that you get more help,' said Mr Telford, 'and if you can billet your workers, so much the better.'

'I can't believe how helpful you've been,' said Janet. 'Thank you.'

'You'll face opposition,' said Mr Telford as he turned to leave. 'The farmers around here will be certain that because you are a woman on her own, you can't do it, but I advise you to listen to old Seth. He's been on the land all his life, and although he may be a bit old-fashioned and his arthritis slows him up, he'll give you sound advice.'

Janet shook his hand vigorously and Mr Telford smiled. 'I'll come back after the Easter holiday,' he told them. 'Any problems, tell me then and I'll see what I can do.'

Janet nodded. That would be the beginning of April. The last thing he had done before he left was to arrange for the billing to be transferred to Janet. Oliver's Farm was now her responsibility, so he'd suggested she write to her husband and ask him to put the bank account in her name while he was away.

They ate their meal eagerly, then sat back to relax for a while. Shirley yawned. She still faced taking another look at her school books before getting ready for bed. Her gaze fell on the mantrap hanging on the wall. 'I really hate that thing,' she said.

'So do I,' said Janet. 'And d'you know what, I think we should change the sleeping arrangements in this house. Why should you and Tom stay in that freezing-cold room when there is a perfectly good room upstairs?'

Shirley blinked in surprise. 'Mr Oliver will go crazy.'

'Mr Oliver isn't here,' said Janet. She pushed her thumbs into the armholes of her floral cross-over apron and grinned. 'I'm in charge now.'

'How shall we do it?' said Shirley eagerly.

'I'll go into Gil's room with Lucy,' said Janet. 'It'll have to be spring-cleaned – it smells like a fox's den in there. Tom can sleep on the landing where I am now, and you can have Elizabeth's room.'

Shirley took in her breath. Was she really going to be allowed to sleep in that lovely room? She could hardly wait.

Tina wasn't at all well. Florrie woke up to the sound of whispered voices coming from the other side of the screen. It was still dark. The big clock on the wall said ten to five. She could hear the nurses pulling together to haul Tina back up the bed, but it did little to help her laboured breathing. A short while later, the nurses wound the bed up so that it was supported on its big wheels, and a few minutes after that, Tina's bed was wheeled out of the ward. When the screen was taken away, Florrie stared grimly at the empty space where her friend's bed had been.

Tina had always struggled with her illness. She'd had the same treatment as everyone else, but people like Edna had gone home for Christmas, and Jill had improved. Even Florrie had made progress, but Tina only seemed to get weaker. About an hour later, when the early morning tea trolley came round, everybody stirred to begin the new day.

Florrie drank her tea, then collected her washbag and towel, and headed for the bathroom. Everyone made polite conversation, but nobody remarked on the big empty space. They didn't need to. While all of them hoped and prayed that it wouldn't be long before Tina was back on the ward, they knew the score. She'd be in a single room on a constant supply of oxygen. She might even be in an iron lung. Experiments were showing that the machine used to help those with polio-myelitis could also help TB patients.

Florrie and the other women washed in silence. When they came back to the ward, no one felt much like conversation. Jill was doing a puzzle. Florrie went to join her. It was then that Florrie noticed a piece of paper on the floor behind her locker. By pushing her locker and balancing over the side of her chair, Florrie managed to reach it. She was lucky not to get caught straining herself or she would have been in trouble. When she finally managed to look at it, she knew it was

Tina's. It was the photograph, the one Tina had shown her of her two little girls.

Pulling on a cardigan, Florrie made her way down the ward. If anyone asked where she was going, she would say this was part of her exercise. The isolation cubicles were at the end of the ward. Each door had a small window that was covered by a sliding door. There was no one around. Florrie peeked through the first window. Empty room. On the other side, a woman was doing her exercises with the nurse. She sat in a chair with the nurse opposite and together they lifted their arms and put them down again.

The third door had the shutter across the window. Florrie slid the wood across silently. Tina was sitting bolt upright in bed with a rubber oxygen mask over her nose and mouth. Her skin was grey, and it was obvious that she was struggling to get every ounce of breath into her lungs. Florrie pushed the door open and slipped inside. As she reached her bedside, Tina opened her eyes.

'Hello, love,' Florrie said cheerfully. She held up the photograph. 'You dropped this.'

Tina's eyes were fixed on the faces of her little girls, but she didn't move. It was only then that Florrie realized she didn't even have the strength to lift her arm and take it. Florrie held the picture in front of Tina for a second longer, and then she tucked it under the fingers of Tina's hand, which was resting on top of the covers. 'Now, you hold on tight,' she whispered.

Tina's fingers fluttered slightly as if she was caressing the picture.

'I'd better go,' said Florrie, squeezing her arm gently, 'or I'll be for the high jump.'

On impulse, as she stood up, Florrie leaned over and planted a gentle kiss on Tina's forehead. Tina didn't speak, but a solitary teardrop fell from the corner of her eye and rolled along the rubber strap of the mask.

Outside in the corridor, Florrie leaned against the wall and struggled not to cry. Damn this disease. It was merciless. It was cruel. It was bloody unfair.

# CHAPTER 19

Janet was right: Mr Oliver's room stank, and when they pulled back the bedcovers, they couldn't believe the colour of his sheets.

'I've no idea when he last changed them,' said Janet, putting them into a pile with her fingertips. 'He never lets me in here.'

'I shall be worn to a frazzle by the time we finish this,' Shirley joked. She was going down to the village later this evening. Although she had no money, the village-hall committee had decided to join a scheme whereby films were shown in the hall. It wasn't quite the same as going to the cinema, but it meant everyone could see a fairly new film closer to home. It was only a shilling to go in, and that included a cup of tea in the interval. Granny Roberts had told Shirley they were looking for someone to help with the teas. Whoever did it would get in free. Shirley had already done it a couple of times. She had to go in early to put out the cups and light the gas under the big kettles. She would miss a bit around the middle of the film while she brewed the tea and then did the washing-up, but she could usually pick up the story, so it didn't matter too much. Tonight, they were showing an Alfred Hitchcock film called *The Lady Vanishes* and she was really looking forward to it.

It took them a couple of hours of hard work to get the room into a habitable state. Months of cobwebs and dust had to be swept away, and they even had to empty a brimming chamber pot they found under the bed. At one point, they started a pillow fight but had to stop when one popped open and feathers went everywhere. They worked hard, and once the windows were cleaned, it made the room a lot lighter, but the curtains fell apart as they were taken down to be washed.

'I shall have to put a blanket over the rail until I can make some new ones,' said Janet. 'Any light here on the hill will have the warden biking up to the house in no time,' and they both laughed.

There was something in the corner covered by an old blanket. Janet pulled it off to reveal a small suitcase. She threw it onto the bed and opened it. It appeared to be empty.

'Hang on a minute,' said Shirley. 'That's my mum's suitcase.' She examined it carefully. 'Yes, there's the scribble picture Tom did when he was about six. He got into a lot of trouble for that. And that nick in the fabric happened when the buckle on my shoe got caught on it when we went to stay with Auntie Doreen.' She looked up at Janet with a puzzled expression. 'We never brought it with us, so what's it doing here? Did my mother come to see us?'

Janet shrugged. 'I haven't a clue,' she said, 'but if she did, I never saw her.'

'So how did it get here?' Shirley ran her fingers along the pocket on the side and pulled out a lipstick with a small luggage label attached. *All my love, Mum xx*. It wasn't her mother's writing. For a second or two, Shirley panicked. Had something happened to Mum? Was she worse? Had she . . . She hadn't . . . No, no, of course not. Of course she hadn't died. She'd written them that letter only a few days ago. Shirley swivelled the lipstick. It was a pretty shade of raspberry pink.

'That's lovely,' said Janet. 'What a great mother you've got – giving you your first lipstick.'

Tears sprang into Shirley's eyes.

'Oh, Shirley,' said Janet, 'I'm sorry. I didn't mean to make you cry.'

'No, it's all right,' said Shirley. 'It just that I can't bear to think that if she came here, I missed her. Why didn't he say something?'

'She could have come, I suppose,' Janet said cautiously. 'You had all those warm winter clothes, remember?'

'But they came by post, didn't they?' said Shirley. 'I opened the parcel on the kitchen table . . .' Her voice trailed off and they stared at each other in bewilderment.

'I bet he took them out of the case and wrapped them in a brown-paper parcel himself,' cried Janet.

'So she was here, wasn't she!' cried Shirley. 'My

mother came to see us and he sent her away and then pretended the stuff she'd brought us came by post.'

'You don't know that for sure,' said Janet.

'What other explanation is there?' said Shirley. She had never felt more frustrated. 'I can't believe it! Oh, he's so horrible, that man. I hate him. I hate him.' She sat on the bed and burst into tears.

Janet had her arm round Shirley's shoulders as Tom came into the room carrying the baby's crib. He stood watching in bewilderment. 'Don't cry, Shirl,' he said. 'I don't like it when you cry.'

Hearing his voice, Shirley pulled herself together. 'It's all right,' she gulped. 'I'm all right now.'

Janet slid her hand into the pocket on the other side of the suitcase. To her surprise, she pulled out three pieces of paper. 'Look at this,' she murmured. 'Three postal orders, all made out to you.'

'Then she definitely came,' said Shirley.

'Who came, Shirley?' Tom wanted to know.

She daren't tell him that their mother had been here and that he'd not been allowed to see her. He'd be devastated. 'A friend,' she smiled. 'A friend came with these.' She studied the date on the Post Office stamp. All were sent before Christmas. Tom lumbered out of the room and went downstairs.

'At least you've got the money now,' said Janet.

'But why?' Shirley asked Janet. 'Why did he do it?'

'To keep you both here, I suppose,' she said.

Shirley frowned. She wished Mr Oliver was here right now and then she could have it out with him, but she quickly realized that if he was here, they wouldn't even be in this room. She stood to her feet to carry on. All Mr Oliver's clothes were in a pile on the floor, and much as they'd like to get rid of them, they couldn't. In the end, they decided to open the trunk he'd used as a bedside table and shove everything in there. When they threw the lid up, they found some lovely bed linen.

'We might as well use this on the beds,' said Janet. 'Shame to waste it all.'

Having pushed all trace of Gilbert Oliver into the trunk, they spread a little lavender polish on the chest of drawers and the room smelled a whole lot nicer. Later in the day, Shirley picked a few early daffodils from the orchard and put them in a vase. They looked nice on the chest of drawers. Now at last, the room was ready for Janet and Lucy.

'One thing I'd really like to do,' said Shirley, 'is to take down that awful mantrap in the kitchen.'

'Good idea,' said Janet. 'Let's do it now.'

They went downstairs, and after a cup of tea, tackled the trap. It was screwed so tightly to the wall it took all their strength and still they couldn't manage to dislodge it. At one point, Shirley dropped the screwdriver and they had to move the chest of drawers to pick it up. There was a drawer on the side that they hadn't noticed before. When Janet opened it, she gasped. There was a large money tin inside, and when she turned the key in the lock, they were dazzled by pound notes.

'Golly,' said Shirley. 'How much do you think is there?'

Janet grinned. 'Enough for us to pay proper wages and to buy whatever we need to keep this farm going.'

'Do you really think you should?' Shirley asked cautiously.

'When I married Gil,' said Janet, 'he made me a promise: "With all my worldly goods I thee endow." I reckon I'm perfectly entitled to use this money for the farm, don't you?'

Shirley grinned. 'I guess you're right.'

She was itching to get into Elizabeth's room, but because the farm work had to take precedence, they could only do one room at a time.

They had a bit of a scare when the village bobby came up on his bicycle to tell Janet that Gilbert had already appeared before the magistrates on a summons for adulterating the milk. They hadn't expected the case to be heard so soon.

'He was fined twenty pounds,' PC Duffy told them, 'with ten pounds in costs. He got off lightly in my opinion. He should have been sent down.'

'Are you telling me he's out of prison?' Janet squeaked.

'No,' said PC Duffy, turning his bicycle round. He was a nice man, quite good-looking. He'd been called up when the war started, but he had damaged his right index finger as a boy and because the joint was locked, it wouldn't bend. 'Not much use when you're trying to fire a gun,' he'd joked.

'He's still in custody regarding the firearms charges,' he went on. 'They've transferred him to Lewes Prison on remand. He'll be back in the magistrates' court next week. Ten o'clock on Tuesday.'

As he cycled away, Janet looked at Shirley. 'For one awful moment, I thought he was going to say . . .'

'So did I,' said Shirley. 'Perhaps we'd better leave changing the other rooms until we know for sure.'

Janet nodded. 'I think it might be best.'

The girls on the ward were subdued. Tina had died in the early hours of the morning. She had no relatives to be with her, so the night nurses had waved the rules and Florrie had taken a turn at sitting by her bedside. As it transpired, the nurse was with her when it happened. Florrie was unbelievably upset. She couldn't bear the thought that Tina's lovely girls would never know their mother, but at the same time she thanked God that they were far too young to understand their terrible loss. They would, she supposed, be told at a later date that their mother had died. As for Tina herself, she'd miss their first day at school, all their birthday parties and Christmases, their first day at work, and she'd never be the mother of the bride – oh, it was too unbelievably awful, too sad.

'Come on now, Florrie,' said Jill as Florrie wept. 'Don't go making yourself bad again. Tina wouldn't want that.'

Florrie nodded miserably and blew her nose. But perhaps it wasn't just for Tina that she cried. What about all her own wasted days and the separation from Tom and Shirley? She missed the corner shop and her dear friends. Much as she complained about it, she wanted to smell the river again and serve tobacco to the dockers. She wanted to chat to Len. Florrie looked up to see a nurse bagging Tina's stuff. A small, flesh-coloured leg stuck out of the top of the bag and Florrie remembered the rag dolls. Tina had so wanted to send them to her girls.

'Excuse me. Those dolls,' Florrie asked, 'can I have them?'

'They're only half finished,' said the nurse.

'I know,' said Florrie. 'She was making them for her girls. I'd like to finish them for her.'

The nurse gave her a sympathetic look. 'The one good thing that's come out of this,' she said cautiously, 'is that her children are still young enough to find a good home. They'll be adopted. They won't even know about the dolls.'

'I know,' said Florrie, her throat becoming tight again, 'but they might be allowed to have a keepsake from their real mother, eh?'

The nurse hesitated for a moment, then handed her the bag. 'Don't be disappointed if the authorities won't allow it.'

Florrie nodded. In the days that lay ahead, it helped to be sewing buttons on for eyes and making felt shoes. She'd found Tina's photograph at the bottom of the bag. Florrie kept it on her locker, and every now and then she showed the girls the progress she had made. Her stitching wasn't as good as Tina's, but everything was being done with love.

\* \* \*

A week before the holiday, Shirley sat the exam. She took a two-hour paper in the morning and a two-and-a-half-hour paper in the afternoon. When she emerged from the classroom, she was exhausted but quietly confident.

Easter came and went. The weather was quite good, even though it was only March. Bank-holiday Monday saw record numbers of day-trippers on the beaches of Worthing. Things seemed to have settled down as far as the war was concerned, and there was a lot less talk of bombing and gas attacks. People still carried their gas-mask box everywhere they went, but these days it was more likely to contain their sandwiches for lunch. Even on Oliver's Farm, there was a period of peace and quiet. True to his word, Mr Telford had found them a farm labourer. Vincent Watts was in his late forties, and although he had worked on the land all his life, he had fallen on hard times. Two years before, he'd got his leg caught in a baling machine. He was lucky, so they told him, that he hadn't lost it altogether, but his recovery had taken so long that his employer had to let him go. Shirley recognized him as the man who, along with the landlord of the Red Lion, had helped her when Tom got stuck in the culvert.

Before he came, Janet got Tom and Seth to put a better door on Shirley and Tom's old room, one that reached to the floor. Tom whitewashed the walls, and Granny Roberts had given them 'a stick or two of furniture' to create a habitable room. It was very humble, but Vince was delighted and Shirley moved upstairs.

One of the first things Vince had them doing, apart from the usual tasks on the farm, was chitting potatoes. The second earlies should have been put into the ground by mid-March, but although they were a bit late, Vince said it would be all right if they got them in now. The maincrop potatoes would take twenty weeks to mature, but they would normally be ready to lift in late August through to October. The work would be labour-intensive because they would have to bank up the rows as the shoots appeared and keep them well watered and pest-free, but they all agreed it would be worth it. The whole crop could be lifted and sold to give them a firm financial footing to take them through the winter.

Janet had decided not to go to Lewes Assizes for the trial, but with Vince in place as the day drew nearer, she began to change her mind. Everyone was convinced that Gilbert would be sent to prison, but she wanted to see it for herself. Of course, if the court was lenient, she would have to leave the farm straight away. As Mr Telford suggested, Janet had written to Gilbert suggesting that he make bank funds available to her, but she held out little hope of getting any. It was a bit embarrassing explaining her concerns to Mr Telford, but he'd seemed unperturbed.

'You can get a loan using the harvest as collateral,' he said. 'It's a bit of a risk, but I think with my recommendation, you'll be all right.' It was a pity that the money in the tin only covered existing debts and a wage for Vince and Seth.

Her head told her it would be better not to go to court just in case it all went wrong, but she dreaded Gilbert walking back in unannounced even more. At least, she told herself, if she saw him acquitted, she would be prepared. She was well aware that her thoughts were confused, but that's the way it was.

Janet arranged for Lucy to stay with Granny Roberts for the day. She had expressed some of her breast milk and put it into a baby's bottle, and she told Granny Roberts that if she was delayed, she was to give Lucy some watered-down evaporated milk. After seeing Lucy settled, Janet caught the early train and arrived in Lewes at nine-thirty.

It turned out that the court, a grey stone Georgian-style building right in the centre of town, was easy to find. Janet ran up the steps and went through the middle door of three. She and the rest of the people waiting to go in entered the public gallery just before ten. The room itself was very impressive. Lined with dark wooden panels, it had a church-like appearance, but the vaulted glass ceiling gave it a touch of the theatrical. Soon after they'd all sat down, the prisoner was called up from the cells into the dock, which was in the centre of the courtroom. Gilbert, looking dishevelled and unkempt, looked around and then spotted her up in the gallery. Their eyes locked, but neither of them showed any hint of recognition. A surge of anger filled Janet's chest. What a fool she'd been. She had certainly jumped from the frying pan into the fire when she had married him. Since he'd been gone, she'd realized that

250

he'd treated her little better than the animals on his farm. Grateful not to have ended up on the streets, she'd made excuses for him for far too long. If anyone remarked on his grumpy moods, she'd say he was still mourning the death of his first wife, or that he was simply desperate to save his farm. She'd spent half her married life apologizing and explaining that he didn't really mean what he'd just done or said, but not any more. All that had changed the moment he'd tried to harm her child.

Someone called out, 'All rise,' which was followed by a low rumble as everyone in the courtroom got to their feet. The judge, Mr Justice Brooks, entered through a door to the side of his chair on the bench and bowed his head. As he sat down so did everyone else.

They began with introductions. Mr John Flowers, KC, neatly turned out in wig and gown, and the bespectacled, much younger Mr Brown, who were both instructed by Messrs Dell and Loader, were speaking for the prosecution. Mr Grayson, KC, a rather tired-looking man wearing a moth-eaten wig, appeared on behalf of Mr Gilbert Oliver. In his opening speech, Mr Flowers told the court that when Mr Bradshaw (on hearing his name, Janet suddenly realized she'd never known the name of the first man from the ministry) arrived at the farm, Mr Oliver had been abusive and aggressive in his behaviour.

At this point, Gil jumped to his feet and shouted, 'They wants to take away my farm, that's why.'

The judge stopped him mid-flow and remonstrated

with him. 'Prisoner at the bar, you will have plenty of time to put your case later on,' he said. 'I would ask you to sit down and wait until your counsel instructs you.'

Gilbert sat down and Mr Flowers continued. 'Mr Oliver, having produced a shotgun, fired it twice, so traumatizing Mr Bradshaw—'

Gilbert was up again. 'It were an accident. The bloody dog bit me.'

The judge banged his gavel. 'Mr Oliver, I have already explained that this is not the time for you to speak. Please do not interrupt King's Counsel again.

Gilbert glowered and sat down once more. Mr Flowers resumed his speech. 'The shotgun was fired twice, so traumatizing Mr Bradshaw that he has been unable to return to his place of work.' Gilbert mumbled something rude, but everyone ignored him.

When Mr Bray, Gilbert's barrister, rose to give his opening speech, it wasn't long before Gilbert was interrupting him as well. 'Tell them they've got no right to take away my place. My family have farmed that land for six generations.'

The judge banged his gavel. 'One more interruption, Mr Oliver, and I shall send you back to the cells and add contempt of court to your list of charges.'

'You call this justice, you dried-up old prune?' Gilbert yelled, incensed. 'It seems to me that it's one law for the haves and another for the have-nots.'

A minute or two later, Gilbert was on his way back to the cells, shouting obscenities and resisting the two burly officers who manhandled him back downstairs. As the judge adjourned the proceedings for a fifteen-minute break, Janet could still hear her husband's protests as he kicked the cell door.

# CHAPTER 20

While they had a fifteen-minute break, Janet took the opportunity to go to the toilet. She felt like a bag of nerves. PC Duffy was talking to another police officer in the corridor. When he saw her, he nodded.

'Mrs Oliver,' he said stiffly.

'PC Duffy,' she replied, guessing that he wasn't more friendly because he was with his superior.

The case continued without Gilbert. In fact, it seemed to be moving along a lot more quickly now that he wasn't constantly interrupting. The jury were sent out late in the afternoon, and less than an hour later, they were back. Gilbert was brought up from the cells into the dock.

'How do you find the prisoner? Guilty or not guilty?'

Janet closed her eyes, knowing that from this moment on, whichever way it went, one word or two words would alter the course of her life forever.

'Not guilty.'

Janet gasped audibly and gathered her things. A murmur in the courtroom grew louder. The judge banged his gavel.

'Mr Oliver,' he said, 'you have been found not guilty of the firearms offences and under normal circumstances would be free to go.' Janet hovered by the door. There was a pregnant pause, and then he continued. 'However, I take a very dim view of your conduct in this court-room. You have a blatant disregard for authority, and your belligerent attitude has shown your contempt for this court. For this reason, I sentence you to three months in prison.'

Gilbert went berserk. As he leaned over the dock shout-ing obscenities to the judge, the usher called, 'All rise' and, gathering his papers, the judge prepared to leave the courtroom. Quick as a flash, Gilbert turned his back and undid his belt. There was an audible gasp in the gallery as his trousers fell and he presented his bare bottom to the bench. As Gilbert bent forward, there was a loud report and a foul odour filled the room. The judge, half out of his chair, sat back down and banged his gavel.

'And for that gross insult, Mr Oliver, I add another three months to your sentence.' There was a slight pause, and then he added, 'With hard labour.'

Gilbert was manhandled back into his trousers and dragged down to the cells by the same two burly officers who had taken him down last time. The judge then left the courtroom. Most people stood in silent and shocked surprise. No one had expected that.

Janet closed her eyes in despair. Six months. Was that all? She was glad he was to go to prison, but six months wasn't nearly enough for her and Shirley to carry out their plan. How could they possibly make the farm a going concern in such a short space of time? He'd be back outside by October. They would barely have time to get in the harvest. Her heart was heavy and she was battling tears of disappointment as she stepped out onto the street and into the middle of an April shower. By the time she'd reached the station, she was beginning to pull herself together. She would have to find another solution. She dared not stay with Gilbert. She couldn't risk putting Lucy in danger. If he'd tried to harm her once, who was to say he wouldn't try again? Some would have said Shirley had imagined what she said she saw, but when Janet had challenged him, he hadn't exactly denied it, had he? No. Which was why she daren't stay. She'd have to think of some other way to survive. The problem was finding a way she could support herself and her daughter. Who would look after Lucy while she went out to work? Where would they live? Most landlords wanted a male guarantor if a woman alone wanted to rent a room – either that or a reference from a bank to say she was a woman with an independent income and flawless character. Janet had neither. Six months. How on earth was she to become a woman of independent means by then? The short answer was, she couldn't.

The train from Lewes terminated at Brighton. The Worthing train was gathering a head of steam on another platform, so she had to run to catch it. She climbed into the ladies-only carriage. The two passengers inside barely gave her a glance as she came in, but Janet didn't care. She sat with her back to the engine and stared out of the window deep in thought. The only other option she had was to . . . No, she couldn't give her daughter up for adoption. She really couldn't. A little noise escaped from her throat.

'Are you all right, my dear?'

The train had reached Lancing and she was alone in the carriage with an elderly lady. She hadn't noticed the others leaving, nor had she seen the old woman get into the carriage. She was neatly dressed in a grey suit with a pleated skirt. Her silver-white hair was pulled back into an untidy bun, and she was wearing a small grey hat with a pink band. It was only as she turned her head to look at the woman that Janet realized she'd been crying. Hastily wiping away her tears with her gloved hand, Janet said brightly, 'Yes, thank you. I'm fine.'

The old woman gave her a concerned look. 'You're Mrs Oliver, aren't you?'

Janet nodded. 'Do I know you?'

'I'm Elizabeth Oliver's mother.'

Janet felt her face colour. 'Oh,' she fumbled. 'I – I'm very sorry for your loss.'

The woman smiled grimly.

'Everyone says she was a lovely girl,' said Janet. She wanted to redeem the situation, but it was so difficult to know what to say.

'She was,' said Elizabeth's mother. 'She was the best daughter a woman could have.'

'I'm sorry,' said Janet helplessly.

The woman went back to reading her book, but Janet, embarrassed as she was, couldn't help stealing a glance in her direction every now and then. She was quite old but still an attractive woman. If her mother was this good-looking at her age, Elizabeth must have been stunning.

The train reached Angmering Station and Janet stood to leave.

The woman suddenly looked up. 'I heard that you had a baby.'

'Yes.' Janet stepped out onto the platform, her hand ready to shut the carriage door.

'Then he served you better than my poor girl,' the woman said quietly.

The door slammed between them and Janet hurried along the platform. All she wanted to do right now was hold her baby, but she still had a couple of miles to walk to the farm.

'He served you better . . .' What did that mean? Puzzled, Janet couldn't make sense of it.

The centre of the village was blocked off when she got there. Some workmen had the culvert open and a policeman was guarding the entrance. A police car waited in the road. A small huddle of women stood outside the village hall. As Janet came up to them, a woman wearing a primrose brooch on her coat lapel turned round.

'They won't let you pass, dear,' she said. 'We all have to wait here.'

'How much longer is this going to take?' grumbled a woman in a bright red coat. 'Only, I need to get to the butcher's before he shuts. I've got unexpected visitors coming for tea.'

'The sergeant told me they have to keep coming back up for air,' said a third woman.

'They should have got it sorted out months ago,' said the primrose-brooch woman. 'It was flooded for days and days in the winter. I complained to the council loads of times.'

'And the smell,' said the red-coat woman. They all shook their heads in shared disgust.

'What's happened?' asked Janet.

The third woman turned to her. 'Haven't you heard, dear? They've found a body in the culvert.'

Florrie could still feel the letter in the pocket of her apron. The hard edges of the envelope dug into her thigh as she moved. It had come that morning, but she still hadn't the courage to open it.

Right now, she was in the potting shed. The doctor had decreed that she should spend the next three weeks working outside. Well, it could hardly be called work, but it was tiring. She sat at a wooden bench with a tray of seedlings in front of her. Her job was to thin them out so that before long they would be ready for planting.

Charlie Fisher, the man in charge of the potting shed, was not a happy man. 'Last year,' he lamented, 'I had the best sweet peas in the village and my lupins were the best in the autumn show. This year, thanks to Adolf bloody Hitler, it's all potatoes, peas and carrots.'

Florrie smiled to herself as she pulled out a straggly, half-formed baby carrot. 'It's just as wonderful watching things growing from scratch,' she said. 'I'd love a bit of your carrot.'

Charlie harrumphed. The woman on the bench beside her sniggered. Florrie hadn't meant it that way, but she couldn't resist a smile. She concentrated on her tray.

When she had seen Dr Scott just yesterday, he'd told her it was time for her to move on. He had, he explained, found her a place in a convalescent home near Fontwell.

'I chose it because it's not too far from your children,' he said. 'You did say they were billeted in Worthing?'

Florrie had nodded.

'Fontwell is only about fourteen miles from Worthing.'

Fourteen miles? Florrie had sucked her bottom lip excitedly. There would be a bus Shirley could catch, surely. 'Thank you,' she'd whispered gratefully.

'It's not expensive,' he'd assured her. 'Four guineas a week excluding doctor's bills. I suggest you stay for three months.'

Back on the ward, Florrie breathed a sigh of relief. She had got off lightly. Had she already been paying for this hospital, she would have used every penny she'd ever had and a lot more. The shop had been doing quite well (God bless dear Betty for all her hard work) and if all went to plan, there was still a chance that she'd come out of this with a little bit put by. Shirley had written to say she wanted to go to college. Even if she won the scholarship, there would still be things to buy, like clothes and books. As for Tom, well, she would cross that bridge when she came to it.

The letter in Florrie's pocket was from Ruth. She knew it was. She didn't recognize the handwriting at the top of the envelope, but the person who had added her address was Mrs Andrews. Florrie had recognized her handwriting at once.

They had exchanged letters over the weeks.

'*Yes, of course I want to meet Ruth,*' Florrie had written earlier. '*How much does she know?*'

'*Her adoptive mother only told her she came from Canning Town. Do you want me to explain everything? She's coming here tomorrow. She's a lovely young woman. You'll like her a lot.*'

Later, Mrs Andrews had written: '*I told Ruth I knew less than nothing about her circumstances except to say that she was born illegitimate.*'

Damn, thought Florrie when she'd read that. I wanted to explain. Why couldn't you leave well alone? She read on:

'*I think she might have already guessed. I took the liberty of telling her it was impossible for her to stay with her birth family. The stigma, you know ... Of course I didn't tell her where she was born. Rest assured, Florence, she knows nothing, but she wants to write to you. I've told her if she gives the letter to me, I shall pass it on.*'

Florrie touched her pocket and felt the letter crinkle.

'You'd better go back to the ward now, Florrie,' said

Charlie, interrupting her thoughts. 'The doc said one hour a day and you've already done nearly two.'

Florrie laid down her trowel. 'I've really enjoyed it,' she said. 'Working in the shop all day, I never did get much time to grow things, apart from a few tomatoes in the summer.' She stood to leave. 'Nothing beats a nice home-grown tomato.'

Charlie harrumphed again. 'Give me a sweet-smelling lily of the valley or a purple lupin any day.'

Florrie took off her garden apron and hung it on a hook by the door.

'Don't forget your letter,' Charlie cautioned.

She didn't go back to the ward straight away. Florrie made for the veranda instead. It was empty. Most people were still having their afternoon nap. As she tore open the envelope, her heartbeat quickened and her hand trembled a little.

'Chickens,' said Shirley as Janet walked through the door.

'Pardon?' Janet had just come from Granny Roberts's place with Lucy in her arms. She was enjoying the warmth of her little body, the smell of her and listening to her small, contented noises. Cuddling Lucy this way made the disappointment of the day fade a little.

'Vince has been telling me some good ways to make a bit of money,' Shirley went on, her bright eyes dancing with excitement. 'We hatch some eggs and advertise the chicks for sale in the village. Apparently, lots of people want to keep chickens now. It's a good way to get fresh eggs, and the birds that don't lay well will make a lovely Christmas dinner later in the year.'

Janet sat at the table with Lucy on her lap.

'And another thing,' Shirley went on. 'When I ran to the village to get help the day Mr Oliver got bitten, I tried to get into the farm on Water Lane, but the geese frightened me. We should get some geese as well. They'd be better than a watchdog, and we'd have goose eggs to sell too.' She became aware that although she was listening, Janet was preoccupied with something else. 'What's the matter?' asked Shirley. 'Has something happened?'

'He's coming out in six months,' said Janet.

'Six months!' Shirley could hardly believe it. 'But PC Duffy was so sure . . .'

'They found him not guilty,' said Janet, shaking her head. 'The six months were because he was rude to the judge.'

Stunned, Shirley slid onto a chair. 'Oh, Janet, what are we going to do?'

# CHAPTER 21

Shirley couldn't help feeling a bit down. The news that Mr Oliver would only be gone until harvest time had scuppered all her plans. Janet seemed to have given up altogether when it came to making the farm viable, and even her enthusiastic idea about the chickens had been met by a blank stare. Vince had shaken his head when she told him.

'That's a shame,' he'd said bleakly. 'If you ask me, it looks like the farm will be requisitioned. They won't allow it to carry on the way it is now.'

Granny Roberts came up to the house the next day.

'You want to know what happened to Gil,' said Janet.

'I do,' said Granny, 'and I've got some news of me own.'

Janet told her everything as she fussed around Granny Roberts, making her tea and offering her the last of the home-made cake.

'What are you going to do for money?' Granny Roberts asked when Janet told her she was leaving as soon as possible.

Janet shrugged. 'I don't have a bean.'

Shirley was washing up at the sink. 'That's why we need to get the chickens under way,' she said.

'Do you really think I want to leave behind anything for that man?' Janet said coldly.

'You won't have to,' Shirley insisted. 'Look,' she said, drying her hands and coming to join them at the kitchen table. 'We've got six months. All right, I know it's hardly long enough, but we could still get something out of it. Like I said, the pullets are nearly six weeks old. What with the war and everything, more and more people are wanting to keep their own chickens. We could make a few bob selling them on.'

Janet glanced at Granny, who was nodding her head. Encouraged, Shirley went on, 'Vince has been telling me how we can hatch the eggs ourselves to make sure we don't lose any. We can even sell them as day-old chicks.'

'If we do that,' said Janet, 'there'll be fewer stock.'

'So?' Shirley challenged. 'You've just said you don't want to leave anything behind.'

Janet glanced at Granny.

'The girl has a point,' said Granny Roberts.

'It would have been fun making a real go of it,' said Shirley, 'but if we can't have that, we can at least take away something.'

'Are you planning to leave as well?' asked Janet.

'I don't know,' said Shirley. 'I shall have the results of the exam in a couple of weeks, but I don't know if I can go to college. I have to think about Tom.'

Janet gave her a sympathetic smile.

'How many hens have you got?' asked Granny Roberts.

'I've done a count,' said Shirley. 'There's fifty-eight good layers and another twenty who are coming up for laying. They're about six or seven months old, and I know the cockerel has been busy, so when they lay, their eggs will be fertilized. As for the rest of them, the ones who aren't good layers, they can go to market for meat.'

Janet grinned. 'It seems that you've got it all worked out.'

'Only because I thought we'd have a couple of years, maybe four, giving us a chance to prove that we could make the farm viable,' said Shirley. 'I did what Mr Telford said. I listened to Vince and Seth.'

'I think you should give the girl a chance,' said Granny Roberts.

'I'd like to,' said Janet, 'but to have good layers, you have to feed them special food. They're going to need bran and maize and sharps. Where's the money coming from for that?'

'My postal orders,' said Shirley.

The three of them fell silent, until Granny Roberts slapped her knee with her hand and burst out laughing. 'Good Lord alive, Janet, this girl has got some pluck.'

'All right,' said Janet with a slow smile, 'you've convinced me.'

'And don't forget you've got the pigs as well,' said Granny.

'Ah yes,' said Shirley. 'Now, I've been reading up on them and the Large Whites are good for bacon, while the Berkshires are better for pork. We can make quite a bit of money with them.'

'And how are we going to pay for them?' said Janet.

'Vince knows a farmer who will let us have them for nothing providing he gets a share of the meat when they're ready,' said Shirley. 'We could start a pig club perhaps, with anyone who is willing to feed it with their scraps getting a share when it's killed.'

Janet looked thoughtful. 'I still can't see how we can possibly look after the cows, the extra chickens as well as the pigs!'

'Tom is good with the bigger beasts,' said Granny Roberts. 'With a little help from Seth, I reckon he could manage the pigs.'

'He'd love that,' said Shirley. 'He's never been trusted to do something like that on his own before.'

'Seth tells me he's shown a lot of interest in the bees,' said Granny. Shirley raised an eyebrow, so she added, 'Seth has got six hives. Tom ain't afeared of them at all.'

'There's a couple of empty hives at the other end of the orchard,' said Janet. 'What if he started another colony there?'

Shirley put her hand to her face. 'That would mean we'd have honey as well.'

'If we go for all this,' Janet told Shirley, 'you and I will have an awful lot to do. I'm a bit worried because you're not so keen on looking after the animals.'

'That's true,' said Shirley, 'but somehow this is different. This is for us. This is for Tom and Lucy.'

Janet's eyes drifted towards Lucy's pram.

'Oh, I can look after the baby,' said Granny Roberts eagerly. The two women looked at her uncertainly. 'I may be slow,' she went on, 'but you can trust me. You two come up with the ideas and work the farm, and I'll look after Lucy.'

Janet's eyes sparkled. 'Then I want us to share everything,' she said. 'Equal parts.'

Shirley looked up at the clock. 'The men will be coming in for their lunch in a minute.'

Granny Roberts stood to make another pot of tea, while Shirley got out the bread knife and began to slice the bread. Janet fed and changed Lucy.

'You said when you came in,' Janet reminded Granny Roberts, 'that you had some news of your own to share.'

Granny Roberts sighed. 'I hates to put the dampener on things, but they found a body in the culvert yesterday.'

'As a matter of fact, I already know about that,' said Janet. 'When I got off the train, I had to wait for ages by the village hall until they'd got whoever it was out. They were saying the body had been down there a long time.'

'The culvert?' said Shirley.

'It's that big drain in the village,' said Janet. 'It runs from the bottom of the hill through the village and comes out near the village hall.'

'I know where you mean,' said Shirley. 'When Tom and I first came here, some boys from the school made

Tom go down there. He didn't get far – less than half-way.'

'They do it for a dare,' said Granny Roberts, nodding. 'It's not that big, but it would have been difficult for a lad like Tom to manage it.'

'He couldn't do it,' Shirley agreed.

'I'm not surprised,' said Granny Roberts. 'He'd have been bent in half.'

'It wasn't so much that,' said Shirley. 'It was the smell.'

Granny Roberts shook her head sadly.

'But that would have been – what, five months ago?' said Janet. 'Don't tell me a body was down there all that time?'

'I reckon that must have been why the village flooded last winter,' said Granny Roberts.

They heard the sound of footsteps and men's voices. Shirley put a plate of doorstep sandwiches in the middle of the table. 'Who was it? Do you know?'

'Reuben Fletcher,' said Granny.

'What on earth was he doing in the culvert?' said Shirley.

'Search me,' said Granny with a shrug.

Janet frowned. 'I know that name.'

'He used to work here,' said Granny. 'When the first Mrs Oliver was alive.' She put the big teapot beside the plate of sandwiches and frowned. 'Come to think about it, he disappeared about the same time as she drowned in the pond.'

'I met Elizabeth's mother when I was on the train,' said Janet.

Granny Roberts shook her head. 'Poor woman. She was all right with you, though?'

'Oh yes,' said Janet. 'It was a bit embarrassing, but she wasn't horrible or anything.'

'Well, she wouldn't be,' said Granny.

'She said she'd heard I'd had a baby,' Janet went on. 'Then she said Gil served me better than her daughter. What do you think she meant by that?'

The men were in the porch taking off their boots. 'All Elizabeth ever wanted was to be a mother,' said Granny. 'She and Gilbert were married all that time, but no babies came along.'

'So she was barren,' said Janet. 'What a shame.'

'But some say that she was pregnant when she died,' said Granny.


In Europe, things were not looking good. In the middle of the month, Germany had invaded Belgium and Holland. When German Panzers came through the Ardennes, the French Army and the British Expeditionary Force were trapped at a place called Dunkirk. The British mounted a fierce rearguard action, with many thousands of Allied soldiers pouring onto the beaches, but the town of Dunkirk itself was almost obliterated by the concentrated bombing raids. Large swathes of the port were flooded to a depth of two feet in an effort to prevent the enemy from sending in its infantry and heavy guns. With the Germans snapping at their heels at the rear and the English

Channel in front, just thirty miles of water separated the British Tommy from his loved ones and home.

As part of the rearguard, Len had been deeply affected when he and the lads arrived on the beach. More than a quarter of a million men crowded the sands, a sight that chilled him to the bone. The noise made him feel he had walked right into the mouth of hell. Whistling shells, machine-gun fire, the thud of anti-aircraft fire, the snarl of enemy planes as they dived towards their quarry, the sound of exploding bombs and the screams of frightened men filled the air. Many lay dead and dying. Others had made foxholes, and whenever an enemy plane screamed overhead, they pressed themselves into the sand and prayed to be missed. At the water's edge, men stood knee-deep, waist-deep and shoulder-high in the sea waiting to be picked up by the flotilla of small boats that ferried them to the bigger ships. The navy was there but far out to sea.

'Looks like they can't get in any closer,' someone said as Len shielded his eyes from the dying sun.

The engines of a German plane screeched as it made its way towards the line of men on the jetty, spraying bullets. A couple of men fell into the water, already bright red with British and French blood. There was nothing anyone could do. The line carried on moving. A thought crossed Len's mind. Only a year ago, this beach would have been filled with French holiday-makers eating ice cream and wearing 'Kiss me quick' hats. (Did they have 'Kiss me quick' hats in France?)

Look at it now. Even the smell of the place was a mixture of cordite, wet sand, vomit and blood.

Len was tired. No, more than that – exhausted. Days of fighting, nights without sleep and all the time knowing that they were fighting a losing battle, retreating, beaten and defeated, had taken its toll. And for what? If he survived all this, he would most likely be a prisoner of war and at the mercy of Hitler's murdering henchmen.

Since they'd been separated from their commanding officer, he and Chalky White had stuck together. The shelling intensified. Taking their cue from the others, they dug into the sands and hoped their foxhole would give them some shelter. Despite the noise and the gathering gloom, almost as soon as he lay down, Len slept. He only woke when Chalky shook him.

In the half-light before dawn, Chalky had spotted a few men climbing from the massive Mole, a sea wall made of stone, onto a pleasure steamer waiting alongside.

'Better get in line, Len,' said Chalky. 'I hear that lot are getting free tickets to see Betty Grable.'

Always the joker, Chalky made his weary way down to the water's edge. Len followed. Eventually, they joined about two hundred other weary men who lay silently on the deck. Apparently, the steamer had been there for two hours under cover of darkness, but now the German battery had trained its guns on the Mole. Behind Len and Chalky, about a dozen other men clambered aboard, but then the captain said he could wait no longer. The shellfire was becoming more accurate. He reversed engines, turned and then they headed out to sea. Len raised his head to watch the French coast get smaller and spotted another group of men running along the Mole. Shellfire crashed all around them, but it was too late. The steamer couldn't risk going back for them. Len watched in horror as some of them fell. Another ten or maybe twelve brave men were left to die in this hellhole called Dunkirk. He couldn't weep. He didn't feel a thing. He was numb. It was at that moment that he thought of Florrie. She'd been in his thoughts a lot just lately. He longed to see her bright smile and hear her voice again.

Nobody spoke, but someone offered him a cigarette. He put it between his lips, but when the match was struck, he was so tired he didn't even have the strength to draw on it. The chilly dawn was giving way to a balmy heat. The sea breeze was pleasant, and the rush of water as the steamer ploughed on was music to his ears. Florrie. The English coast appeared at last – not the White Cliffs of Dover but the Seven Sisters near Brighton and the coastal waters of Worthing and, finally, Little-hampton, where they docked.

Mustering what little energy he had, Len followed Chalky onto the quayside, where a group of WVS women were serving tea and buns and cigarettes. His heart lurched as a slim woman picked up a tray of buns to hand them out. Florrie? She turned, but it wasn't her. He drank the scalding tea as if it were nectar from the gods; then a sergeant called them into line. They were to march to the station, where, they were told, a train would take them to a fleet of army trucks waiting in Chichester and on to the barracks. As they marched, the people of the town came out of their shops and houses and lined the streets. Len could hear applause and cries of 'Well done, lads' and 'Good luck'. What began as a weary dragging of the body became a firmer step and finally, as the station came into view, he and the others had their heads held high and even managed to give their arms a bit of a swing. As he sank down in the seat of the railway carriage, all he could think about was Florrie. What a fool he'd been. Life was too short to wait any longer. He'd held back for too long. Somehow or other he'd help her to get that divorce, but if she couldn't, he'd do his best to persuade her to live with him. If it embarrassed her, he'd suggest that she change her name by deed poll. What did it matter what people thought? She had been his guiding light. It was just the thought of seeing her again that had got him through all this. He couldn't let her go, not now, not ever. For the first time in his life, he owned up to the fact that he was totally, hopelessly in love with her.

'Um?' said a sleepy Chalky beside him. 'What was that you said?'

'Night, Florrie, love,' murmured Len as he fell asleep.

# CHAPTER 22

It was the twins' sixteenth birthday. The postman was late, but when he finally arrived, he brought several cards and a letter addressed to Janet. As soon as she saw the stamp in the corner, Janet knew who the letter was from. *His Majesty's Prison*. She slipped it into her apron pocket until she was sure she was alone. She had mixed feelings. Contempt that Gil had embarrassed her in public at the trial; shame that he'd been in the dock in the first place; frustration that he would soon be out; worry that he posed a real danger to herself and her daughter; and finally, frustration that justice had hardly been served. She was also scared of the future.

Shirley had gone to the potato field to bank up the rows and clear the weeds. Tom was grooming the horses and mucking out the stables, and Granny Roberts, who surprisingly seemed a lot more spritely these days, had taken Lucy into the village in the battered old pram Janet had bought from the Red Cross shop. Having made herself a cup of Camp coffee, Janet took out the letter and laid it on the table. She stared at it for some time before taking two flimsy sheets of paper out of the envelope. She could see at once that it had been heavily censored. Thick inky patches littered the page, obliterating word after word. It didn't take long to understand why.

It began, '*I had a letter*' – no '*Dear wife*' or '*Dear Janet*' – '*from my solicitor saying you want your name on my bank account. Keep your — fingers off my money. You can go to — before you'll ever get a — penny of mine. You're nothing but a — —. That's my — farm not yours. So — —.*'

Janet laid down the page. She didn't bother to even look at the second. How on earth Gil thought she could keep the place going without money was beyond her. The man was a complete idiot. When he'd turned on all his charms to get her, she'd honestly thought that if she did her best to be a good wife to him, eventually they could have a happy life together. She felt her eyes smarting, but she refused to allow herself to cry. What a hateful person he'd turned out to be. She stuffed the pages back into the envelope and squared her shoulders. 'Right, Gilbert Oliver,' she said aloud. 'I'm telling you now, before I leave this place, I'm taking you for every penny I can.' She got to her feet and put the letter behind the clock on the mantelpiece, then having gulped down her now lukewarm coffee, she pulled on her wellington boots and went to call Shirley and Tom.

Apart from Christmas, Shirley had never had so many cards waiting for her when they both came in for their mid-morning break. She and Tom were used to getting a card from Mum, Auntie Doreen and Auntie

276

Betty, but apart from the odd friend at school, that was it. This year, she had the usual three, plus cards from Granny Roberts and Seth, Janet, Vince, Hazel Freeman, Gwen Knox and Miss Smith.

'We're sixteen,' she told Tom. 'We could have gone at Easter, but now we have officially left school.'

'Will I have to go out to work now, Shirl?'

'You already have,' said Janet. She handed him a small brown envelope. 'This is your first proper wage and you've earned every penny.'

Tom was thrilled to bits. Janet had already taken out a small amount for his board and lodging, so everything in the envelope was his to do with as he wanted.

'I want to send it to Mum,' he said, 'to help pay for her to get better.'

Shirley's eyes smarted. 'She won't need all of it,' she said, glancing at Janet, 'but we'll get a postal order and send it to her the next time we go down to the village.' And he was happy with that.

The day was much the same as any other until the afternoon. Shirley was hoeing in the fields when she spotted a small gaggle of people coming along the lane towards the farmhouse. Coming indoors, she discovered that Janet and Granny Roberts had arranged a surprise tea party for them.

'Is it me,' asked Granny Roberts, looking at the wall, 'or is that mantrap crooked?'

'We were trying to take it down,' said Janet. 'Shirley and I can't stand it, but it's too firmly fixed.'

'I've got an idea for it,' said Granny.

'What's that?' asked Shirley.

Granny Roberts thumbed her nose. 'Wait and see.'

By the time Shirley and Tom had washed and changed, it felt as if half of Angmering was crammed into the farmhouse kitchen. Bobbi Mackenzie and Hazel Freeman came, and Gwen Knox, although she kept apologizing because she had to dash back into Worthing before five because she was in a show at the Pavilion. Everyone was very impressed.

'I'm only in the chorus,' she said modestly, 'but it's a start.'

Shirley was delighted that her teacher, Miss Smith, had come too. Shirley noticed her looking around. 'Would you like to take a walk around the farm, miss?'

'Oh, I know it like the back of my hand, Shirley,' she said.

'You do?'

Miss Smith leaned forward and whispered confidentially in her ear, 'I used to come here when Elizabeth was alive. She was my best friend.'

Shirley was about to ask more, but Miss Smith stepped back and said loudly, 'No news of the exam yet, Shirley, but as soon as I hear, I'll let you know.'

'It's a long time coming,' Janet remarked.

'Don't you know there's a war on?' Miss Smith said, mimicking one of the characters from a radio programme, and everyone laughed.

'What on earth have you done with that trap thing?' cried Janet, looking up and noticing it for the first time.

Granny Roberts had draped the mantrap with an

enormous pair of men's underpants, and Vince had drawn a cartoon face of Hitler on a piece of brown paper which they'd stuck to the wall next to it. It looked as if the Führer was turning his head to look at his big bottom. By now, everybody was laughing. 'If you don't like something,' said Granny, 'give everybody a good laugh, I say.'

'Come on, Shirley,' Janet cried. 'Open your presents. We're all dying to see.'

The twins opened present after present, but best of all was when Auntie Doreen walked through the door. Dressed in a WAAF uniform, she had been driven down from London by a small, slightly balding man, who was also in uniform.

'This is Popeye,' she said, and when Shirley looked slightly surprised, she added with a laugh, 'His real name is Ernest, but the boys call him that because he likes his greens.'

Shirley wondered if it was more to do with his jutting jaw and the pipe he had in his mouth, but she said nothing. Popeye gave everyone a hearty handshake. Shirley took to him straight away. He had merry eyes and a hearty laugh. Auntie Doreen hugged Shirley to death and even managed to give Tom's arm an affectionate rub before he moved out of the way. 'Oh, it's good to see you at last,' she cried. 'I was so disappointed to miss you last time.'

'You came here?' Shirley gasped. 'To the farm?'

'Not exactly,' said Doreen. 'Didn't Mr Oliver tell

279

you? He met me at the station because you were on a school trip and he wanted to save me the walk.'

Shirley glanced at Janet. 'We've never been on a school trip.'

Doreen frowned. 'That's odd.' As they discussed it further, they realized it must have been the time when Shirley was rehearsing for the pageant and that it was Auntie Doreen who had brought the suitcase full of clothes. Shirley was hugely relieved that she hadn't missed her mother but cross that she'd been denied seeing Florrie's oldest friend. She was keen to hear how her mother was doing.

'I haven't seen Florrie for a while,' Doreen admitted. 'I was in the WVS, but then I joined the WAAF, and would you believe it? I'm stationed at Tangmere, just down the road from here.' She glanced at Popeye and grinned. 'Best thing that ever happened to me.'

'That's where you're stationed too?' said Seth, looking at Popeye.

Popeye nodded. 'Best damned station in the South.' With a nickname like Popeye, his cut-glass accent took everybody by surprise.

'We've seen a few of your dog fights around here,' said Vince. 'You seem pretty good at seeing Jerry off.'

'Oh, I don't fly,' said Popeye. 'I'm only in the office, but yes, our boys have their work cut out.'

'Did you have a card from your mother?' said Auntie Doreen, changing the subject.

'I did,' said Shirley. 'We both did. She says she's

moving to a new place, but she doesn't have the address just yet.'

'Right, come on,' said Janet, putting the big teapot on the table. 'Let's get this party under way.'

While they ate, Shirley caught up with the London news. Auntie Betty was still in the shop, but she'd handed it over to Phyllis Walters for a week because her husband ('Uncle Raymond' to the twins) was home on leave. Most of those who had been evacuated with Shirley and Tom were back home now, and a lot of them were already going out to work. Joseph Harper was a telegram boy with the GPO, but as soon as he was old enough, he planned to join the fire service. Helen Starling, who had been sent to an approved school for shoplifting after the day the whole school went to Southend-on-Sea, hadn't learned her lesson. She was currently on remand for stealing something from an old lady in the borough. Auntie Doreen didn't know what had happened to Ann Bidder. After the shame of the shoplifting incident, her whole family had moved away. Len? No, Auntie Doreen had no news of him except that he had been in France with the British Expeditionary Force.

'Terrible business, that,' said Popeye.

'They've been bringing the poor devils in at Little-hampton,' said Granny Roberts. 'Mrs Beecham from the post office said she saw some being marched to army trucks near the station with their clothes all soaking wet, some of them wounded and all of them half dead.'

'Still, at least they're back home,' said Janet.

Everyone nodded in agreement.

'I've just come back from Coventry from seeing my mother,' said Auntie Doreen.

'Oh,' said Shirley, 'and how is she?' She was only being polite. She didn't really like Mrs Kennedy. In fact, the feeling was mutual. Mrs Kennedy only ever spoke to her to criticize. 'Why are you wearing those awful ankle socks? For heaven's sake, sit up straight, girl, and stop swinging your legs like a barn door.' Tom was terrified of her.

'She's in good health,' said Auntie Doreen, 'but she's not a happy bunny.'

When was she ever? Shirley thought acidly. 'Oh?'

'She doesn't like me in uniform,' said Doreen.

'Well, I think you look fantastic,' Shirley cried.

'So do I!' Popeye agreed enthusiastically.

Auntie Doreen glanced shyly at her friend. 'Why, thank you, Ernest.'

There was the sound of planes overhead, so they rushed outside to watch another dog fight. This time, the German got away, but the RAF boys chased him back towards the sea. As they stood watching, Hazel stuffed some straw down Shirley's back and she chased her to do the same. After a few minutes, everyone had joined in, whooping, screaming and laughing. It was good to be silly for a while. When they'd had enough, they went inside to eat.

When most of the food was gone, Janet produced a huge birthday cake. They'd even managed to get enough candles. Granny Roberts had made the cake, which despite her arthritis, was as light as a feather. When the cake was almost gone, Seth put a shove-halfpenny board onto the table, and Vince hung a dartboard on Hitler's underpants and everybody couldn't wait to aim and fire. The two men insisted on doing the milking by themselves, and by the time they came back, Gwen and Bobbi had already left. Of those remaining, Auntie Doreen and Popeye went first, with everyone waving after them and calling out their goodbyes, even Tom. A little later on, the others said they were keen to be back in the village before the blackout. It was only later that Shirley realized she hadn't asked Miss Smith to tell her more of her friendship with Elizabeth.

Alone in the kitchen, Shirley suddenly felt that she had never been happier. What a terrific day. She piled the plates next to the sink while she waited for the kettle to boil. As she stood there with the dishcloth, Shirley felt a mixture of emotions. She liked it here. It had taken a while to get used to it, but she was happy being part of village life. Now that she'd officially left school, though, she guessed she would be expected to go back home and take over the running of the shop. She sighed. It was the last thing she wanted to do. Tom wouldn't want to go either. She emptied the teapot and made up her mind that as soon as she got her mother's new address, she'd ask her if she could stay a little longer – at least until Mr Oliver came out of prison and Janet left the farm.

\* \* \*

France had fallen. Florrie had been looking for a letter from Len for more than two weeks now, but she was disappointed. In her head, she kept going over old ground. If only things had been different. If only Mum hadn't . . . But what was the use? It didn't alter anything. What was done was done. Her mind drifted back to Ruth. She had agreed to see her when she got to the new convalescent home. She didn't know why, but somehow she felt it would be better to meet her in her new surroundings. The place sounded lovely. Countryside, big house, lovely grounds. Florrie shivered. Her bag was packed. She'd written to Betty, Doreen and of course to Shirley and Tom to tell them of her new address. Betty, dear Betty was still looking after the shop, and wasn't Doreen visiting her mother in Coventry? Florrie hoped that she didn't stay too long. She knew Doreen would visit her in the new convalescent home whenever she could. Doreen was all too easily manipulated by her mother. It worried Florrie when Doreen hinted in her last letter that she had some unexpected news to tell her when she came to visit.

Now that they were both sixteen, the twins had officially left school and there was every possibility that they'd want to go back home. She wouldn't stop them. Why should she? Shirley could help Betty in the shop, and Tom would be in familiar surroundings. Florrie couldn't wait for them all to be together again. She'd missed them both so much.

The journey was very pleasant. Florrie enjoyed looking out of the car window as the leafy Sussex countryside, miles and miles of rolling hills, sheep and blue skies, sped by. If only the war and the horrors she'd heard about on the radio in Dunkirk were a thing of the past too . . . She wondered again what Len was doing. She wished her answer all those years ago could have been different. Just recently, she'd kicked herself for caring more about what people thought than how much she'd cared about him. After what had happened to Mum, she'd moved away. She'd been in service for a while and there she met Sid. It didn't take long before they'd courted and married. He'd been all right to start with and they'd been happy, but when the twins were born, and it became apparent that Tom wasn't quite right, she'd blurted out everything about the past. Of course, the minute she'd done it, she'd wished she hadn't, but she was upset and wasn't thinking straight. She'd always blamed herself for Tom. God must have been punishing her because of Ruth. As soon as she saw the expression on Sid's face, she knew everything had changed, but she couldn't take it back.

'My God,' he'd gasped. 'Wasn't that in all the papers?'

Florrie had nodded miserably. He gave her a look so filled with anger and disgust she almost felt like he'd stabbed her in the heart. 'But it doesn't change anything, love,' she said. She'd reached out her arms to him, but he'd butted her away.

'Don't you touch me,' he'd snarled. 'Don't you ever touch me again.'

She'd been devastated. She'd pleaded with him, but

he'd grabbed his coat and left the house. He was drunk when he came back home and he didn't come to bed. He'd slept downstairs on the sofa, and when she'd got up in the morning, he'd already gone to work. The next few days were very difficult. They shared the same house, but Sid refused to speak to her. She tried to talk to him, but he acted as if she was completely invisible. Florrie had done her best to keep the horrible atmosphere from the twins, and a week later, she'd come back from the shops to find all his things gone as well. It was only then that she'd discovered their father had moved in with the publican's wife from the Cross Keys.

Florrie felt embarrassed now about the way she'd handled the situation, but back then she really didn't think she could survive without Sid. She'd gone round to see him, even falling on her knees and holding on to his legs, but to no avail. She'd begged and pleaded for him to come back, but instead he'd literally thrown her out onto the street. She'd honestly thought she'd fall apart without him. How wrong she was. As far as she knew, he never told anyone her terrible secret. She'd guessed it was a mixture of fear of the unknown and fear of exposure, but certainly the local gossips never found out the real reason why he'd gone. Within a month, Sid and his mistress had gone to Bristol, some said; Wales, according to others. Wherever he'd gone, she'd never heard a word from him from that day until this. Her luck had changed when she'd inherited the shop. It was even better that it was in a different part of London where nobody knew her maiden name. Len had been a brick right from the word go. He'd wanted to marry her, but of course she couldn't. She'd explained that there was no possibility of divorce and that she wouldn't live with him without being married. She'd given Ruth away and then she'd had Tom. Poor Tom. She'd couldn't bear it if anything bad happened to Len.

'God is punishing me,' she'd told him.

'Now you're talking complete tommyrot,' he told her, but he didn't know the whole truth, and back then Florrie couldn't bring herself to take the risk. And now that Ruth was back in her life, she wished . . . Florrie sighed. What did she wish?

'Here we are, love.' The driver of the car had pulled from a winding lane onto a long driveway. At the end, she could see what looked like a country house. Built possibly as early as the eighteenth century, it was a pretty place made of white brick over two storeys. There was an attractive cornice and a parapet on the roof. At the front, she saw a large veranda and lacy ironwork in front of the curved windows. The property of Sussex County Council since the 1920s, the house's surrounding grounds were cultivated not with flowers but were kept as a smallholding. She could see fruit trees and rows and rows of neat vegetables. Florrie smiled. Not bad for four guineas a week. She was going to like it here.

Shirley loved being in Elizabeth's room. It was perfect. So perfect she could hardly believe that Janet preferred Mr Oliver's room over this. Of course, Janet's room was a lot bigger, but wasn't a patch on this pretty place.

When she got ready for bed that night, Shirley found herself just sitting on the edge and looking around. It was odd that Elizabeth, like Janet, hadn't shared the same room as her husband. Shirley knew little about the facts of life, but she knew enough to understand that husbands and wives usually shared the same bed. It was also odd that Elizabeth had such a feminine room. She had obviously been allowed free rein when it came to making choices in here. Pretty floral curtains, fat pink cushions and pillowcases edged with white lace. It was only on closer inspection that Shirley realized that these added touches were entirely home-made. Elizabeth was a home-maker. Given a chance, she could have made a real difference to the cold, functional farmhouse, but perhaps miserable old Mr Oliver didn't want that.

When she came to put her own things in the drawers, she could see that although there wasn't a lot inside, the contents had been disturbed by somebody else. She couldn't believe that Elizabeth would leave them in such a higgledy-piggledy state. Someone had been looking for something. Even though the first Mrs Oliver was never coming back, Shirley decided out of respect to put her things in one place. She found a suitcase at the bottom of the wardrobe, but it was already full of stuff. That was funny. Someone had gone through the case as well. Neatly folded clothes had been tossed around before the lid was closed. She couldn't put her finger on it, but something wasn't quite right.

Shirley took everything out and repacked the case.

She opened the half-empty drawers and carried on filling the case until it was difficult to close the lid. That was when she noticed another strange thing. Elizabeth had gone in winter and slipped into the icy water of Patching Pond and yet the stuff in the case was for summer. Could it be that Elizabeth had simply packed her summer clothes away for the winter? That was entirely possible, she supposed, but why pack a washbag and toothbrush into the same case? They said she'd gone to the pond to pick greenery for Christmas wreaths, yet she was all packed and ready to go. It didn't make sense.

Dog-tired after another hectic day on the farm, Shirley could hardly keep her eyes open. She'd added two more money-making schemes to her already overfilled day. Having picked and sold a basket of primroses from the hedgerows, she'd gone round the village with a basket of fresh eggs as well. Both proved to be very popular, so she'd decided to build on the idea. When the primroses were over, it would be bluebell season. Of course, selling stuff door to door only brought in pennies, but every one counted and already the communal pot was growing. After all that work, and two rounds of the village with the baskets, her legs were so tired she had a bit of a wobble. When she grabbed the iron bedstead to steady herself, the knob came off in her hand. It was only as she tried to screw it back on that she realized there was something inside the hollow tube.

It was difficult to get out because her clumsy fingers kept accidentally pushing it further down. In the end, she took a pin from Elizabeth's workbox and used that to pull it up. It was only a piece of paper, but when she unrolled it, she was surprised to find a picture of a ship, the *Dunnottar Castle* from the Union-Castle Line. Shirley gazed in wonder at the swimming pool, the library and the sports facilities on offer for passengers going from Southampton to Cape Town.

She looked down the tube again, but there was nothing else. How odd. Why hide your holiday poster inside the bedstead? But by the time her head hit the pillow, Shirley had convinced herself that any unease she felt was only because of her overworked imagination.

# CHAPTER 23

Florrie sat in the big winged chair facing the door. She wanted to see her visitor from the moment she came in. She had taken a great deal of trouble with her appearance. Barbara had helped her with her hair, and she was wearing her best dress. It wasn't so attractive as it had once been, because she had lost so much weight, but it was the best she could do. Mavis, two beds down the ward, had loaned her a brooch, and Florrie had bought a small potted plant from the shop on the smallholding the day before to give to Ruth as a present.

When the door swung open, the first person to come in was Dick, Barbara's gentleman friend. He was closely followed by a string of other people who had relatives or friends in the home. The air was soon filled with noisy and excited conversation. The clock said twenty past three. The doors closed and Florrie waited. Her heart sank. After all this, Ruth wasn't coming. A few minutes later, her heart leapt as the doors swung open again, but it was only one of the nurses. Florrie bit back the tears and got up. She went and sat on the veranda. It was a little more private. No one else was here and she could dab her eyes without anyone noticing and making a fuss. Sitting by the window, she stared miserably out onto the gardens.

She had settled quickly into her new surroundings. There was a fairly strict routine, but she was allowed to move around at will. After breakfast, she had a choice of activities, all of which were designed to help strengthen her body and increase her muscle power. She could do keep-fit in the library, in which patients did exercises on a mat to music played on a wind-up gramophone, or she could join the others on a walk around the grounds. It was only when she realized how physically tired she was after such activity that Florrie understood how weak her body had become after months of lying in bed. She didn't suffer from bouts of coughing any more, but for the first week she needed to lie down before lunch, and sometimes she slept. The meals were plain, but there was plenty of food. Good old-fashioned things like mutton stew, liver and bacon, bacon and onion suet pudding were followed by rice pudding, apple pie or steamed jam roly-poly and custard, all designed to build her up. And they did. Slowly but surely her energy levels grew and she began to feel stronger. After lunch, everyone had an afternoon nap, and then they read, played cards or chatted until teatime.

The people living there were a mixed bunch. Some were quite well off, but others, like herself, were working people with limited funds. Florrie made a special friend of a woman called Barbara who had worked in a large department store in Portsmouth before she was taken ill.

'I belong to a friendly society,' she confided in Florrie. 'A lot of my treatment has been paid for by them.'

Barbara was about the same age as Florrie. She wasn't married, but she had what she called 'a gentleman friend'. Visiting hours were from five until six on Saturday evening and three till six on Sunday, and Barbara's gentleman friend was always the first to come through the doors. It seemed that everyone had someone, all except Florrie. She had written to tell Shirley and Tom of her new address and the twins were coming next week. Florrie could hardly wait. It had been nine months since she'd seen her children, and oh, how she had missed them.

Florrie closed her eyes. She couldn't blame the girl for not turning up. It was a long way to come. Perhaps she'd been put off when she'd learned that Florrie had been ill with TB. There were still some people who believed you could catch it just by a handshake.

'Florrie?' said a soft voice beside her. 'Florrie Jenkins?'

Florrie opened her eyes to find herself looking into the face of a young girl with pale hazel eyes and light brown hair. 'I'm Hannah,' she said, 'but you remember me as Ruth.'

Florrie leaned forward to get up, but the girl said, 'No, no, don't get up, please. Sit still and I'll fetch a chair.'

Florrie sank back and watched her heading towards a

wooden chair on the other side of the room. She was beautiful, slim with an easy sway to her body. She turned to come back. Under a plain cotton jacket, she was wearing a pretty button-through dress in a striped material. Florrie spotted a small pocket with an imitation handkerchief on her left breast, and the knee-length skirt was tight over her hips but burst into neat pleats from the hip down. Round her waist, she wore a plain blue belt. Her hat, the same colour as her jacket, sported a pretty spray of summer flowers on the brim. She carried a cream clutch bag and cream gloves.

'How was your journey?' Florrie asked as she sat down.

'Fine,' said Ruth. 'I got a friend to bring me.'

'That's good,' said Florrie. 'At least you haven't been hanging around bus stops all day. They say that the government might stop civilian cars having petrol altogether soon. That would be a disaster, wouldn't it? I mean, you would have to rely on the bus or the train for everything, wouldn't you? And if you were a soldier on leave, it might not be possible to get home to the family and back to barracks in time. People won't be very happy about that, will they?' She stopped, suddenly embarrassed that she was gabbling on and on about nothing. It was only because she was flustered and nervous. 'I'm sorry.'

'It's all right,' said Ruth, 'and you're right.' They looked at each other and then Ruth fiddled with her gloves, while Florrie stared at her own hands, resting in her lap. She felt awkward. What should she say? What should she ask?

'Before I forget,' said Ruth, handing her a slip of paper, 'here's my new address. I'm working in an orphanage now, so I've decided to live in. The army requisitioned Mother's house anyway.'

'Oh,' said Florrie. 'You're a nurse?'

'A nursery nurse.'

Ruth smiled shyly. It was so unnerving looking at her. The girl was a younger version of her mother – the same tilt of her head, and her lips moved in the same way as she formed words like 'friend' and 'requisitioned'. Florrie was suddenly filled with a gnawing sense of loss.

'Can you tell me about my father?'

Florrie shook her head. 'I hardly remember him,' she said dismissively.

Ruth seemed surprised. It was hard for Florrie to think of her as Hannah. She was still Ruth to her.

'Then tell me about yourself,' she said. 'I want to know all about you.'

'Me?' said Florrie. She took a deep breath. 'Well, until I was ill, I looked after my shop.'

'Mrs Andrews said you were a shopkeeper.'

'A tobacconist and newsagent,' said Florrie. 'I inherited it from Father's estate. He knew about this shop, but he was far too ill to run it himself. A stranger left it to him. Apparently he did something very brave trying to help the man's son. The soldier died of his wounds and so the man left my father the shop.'

'That was very nice for you,' said Ruth.

Florrie blinked. Was that a hint of sarcasm in her voice? 'As a matter of fact,' she went on, 'it couldn't have come at a better time. My husband had just left me with two small children.'

Ruth stared at her. 'You're married, then?'

Florrie nodded. 'My son, Tom, is what you might call simple,' she went on. 'There's no harm in him, but he doesn't grasp things as he should. On the other hand, Shirley, his twin, she's as bright as a button.'

'But you kept them,' said Ruth.

'Of course,' said Florrie, puzzled.

'When did you marry?'

Florrie was confused by the note of hostility in her voice. Why was Ruth angry? 'When I was eighteen,' she said. 'In 1919.'

'Two years after I was born,' said Ruth. 'And when you got married, did your husband know about me?'

'No,' said Florrie. 'Mrs Andrews thought it best not to say anything.'

Ruth's face clouded. Florrie leaned forward to touch her hand, but Ruth moved herself out of reach. 'We did it to protect you,' Florrie protested mildly. 'We thought it was for the best.'

'I'm sure you did,' said Ruth stiffly.

'I've never stopped thinking about you,' said Florrie. 'Mrs Andrews said you'd been well looked after and that you had a good life.'

'I did,' said Ruth. She was tight-lipped now.

Confused, Florrie said, 'Ruth, what's wrong?'

'Nothing,' said Ruth haughtily. 'Nothing at all.'

They both fell silent, and when Ruth looked up again, Florrie was alarmed to see tears standing in her eyes. 'I knew this would be a mistake,' she said, gathering her things.

'I don't understand,' cried Florrie. 'What did I say?'

Ruth rose and began moving the chair back to its proper place.

'Mrs Andrews said you wanted to see me,' said Florrie, battling with tears herself now. 'I would never have agreed if I'd thought it would upset you this much.'

'Of course it upsets me,' Ruth hissed. 'You have me with some chap you hardly remember, then hand me over like a piece of cheese . . .'

'It wasn't like that,' said Florrie, her voice rising.

'Then you get married,' Ruth went on, 'and carry on with your nice little life in your nice little shop . . .'

'No, no, you've got it all wrong,' Florrie cried desperately. She was beginning to feel very hot, and her head was all swimmy.

'And then you have two more children without even a backwards glance in my direction . . .'

'No, listen to me, please. You've made a terrible mistake—'

'That's right,' Ruth spat. 'For one glorious minute I thought you might actually feel something for me. I thought,' she laughed sardonically, 'God forgive me, that there might be just a small spark of love and affection, but you're as cold as ice.'

A nurse appeared in the doorway. 'What's going on?'

297

She went to Florrie's side and picked up her wrist to feel her pulse. 'I'm afraid I must ask you to leave,' she told Ruth. 'This patient is still far from well. You can't be allowed to upset her like this.'

Ruth turned towards the door. 'Oh, don't worry,' she said haughtily. 'I'm leaving.'

Florrie tried to stand up.

'Mrs Jenkins,' said the nurse, 'let's get you back in bed.'

'Ruth, don't go,' Florrie cried. 'You don't understand. I never meant to hurt you.'

But Ruth wasn't listening. With the nurse doing her best to slow her down, Florrie staggered to the veranda door. 'Come back,' she shouted after Ruth's receding back. 'Please.'

'Back to bed now, Mrs Jenkins,' the nurse insisted. 'All this upset isn't doing you any good at all.'

'But she mustn't go,' Florrie said, trying her best to push the nurse away. 'Not like this. She doesn't understand. Please make her come back. I need to explain. Ruth, Ruth . . .'

As the doors to the ward swung on their hinges, Florrie let out such a heart-rending wail it brought the happy buzz of visiting time to an abrupt standstill.

# CHAPTER 24

'Mrs Oliver?'

A man in his forties had come up the lane. He was dressed in a rather tired-looking, old-fashioned suit, but he looked clean-shaven and tidy. The cuffs on his shirt were frayed, and he carried a small suitcase. Seth, who was sharpening a scythe in the barn, came out and, standing by the doorway, called Vince softly. He was at the other end of the barn hanging up some dead rabbits. Later on, he would take them down to the village and sell them to the local butcher. It was a good arrangement. He'd got rid of a nuisance and tomorrow somebody would get a decent rabbit pie for tea. Seeing Seth's anxious expression, Vince left what he was doing.

Janet had been putting Lucy into her pram for an afternoon nap. She turned at the sound of her name. 'Yes.'

'My name is Eddie Keller. I shared a cell with your old man.'

Vince came out of the barn, wiping his hands on an old rag.

Janet's eyes grew wide. 'What do you want?'

'I've got a message from him,' said Eddie.

As Janet grabbed the prop from the washing line, Eddie lifted his hand. 'There's no need for that,' he said quickly. 'He just wants you to know how much he misses you.' Eddie reached into his pocket and drew out an envelope. 'And he asked me to give you this.'

Janet edged nearer, but only close enough to snatch the envelope, and then she put herself between Eddie and her baby.

'I don't understand why you're so scared,' Eddie complained. 'I may be an ex-jailbird, but I've never lifted a finger to anybody, much less a woman. Gilbert seems a really nice bloke.' He looked around, but confused by their cold stares, he turned to go. Seth and Vince stuck out their chests as if to make themselves look bigger. Eddie walked out of the gate cautiously as if he was afraid that they would chase after him.

Janet had paled.

'You all right, lass?' asked Seth.

She nodded and went inside. She glanced up at the mantelpiece. Every time a letter came, Janet slipped the unopened envelope behind the clock with the others. After the first one, she hadn't bothered to open any of them. Why should she subject herself to his tirade of abuse? He meant nothing to her now, and his farm was only a means to an end.

The reminder that Gil was still very much around had upset her. For some time, she simply stood still and tried to stop trembling. It wasn't fair. Life was so much better without him. She never thought she'd say it, but she liked being on the farm. Of course, it would be far more of a going concern if she had a husband who was more committed to making it a success. It would be better if she had a proper husband, full stop.

She looked around the room. Only a few more weeks and she'd be gone from here. She'd miss all her friends, but it couldn't be helped. They'd made such a difference, Shirley and Tom. She wondered about their future too. It wouldn't be long before they were back in London with their mother. Janet sighed. What was she going to do when Gil got out? Mrs Dyer had offered her a live-in cook-housekeeper's post, and had said she would let her keep Lucy. It sounded like a generous offer, but Mrs Dyer was a shrewd woman. The exceptional wage she'd offered would be somewhat diminished once her board and lodging were taken into consideration, and Lucy's board and lodging would be extra. She would end up with a lot less than Mrs Dyer first said, and Janet couldn't help thinking that the doctor's wife was getting the better end of the deal. But the biggest problem was that she would be too close to Gil. Janet knew in her heart of hearts that he would turn on that charm of his and she'd end up the villain in the eyes of the village, or worse still, he'd make himself a nuisance and she'd be out of a job in no time. Out of a job and nowhere to go. Except back to the farm. No, if she went, she'd have to go far, far away, and probably leave no forwarding address.

She became aware that her cheeks were wet and her nose was running, so she lowered herself into a chair and got out her hanky. 'No good ever came of boo-hoo-ing,' she told herself crossly.

The letter was written on that same prison paper, but there was no stamp in the corner of the envelope. Eddie had obviously got it past the censors. She glanced up at the mantelpiece, where the dozen or so unopened letters were tucked behind the clock. Should she open this one? Supposing it was filled with the same disgusting words the prison officers had blanked out in his other letters. Supposing he was just as nasty. Then it occurred to her that by putting a letter into the hands of a fellow prisoner, he might be a little more circumspect. He would have turned on the old charm to persuade Eddie to risk getting into trouble by bringing it out, so perhaps this letter was different. After all, there was always the possibility that Eddie might steam it open and take a look for himself. Janet turned it over in her hands, then, picking up a knife from the kitchen table, she slit it open. Her heart was in her mouth as she opened the folded page. It was upside down. She turned it the right way up, and then her whole world was turned upside down.

*When I get out, bitch, you and that brat are dead.*

\* \* \*

Florrie opened her eyes, but it was hard to focus. She could hear voices through the fog, but for a second or two, she couldn't remember where she was. Her whole body hurt, and her head was thumping. Her nose was sore, and her eyes felt puffy. She must have been crying. Why was she upset? What had happened . . . ? And then it all came rushing back. Ruth. Lovely Ruth. She had been so cross she'd walked away. If only she had stayed long enough for her to explain, and yet how could she tell her the whole truth? It would destroy her. Florrie could feel her eyes smarting again. What was the use? Everybody had opinions, and even at that time they'd blamed her, but what could she do about it? It really wasn't her fault.

She sensed someone leaning over her. 'Mrs Jenkins?' The nurse's voice was gentle, but Florrie turned away from her. They meant well, but all she wanted to do was curl up and die.

'Mrs Jenkins, someone rather special has come to see you.'

Florrie lifted her head. 'Ruth?'

'No,' said the nurse. Florrie sank back down dejectedly on the pillow. 'But one of our brave boys from Dunkirk is here, and Matron has let him in even though it's not visiting time.'

There was a slight pause, and then she heard him say, 'Hello, my lovely.'

Her heart leapt. Was he really here? She pulled herself up on her elbow and her eyes met his. 'Oh, Len.' She struggled to sit up.

The nurse was pulling the screens round the bed. 'She's been like this for four days,' the nurse was telling him. 'She had a visitor last Sunday, her daughter, I believe. Whoever it was walked out and Mrs Jenkins hasn't been the same since.'

Len nodded and lowered himself onto the chair beside the bed.

'I'll go and get you some tea, but if you could get Mrs Jenkins to eat something, that would be good,' the nurse whispered conspiratorially. 'We can't persuade her to do anything. It's as if she's completely shut down.'

She plumped up Florrie's cushions and left them alone.

Florrie and Len hadn't taken their eyes off one another.

'So what's all this about, my lovely?' said Len, taking her hand. 'What's up with Shirley?'

Florrie shook her head. 'It wasn't Shirley. It was Ruth.'

'The baby you gave up?'

Florrie nodded, and suddenly aware of how dry her mouth was, she reached for some water. Her hand was shaking so much Len held the glass steady for her.

'How did Ruth know you were here?'

'Mrs Andrews told her.'

Len's brow furrowed. 'Some bloody do-gooder interfering again?'

'No, no,' cried Florrie. 'It wasn't like that.' She looked away, aware of how fragile she was, and the realization dawned. 'Just a minute . . . How did you know about Ruth?'

'I know more than you think,' said Len.

Florrie smiled wanly. 'You think you do, but you don't.'

'I know Ruth isn't your daughter, for a start.'

The revelation almost took Florrie's breath away. 'You knew?'

'Some bloke from Shoreditch told me,' said Len. 'I helped him aboard ship. On his way to Australia, I think.'

Florrie made a small sound. Sid's family came from Shoreditch way. Didn't his brother emigrate to Australia? She'd been so careful not to let on to anyone.

'I've known for years,' said Len. 'Look, Florrie, I've been a fool. We've both been fools. We should have brought all this out into the open years ago.'

Florrie put her hand to her head. She'd known Len since before she'd had the twins, but it had been six years before that when the whole thing came about. Even though she was only sixteen, as soon as the trial ended and the verdict was announced, she had been subjected to a tirade of abuse. It seemed that she couldn't go anywhere without somebody taking out their feelings on her. She'd been buffeted on the tram and spat at in the street. As for friends and neighbours, every one of them was angry, disappointed or disgusted, and they made no bones about telling her what they thought. She'd had buckets of horse manure smeared on the windows and pig's blood poured all over the front step. It was hard enough dealing with what her mother had been accused of, let alone having to deal with the wrath of others as well. 'When did you find out?' she asked.

'Soon after Sid went,' he said. He rubbed her hand gently and she stared at the top of his head as he bent to kiss her fingers. Her thoughts were immediately turned from her own misery to what he'd been through.

'You've had a terrible time, haven't you?' she said tenderly. 'Dunkirk. We've heard so much about it on the news and in the papers. Was it really bad?'

'Worse,' he said.

'Oh, Len, I'm sorry. Do you have to go back?'

He shook his head. 'I'm on two weeks' leave and then I have to report to Doncaster, of all places. I don't even know where it is. Up North somewhere.' He looked up and they both laughed.

'I missed you,' she said.

'I missed you more,' he said.

The nurse bustled in and put two cups of tea onto the bedside locker. As she'd pushed past him, Len had stood up to get out of the way. When she left, he leaned over Florrie and brushed his lips against hers. The sensation made every fibre of her body respond to him. Such a gentle touch, but her heart pounded. He sat back down.

'While I was on that beach,' he began, 'I did some serious thinking. Half of my pals got shot to pieces and I decided there and then that life is too short to keep waiting for something that might never happen. Listen, love, I know you can't marry unless you get a divorce from Sid, but for all we know in these uncertain times, he could already be dead.'

She nodded, her eyes smarting with unshed tears.

'Florrie, I want us to be together. I know if you haven't got a wedding ring, it's not what you want. It's not what either of us wants, but I'm tired of waiting. We've already wasted half a lifetime, and after what I've seen in that hellhole, I don't want to wait any longer.'

'Neither do I,' she said softly.

'I reckon if we made our vows to each other, in church if you like, just you and me . . . well, that should be enough, shouldn't it?'

Florrie chewed her bottom lip anxiously.

'I know we won't be man and wife in the eyes of the Church,' he went on, 'but we can still make that promise, and if we did, God knows I for one would mean every word.'

She blinked. 'I'm not much of a catch.' How could she explain that even her neighbours, people she had known all her life, had turned against her because of Ruth? It had taken years of hard work to build a good reputation, and there was always that ever-present dread that somebody from the past would undo everything and ruin her future. She could still hear the voice of Mother's old neighbour, Mrs Jefferson, ringing in her ears. 'Shame on you, Florence. How can you have anything to do with that wicked, wicked woman? Shame on you, I say.' But what could she do? Whatever her mother had done, Florrie couldn't turn her back on her.

'That's enough of that,' Len said firmly, at the same time squeezing her fingers. 'You're my best girl and you mean the world to me.'

Florrie's throat constricted. 'Len, you may know

307

about Ruth, but I promise you don't know the half of it.'

'Then tell me,' he said earnestly. 'Whatever it is, it won't make any difference to how I feel about you, Florrie.'

They could hear the rattle of a trolley coming down the ward. It was almost suppertime.

'When I told Sid, he walked out on me,' she said, looking away. 'I'm afraid to say the words.'

'I'm not Sid,' he said firmly. 'I may not be the most romantic man in the world, but once I've set myself on something, there's no going back.'

The nurse burst through the screen again. 'I'm afraid you'll have to go now, Mr Greene. We don't want the other patients getting jealous, now, do we?'

Len rose to his feet. 'Nurse,' he began, 'you've been very kind and we appreciate all that you've done for us, but five more minutes, please.'

The nurse hesitated.

'It doesn't matter, Len,' Florrie interjected.

'Just five more minutes and I'll give you the old Florrie Jenkins back,' Len insisted.

A small smile edged its way onto the corners of the nurse's mouth. 'You'll get me shot,' she said. Then blushing a bright crimson, she added, 'Oh, I'm sorry. I didn't mean that. It was a slip of the tongue. I'm so sorry.'

'Don't worry,' said Len. 'Five minutes?'

She nodded and put the screen back in place.

Len sat back down. 'Tell me now, Florrie, and tell me everything.'

Florrie stared at him hopelessly. 'When Mother had Ruth,' she began, 'I had to go and collect her from the prison. Did you know she was in Holloway?'

Len shook his head. 'What did she do?'

'She was accused of betraying her country,' said Florrie. 'But she didn't do it.' Len must have looked slightly sceptical because she added, 'People always look like that when I tell them, but I know my mother and she didn't do it!'

'Then that's good enough for me,' Len said stoutly. 'So while she was in prison, you were left alone with Ruth.'

'I wanted to look after her,' said Florrie, her eyes misting over again, 'but how could I? I was sixteen, I had no job, and the landlord kicked us out when he heard what Mother had done.'

'You mustn't blame yourself,' said Len.

'That's what Mrs Andrews said,' said Florrie, 'but I can't help it. I keep wishing there could have been another way.'

'Florrie, love,' Len said gently, 'you have to let it go.'

'It wasn't that I didn't trust you,' said Florrie, her voice thick with emotion. 'I was just scared to say the words.'

'I understand that now, my lovely,' said Len. 'There's no need to be scared any more.'

'Thank you,' she said huskily.

'Let's leave the past in the past.'

'But what am I going to do about Ruth?'

'She'll come round,' said Len. 'She just needs a bit of time, that's all.' He stood to his feet. 'I'd better make tracks or I'll have Matron after me.'

She nodded, her chin quivering.

'Have you seen Matron?' He gesticulated with his hands. 'Big woman. Big, bushy beard and all. Ten times more scary than old Hitler.'

Despite herself, Florrie laughed.

'They tell me visiting is Wednesday and Sunday,' he went on. 'I'll be back on Sunday.'

'Shirley and Tom are coming Sunday,' said Florrie.

'Then I'll give Sunday a miss,' he said.

'No, no,' she smiled. 'I'd like to see all of you.'

'And you will, my lovely, but let Sunday be for your children, eh? You haven't seen them for so long. They deserve to have you to themselves.'

Florrie could hardly breathe. It was happening again, wasn't it? The brush-off. 'But when will I see you again?'

'I'll come on Wednesday,' he said.

'Promise?'

'Promise.'

They could hear the nurse coming back. 'All right, then, my lovely,' he said as he bent to kiss Florrie's cheek. 'See you then' and, aware that the nurse was watching them, he added sternly, 'And make sure you eat something, woman.'

* * *

310

On Oliver's Farm, the main potato crop was looking good, although they had been a bit late getting it in. It was a lot of hard work, but Janet and Shirley didn't mind spending the day in the fields when the weather was so pleasant. Whit Monday had been a complete washout. The weather was cold and wet. As it turned out, had it been fine, it wouldn't have helped Worthing day-trippers, because the town had been declared a military area and was closed to visitors. Of course, now that the holiday was over, in typical fashion, the weather had picked up and today it was glorious. Apart from the occasional buzz from a passing bee or fly, it was very quiet. In the distance, they could hear the trains as they pulled into Angmering Station and the judder of steam as they set off again. It didn't last long. Several fighters came roaring out of the skies to see off some German planes coming in over the Channel and a couple of times they had to dive for cover in the ditch.

According to Seth, the second earlies would be ready for harvesting in three or four weeks' time. Mr Oliver was due for release after six months. They had worked out that he would be back on the farm in late October, so it was possible that they could lift the main crop before he came back. Shirley had found a buyer, so they knew they could both leave with a fair bit of money – enough to keep Janet and Lucy going for a few months, and Shirley would have some money towards the extra expenses she would have, should she ever manage to get to college. The yield from the cows was up, even though they had lost two of the herd. Buttercup got an

311

infection, and Iris sustained an injury to her leg and had to be put down. The sales of eggs, day-old chicks and six-week-old pullets brought in a healthy income. They'd rented the bottom fields out to a lady with horses, and together with the other little schemes they'd devised, they'd made a fair bit of cash. Right now, the pair of them were spraying the crop with a compound of copper to prevent fungal attacks and mould. Tomorrow, they would be dusting DDT on the cabbage field to keep down the infestation of cabbage-white caterpillars.

Once the maincrop potatoes were lifted, Janet planned to be on her way, but although she had applied for several posts from magazine and newspaper ads, so far she hadn't been lucky. Having Lucy with her was proving to be a problem.

Shirley's future looked more settled. Her mother wrote to say she was getting stronger every day and before long she would be able to go back home. That meant she and Tom would go back too. After all this lovely fresh air, Shirley didn't relish being back in London, with its river mists and the sulphuric smog in winter, but it was better than nothing. Although she had shelved her dream of college for the time being, it hadn't died altogether. She had passed the exam with flying colours, but her mother would need help for a while. As for Tom, he didn't want to go back home at all. He had an easy rapport with the farm animals, especially Darby and Joan, the percherons, and they had absolute trust in him.

The silence in the field was suddenly broken again by

the sound of aircraft. Shirley stood to shield her eyes as a German plane hurtled across the almost clear blue skies with two Hurricanes in hot pursuit. They flew around each other like birds, weaving, pitching and soaring as if they were caught up in some beautifully choreographed dance, except that this one was deadly. All at once, the enemy plane began to spiral towards the ground, with thick smoke following in its wake. Shirley and Janet watched in horror as it disappeared into the distant horizon, and seconds later, they heard a deep boom and saw a cloud of black smoke coming from somewhere beyond the village.

'Poor sods,' Janet muttered.

Shirley raised an eyebrow.

'I know I should hate them,' said Janet, 'and I do really, but we've just seen somebody's son, or brother, or husband die.'

Shirley hadn't thought of it like that and it was sobering. Then the two Hurricanes reappeared, obviously heading up country towards their own airfield. One swooped down low and they could clearly see the pilot waving. The two girls waved back and cheered. The pilot soared again, did a victory roll and set off to join his companion.

'Are you going to the dance on Saturday?' Janet asked.

'What dance?'

'Oh, Shirley,' Janet teased, 'do keep up. There's one in the village hall. All the Canadians will be there, and' – she gesticulated towards the sky – 'maybe a few of our boys too. Granny Roberts is babysitting. I'm going. Fancy it?'

Although Shirley felt a tingle of excitement, she shrugged her shoulders. 'Dunno. Might do.'

# CHAPTER 25

The night of the dance, Shirley could hear the music as she and Janet made their way across the triangle. A group of Canadian soldiers hung around the door, and as they parked their bicycles, they wolf-whistled before following them in. The village hall was moderately full. The girls sat on chairs round the edge. Shirley spotted her old school friends Hazel and Bobbi and went to join them. There were a few others she knew as well, girls she had seen behind the shop counter or met on the bus the few times she had been into town. Angmering was a small place where almost everybody knew everybody. The boys, mostly Canadian soldiers, stood in huddles at either end of the room.

'Shirley, you look fantastic,' said Hazel as she sat next to her.

'Why, thank you,' Shirley said teasingly. She did feel rather good. She was wearing a red and white dress that she'd picked up at a jumble sale for tuppence. When she'd bought it, it had long, tapering sleeves, and the skirt came down her to ankles. Now, it had a snugly fitting yoke with a small bow at the front. The sleeves were more fitted than before and only three-quarter-length. The material under the bust had been smocked, and the skirt, which ended at the knee, was joined to the bodice with soft pleats. Janet had picked up a bargain at the same sale. She was wearing a plain yellow dress, which she had changed by embroidering a flower motif round the neckline and down the bust. The pattern was repeated round the hem, and she had picked out the colours from a silk scarf that she had trimmed and wore as a sash round the waist. The people who had donated their dresses to the jumble sale would be hard pressed to recognize their own garments.

The music was being played not by the usual gramophone but a three-piece band called the Scallywags. They were quite good, not only playing the old familiar tunes but some of the more modern songs too. They did the old favourites like the foxtrot, the Dashing White Sergeant, which was more like Scottish country dancing, and of course the waltz. Everyone stuck to the dance-hall tradition of three dances in a row and then a short interval when everybody cleared the floor.

'Shirley, how nice to see you again.' It was Miss Smith, her old teacher. Dressed in a pale blue sparkly top with a long chiffon skirt, her hair was piled on the top of her head, Betty Grable-style. Shirley had never seen her looking so attractive.

'Miss Smith!'

'Call me Marilyn,' she said. 'Now that you've officially left school, I think we should dispense with the formality, don't you? How are you?'

Hazel and Bobbi were invited to dance, and Janet was already on the floor. Shirley and Marilyn were alone. 'Fine.'

'Are you still at the farm?'

Shirley nodded. 'I shall leave after the harvest,' she said. 'Janet needs all the help she can get.'

'Just give me a shout when the time comes,' said Marilyn.

An eavesdropping soldier standing next to them said, 'Count me in to help, ma'am. My folks are farmers back home.'

The girls laughed and Shirley accepted his offer of a dance.

'I suppose you used to help on the farm when you were friends with Elizabeth,' said Shirley when she came back to her chair.

Marilyn Smith's face clouded. 'No, I didn't do anything like that,' she said. 'He wouldn't let anyone help. I went there because Elizabeth needed someone to confide in.'

'So you were very close,' said Janet.

'The three of us were going away together,' said Marilyn with a sigh.

'Going away?' said Janet. 'Where?' But another Canadian was tugging at her arm and the next minute she was on the dance floor again. Marilyn wasn't far behind, dancing with his pal. Three dances later, they were back together once more.

The music started, but the three girls preferred to sit and talk. They were all feeling hot, so Janet went to get them some water. Bobbi and Hazel were at another table with some Canadians.

'You were saying that the three of you were going away together,' said Shirley. 'Did that mean Mr Oliver was leaving the farm?'

'Heavens, no!' cried Marilyn. 'Elizabeth hated Gilbert.'

'I don't understand,' said Shirley.

'It was all very hush-hush,' said Marilyn, her eyes filling with tears, 'but Reuben, Elizabeth and I were going to South Africa.'

Shirley's jaw dropped. 'So she was having an affair with Reuben Fletcher?'

Marilyn laughed sardonically, and the dance hall cleared. Janet was back with some cups of water. 'What have I missed?' They arranged them on the window ledge.

'Elizabeth was having an affair with Reuben,' said Shirley.

'What!' exclaimed Janet. The music started again and several soldiers came to where they were sitting, but they stayed in their huddle.

'That's not what I said,' Marilyn insisted.

Janet frowned. 'Let's go to the cloakroom.'

In the safety of the ladies' cloakroom, Shirley said, 'Are you all right? I didn't mean to upset you.'

Marilyn, her face slightly flushed, put up her hand. 'You've got this all wrong,' she said. 'Elizabeth stayed faithful to that dreadful man . . .'

'But you've just said she was running away with Reuben,' Shirley protested.

318.

'The three of us were going together,' said Marilyn, blowing her nose into her handkerchief. 'Not running away. At least, I wasn't. Reuben and I were going to get married as soon as we reached Cape Town.'

Janet and Shirley stared at her in disbelief as all at once Marilyn began to cry. Shirley put her arm round her shoulders, and they waited for a few minutes for her to calm down.

'I'm sorry,' said Shirley. 'I didn't mean to—'

'No, no,' said Marilyn. 'I'm all right. It's just that I've held everything in for so long.'

'When you're feeling better,' said Janet, 'we'll forget all this and go back in.'

'I don't mind talking about it,' said Marilyn. 'It's a bit of a relief, really.'

'I'm totally confused,' whispered Shirley.

'I think you'd better start from the beginning,' said Janet.

Although they were interrupted by the occasional girl wanting the toilet or to patch up her make-up, Marilyn carried on speaking in hushed tones, as she did her best not to weep. 'Elizabeth and I were friends from way back. She was very unhappy. I know people said she was expecting a baby when she died, but she wasn't.'

'How do you know?' whispered Janet.

Marilyn waited until she was sure the toilets were empty, then leaned towards them. 'Because she was still a virgin.'

Janet frowned. 'But they were married for years.'

'And he never touched her,' said Marilyn. 'Not once.'

The appalling shock of what she was saying wasn't lost on Shirley, but they had to wait for someone else to come out of the cubicle.

'All Elizabeth wanted was to be a mother,' said Marilyn when they were alone again, 'but in the whole time she was with Gilbert, she had her own bedroom and he had his. They lived completely separate lives.'

'Then why marry her in the first place?' said Shirley. 'If he didn't love her, why take her as his wife?'

'Money,' said Marilyn. 'When they got married, she had quite a bit of money.'

'Oh, don't tell me,' said Shirley angrily. 'He took it for the farm.'

'But if that farm means so much to him, you'd think he'd want a family,' Janet mused. 'Someone to hand it on to.'

'Personally,' said Marilyn, 'I don't think he knew what to do with it.'

'He probably bought animal fodder or something,' said Shirley, completely missing the point.

As her older friends sniggered, Shirley felt her face colour. When Janet gave her a hug, she guessed that they must have been talking about having babies, so she giggled along with them rather than confess she didn't understand.

'Why didn't she just run?' said Janet.

Marilyn pulled a face. 'Anywhere in this county and he would have gone after her. South Africa was too far for him to come.'

'But I don't understand why *you* were going in such

320

secrecy,' said Shirley. 'Why didn't you want to tell everybody? They'd have loved to have given you a good send-off.'

'Reuben and I were secretly engaged,' said Marilyn. 'He was such a lovely man, but my parents disapproved of me, a teacher, taking up, as they put it, with a "common labourer". They would never have sanctioned our marriage, so when we saw the wonderful opportunities in South Africa, we decided to make a completely new start.' She wiped her eyes again and blew her nose.

The two women looked at her. 'I found a poster hidden in her bedroom,' said Shirley. 'It was all about the *Dunnottar Castle* from the Union-Castle Line.'

'That was our ship,' Marilyn nodded. 'We were due to sail the day after she died.'

'People say they found two tickets in Reuben's pocket,' said Janet.

'I heard that too,' said Shirley, 'but nobody knew who they were for, because the water had washed away the names.'

'Hers and his,' said Marilyn, looking away sadly. 'Reuben was looking after Elizabeth's ticket for safety. I still have my ticket at home.'

'Didn't you think it suspicious?' Shirley asked. 'Her death?'

'What are you saying, Shirley?' said Janet, alarmed. 'From what Marilyn has just said, nobody knew she was going. Why would her death be any more than a horrible coincidence?'

'I'm sorry,' said Shirley. 'I just thought with Reuben in the culvert and Elizabeth in the pond . . .'

'To tell you the truth, I didn't know what to think,' said Marilyn. 'I went all the way to Southampton on the train, but of course neither of them turned up. After that, all I cared about was that Reuben was missing. For ages I couldn't even think straight. I did go to the police, but they didn't think anything was wrong. They said he was a casual labourer and he must have moved on.'

'How awful for you,' said Janet.

'When I came back to Angmering and heard about Elizabeth's death, I did go and see Gilbert,' said Marilyn. 'He seemed to know Elizabeth wasn't happy, but he said he'd persuaded her to give their marriage one last try. He said that the fact she was by the pond looking for bits for her Christmas wreaths proved she intended to stay.'

The door banged against the wall and they all jumped. 'Are you lot coming in or what?' Hazel was holding the cloakroom door open. 'Come on, girls. There's loads of blokes waiting for dances out here.'

Their little chat broke up, and when they got back in the hall, Janet hardly had time to sit down before someone else was coming up to her to ask for a dance. Shirley and Marilyn, who put on a very brave face, had their fair share of dances as well. Shirley accepted most offers and had great fun. Halfway through the evening, the tea hatch was opened and for once she didn't have to go into the kitchen. Tea and biscuits were served, but neither Janet nor Shirley had to pay. In fact, they could have had six or more cups each, the amount of offers they had.

Janet leaned over towards Marilyn. 'I'm so sorry about what you went through,' she said.

Marilyn shrugged. 'At least I know now that Reuben didn't desert me.'

After the interval, the local lads turned up and they seemed rather put out. Apparently, the visitors didn't understand the English strategies for getting a girl, namely that it was unmanly to go into the hall before the interval and it was expected that you should be tanked up before asking anyone to dance. The Canadians had already made their mark, and few girls were interested in a half-cut local when they had glamour from Toronto, Calgary or Ontario.

'Enjoying yourself?' Hazel asked in a rare moment when she and Shirley had time to talk.

'I'd say,' said Shirley.

'They have a dance every month,' said Hazel. 'You must put a note in your diary.'

'I wouldn't miss it for the world,' Shirley laughed as a handsome Canadian called Clay whisked her off again, this time to dance the quick-step. She had very little knowledge of the dances, but she was learning fast.

'Where do you come from?' she asked Clay.

'Newfoundland,' he said.

'You're a very good dancer,' she said.

'We do a lot of what we call Newfy dancing,' he said.

'It's a bit like Scottish dancing or English square dancing, so this is easy to me.'

At ten, when the dance wrapped up, Marilyn had already slipped away. Hazel and Bobbi were walking home with a couple of Canadians, while Shirley and Janet made for their bicycles. They had plenty of offers to walk home, but they had agreed beforehand that they would refuse them all and bike back together.

'Can I see you again, Shirley?' Clay asked as she headed round the back of the hall, where the bikes had been left.

Shirley's heart was racing, but she wasn't sure what to say. He was very good-looking.

'They tell me there's a dance at East Preston Village Hall next week,' he persisted. 'Can I meet you there?'

Shirley nodded shyly and he leaned forward to kiss her on the lips. His kiss was soft and gentle, and she breathed in the smell of him. It wasn't like the smell of carbolic soap or of stale underarm sweat that she was used to from English boys. He smelled of cinnamon and spice, an altogether intoxicating smell. She felt her knees buckle slightly.

'Are you sure you wouldn't like me to walk you home, honey?'

'I'm fine,' said Shirley a tad reluctantly, 'but I may see you next week.'

'That was amazing,' said Janet, when they were well away from the centre of the village. 'I had the best time.'

'Me too,' Shirley said dreamily. The memory of Clay's kiss was still on her lips. She caught sight of Janet looking at her and laughed. 'And I'm worn out as well. I don't know how I'm going to catch the bus tomorrow to see Mum.'

Shirley was still holding her mother's hand. She had been sitting next to her in the convalescent home for the best part of half an hour and she still couldn't let go.

The bus ride had been enjoyable. After dancing until ten and then having the bike ride home and the chores to do in the morning, Shirley thought she would doze for a while, but in fact she enjoyed looking out of the window at the passing English countryside. Because the bus route was designed to attract as many customers as possible, they had gone through several pretty villages: Arundel, Ford, Yapton, Walberton and, finally, Font-well. When they got out, the conductor told them to cross the road and turn left off the lane. There were no road signs: they had all been removed in case of an invasion. Tangmere and Ford airfields were very close by and the constant drone of engines filled the air. However, after a ten-minute walk, they could see the big house in the distance.

Tom, who had been very restless on the bus, managed to give his mother a quick hug, and although he hadn't stopped smiling, he couldn't manage eye contact with her. Once the greetings were done, he stood by the window looking out over the grounds, every now and then turning his head to steal a glance at his mother. If she looked up at him, he'd look away quickly.

Shirley was really worried about her mother. She had

lost a lot of weight and she still seemed rather weak. It was only now that she began to appreciate just how ill Florrie had been.

'So,' said Florrie, relaxing back in her chair, 'what have you two been doing?'

Shirley hardly knew where to begin, but anxious not to worry her, she was selective in what she told her. She began with the potato crop and how they hoped to lift it soon. When she mentioned the cows, Tom turned round.

'I milk the cows,' he said, 'but we've only got six now.' He reeled off their names, ending up with 'Buttercup died, and Iris hurt her leg.'

'I'm sorry to hear that,' said Florrie.

'And I take care of the pigs,' Tom announced proudly. He told his mother their names as well. 'They have to be fattened up to give us bacon.'

'Seth and Vince are very pleased with what Tom has done with the animals,' said Shirley. 'He really loves life on the farm.'

'And what about you?' said Florrie.

A small smiled edged its way onto Shirley's mouth. 'I don't like the mess,' she admitted, 'but I've enjoyed organizing things, and I've been trying my hand at growing a bit of veg and stuff. It's very satisfying.'

'I know what you mean,' said Florrie. 'I've been doing the same. Shall I show you?'

They stood up and Florrie took them outside.

'How long do you reckon you'll be here, Mum?' Shirley asked.

'I can't afford to stay much longer,' her mother admitted. 'It's expensive and I don't want to use all our savings. Maybe another week or so.'

Shirley looked thoughtful. 'Is Auntie Betty still at the shop?'

'Yes, but I was wondering if you would help out when I get home,' said Florrie. 'I don't think I can do it all on my own. Not just yet.'

Shirley's heart sank. She had expected as much, but she'd hoped against hope that it wouldn't happen. It would probably be the end of all her dreams for the future. They had reached a greenhouse and Florrie showed her children where she pinched out the tender plants and potted the stronger ones on. Her pride and joy was a tomato plant that groaned with ripening fruit.

'I like tomatoes,' Tom said.

'These are amazing, Mum,' said Shirley. 'Much better than the ones you grow at home.'

'I've learned a lot since I've been here,' said Florrie. 'You know, about feeding them properly and looking out for disease. Before, I just used to stick them in the pot and hope for the best.'

They laughed.

'I was so proud when you passed that exam,' said Florrie as they strolled back. She'd threaded her arm through Shirley's. 'Do you still want to go to college?'

'Yes, I do, but can I ask for something else first? Would you mind if Tom and I stayed on at the farm until the harvest? Janet needs all the help she can get. It's a big job for a woman on her own.'

'On her own?' said her mother. 'But where is Mr Oliver?'

Shirley felt her face flame. Blast! She hadn't meant for her mother to know that. As soon as the words left her mouth, she regretted them. 'On holiday,' she said, but at the same moment her brother said, 'In prison.'

Florrie stopped walking and stared at them wide-eyed.

'He shot the dog,' said Tom.

Florrie took in a breath. 'Shirley?'

'Let me tell Mum, Tom,' said Shirley. 'Mum, it's all right. The dog bit him and his gun went off, but somebody thought he was trying to shoot them, so they arrested him. He was found not guilty, anyway.'

'But Tom said he was in prison.'

'He was sent to prison because he was rude to the judge, Mum, that's all.'

Florrie continued to stare. 'How long before he's out?'

'He gets out at the end of October,' said Shirley. 'Janet needs help for the harvest before then. I thought, considering how kind they've been to Tom and me . . .'

'Yes, yes,' said Florrie. 'Of course you must help.'

'We'll leave straight after.'

'I don't want to leave the farm, Shirley,' said Tom.

'I know,' she said, 'but we have to go home to help Mum.'

Florrie's heart constricted.

They sat for a while longer; then Shirley said they had to go for the bus back. It was hard saying goodbye again, but all of them felt better for the visit. Florrie was on the mend, and her children were thriving in the fresh country air. She watched as they ran down the drive and into the lane. Good job Len was coming soon. She desperately wanted someone to talk to.

# CHAPTER 26

'I've got somewhere to go,' said Janet.

They were sitting at the table in Granny Roberts's place. The old lady looked up from her sewing. She was making a dress for Lucy out of the skirt of an old dress. The dress itself was old-fashioned, but the material was attractive. Lucy was asleep in her pram, and Shirley and Janet were waiting for Hazel and Bobbi to come up from the village; then they were all going to another dance. This time, the Canadians were sending a truck for them, but they had to be by Patching Pond at six-thirty, where they would be picked up. It was already ten past six. Bobbi and Hazel were late.

'What do you mean, you've got somewhere to go?' asked Granny.

'When I leave here,' said Janet. 'I've been accepted as a cook in a residential nursery in Surrey.'

'Gosh,' said Shirley. 'That was quick.'

'Not really,' said Janet. 'Gil will be out in a matter of weeks.'

'Where exactly?' asked Granny.

'I don't want to tell anyone,' said Janet. 'I still want

to keep in touch with you, but I'll set up a Post Office box number you can write to. That way, what you don't know you can't let slip. I'm scared Gil will come after me, especially when he finds out we've used the money from the tin.'

'Only to keep the farm going,' said Shirley.

'He won't see it like that,' said Janet.

'What's it like?' said Granny. 'The nursery.'

'Lovely,' said Janet. 'It's a big house set in its own grounds. Lucy and I will have our own room.'

'But you can't look after her while you're working in the kitchen,' said Granny. 'She'll be crawling about soon.'

'I won't have to,' said Janet. 'She'll be with all the other children in the nursery during the day. I'll have her when I finish work and on my day off.'

'Sounds ideal,' said Shirley. 'When do you go?'

'If we start lifting the potatoes next week,' said Janet, 'I'll go as soon as everybody's been paid.'

'Loads of people say they're going to help,' said Shirley.

They heard the sound of a bicycle bell outside. 'About time too,' said Janet. 'Come on or we'll miss the truck.'

Shirley set off behind her with a feeling of foreboding. It was fun going to the dances, but Clay wanted to monopolize her all the time and that spoiled it a bit. She liked him and he was very good-looking, but she didn't want to be 'his girl', as he put it. She didn't want to be anyone's girl. As they hurried down the road to meet the truck, she had made up her mind. Tonight, she

331

wasn't going to beat about the bush any more – she was going to tell him straight and he could like it or lump it.

It was Wednesday again. The sun was in her eyes when Florrie looked up, but her heart leapt almost out of her body. Len stood in front of her. For days she had dreaded that her disclosure the last time they'd met would have driven him away, but here he was. He'd come back!

'Hello, my lovely,' he said. 'How are you?' He kissed her forehead. 'I've brought someone to see you.'

She became aware that someone stood directly behind him, totally obscured by him. He stepped to one side and there was Ruth. 'But how . . . ?' Florrie began.

'I saw her address on the piece of paper she'd left on your locker,' he said with a grin.

'Oh, Ruth,' cried Florrie. 'I'm so glad to see you.' She pulled herself up straight and leaned forward, but Ruth stood rooted to the spot. The expression on her face was frozen, but her eyes were less hostile than they had been last week.

Len fetched a chair. 'Have a seat, Ruth,' he said, manoeuvring the chair so that it was directly in front of Florrie.

Ruth pushed the chair back a few feet before lowering herself onto it. 'Len says you have something more to tell me,' she said stiffly. 'I've agreed to listen, but I don't think it'll make much of a difference to the way I feel.'

Florrie hardly knew where to start, but with a little coaxing from Len, she tried to do her best. It wasn't easy voicing things she'd never spoken of, things that had churned around her head for years and yet she'd never breathed a single word about them to a living soul. When she'd tried to tell Sid, his reaction had meant she'd never told him the full story. Would Len and Ruth be willing to wait until she'd finished?

'Ruth, I'm not your mother,' she began. 'I'm your half-sister.'

Ruth took in her breath and her face coloured.

'Father went to war in 1915,' Florrie went on. 'I was fourteen years old. I didn't understand everything, but after he had a period of training, he went to France.'

Ruth took off her white cotton gloves and laid them on her lap. She looked very elegant in her pale green dress. At first glance it looked as if it had its own light-weight coat with a green and white striped dress peeping out at the front, but that was the way it had been made. Her hat matched perfectly, and she had white peep-toe shoes. Seeing the relaxed way Ruth crossed her legs as she sat helped Florrie to relax too. Perhaps she was going to stay after all.

'Father only came home on leave twice,' she continued. 'The first time, he slipped back into normal life quite easily, but the second time, he was a changed man.'

Ruth's expression was impassive. Len seemed more sympathetic.

'He paced the floor for hours,' Florrie went on. 'He cried a lot too. I'd never seen a man cry before.'

'This is all very sad,' said Ruth stiffly, 'but what has it got to do with me?'

'There is a reason,' said Florrie. 'You need to know everything.'

Ruth sighed pointedly.

'Some time after my father went back to the trenches at the end of 1916, he went AWOL. He was captured and put in prison.'

Neither of them said anything, but she knew what they were thinking. Back then, people had only contempt for deserters and cowards. 'He was lucky they didn't shoot him,' said Florrie, voicing what she was sure was going through their minds. 'I think it was because he'd saved the life of an officer not long before he walked away, but he had to be punished as an example to the other men, so he was sent to prison and his army pay was stopped for three months.'

Len frowned. 'But that would have left your mother destitute.'

Florrie nodded. 'I had to leave school and go into service. Mother took in lodgers.'

'It seems a bit harsh,' said Ruth, mellowing a little.

Florrie shrugged. 'And one of our lodgers was Captain Faversham-Wood.'

Ruth took in her breath and leaned forward eagerly. 'My father? What was he like?'

'Very good-looking,' said Florrie. 'Charming, witty, kind. He'd been invalided out of the army with a

wound to his leg. He worked for the Foreign Office.'
She paused. 'It didn't take long for Mother to fall in
love with him, but they were very discreet. At the time,
not even I knew what was going on.'

Florrie's narrative was interrupted by the nurse
coming round with the tea trolley. When she saw her
patient's visitors, she eyed them suspiciously. As she
poured three cups of tea, she asked, 'Are you all right,
Mrs Jenkins?' Florrie nodded, but it was obvious that
the nurse was still concerned. Looking directly at Ruth,
she added, 'Only, we'd rather not have a repeat of what
happened the last time your visitor came.'

Ruth's face coloured, but she said nothing. When the
nurse had moved on to the next patient and her visitors,
Florrie continued as if nothing had happened.

'One day, Captain Faversham-Wood asked my mother
to take a letter to a friend of his. He explained that the
friend lived in a house with a long flight of steps leading
up to the front door and walking up them aggravated
his bad leg.'

'Why didn't he post it?' Ruth asked.

Florrie shrugged. 'I said that, but he said he didn't
trust the post and wanted a cast-iron guarantee that it
was delivered.' She sipped her tea. 'Posting those letters
became a regular thing for my mother.'

'What became of him?' asked Len.

'Captain Faversham-Wood?' said Florrie. 'He left our
house in June of that year. Later on, we heard a rumour
that he'd died in the flu epidemic.' Ruth made a small
sound and Florrie looked up. 'Oh, I'm sorry, dear. That

was thoughtless of me.' Embarrassed, she looked away as Ruth sniffed loudly.

'Go on, then, my lovely,' said Len as the silence between them grew. 'What happened next?'

'Mother was arrested.'

'Arrested?' cried Ruth. 'But why?'

'It turned out that the letters were being delivered to a German spy,' said Florrie. 'Captain Faversham-Wood was a traitor.'

Ruth leapt to her feet. 'No!' she cried. 'That's not true. You're making it up.'

Len was on his feet too and Florrie burst into tears. However, he wasn't getting ready to run, as Florrie had feared. Instead, he spoke in low tones to Ruth. Florrie couldn't hear what he was saying, but eventually Ruth, stony-faced, sat back down.

'Go on,' said Len softly. 'Tell us the rest.'

Florrie gulped. 'There was a trial and Mother was found guilty of aiding and abetting the enemy.' She took another breath. 'She pleaded her belly, but they said she had known what she was doing and that she condoned Captain Faversham-Wood's conduct, so she was sent to prison.'

'So now I have a criminal for a mother and a traitor as a father,' said Ruth bitterly.

'Our mother was totally innocent,' Florrie retorted.

'What did you mean, "she pleaded her belly"?' said Ruth.

'She was carrying you,' said Florrie.

'So I was actually born in prison?' Ruth squeaked.

Florrie nodded miserably. 'It was just before my father came back home.'

'Did he know about me?'

Florrie shook her head. 'I don't think he even knew what day it was. He came back a broken man. He couldn't stop shaking, and if he heard the slightest noise that was out of the ordinary, he would fling himself under the table or behind a chair.'

'So you had to look after him,' said Ruth, her voice softening for the very first time. 'But no thought of me, then.'

'I went to fetch you when you were a week old,' said Florrie as her mind drifted back. How could she forget that day? She had been part of a small crowd waiting on the pavement outside the prison when the door within the much larger one opened to let them in. It had all seemed so unreal. She'd had to pinch herself to believe that she was really here and that she was on her way to see her mother. Everyone shuffled along in silence, their heads bowed, each lost in his or her own thoughts.

Then someone had said, 'This is no place for a young girl like you,' and Florrie had looked up to see a burly prison officer standing in front of her. 'Who have you come to see?'

She'd handed him her permission papers. He'd read them, then given her a long, hard stare. Even now, all these years later, she had no idea if it had been sympathy or contempt in his eyes, but whatever it was, the

337

look he gave her made her feel like shrivelling up and dying. 'Why would you want to see the likes of her?'

Instinctively Florrie had lowered her eyes. 'She's my mother.'

'Florrie? Florrie, love.' She was suddenly brought back to the present day and Len was standing in front of her with a glass of water. 'Are you all right? You looked as if you were about to pass out, my lovely. Shall I call the nurse?'

Florrie glanced at Ruth again. 'We shared the same name, you see,' Florrie said quietly. 'Florence Lincoln. That's why you thought *I* was your mother.' Taking the glass and a gulp of water, she shook her head at Len. 'No, I'm fine.' Refreshed and revived, she turned to Ruth. 'Sorry. Now, where was I?'

'You collected me from prison but couldn't keep me.' Ruth's tone was a tad accusatory.

'You know, all my life I've been made to feel guilty about this,' said Florrie, slightly irritated. 'You ask me: how could I have done it? My father was totally useless and everybody hated us. When they saw me coming, people would spit on the ground in front of me. I was pushed over on more than one occasion.' She held Ruth's gaze. 'I had no money and no job – I lost that when my employer read his newspaper. Everybody is so quick to judge. I was sixteen. It wasn't that I didn't want you. I *couldn't* look after you.'

Len gave her shoulder a gentle squeeze. 'Perhaps we'd better stop now, Florrie, love. I can see that you're getting upset.'

'I took you to Mrs Andrews,' said Florrie, ignoring him. 'She told me she knew a lovely couple who would give you a good home and that they'd keep you from ever knowing the truth. We just wanted you to have a proper chance in life.' Florrie turned her head, a hurt look on her face.

Ruth dabbed her eyes. 'And I did,' she said, her voice choked with emotion.

Florrie looked back at her half-sister. 'Our mother loved you very much,' she said, her voice softening. 'It broke her heart to give you up. She said, "I want you to go far away from here, Florrie, and never come back." She said to me, "I am so sorry for what I've done. I was a fool. I was deceived and I was unfaithful, but I promise you I never knew what was in those notes, and I certainly never intended to betray my country." Then the prison nurse came in and handed me a bundle – you. Mother kissed your little forehead and said, "I want you to call her Ruth, after the Ruth in the Bible. She made a home for herself far away from her own family, and that's what my baby must do."' There was a pregnant pause. Then Florrie said, 'I didn't know what to say. I just stood there like a lemon and they took Mother away. I didn't even get to kiss her goodbye.'

Ruth's chin was quivering as she dabbed her eyes with a lace handkerchief. 'I've treated you badly, Florrie, and I'm sorry. Our mother got her wish. I *was* well looked after, and I loved my parents.'

'Then I'm glad,' said Florrie, looking up at her. 'She

339

said she would pray for you every day for the rest of her life.'

Without breaking her gaze, Ruth reached out and grabbed Florrie's hand. The two of them squeezed hard, and then Ruth stood and, leaning over, gave her half-sister a hug. Len moved to the window and stood with his back to them. He knew this was a very private moment.

'They found out she was telling the truth in the end,' said Florrie as Ruth sat back down.

Ruth gasped, and Len spun round. 'How?'

'It turned out that the captain didn't die after all,' said Florrie. 'He wrote a memoir, which was published by the Blackshirts in 1934.'

Ruth took in her breath audibly. 'Have you seen it?'

Florrie shook her head. 'A friend of mine told me about it without realizing it was anything to do with me,' she said. 'Apparently, he had been educated here in a public school. He had an accent so English you would never have guessed in a million years that he was of German descent, but whatever we think of him, he was loyal to his own country and decorated for his achievements.'

'So your mother was exonerated,' said Len, smiling with relief.

'Fat lot of good it did,' said Florrie bitterly. 'She was already long gone.'

Ruth's face fell. 'So she died in prison?'

Florrie looked up at them, surprised. 'Don't tell me you didn't know? My mother was notorious. You must have heard of her. She was called the English Mata Hari. It was in all the papers. A week after I'd collected you from the prison, she was hanged.'

# CHAPTER 27

Florrie stared out of the window. Tomorrow, she would be seeing Dr Scott for the last time. He had written to tell her that he was coming by and that he wanted to check up on her. For a second or two, she'd been alarmed, afraid of the cost of his visit, but as a post-script at the bottom of his letter, he'd written, '*No charge.*'

It was almost time to go home, but after all these months, Florrie didn't want to go back to London. Although life was quite often disturbed by enemy bombers going over, or the sound of dog fights in the clouds, it was so much better being in the country. Florrie had lost count of the times she heard the sirens in the distance followed by the all-clear, but there were few incidents. If a bomb was dropped, it was usually in a field somewhere. Of course, she realized that in this part of Sussex, they were in the front line as far as the enemy invasion went, but she still preferred to be here rather than in the capital. The news, wherever it came from, wasn't good. Portsmouth and Southampton seemed to be bearing the brunt of things, but the RAF had downed eighty-six German planes with only fifteen losses of their own. It was a small crumb of comfort, but she couldn't get those brave boys out of her mind. Fifteen planes (she was willing to bet that it was probably a lot more) represented at least fifteen families going through hell. But it wasn't the fear of bombing that made her reluctant to go back to London. She loved Sussex. She loved the clean air and the beauty all around her. Most of all, she loved the people. This was the place to make a completely fresh start.

With no one around to talk to, she'd resorted to writing long letters to share her thoughts. She started with Len. He was back with his regiment and about to be shipped out to God knows where. Just the thought of him created a hollow feeling in her heart. His letters were wonderful and she read them over and over again. For a man of few words, he always said the right thing. The radio was on in the other room. An American girl, Jo Stafford, was singing a lovely song. Florrie couldn't catch all the words. '*To hold you ever so tight . . . and to feel . . . the nearness of you . . .*' Oh, how she longed to be nearer to Len.

When she'd told her friends what she planned, Doreen had been enthusiastic: '*Sounds wonderful. Just do it.*' Betty's comments had been more thoughtful. '*I'm not keen to stay here much longer myself,*' she'd written. '*The bombing is getting much worse. I enjoyed looking after the shop up to now, but I want to do my bit as well. I'm thinking of joining the WVS canteen. They do such a valiant job in helping people who have*

343

*lost absolutely everything and I'd like to be a part of that. Your idea sounds really good, and I know a couple of people who would jump at the chance.'*

Although Florrie didn't need it, their encouraging comments felt like she'd got their blessing.

Shirley and Tom were coming up the drive. Florrie grabbed her cardigan and, for the first time in many months, hurried to meet them. The three of them swapped their news, and by the time they'd reached the nursery garden and found a seat, Florrie could hardly contain herself with excitement.

'I've had a letter from Mr Mills,' she said. Her son was preoccupied with a bumblebee that was crawling along the back of the seat. 'Tom, I want you to listen too. This is important.'

'Do we know a Mr Mills?' asked Shirley.

'No,' said Florrie, 'but he is very keen to run the shop.'

'You mean I don't have to go back to London to help you?' cried Shirley.

Florrie shook her head.

'Oh, Mum, does that mean I could take up that scholarship?'

Florrie laughed. 'If that's what you want,' she said. 'Mr Mills has offered me far more than I expected – four hundred and ten pounds – so I'm selling it.'

Tom froze. Shirley's jaw dropped. 'Selling?' said Shirley. 'But, Mum, you love that shop. You're not selling it because of me, surely?'

'No, love,' said Florrie. 'I did it for all of us. I enjoy

working outdoors, and Tom loves the farm, so it seemed the next logical step. That's a good price, and as soon as the money is in the bank, I'm going to look for a place around here.'

Shirley seemed to have lost her voice.

'Near Angmering, if you like,' said Florrie encouragingly. 'You've made a lot of friends there, haven't you? If I can get a place with a bit of land, we could keep chickens.'

'And pigs,' said Tom. 'I'm good with pigs. Seth says so.'

Florrie laughed again. 'Well, maybe one pig.'

Shirley chewed her bottom lip. Clearly her mother thought that Tom could carry on at the farm, but she wasn't so sure. Once Mr Oliver was back and he knew Janet was gone, he would be angry. He'd probably blame her and take it out on Tom. Oliver's Farm wouldn't be a safe place any more. Yet looking at her mother's bright smile, she couldn't bring herself to say anything. Let her enjoy this moment for now. Explanations could wait a while. Mr Oliver wouldn't be out for several more weeks.

'Shirley?' Florrie seemed concerned.

Shirley gave her mother a big hug. 'Sounds wonderful,' she cried. 'I can hardly believe it.'

'Then that's settled, my darling,' said Florrie, relaxing. 'It's going to happen.'

August was hot. It should have gone down as a lovely summer, and it would have done had it not been for the constant news of the misfortunes of war. The Battle of

Britain was raging overhead, and although everyone did their best to stay cheerful, they all sensed that it would only take one small error of judgement to lose the war. Having already been active in the North, the German Luftwaffe now came across the Channel in droves, bombing large swathes of southern England. Much to the delight of small boys, the battle-scarred remains of Dorniers, Heinkels, Messerschmitts and Junkers littered the countryside and they ran or biked to get to them first before the Home Guard or the local policeman stopped them taking souvenirs. Most of the rest of life carried on as usual. While the brave boys of the RAF struggled to keep the enemy away from Britain's shores, on Oliver's Farm it was time to lift the potato crop.

Until she came to the farm, Shirley had no idea what a labour-intensive job digging up potatoes was. It sounded simple enough – plant them in rows, then, when the time came, put in a fork and shove the potatoes in a bucket. However, with such a large field full of them, it was going to take a lot more than that. During the growing season, she'd weeded the furrows and banked up the plants. A couple of times, she'd been asked to dust the whole crop with DDT to deter pests. Now that it was time to lift them, Seth and Vince had dug a long trench at one end of the field. The plan was to put some of the newly dug potatoes into it, then cover them with straw and another layer of earth. It was by far the best way to store them for a short period until they could get around to bagging them up and putting them into the barn. The rest of the field was earmarked for market.

On the day they were to do it, Hazel and Marilyn had mustered quite a bit of help from the village. Several schoolchildren and a few young men who were not yet old enough to be called up came along as well. Tom brought the horses up to the field. He was to go along the furrows turning the soil to release the potatoes. Everybody was given an area to work on, and once the potatoes were exposed, they had to put them into their molly. The full mollies were emptied into the cart, and by the time Tom and the horse came down the other side of the furrow, everyone was ready to pick up the next batch. Being so dry made it a lot easier, but it was still back-breaking work.

Janet and Shirley spent their time putting the potatoes into hessian sacks and weighing them. If all went well, they would be on their way to Covent Garden on the late-afternoon train from Angmering Station.

Because of Shirley's careful budgeting, Janet was able to pay each adult the going rate for the work – three shillings a day. The children were paid one and ninepence. No health or unemployment insurance was payable in respect of the children, but Janet had to insure everybody against accident while they worked for her. Seth and Vince were on the normal rate for a farm labourer. They both got three pounds a week.

There wasn't a lot of time for conversation, except at lunchtime, when everybody took a half-hour break. They sat in the barn for a little shelter from the sun, and

Shirley found herself sitting next to her old teacher. Granny Roberts was going round with the big teapot, but everyone was eating their own sandwiches.

Marilyn was thrilled to hear that Shirley's mum had decided to move to the country. 'There's a cottage for sale in Clapham,' she said. 'It's on the main road about halfway up the hill.'

'Where's Clapham?' Shirley asked.

'It's not far from Patching Pond,' said Marilyn. 'Virtually opposite Patching village.'

Shirley's eyes glistened with excitement. 'Do you know how much it is?'

Marilyn shook her head. 'I can't tell you, but most places around here are in the region of two hundred pounds.'

Two hundred pounds! If her mother got £410 for the shop in London, she'd have plenty to live on until she found her feet. 'Do you know who owns it?'

Again Marilyn wasn't sure, but she promised to find out. 'Someone told me Janet is moving,' she said.

Shirley nodded.

'Do you know where?'

'She's not saying.'

'Isn't Gilbert getting out of prison soon?'

Shirley was beginning to feel a little awkward. She didn't want to be drawn into a conversation about Janet. It would be all too easy to let something slip that might be repeated and give Mr Oliver a clue as to where Janet was. 'He's due out in October,' she said, looking at her watch. 'Gosh, it's half past one. I guess we'd better get back to work.'

'It sounds to me as if he's treated Janet the same way he treated Elizabeth,' said Marilyn, dusting the straw from her behind.

Although she was dying to know more, Shirley said nothing.

When four-thirty came, they were done. Although it had been a long, hard day, everyone had enjoyed themselves, and most of them had caught the sun. The trench was full and the rest of the potatoes were on their way to London. Tom went into the stables to give the horses a good rub-down and some oats as a special treat. Janet and Granny Roberts had arranged for everyone to share a meal on the meadow. While everyone took turns to have a wash in the scullery, Vince put some planks of wood across some old oil drums for a table and Granny Roberts covered it with a white sheet. Everybody sat around on whatever they could find. Some had chairs, but others managed on an old log or an upturned box. One girl had an upside-down bucket with a cushion on the top to protect her bottom from the rim, and the rest sat on blankets spread out on the grass. Some of the mothers came up from the village, bringing with them an array of dishes or plates of food, which were all put on the table. There were few men present – only the young lads and a couple of older men. The rest were at war, but that didn't stop the working party from having fun after they'd eaten. When the meal was almost finished, Vince got out his fiddle, and Seth played the spoons. Much to everyone's delight, Gwen sang a couple of songs, and while the women danced with each other, the children played kiss-chase or hide-and-seek.

At one point, they had to make a dash for it when a couple of German planes flew over, hotly pursued by two Spitfires. They were soon seen off, and everyone waved and cheered as the RAF boys disappeared over the horizon. The party broke up at around nine-thirty and they all began the long walk back to Angmering.

As Shirley lay in her bed that night, it was almost too hot to sleep. She only had a sheet over her and she had taken her nightie off, but even with the window wide open, the room was stifling. She stared at the ceiling and thought about her day. Tomorrow, Clay and some of the other Canadians would be coming to help move the pigs.

She wished Clay wasn't coming, but when she'd asked some of the other lads for help, he'd taken over, even though she'd told him time and again that she wasn't interested in him as a boyfriend. She'd tried telling him at the dance that she liked him as a friend and didn't want anything else, but he hadn't been listening. The last couple of times, he'd been on duty and unable to come to the social and she'd had a much better time. But then he'd started hanging around the farm and he was beginning to annoy her. He was critical too. 'Why have you put on that dress? You look much nicer in the blue one.'

As she thought about it, she began to bristle. He didn't own her. Nobody, she thought crossly, had the right to dictate to her what she should do. The trouble was, the pigs were too difficult for them to manage on their own. One was going to be slaughtered, but those belonging to the Pig Club were being moved to a new home. Janet was worried that when he got back, Mr Oliver would keep them for himself, so she'd found a small field next to the nursery on Station Road where the nurseryman said they could keep the pigs for a share of the meat at Christmas. They would have to make pens for them and make the area secure, which would mean a lot of hard work. The pigs were already big, so it would take every bit of muscle to keep them under control while they were being moved, and the Canadians were always boasting how strong they were, so let them get on with it! She and Janet would be in the orchard picking apples. Several ladies from the WI were coming to pick as well. There were few windfalls. The pigs had made good use of them, and although it was a tad too early to pick from the branches, she and Janet wanted some return on all their hard work.

Shirley was sure they'd make a tidy profit all round, certainly enough to give Janet and Lucy a decent start in their new life. What a pity Mr Oliver was such a dinosaur. With a little imagination, Oliver's Farm could be a really profitable business, as she, Janet and Granny Roberts had proved. On his last visit, Mr Telford had been delighted.

'I am impressed, Mrs Oliver,' he'd said. 'No, I'm more than impressed. You have done a magnificent job here, and because of that I am in a position to offer you a place on the government scheme for the share of a tractor. The horses have done a wonderful job, but a machine doesn't get tired and it doesn't need stabling.'

He'd been devastated when Janet had told him she and Lucy were leaving.

'The country needs people like you, Mrs Oliver, people who work hard and are willing to take advice. Are you sure I cannot persuade you?'

''fraid not,' said Janet.

Shirley sighed. She and Granny knew the reason Janet was going, but Mr Telford was no fool and he'd probably worked out that once Mr Oliver was back in charge, his wife would have no say in the matter. Shirley's mind drifted back to Elizabeth. She'd miss being in this lovely room, but she was glad that there was a real chance she would be staying in the area. She'd made some good friends here. She'd write to her mother tomorrow and tell her about the cottage.

Her gaze wandered towards the bedpost and the place where she'd found that poster. Odd that Elizabeth had put it there. A sudden thought struck her. There were four bedposts on this bed. What if Elizabeth had put something in each of them? Wide awake now, she knelt up and looked in the ones at the head of the bed. Nothing. They were quite empty. She stepped off the bed onto the floor and reached for the post at the foot

352

of the bed. It was a struggle getting the knob off, but when she looked inside, her heart almost stopped. It was just as she'd thought. Something else had been hidden down there.

# CHAPTER 28

It took some time to get the rolled-up paper out. Shirley had to resort to the pin from Elizabeth's workbox again, and she had to be careful not to tear it. As it emerged, she could see it was a newspaper cutting. She smoothed it out on the bed. One side was a jumble of bits and pieces, including part of an advertisement for a summer sale at Plummer's department store. Where was Plummer's? She didn't recall a shop in Worthing with that name. Smith & Strange, Hubbard's & Bentall's, but not Plummer's.

On the other side, she found a story about an inquest into the tragic death of a twin. Apparently, a young man, Stephen Oliver, aged twenty-seven and newly returned from the horrors of war, had bought a farm. The older brother to his twin, he had lost his leg after an injury refused to heal, and after all that he'd been through, this was to be the fresh start. The brothers had been estranged some years before because the younger one had brought shame on his family by trying to cheat an ageing relative out of some money. He had received a custodial sentence. Sadly, within a year of their reunion, the older brother, Stephen, was killed, trampled to death by cows. As it happened, the younger brother had been visiting his brother at the time. 'My brother and I patched things up,' he'd told the coroner. 'I was returning to my car when I heard a shout. I ran to the gate where the cows had gathered. That's when I saw my poor brother under their hoofs.' The article went on to describe how the witness had broken down and needed medical assistance before the court could proceed. The verdict was accidental death, and having died without a will, the farm had gone to his next of kin, Gilbert Oliver.

Shirley sat back and frowned. So what was all that stuff about the farm being in the family for six generations? She read the article again. The older brother *bought* the farm. He didn't inherit it, and if he was a cripple, what was he doing surrounded by cows, anyway? When she'd first come to the farm Shirley hadn't realized how dangerous cows could be, especially if they thought their young were under threat. If Stephen Oliver only had one leg, surely he would have known to be extra careful, and if he'd already been on the farm for a year, he would have known how to keep himself safe.

Shirley was puzzled as to why the cutting was there. The reason why Elizabeth had hidden the brochure was obvious. She'd wanted to look at it and remind herself of her wonderful future, but apart from the fact that it was about her husband, why keep this cutting hidden? There had to be something more significant about it. She wanted to talk to Janet, but somehow she felt she might worry her for nothing. It was then that she noticed a pencilled note written down the side of the cutting. It was as plain as a pikestaff once she'd seen it, but what did it mean?

'*Peach & Lemon Liverpool*,' then some unreadable blob, followed by '*573A64.*'

Peach & Lemon – was that some sort of crop? That didn't seem likely. Why hide it? Why write it on this particular cutting? 'Liverpool 573A64' looked a bit like a telephone number, apart from the 'A', and it couldn't be a number because there were too many digits. Most telephone numbers only had three digits. Dr Dyer's was Goring 952.

There was an indecipherable smudge after the word 'Liverpool'. Was that important? She got off the bed and looked down the tube again, but it was empty. When she climbed back into bed again, Shirley felt a kind of presence in the room. It wasn't spooky or upsetting, but she was sure Elizabeth was trying to tell her something. If only she knew what it was.

Granny Roberts had offered Florrie a room in her cottage until she could find a cottage to buy. It was a wonderfully generous offer and Florrie couldn't wait to meet the kind-hearted people who had cared for her children so well. She had accepted Len's offer to help her move over to Angmering. He'd managed to get compassionate leave and as soon as he saw her, he said he'd put in for a transfer to be closer to her. Whether he got it or not was anybody's guess. Being in the army, he didn't get much choice, but Len thought it worth a try. He'd borrowed someone's car and driven down from Yorkshire overnight. Dog-tired, he perked up as soon as he saw Florrie. She was wearing her best dress, the one she had worn when she'd first left home, a pink and blue striped dress with short sleeves and little buttons down the front. It was a good job the dress had a small belt at the waist. She had lost so much weight it hung on her. She had to make a new notch in the belt to make it fit snugly. Florrie felt a bit like a sack of potatoes tied in the middle, but what could she do? She had nothing else.

Florrie said her goodbyes on the ward and she and Len went out into the grounds. 'Oh, how I've missed you, my love,' he said, sweeping her up into his arms.

'Put me down, you great lummox,' she laughed, and he lowered her gently to the grass. 'You do think we're doing the right thing, don't you, Len?'

'Course we are.' He cupped her face in his hands and kissed her tenderly. Florrie's senses were reeling and she went weak at the knees. Her heart was pounding in her chest like a silly young girl's, and every part of her wanted more of him.

'From now on, you're Mrs Greene,' he said. 'My darling wife.'

Tears rimmed her eyes as she nodded. 'I'd really like to do what you said.'

He gave her a puzzled look.

'Go to church,' she reminded him, 'and make all those promises.'

'Then so we shall, my lovely.'

They held hands as they walked to the car.

'When do you have to go back?' she asked.

'Day after tomorrow,' he said, and her heart sank a little. 'I shall have to leave in good time if this Rolls-Can-'ardly is going to get me back.'

Florrie gave him a quizzical look.

'You've heard of a Rolls-Royce,' he said, grinning. 'Well, this is his younger brother. It can 'ardly start, can 'ardly get up a hill and can 'ardly stop when I brake.'

Florrie slapped his arm. 'Oh, Len,' she laughed.

As they drove away from Fontwell, she explained about the offer she'd had of a room at Mrs Roberts's place. 'It's just until I can find a place of my own.'

Len nodded. 'That's fine,' he said, 'but for the next couple of nights, I'm taking you to a hotel.' He leaned over and squeezed her hand. 'I'll help you look for a place tomorrow, but after all this time, I want you to myself.' He lifted her fingers to his lips and kissed them.

Florrie couldn't contain her smile. How wonderful. How exciting.

When they reached Angmering, they went straight up to the church. It was easy enough to find. There was nobody about, although the noticeboard said there was Holy Communion on a Wednesday. They pushed open the little door and stepped inside. For a moment or two, she wished she was wearing a better dress and that Shirley was her bridesmaid. Tom could have given her away if this was real. It was cool and shaded as they walked silently towards the altar. When they reached the front-row pews, Florrie bobbed a curtsey and Len bowed his head out of respect for the cross.

As they sat down together, a woman with a mop and bucket appeared. She gave them a quick smile and said, 'Good morning' as she went by. They watched her as she disappeared into what they supposed was a kitchen.

Florrie and Len sat in silence, each lost in their own thoughts. Florrie stared at the stained-glass window and wondered how many eyes had admired and learned from the message they'd brought over the centuries that the church had been in existence: the birth of Christ, the crucifixion and the empty tomb. Len looked up at the vaulted archway, where a hundred years before, some Victorian artist had painted the Ten Commandments, the Lord's Prayer and the Creed down the sides and across the top.

After the sound of running water and the clanking of her bucket in the sink had stopped, the cleaning woman reappeared. She wore no hat, but she had a shopping bag over her arm. They made no eye contact as she padded past them and out of the church. The door closed softly behind her and Len took Florrie's hands in his.

'I don't remember all the words, Florrie, love, but as God is my witness, I love you with all my heart.' He let go of her hands and reached into his pocket to pull out a small box. His hand trembled as he put the ring on her finger. 'With my body I thee worship, with this ring I thee wed, and I promise to love you all the days of my life.'

Florrie looked up at him with tears in her eyes. 'And I promise always to be faithful to you, Len,' she said, 'all my life until death do us part.'

He leaned over and whispered in her ear, 'And I promise that as soon as we can, we'll make this all legal and proper, but I'm saying before God, you are my wife.'

She laid her head on his shoulder and they sat for a while enjoying the warmth of each other's bodies and the glow of what they'd just done.

'Is everything all right?' The vicar's interruption made Florrie and Len jump. They sat up straight.

'The wife and I just came in for a few minutes in the peace and quiet, sir.'

The vicar nodded. 'Soldier, thank you for what you are doing to protect our country,' he said. 'I for one appreciate your sacrifice and dedication.'

Len was taken by surprise, but he said, 'Thank you, sir.'

The vicar held out his hand for Len to shake. 'My name is Reverend Theodore Wright. May I offer you a prayer of blessing?'

Len glanced at Florrie. 'Much appreciated, sir.'

Later, as they strolled back to the car, Florrie said, 'Do you think that was a sign?'

He patted her hand, which was threaded over his arm, and grinned. 'Most definitely, my lovely.'

When her mother appeared at the gate, Shirley let out a whoop of delight, which brought Tom from the stables.

They all greeted each other with hugs and dancing on the spot.

'Come into the house,' Shirley cried. 'We thought you'd be here a lot later, so Janet and Lucy have popped down to the village. I'll make us a cup of tea and then I'll take you to meet Granny Roberts.'

'What on earth is that?' cried Florrie when she saw the dartboard on the wall.

'That's Granny Roberts's idea of a good laugh,' said Shirley, explaining how it all came about, and she was pleased to see that her mother enjoyed the joke.

Florrie was impressed with Shirley's room and the farmhouse in general.

'Does Tom mind being on the landing?' she whispered anxiously.

'No,' said Shirley, wondering if she should tell her where they had slept when they'd first come here.

'I can see the stars,' said Tom, coming up the stairs behind them. He threw himself onto the bed to demonstrate how the skylight window was directly above him. 'Sometimes I see the Spitfires too.'

'I'm glad you like it,' said Florrie.

'Come and see where I work,' said Tom. 'I want to show you the horses. The pigs have all gone now . . .'

Shirley smiled as she heard him clatter downstairs with her mother and went to put the kettle on. Half an hour later, as they swapped more stories, Shirley noticed her mother's ring. 'Is that new?'

Florrie nodded. 'Len gave it to me.'

Shirley seemed puzzled. Why would Len give her

mother a new wedding ring? Florrie glanced anxiously at Len.

'I've only got a couple of days,' he began, 'so your mother and me went to the church before we came here.'

'You got married?' Shirley squeaked.

'We said our vows,' said Len, glancing at Florrie, 'and the vicar gave us his blessing.'

Shirley's face fell. 'But I don't understand,' she said crossly. 'How could you get married without even bothering to tell us? Surely you must have known we would have wanted to be there.'

Tom looked confused.

'I know,' Florrie began, 'but you see—'

'It was all my fault,' Len interrupted. 'I persuaded her. We had a special arrangement. I know I'm being selfish, but' – he took Florrie's hand in his – 'I've got to go back the day after tomorrow and I wanted your mother all to myself for as long as possible. A big day and a party would mean we wouldn't have much time together.' He looked contrite. 'I'm sorry. I hope you can both forgive me. It's only for two days and then she's all yours.'

Florrie could see the indignation in her daughter's eyes fading.

Len continued to look sheepish. 'Perhaps we could have a bit of a shindig the next time I come home?'

Shirley hesitated for a second; then she hugged Len's arm. 'Oh, all right. You're on, but you're still very naughty.'

'That I am,' said Len, giving Florrie a wink.

'Is it all right, then, Shirl?' said Tom.

'Course it is,' said Shirley. 'Mum and Uncle Len have just got married.'

Len held out his hand and Tom shook it warmly. 'Does that mean you're my dad now?'

Len clapped him on the shoulder. 'If that's what you'd like, son, then I'd be honoured.' He looked at Shirley again. 'There's one more thing. I'm taking your ma away with me on honeymoon. It's all booked and I'll bring her back first thing the day after tomorrow.'

It seemed strange to wave them goodbye almost as soon as they'd got here, especially as they didn't even wait to meet Janet and Lucy, but Shirley couldn't be upset. It was obvious Uncle Len adored her mother and she'd never seen her looking so relaxed and happy.

# CHAPTER 29

When Marilyn came over to see Shirley late the next day, the pair of them biked up to Clapham to have a look at the cottage for sale. Sadly, it wasn't at all suitable. Neglected for far too long, it had grass at the front a mile high, ivy growing inside the front door, a broken window had let in the rain, and it was obvious when they peered through the window that the floorboards were rotten. What's more, judging by the amount of mouse and rat droppings, the place was infested.

'That's a shame,' said Marilyn. 'I'm sorry to have dragged you up here.'

'Don't be silly,' said Shirley. 'It was worth a try, and it was a nice ride.'

'There are other cottages around here,' said Marilyn. 'A lot of them belong to the Castle Goring estate and can only be rented, but some belonged to woodlanders. They would have lived in them when they worked the copses making hurdles.'

'Hurdles?' said Shirley.

'Fences,' said Marilyn, 'for sheep pens and stuff. Did you know there's a copse called Olliver's Copse?'

'Really?' said Shirley. 'Does it belong to the farm?'

'I shouldn't think so,' said Marilyn. 'The spelling is different. It's got two "l"s. It's the same as the spelling on the miller's tomb on Highdown Hill. Tell you what, let's bike back that way and I'll show you.'

Olliver's Copse was close to Swillage Lane. Even though it was overgrown and unmanaged, Shirley could see at once that it had potential. This was a sheep-farming area. The Findon Sheep Fair, held in September, was famous, and Findon was less than three miles away. This year, because of the war, the fair itself was to be moved to West Grinstead, presumably to be well away from the Battle of Britain, but why on earth were shepherds buying their pens from elsewhere when, with a little work, they could have local hazel hurdles? She sighed. If only they had a few years instead of a few weeks left at the farm, she could perhaps approach the manager of the Castle Goring estate and revive some of the old skills.

The two girls found a shady tree and parked their bicycles. Shirley took out a blanket she'd put in the clip over the back wheel. They spread it out and sat down to enjoy their sandwiches and an apple. The views were fantastic. It was only now that Shirley appreciated that the village of Angmering itself was in a dip.

'This is the life,' sighed Marilyn, leaning back against the tree. 'Are you still seeing Clay?'

Shirley shook her head.

'Oh dear,' said Marilyn. 'What happened?'

Shirley shrugged. 'He's a nice boy, but I'm only sixteen. I don't want to be tied down.'

'Have a bit of fun first, eh?' Marilyn teased.

'Something like that,' said Shirley, although she had no intention of having fun with Clay. They drowsed in the warm sunshine. 'I want to show you something,' she said, taking out the newspaper cutting she'd found stuffed down the bedpost. 'It's about Stephen and Gilbert Oliver. Did you know Mr Oliver had a twin?'

'No, I didn't,' said Marilyn. She read the cutting quickly. 'Well, I'm blowed.' As she handed it back, she noted the expression on Shirley's face. 'You think there's something more to it, don't you?'

'Let's go over what we know,' said Shirley, sitting up and hugging her knees. 'Elizabeth was your friend. You and Reuben were going away with her, but then someone kills Reuben and puts his body in the culvert.'

Marilyn nodded uncertainly. 'Yes.'

'Reuben, a man whom everyone likes, a man who has no enemies,' Shirley continued. 'And at the same time, Elizabeth, another popular person, falls into Patching Pond and despite a valiant attempt by her husband, she drowns.'

'I see what you're driving at,' said Marilyn as she sat up, 'but it's a coincidence. Gilbert didn't know anything about us going to Cape Town.' She paused. 'Are you thinking that the two are connected?'

'I think you do too, if you're honest,' said Shirley.

Marilyn looked away. 'You're right. I just didn't want

to put it into words.' She sighed. 'Once you voice it, there's no going back.'

Shirley leaned forward. 'But now that you know Reuben didn't run off and leave you, don't you want to find out what happened to him?'

'The police are convinced that he was set upon by some roaming gypsies,' said Marilyn.

'How very convenient,' said Shirley sarcastically. She held up the cutting. 'I have read and reread this cutting and some things just don't add up. What was Stephen doing in the middle of a herd of cows? You watch Vince and Seth when they're herding. They always stay on the outside of moving cattle.'

'He was a novice farmer.'

'One who had at least a year's experience,' Shirley pointed out. 'He would have known how to stay safe by that time.'

Marilyn's eyes grew wide. 'If you're suggesting what I think you're suggesting, we're talking about a serial killer.'

Shirley nodded.

'But this is Angmering,' cried Marilyn. 'A sleepy Sussex village where nothing ever happens. Murders happen in London and Manchester.'

'We're the same people wherever we live,' said Shirley sagely.

Marilyn smiled reluctantly. 'For one so young, you're a wise old bird, Shirley Jenkins.'

'And another thing,' Shirley went on. 'Why was Elizabeth at the pond that day? Don't give me all that stuff about holly trees and Christmas wreaths. I walked right round that pond and I couldn't find a single holly tree.'

Marilyn's eyes grew wide.

Shirley held out the cutting again. 'What do you make of that?' She was pointing to the pencilled note at the side.

'I didn't notice that,' cried Marilyn.

'It took me a while to see it,' said Shirley. 'Peach and lemon – they hardly go together.

'There's a solicitor called Mr Lemon in Worthing,' said Marilyn. 'Yes, that's it! He's in Liverpool Gardens. That's where all the solicitors are.'

'So that blob there is the word "Gardens"? It's not long enough.'

'You can write it "Gns",' said Marilyn.

Shirley felt a tingle of excitement. 'What do you make of the numbers? 573A64.'

'They could be the number of the street,' Marilyn mused. 'No, that's ridiculous. Maybe a file number?'

They looked at each other, startled. 'Oh my goodness,' cried Shirley. 'That's it. It's a file number. Elizabeth wanted whoever found this cutting to take it to Peach & Lemon in Liverpool Gardens.'

Marilyn frowned. 'What for?'

'I have no idea,' said Shirley, 'but you can bet your life I mean to find out.'


This stone had to be really special. Florrie and Len were walking on the seashore near Ferring, one of the few remaining parts of the beach not covered in barbed wire. The day was overcast, but there was a gentle breeze coming off the sea. Two dogs were running ahead of them, one barking at nothing at all and the other, a much older animal, loping along behind him. The owner kept to the grass verge and hardly noticed Florrie and Len passing by.

The tide was out and their feet pressed water from the sand as they walked. Florrie turned to watch the water bleed back into their footprints, leaving a shallow imprint, a record of where they had been. It looked solid enough, but of course the little marks would be washed away once the tide came back in and there would be no sign that they had ever been here.

She recalled part of a poem she'd once read. *But all shall be well and all shall be well and all manner of things shall be well* ... Comforting words, but she couldn't remember where she'd seen them. Florrie was in maudlin mood, which was why she was looking for a memory stone.

She hadn't collected one for years. She'd started collecting them when she was young, and up until the time Sid left, she had done it for every landmark occasion in her life. She'd kept them in her drawer in her bedroom. She hadn't opened that drawer for at least a year, but they were still there. One for the day she'd met Sid, one for the day she married, a few others scattered in between and another for the day Shirley and Tom were born. After that, she hadn't wanted to keep her memories, but she did today.

'What about that one?' said Len, pointing to a distinctive-looking stone at his feet.

Florrie shook her head. It was nice but not quite right for the occasion. 'It's too dark,' she said as she slipped her arm through his.

Last night had been wonderful. The hotel, just across the road from the beach at East Worthing, had been warm and inviting. They had dumped their things and then Len had taken her to a swanky hotel for dinner. She dreaded to think how much their meal cost, but it was delicious. Just before they'd gone in, he'd sprinkled a little confetti over them. Of course, as Len had intended, the waiter spotted it, and much to Florrie's embarrassment, the manager had offered them a free drink to celebrate.

'You are naughty,' she'd whispered when he'd gone.

'Aren't I just,' he grinned as he leaned back in the chair.

They'd strolled back in the half-light. There were no street lights, of course, but it wasn't pitch-black or anything like it. Where it was difficult to see the pavement they were guided by the white bands painted onto the bottom of the trees and lampposts to keep them safe from the edge of the road, and there were hardly any cars, anyway.

She'd felt quite shy when they were alone, but Len was a considerate lover. She could tell he was holding back until she was ready, and when he finally entered her, she felt as if her whole being melted into his. The first time was over quickly, but there were two other

370

occasions before they got up for breakfast, each one more delicious than the last.

After a breakfast fit for a king, they walked into town. It was a pretty place, perhaps a little old-fashioned, but Florrie liked it. They came down Warwick Street and into the main shopping area. Of course, the preparations for invasion had scarred the town hall, which had a large bunker right in front of it and an above-ground air-raid shelter in front of that. Even the kerb stones had been painted black and white to aid motorists and pedestrians in the blackout, but Florrie and Len did their best to ignore the reminders of war as they held hands and peered in shop windows.

'I want to buy you a dress,' he said suddenly.

'I'm not sure if I have enough coupons,' she said, laughing.

'Then use mine,' he said, dragging her into Hubbard's at the end of South Street.

The lady in the dress department was quite snooty until Len told her they were on their honeymoon and then she couldn't have been more helpful. In the end, Florrie chose a delightful print button-through short-sleeved dress with a white collar and cuffs. At Len's insistence, the woman bagged up Florrie's old dress and she wore the new one right away. It was beautiful, and best of all, it fitted properly.

They couldn't walk along the seafront in town. Large concrete anti-tank blocks, each about six feet square, had been put up all along the shoreline. They couldn't go onto the pier either. A huge hole had been blown in the middle to stop enemy ships unloading supplies at the pier-head. It didn't matter. Len and Florrie were content to keep walking.

This was the first time since they'd known each other that Florrie and Len were on their own. When they'd talked after making love last night, she'd finally understood how much he'd longed to tell her that he loved her. At first, she'd wept for the wasted years, but he'd held her close and told her they mustn't think of that. 'We still have the future,' he'd told her. But what future did they have? She stared out to sea and the distant horizon. What if Hitler really did come over the Channel? What if, like Churchill said, they'd end up having to fight them on the beaches and the streets and the hills? What if Len got killed? She gave a little shudder.

'Cold?' he asked anxiously.

She linked her arm through his and moved closer. He bent down and kissed her tenderly.

The beach was deserted, but how could she enjoy all this peace and tranquillity when her brain was going nineteen to the dozen? If she wasn't worrying about the future, she was letting her imagination run riot and fretting about what might have been. She brushed a renegade tear from her eye. 'Gosh, that wind is keen,' she said as she noticed Len's anxious look.

They reached the pebbles near the cafe and Len sat down. Florrie flopped close beside him, longing for the warmth of his body.

'When we're old and grey,' Len said, putting his arm

round her shoulders, 'I'll bring you back here and we'll remember this day.'

Florrie scanned the beach and spotted a dusty-pink stone. What an unusual colour. Every other stone was speckled or grey or black or chalk-white. It felt special. It felt like a memory stone. She picked it up and showed Len.

'Pretty,' he said, and then he gave her a long, hungry look. Without a word, they both got to their feet.

On the long walk back to the hotel, their urgency grew. Back in their room, Len locked the door and Florrie pulled the curtain before they lay down on the bed. And later, as he ran his finger down her naked thigh, Florrie knew they wouldn't be going out again today.

# CHAPTER 30

It seemed that Mother Nature had been particularly kind this year. Even the hedgerows were bursting with fruit. Towards evening was the best time to go blackberrying, so armed with a walking stick and an old umbrella, Florrie and Shirley set out. Granny Roberts was in her kitchen, busy bottling jams and chutney and putting fruit into Kilner jars ready for the winter, so they worked their way along the hedgerows towards the woods.

The countryside wasn't without its hazards. The Canadian soldiers had been digging anti-tank trenches, and several fields had big skull-and-crossbones signs in both English and German warning of minefields. There were no mines, of course. It was merely a ruse designed to make life as difficult as possible for any invader.

Just back from her two-day honeymoon, Florrie had a lot of catching-up to do. 'So what exactly is Mr Oliver like?' she asked.

Her question took Shirley by surprise, but at the same time she was glad to be given the opportunity to get everything out in the open. She decided not to hold back anything of real importance, and Florrie did her best to listen without interruption, although several times surprise got the better of her.

'You don't mean he made both you and Tom sleep in that tiny space beyond the scullery? Oh, Shirley, that's awful. If only I had known.'

'It looks a lot better now,' said Shirley. 'We did it up when Vince came. When Tom and I were in there, the door didn't fit and half a gale blew under it.'

Florrie was shocked.

'It's all right, Mum,' said Shirley with a chuckle. 'We survived, and besides, what could you have done about it?'

'Couldn't they have sent you somewhere else?'

Shirley pulled a face. 'Nobody else wanted us.'

Florrie was stricken.

'It turned out all right in the end,' said Shirley reassuringly, 'and Tom loves being a farmer. Vince and Seth only have to show him what to do once and he takes to it straight away.'

'Do you really think he's happy?'

'I know he is, Mum,' said Shirley. 'You remember how, when he was worried about something, he always wanted a story? Well, he hasn't asked me for one in months.'

'He certainly looks happy and settled, and yet you're all planning to leave.'

'Mum, there's something about Mr Oliver I need to tell you.'

'Ooh, mind that bramble,' said Florrie. 'You're all

caught up in it. Let me help you or you'll tear your frock.'

'You know I told you Mr Oliver is in jail,' Shirley said as they extricated the skirt of her dress from the bush. 'Well, Janet's marriage isn't a proper marriage.'

'What on earth do you mean?' said Florrie, echoes of her own marriage immediately coming to mind.

'Janet hates him,' said Shirley. 'She only married him to get herself out of a hole. You see, she was having a baby and her stepmother threw her out. Marriage to Mr Oliver gave her a roof over her head, but she regrets it now. Oh, look – there's loads on that branch up there. Can you reach them?'

'She seems like a nice girl,' said Florrie as she used the umbrella handle to pull the branch down while Shirley picked the fruit.

'She is, Mum,' said Shirley, 'and she deserves better. He's horrible to her.' She toyed briefly with telling her mother about her suspicion that he'd meant to do Lucy harm that day on the landing, but in the end decided not to. By the time Mr Oliver got back home, they'd all be long gone, and in the meantime, if she knew, her mother would only worry. And as for the rest – Elizabeth's death and the discovery of Reuben's body – she kept that to herself for now. She had an appointment with Mr Peach in Liverpool Gardens for the following Wednesday at 2 p.m. Whatever Elizabeth had left in his keeping might throw a different light on the matter.

Her mother said nothing, so Shirley didn't pursue it.

'How's the sale of the shop going?' she said, changing the subject.

'Slowly, but it seems the right thing to do,' said her mother. 'You and Tom have taken to country living, and the fresh air is so much better for my health too. I really enjoyed being in the glasshouse at the convalescent home, so it seemed like a logical step.' She didn't mention that here in Sussex she could start afresh much more easily with a different name without people questioning her. As far as the folks around here knew, she really was Mrs Greene. There was a slight pause; then Florrie said, 'Now that you've told me about Janet, I understand why you think it's a bad idea to stay at the farm.'

'Is Uncle Len happy about leaving London?'

Florrie's expression softened. 'He says he'll be happy wherever we are.' She glanced over at her daughter. 'You don't mind us being together?'

'Oh, Mum,' said Shirley, putting her bowl down on the ground, 'I'm absolutely thrilled.' She threw her arms around Florrie and gave her a hug.

Returning the hug with one of her own, Florrie smiled. 'Shirley, there's something else I have to tell you.'

'Oh dear,' Shirley joked. 'This is beginning to be a bit like a priest's confessional.'

She stepped back and her mother's expression was so serious that for a minute Shirley was seized with panic. Dear Lord, she wasn't ill again, was she? 'Mum? What is it?'

'It's about your grandmother,' Florrie began. She held both her daughter's sticky hands in hers and looked her in the eye. 'I think you're going to be shocked by what I'm about to tell you, but I hope you will find it in your heart to understand.'

Shirley could see this was going to be a long story, so she backed towards an old tree trunk and they both sat down.

'When I was your age, my father had been in the war for two years and apart from ten days' leave in 1915, I hadn't seen him,' Florrie began. Leaving out the bit about him going AWOL and being put on a charge when he was caught, she went on, 'Money was tight, so to make ends meet, Mother took in lodgers: first, Mr Payne and then Captain Faversham-Wood. I had little to do with them. I had been taught to be polite, so I answered their questions, but I kept out of their way. After six months, when Mr Payne left, Mother didn't get a replacement. I never questioned anything she did. Apart from the war, life was quite good. My friends and I went roller-skating whenever we could. I'd got plenty of pretty dresses, which attracted admiring looks wherever I went.' She let out a wistful sigh. 'There were church socials, and we used to go for walks by the river. I loved reading romances and I always dreamed that some handsome knight in shining armour would carry me off on his white horse.'

Shirley squeezed her mother's hand. Florrie hurriedly wiped a tear from her cheek with her hand, leaving behind a blackberry-stained smear. 'I had noticed that

378

Mum and Captain Faversham-Wood got on particularly well. I would often hear them laughing together, and occasionally they went to the music hall or out for a walk of an evening. Mother often ran errands for him as well. He would give her an envelope and she'd have to deliver these letters to somebody. "Just a little favour your mother does for me," Captain Faversham-Wood used to tell me when he saw me watching my mother setting off. I just shrugged. It was nothing to do with me.'

She gave Shirley a wobbly smile. 'It wasn't until a few months later, when my best friend, Edna, made a remark about Mother putting on weight that I began to put two and two together. "They say your mother is carrying on with your lodger," Edna said. Of course, I was furious.' Florrie sighed. Shirley slipped her arm round her mother's shoulders. 'The sad thing is, I really liked Edna, but I never spoke to her again.'

Shirley said nothing.

'Then one night, there was an almighty row,' Florrie went on. 'When it was over, Captain Faversham-Wood had gone and Mother was distraught. A little later, the police turned up and arrested her.'

'Arrested her?' Shirley gasped.

Florrie nodded. 'As you can imagine, it was an awful shock. The trial lasted four days. I went to the court every day. I could hardly believe it. Mother was accused of passing information to the benefit of the enemy, but not only that, she was expecting Captain Faversham-Wood's baby as well. The shame and disgrace were terrible.'

'Oh, Mum,' said Shirley.

Florrie gulped and blew her nose. 'When the guilty verdict came,' she said, stuffing her hanky up her sleeve again, 'the neighbours took it out on me. My father came back home, but he was so terribly ill I had to do everything for him. I couldn't look after Mother's baby as well, so she had to be adopted or grow up in a home for destitute children. Then someone told me about Mrs Andrews. She sometimes helped distressed women.'

'I can't believe this,' said Shirley. 'I had no idea . . .'

'The last time I saw my mother,' Florrie went on with a sad smile on her lips, 'she said, "You've been a good daughter to me. Please don't tell your father what I've done," and I never did. He wouldn't have understood anyway. He was a wreck of a man.'

'But Mrs Andrews found the baby a home?'

Florrie nodded. 'She found a lovely couple who were just dying for a baby. It was of some consolation that when we met, Ruth told me she'd been well looked after.'

'You've actually met her?' said Shirley, her eyes widening.

'She came to the convalescent home,' said Florrie. 'She's awfully nice. She was upset with me at first, but she's all right now.'

'Why was she upset?'

'There was a silly misunderstanding,' said Florrie. 'She thought I was her mother.'

'So she's my aunt,' said Shirley.

Florrie nodded.

'And my grandmother, where's she?'

'They exonerated her in the 1930s,' said Florrie, her voice tight with emotion, 'but of course by that time it was far too late.'

'She'd died,' said Shirley sadly.

Florrie brushed an imaginary crumb from her lap. 'Your grandmother had been found guilty of high treason. The penalty for that was hanging,' she said simply.

The long, hot summer gave way to the more balmy days of autumn. In keeping with farming tradition, Shirley, Tom and Janet repaid the kindness shown to them when lifting the potato crop by helping other farmers in the area get their harvests in. Some days, they would be lending a hand in the fields, and other days picking fruit. The Battle of Britain was still raging and they often had to dive for cover into ditches or a purpose-built air-raid shelter (if they were lucky) to avoid the fighting overhead. Despite the difficulties they faced, everyone worked hard, loving the sense of all pulling together.

The first week in September saw the beginning of the harvest festival services in the local churches, and on Sunday September 8th, the king called a National Day of Prayer. It couldn't have been more timely. The night before, starting at 6.30 p.m., the skies over the Channel were thick with German planes. They came over, wave after wave of them, for hours and hours. There was little activity in Sussex, but when Janet switched on the wireless, each bulletin seemed to bring worse news. By morning, the heaviest bombardment of the war had left three hundred dead and more than a thousand people injured. Not only that but a large part of London was ablaze, and because it was only sixty miles away, when she'd padded outside to the lavvy last night, Shirley had seen a red glow on the distant horizon.

In Angmering, everybody set out early for St Margaret's, including Florrie and her children and Granny Roberts. As they walked, they passed the place where just the day before, Florrie had told Shirley about her grandmother's conviction and Ruth. It hadn't been easy, but Shirley had been overwhelmed with sympathy for her mother's predicament. When she'd stood up from the tree stump, they'd held each other for a long time and wept.

For Florrie, it was a moment of tremendous release. Now all the people who mattered the most to her, with the exception of Tom, who probably wouldn't understand, knew the whole truth. She didn't have to hide her heartache, or feel guilty any more; she didn't even have to hold on to her regrets. She had done what she could and it was all in the past now. When Ruth had had a bit of time to nurse her wounds, she would invite her to meet her family.

As for Shirley, the revelation had been the stuff of a mystery writer's imagination. It was a lot to take in. She'd mulled it over for hours, and although she had always respected her mother, now she held her in the highest esteem. If Shirley thought she'd had it tough for her age, it was nothing in comparison to what her mother had had to deal with. It must have been awful for her. As she'd lain in bed that night, another thought had crossed Shirley's mind. She would never say it to her mother, but it was all rather exciting too. Everybody had a skeleton in the family cupboard, and hers was quite something compared to other people's.

As they reached the end of Dappers Lane, Florrie said, 'I heard someone on the radio saying that last night's raid in London was worse than the Silvertown explosion.'

'Whatever was that?' Janet asked.

'A whole lot of TNT went up at Brunner Mond back in 1917,' said Florrie.

'I remember that,' cried Granny Roberts. 'It was in all the papers at the time. Something like nine hundred homes were destroyed, weren't they?'

Florrie nodded. 'They said it was the largest explosion in history,' she said.

'Will everybody move to the country like us now?' asked Tom.

'I shouldn't think so, love,' said Florrie. 'It'd take more than a few bombs to shift them out of London. And if I know the people of Canning Town, it'll make them all the more determined to stick it out no matter what.'

'But you won't go back, will you?' asked Granny Roberts.

Florrie shook her head. 'I've already found a buyer for my shop. I've signed the papers at my end, so as soon as Mr Mills signs at his end, I shall be free to make new choices.'

Janet raised an eyebrow. 'And how was the honeymoon?' she teased.

Florrie laughed. 'All too short,' she said, 'but we went to a lovely place called Worthing. Ever heard of it?'

'I think I might have done,' said Janet with a grin.

'Have you found anywhere you'd like to buy, Mum?' Shirley asked.

'Not yet,' Florrie confessed, 'but I'm going to look at a cottage over the bridge at Rustington tomorrow.'

'Um, that's not far away,' said Janet.

'I'm not sure if it's suitable,' said Florrie, 'but it is a very reasonable price.'

'I don't want to leave the farm,' said Tom. 'I like the animals.'

'I know, love,' said Florrie, 'but we'll find you another job.'

'With animals?'

Shirley glanced anxiously at her mother as she nodded. 'With animals.'

They arrived at the church in good time for the service, but it was already packed, with standing room only. They squeezed down the side and stood at the back, although a younger man did give up his seat for Granny Roberts. The service included prayers for the Royal Family, for Mr Churchill and the government, and for the people of London. After each was said, every 'Amen' from the congregation was heartfelt and sincere.

They all went back to Granny Roberts's for lunch. Janet had contributed to it as well, so they sat down to rabbit stew and dumplings, Oliver's Farm potatoes and carrots, followed by apple pie and custard. They squashed themselves into her little kitchen, although after a few minutes, Seth and Vince decided to sit outside, complaining that they couldn't get their arms up to put their forks in their mouths.

'Huh,' said Granny, when they'd gone. 'They want to have a beer more like.'

After such a busy period, it was good for the women to relax during the afternoon. They didn't talk much. It was nice just to sit and do nothing, to knit or read a book. At milking time, the men and Tom went back to the farm to see to the cows, while the women laid the table for tea. By the time they came back, it was groaning with sandwiches and a cake, even though no one was particularly hungry after such a large dinner.

'Telegram for you, Florrie,' said Vince.

Florrie thought he was joking at first, but then she saw that his face was deadly serious. The colour drained from her cheeks and she clutched at her throat. Oh God, don't tell me something has happened to Len, she thought darkly.

'I didn't think they delivered telegrams on a Sunday,' Shirley remarked.

'Sunday mornings they do,' said Janet.

'The telegram boy was too scared to go back with it undelivered, so he was sitting outside the back door waiting for you to come home,' said Vince. 'I think it might have been his first job.'

'He looked really worried,' said Seth, 'but he felt a bit better when Vince slipped him a bob for his trouble.'

Florrie lowered herself down onto a chair and opened the telegram with trembling hands. Everyone watched her anxiously. As she read the first few words, Florrie took in her breath noisily, and then covering her mouth with her hand, she burst into tears.

'What is it, Mum?'

The flimsy paper fluttered onto the table. They all looked from one to another, but it was Shirley who picked it up and read it out loud.

'*Terrible bombing last night stop. Shop took direct hit stop. Betty missing stop. Love Doreen.*'

# CHAPTER 31

The next few days were pretty fraught. Understandably, Florrie was distraught by the news from London. It was bad enough that her shop had been blown to bits, but she was far more upset about Betty. She had been such a wonderful friend, and the thought of her going like that was almost too much to bear. A day or two after the telegram came, Doreen had written to say that Betty had been packing up Florrie's things in anticipation of the sale when the air raid had sounded. There had been air raids before, but this one had begun in broad daylight. The ack-ack guns had done their best, but the sheer numbers of German bombers overhead had meant it was hopeless. No one could be absolutely sure what happened, because Betty was on her own, but the educated guess was that she never even made it to the air-raid shelter in time. The docks were the main target, and of course they were in a tightly packed residential area, so by the end of the first day, it was said that over four hundred people had been killed and more than thirteen hundred injured. Apart from a two-hour reprieve at six o'clock in the evening, the raid had continued until four-thirty the next morning.

*It seemed like the blighters were coming over every two or three minutes*, Doreen wrote. *The racket was just awful, and what with the sound of the engines and the bombs dropping, not to mention the guns, I thought my poor head would split in two.*

To Florrie's immense disappointment, a couple of days later, her solicitor wrote to say that Mr Mills hadn't signed the papers, so the loss of the shop was hers. In one fell swoop she'd lost everything.

Shirley comforted her as best she could, but she could see that her mother was in no fit state to make decisions about her future. She shared Florrie's sense of grief over Betty, and the loss of the shop made it quite apparent that teacher training would have to wait. From what she could gather, her mother had a bit put by in the bank, but nowhere near enough to buy a property. Perhaps it was just as well. Right now, Shirley was angry enough to take Hitler on single-handed.

It seemed somehow fitting that Shirley should arrive at the offices of Peach & Lemon on the brink of a thunderstorm. Thick, dark clouds had been gathering out to sea ever since the early morning, and as she dashed inside, the skies opened.

The reception area was empty. Good. That gave her time to slow her breathing and compose herself. She glanced around the dingy office as a brilliant flash of lightning suddenly lit the dark green and cream walls.

With the exception of one photograph, framed and faded certificates hung from the picture rails. Shirley's laboured breathing slowed as she moved closer to look at the photograph, which was of a large crowd of sombre townspeople standing in front of a monument outside the new town hall. In the foreground, a woman was making a speech, but every eye was on the drapes that were being pulled away from the life-size figure in bronze, the British Tommy, his arm raised above his head and his tin helmet in his hand to represent victory. The impressive statue had been paid for by the ordinary people of the town with their hard-earned shillings. The date underneath said, '1921,' and the names of the dignitaries present were recorded on a gold-painted plaque. The mayoress, who was making the speech, was Mrs Chapman, and the man who had officially unveiled the memorial was Field Marshal Sir William Robertson. As the thunder growled above the building, the irony wasn't lost on Shirley and she sighed. There they were, commemorating those brave men who had died in the war to end all wars when, less than twenty years on, the country was at war again.

She heard footfall behind her, and taking a lungful of air, turned as a soberly dressed woman wearing a small brooch on the lapel of her navy dress came up behind her. Her hair was held in a roll at the nape of her neck, and she peered at Shirley over her tortoiseshell glasses. She was smart, but her shoes, black brogue-fronted lace-ups with a small heel, although highly polished, had seen better days.

'Good afternoon,' she said. 'I apologize for keeping you waiting. I didn't realize anyone was here. Do you have an appointment?'

Shirley smiled. 'With Mr Peach at two-thirty,' she said.

'Did I hear someone taking my name in vain?' said a voice behind her.

'Your afternoon appointment, Mr Peach,' said the woman as Shirley turned to see who it was.

'Thank you, Mrs Webb,' he said, and extending his hand towards Shirley, he added, 'Miss Jenkins? Come this way, will you? Oh, and could you bring us some tea, Mrs Webb?'

Shirley followed as he walked from the reception area down a dark corridor. He was younger than she'd expected. He looked about thirty-five or forty, clean-shaven, roughly five foot six, slim rather than thin, and he was dressed in a tired-looking brown pinstriped suit. She wondered vaguely why he wasn't in uniform, but then noticed his profound lurch to one side as he walked and realized why he hadn't been called up. He had a built-up shoe because his left leg was at least five or six inches shorter than the right.

'Filthy weather,' he remarked as they reached his office, and Shirley agreed. If the rain didn't ease up a bit, she was going to get soaked running for the bus.

The room itself was rather poky, very cluttered and dominated by a huge desk, which was covered with bits of paper, biscuit crumbs and an overflowing ashtray. A pile of casually stacked paper almost obliterated a typewriter. It was noisy too. She could hear the rain pummelling down on a corrugated-tin roof somewhere close by. As he walked round his desk, Mr Peach indicated that she should sit on the chair opposite. 'Now, what can I do for you?'

Shirley showed him the cutting and waited patiently while he read it.

For a second or two, Mr Peach seemed confused, and then his face lit up. 'Ah yes, Mrs Oliver. I remember her. A charming woman. You should have had a letter with this. Do you have the letter?'

Shirley shook her head.

'No matter,' he said. 'You're fortunate that I remember the lady and her instructions well. It wasn't a legal document, more of a favour really.'

Shirley stared at him with a blank expression as he began to clear a space on the top of his desk. The door opened again and Mrs Webb came in with a tray of tea. She put it down in the space he'd cleared, and scribbling the number from the side of the cutting on a piece of paper, he said, 'Mrs Webb, would you get me this file? It will be in the second basement, I believe.'

As she hurried to do his bidding, Mr Peach poured some tea. 'If I remember correctly,' he went on, 'she was going to South America . . . no, no, South Africa. Do you ever hear from her? Has she settled in well?' He pushed a cup towards Shirley and indicated the sugar bowl on the tray. Although she didn't have sugar in her tea, Shirley was amused to notice what looked like a

391

salt spoon in the sugar. Clearly Mr Peach didn't want his clients helping themselves to too much.

Shaking her head, Shirley carefully avoided his eye. 'Mrs Oliver never went to South Africa,' she said quietly. 'She died two and a half years ago.'

'Died?' Mr Peach's voice had become hushed.

'She drowned,' said Shirley.

There was a short pause; then Mr Peach said, 'Oh dear, dear. I'm so sorry. Are you a relative?'

'No,' said Shirley. She went on to explain how she'd come by the cutting. 'When I realized that Peach & Lemon must be you, I made an appointment straight away.' Mrs Webb's prompt reappearance negated the necessity of explaining any further.

She was handed a single envelope. Then Mr Peach got to his feet. 'I shall leave you to peruse the document for a few minutes, Miss Jenkins. If you require any assistance, I should be happy to help.'

Shirley hesitated. 'Can I take it away with me? I should like to be on my own when I open it.'

'I don't see why not,' said Mr Peach after a moment's consideration. 'So far as I remember, I was merely instructed to give the envelope to whoever gave me the number on the document.'

'Then that's what I should like to do,' said Shirley.

As she travelled back to Angmering on the bus, it felt as if the envelope were burning a hole in her pocket. She had managed to stay fairly dry. The worst of the storm was over by the time she came out of Peach & Lemon's offices, and although it rained while she was on the bus, it had eased off again by the time she got to the village. The brief respite had given her a chance to think what to do. She decided that she would open the envelope when she and Janet were together. Whatever Elizabeth had said would affect Janet more than anyone, so she had a right to know.

Everything was put on hold when she got back to the farm. When Shirley saw that Dr Dyer's car was outside the house, she ran indoors, scarcely able to breathe for the panic in her chest. Several ladies sat round the table drinking tea. They turned as she burst through the door.

'What's wrong?' Shirley blurted out. 'Is it my mother?'

'Is what your mother?' said Florrie, standing up from where she'd been bending over a cupboard to put some clean plates away.

Shirley's relief was palpable until a second thought crossed her mind. 'What about Tom? Is he all right?'

She heard some soft laughter, and then Janet said, 'Calm down, Shirley. Everything's fine.'

'I brought the ladies from the WI up for the afternoon to do some fruit-picking,' said Mrs Dyer. She was sitting with her back to Shirley.

'They came for anything going spare for their jams and chutneys,' said Florrie.

'But we've been horribly rained off,' said Marilyn with a chuckle, 'so we've been having tea and cake instead.'

Shirley felt a little foolish. 'When I saw the doctor's car outside, I thought . . .'

'Here,' said Marilyn, getting to her feet. 'Put your

body down there for a minute. You look as if you could do with some reviving yourself.'

As Shirley sat at the table, Mrs Dyer and the other ladies stood up and began to make their apologies. After some cheery goodbyes, they piled back into the doctor's car and set off for the village. While Janet and Marilyn waved goodbye by the door, Florrie gave Shirley a fresh cup of tea and then a hug. 'You mustn't worry about me,' she whispered in her ear. 'I'm fine, really.'

'I know it was daft,' said Shirley, 'but you've been through so much and I panicked.'

Florrie kissed her forehead. 'I have to go myself,' she said. 'I'm only here because Granny Roberts wasn't feeling too good. She was supposed to be looking after Lucy.'

'Oh?' said Shirley.

'A bit of a cold, that's all,' said her mother, putting on her raincoat and wellingtons. 'I'd better go. If that cloud is anything to go by, we're going to have another downpour before long.'

'I came on my bike,' said Marilyn, coming back inside. 'If you hang on a minute while I get my coat on, I'll walk with you as far as Granny Roberts's.'

'It's all right,' said Florrie. 'No offence, but I should like to be alone for a bit.'

'Well,' said Marilyn cautiously, 'if you're sure.'

'I am,' Florrie said firmly.

As the door closed, Shirley put a restraining hand on

Marilyn's arm. 'Can you stay for a minute? I have something to tell you both.'

Janet put Lucy into her playpen. The little girl protested loudly until her mother gave her some toys. It didn't take Shirley long to bring them both up to speed about the cutting, although she had to backtrack a little to explain everything to Janet.

'I'm sorry I didn't tell you,' she said, 'but I didn't want to worry you.'

When they had both familiarized themselves with the cutting, Shirley laid the envelope on the table. 'I've just come back from the offices of Peach & Lemon.' She raised an eyebrow in Marilyn's direction. 'You were right. They are in Liverpool Gardens.'

Janet looked at the envelope. 'What's that?'

'This is what Mr Peach gave me. This is the envelope Elizabeth left in his care.'

'And he gave it to you on the strength of that cutting?'

'There should have been a letter as well,' Shirley went on, 'which of course I didn't have, but the arrangement between Elizabeth and him wasn't anything legally binding. He apparently kept it as a favour to her.'

'Did you look for a letter?' Marilyn asked.

'When I moved into Elizabeth's room,' Shirley said, 'it was neat and tidy on the surface, but every drawer have been rifled through. I think after she died, Mr Oliver must have gone through them looking for something.'

'Possibly a letter,' said Marilyn.

'And he probably found it,' said Janet.

'I'm not so sure,' said Shirley. 'I was thinking about it on the bus on the way back home. If he'd found it, he would have gone to Peach & Lemon himself. As her grieving husband, he'd have had more of a claim than me.'

Janet pulled the corners of her mouth down. 'You might be right there.'

'I think that's why he didn't want anyone in her room,' Shirley went on.

'In case they found the letter he couldn't,' said Marilyn.

The other girls nodded sagely as they stared at the envelope.

'Aren't you going to open it, then?' said Marilyn.

'I think Janet should do that,' said Shirley.

Janet chewed her bottom lip anxiously, then picked up the envelope. Sliding a clean knife under the seal, she slit it open.

# CHAPTER 32

It was spotting with rain, and the dark clouds in the sky looked ominous. Florrie wasn't feeling so good. As she walked back to Granny Roberts's place, she kept telling herself she'd done her best to stay positive, but the loss of a dear friend like Betty was a bitter blow. It didn't help that she felt in some way responsible for her death. One part of her mind told her that was ridiculous – Betty's death had come about because a megalomaniac warmonger was trying to take over the world – and yet time and again she found herself travelling the 'if only' path. If only she'd decided to sell up a few months ago when she'd first thought about it. If only she'd gone straight back home instead of coming to Sussex. If only Betty had started the well-earned rest she'd planned for the week after. If only she hadn't been in the shop to finish off the packing. If only she'd had half-day closing that day. If only, if only . . . It went round and round her head until she had to reach for an aspirin to take away the headache.

Alone in her bed at night, she cried silently in the darkness as she relived the last time they'd all sat on the pavement outside the shop with a pot of tea. War hadn't been declared then, and she didn't know it but she was on the brink of going to the sanatorium. That was the last time she'd seen Betty, and the thing that stuck in her mind was the moment she'd laughed at that silly joke. What was it, now? Ah yes, the one about a farmer who put up a notice in his field. She sighed and brushed away a tear. Oh, Betty, Betty . . .

It wasn't just Betty's death that had pulled her down into the doldrums. With the shop gone, her dreams of a little place in the country had gone with it. She had a bit put by, but it was only a bit. She couldn't stay with Granny Roberts without paying her way, and if she found a place to rent, her meagre nest egg wouldn't last long. She'd have to go back to work, but what could she do? There were plenty of voluntary jobs available – fire-watching, WVS, Red Cross – but where could she find paid work? And would she be fit enough to do a normal ten-hour day? She was still quite delicate, and although she had experience of shop work, she had no other qualification. And what of Shirley? Tom would stay with her no matter what, but her daughter had dreams of her own. After all she'd given up in the past few months to keep Tom happy, Shirley deserved the chance to do something she really wanted to do, but where was the money coming from? Yes, she'd won a scholarship, but that didn't cover absolutely everything. There was always something unexpected: her bus fares from her lodgings to the college, for example.

The few raindrops had become a steady rainfall. Her

shoulders drooped and she knew she was feeling sorry for herself. No good ever came of self-pity, she knew that too, but just for once she wanted to indulge herself. She was feeling miserable and she didn't want to be sensible. What was the point of putting on a brave face, anyway? Nobody cared about her or her problems. They had enough of their own.

To go through the back door of Granny Roberts's place, she had to pass the kitchen window. As she did, she caught sight of two men in khaki uniform and her heart went into freefall. The army always sent two men when something dreadful had happened. What did they want? Someone must have died. Her chin quivered uncontrollably. Oh, not Len . . . Please not Len too. She stood at the door, her heart pounding with fear and her eyes brimming with unshed tears. If she went inside, they would tell her and she would know the awful truth. If she ran away, she wouldn't have to hear it.

'Ah, there you are,' said Granny Roberts, coming up behind her with an armful of washing she'd just brought in. 'There's someone here to see you.'

Florrie stared at her helplessly and a tall man came out to meet her. 'Hello, Florrie,' he said as she stared at him in disbelief. 'Nice to see you again.'

'Popeye!' she squeaked. He was the last person she'd expected to see. They had met a couple of times in the hospital, once when he'd brought Doreen down for a flying visit and another time near to the end of her stay. Florrie liked him a lot and it was obvious that Doreen was totally smitten. 'What are you doing here?'

'I'm the one with the car, don't you know.' He chuckled. 'You'd be amazed how many trips I do all over the flipping country.' He put his hand on Florrie's shoulder and leaned towards her to peck her cheek. 'I was so sorry to hear about poor old Betty. Doreen was really cut up about it, but I told her straight, "There's one blessing, old girl: she wouldn't have felt a damned thing." Doreen sends her love, by the way.'

She became aware that there was someone else behind him. Popeye stepped to one side and a voice said, 'Hello, my lovely.'

'Len!' Florrie cried. 'Oh, Len . . .'

There were several sheets of paper in the envelope when Janet opened it.

'*If you are reading this*,' Janet read aloud, '*I have either left or I am dead.*'

A chill descended over the room. Marilyn clutched her chest and took in her breath. 'She knew? She knew she might die? But why didn't she say something? Why didn't she get help?'

'Perhaps she thought no one would believe her,' Shirley suggested.

Janet turned back to the page and began to read again. '*All he wants is money*,' she continued. '*It's taken me a long time to work it out, but I think he only married me for my money. I have nothing now. Not so much as a farthing, but I must begin at the beginning.*'

Shirley and Marilyn leaned forward, anxious not to miss a word.

'Gilbert and Stephen are twins. There was always rivalry between them. I was with Stephen before I married Gilbert. He was a bit older than me but a wonderful man and he'd lost a leg in a motor vehicle accident. When he was well again, he bought the farm and we were to marry in the spring. When he died, Gilbert was his next of kin, so the farm automatically went to him. He was attentive and kind, and once I'd come to terms with my grief, we got married, in February 1937. It was never a real marriage, although I did try to make it so. Gilbert wanted us to live separate lives. Once the ring was on my finger, he didn't want to share anything. I couldn't believe he was the same man who had courted me and I grew to hate him. I found a cutting about Stephen's death hidden between the pages of a book. I don't know who put it there, but I'm sure it was meant for me. Gilbert never reads. It made me worry, but I had other things to think about. Money was tight. Even my little trinkets were sold for the farm.'

'What on earth does he do with all the money?' Shirley muttered.

Janet went on reading:

'When he took out the life insurance policies, he said it would give us both peace of mind. If one of us dies after two years, it pays out in full. I would have a lump sum if he died before me, and he if I died. That's what we agreed. I've only just found out that he cancelled his life insurance policy soon after we took it out.

*'Now I am afraid. I have no proof of anything, but I fear he means to do me harm, so I have decided to go with M and R to South Africa. I'm sure he's suspicious. He keeps asking me questions.'*

The three girls stared at each other.

'What is she saying?' asked Marilyn. 'Did she think Mr Oliver was going to murder her?'

'I think she did,' said Shirley. 'Elizabeth was supposed to be collecting holly for Christmas wreaths, but I've been right round that pond and there are no holly trees there at all.'

Marilyn put her head in her hands. 'Oh God, what do we do? Is there enough evidence for them to make an investigation?'

'It's all circumstantial,' said Janet.

'She says in the letter she hasn't got any money,' said Shirley, 'and yet she was going to South Africa with you. Where did she get the money for that?'

'Reuben lent her enough money to travel steerage,' said Marilyn. The two of them gaped. 'And as for the rest, she was sort of working her passage anyway. She'd got a job in the ship's laundry room.'

Shirley nodded. 'Another thing I don't understand – Mr Oliver gets all this money, but he has nothing to show for it. It doesn't make sense.'

Nobody spoke for a couple of seconds, and then Janet said quietly, 'He took out a life insurance policy on me soon after we were married.'

They stared at her in disbelief.

'It pays out five hundred pounds if I die prematurely.'

'Oh God,' Marilyn gasped. 'Janet, you really need to get away from here.'

'She's going,' said Shirley.

Marilyn looked at Janet.

'I've got a job in a children's nursery,' she explained, 'but I'm not saying where it is. It's not that I don't trust you, but Gil has a way of finding things out, and what you don't know you can't tell.'

'So we all agree that he's really dangerous,' Marilyn said darkly.

'Tell him about Lucy when she was little,' Janet said to Shirley as she got to her feet. Shirley told Marilyn what she'd seen on the upstairs landing and Marilyn's eyes grew wide. 'I can't say for sure he was doing her harm,' Shirley admitted, 'but Lucy was very cross and all hot and sweaty. There was a wet mark in the centre of the pillow as well.'

Janet came back to the table with the pile of letters she'd left behind the clock. 'He writes to me from prison, but I never open them.' There were probably ten or twelve letters by now, all with the prison stamp on the outside. Beginning with the first, Janet slid the knife along the edge and pulled the letter free of the envelope. They were all the same: angry, abusive and some quite frankly terrifying. He was clearly obsessed that she was going to take his money and he threatened that they would all suffer dire consequences if she did. In one letter, he sounded a little more conciliatory as he asked her to remember to pay the insurance policies.

'I stopped paying them soon after he went into prison,' said Janet. 'That's when I discovered he'd already cancelled the one on his life. I had no money for food, so I thought why worry about what was going to happen when I die? So I cancelled the other one too.'

'None of these letters is very nice,' Shirley observed, 'but he doesn't actually admit to anything.'

'I still think she shouldn't be around when he gets out of jail,' said Marilyn.

'Absolutely,' said Shirley.

'I don't intend to be,' said Janet firmly.

It was so wonderful to be with Len again. When the rain had stopped, he'd taken Florrie up Selden Lane and away from the houses. They'd walked with their arms around each other, and every now and then, he'd bent his head to kiss her. Eventually, he found a flat area at the base of a huge tree and, taking off his jacket, invited her to sit down.

'How are you feeling?' he said as he leaned against the trunk. She was just about to say, 'Fine,' when he stopped her. 'And I want the truth, mind.'

So she told him that Betty's death had hit her hard, that with the shop gone, she'd lost everything and that she didn't know which way to turn. Len listened without interruption and held her close to him as she wept. When his handkerchief as well as her own was well and truly sodden with her tears, he said quietly, 'And where do I fit into all this, my lovely?'

His question startled her. It wasn't remonstrative or critical, but he had a point. She hadn't given him a thought, apart from wanting to spare him the worry.

'If we are going to be together,' he went on gently, 'I want to be included. You don't need to do this on your own.'

'I'm sorry,' she said, 'and you're right. I should have talked things over with you. It's just that I'm so used to being independent.'

'I understand that, Florrie,' he said softly, 'and let me make it quite clear now – I am not like some husbands. I will never insist that you do what I want all the time. It was your confidence that attracted me to you in the first place, but I should like us to tackle our problems together.'

Florrie relaxed against his chest. What a lovely, lovely man. She could hear the steady thud, thud of his heart beating beneath her ear. 'You're right,' she said, looking up at him. 'I just didn't think—' The rest of her sentence was silenced by his tender kiss, arousing within her the deep, deep love she felt for him.

After a minute or two, they relaxed in each other's arms again. 'I have a bit put by,' he said. 'It won't be enough to buy a house, but it will get us a nice place to rent, and you won't have to go out to work.'

Florrie sat up. 'Oh no, Len, I can't—' she began, but then seeing his raised eyebrows and the teasing smile on his lips, she laughed. 'All right. We'll do it together.'

He stroked her chin with his thumb and she knew what was coming, but before his lips covered hers, he whispered, 'I'm glad that's settled, my lovely.'

# CHAPTER 33

The next few days were very busy. Janet and Shirley counted the days of Mr Oliver's sentence and worked out that he would be released on October 22nd. Janet's new job commenced on October 1st. That gave a decent hand-over period and she would be well away from the farm before her husband turned up.

Florrie and Shirley spent their time looking around for a place to live, and eventually Florrie settled on a two-up, two-down fisherman's cottage in Jefferies Lane in Goring-by-Sea. It was perfect. It needed a bit of work doing to it, but nothing more than a lick of paint, a broken window latch to mend and a few missing tiles on the roof to be replaced. The owner promised to get the repairs done before Florrie signed the rent book.

She was already dreaming of what it might become. The garden was very long, and in her mind's eye Florrie could see the potential. It would take a couple of years to get it established, but she was confident it could become a smallholding. Cabbages, runner beans, peas and carrots would make the bulk of her produce, but she might keep a few chickens and sell the eggs. It wouldn't make her rich, but she could keep the wolf from the door and make a home for Len to come back to once the war was over. He was back with his regiment working for the Pay Corps in Aldershot. It wasn't on the doorstep, but it was certainly closer than Yorkshire, and they were both hopeful that if he had the occasional forty-eight-hour pass, he would have time to get home to see her.

There were glasshouses and open fields all around Goring, and a chance conversation opened up an opportunity for Tom. About half a mile down the road was a blacksmith's forge owned by Sam Haffenden, who was looking for someone to take care of the horses when they came to be shoed. What could be more perfect? The cottage was also within walking distance of the station, and the frequent trains meant that it would be convenient for Shirley to do her training. The family were to move in on the first of the month.

Because Janet was leaving before Gilbert returned, arrangements had to be made for Oliver's Farm. Janet contacted Mr Telford again. Although he was still upset that she was going, and did his best to persuade her to stay, he soon found a temporary tenant farmer who would arrive on September 26th and take over the place as soon as possible.

'I want a cast-iron guarantee that he'll keep Seth and Vince on,' said Janet. 'I want it written into the contract.'

'Fair enough,' said Mr Telford. 'I've seen their work and I'm happy to let them stay.'

'What will happen when Gil gets out?' she asked.

'We'll discuss the situation with Mr Oliver,' said Mr Telford, 'but judging by his past record and his lack of cooperation, I doubt that the government will allow him to stay.'

'He does own the property,' Janet cautioned.

'We are aware of that,' said Mr Telford, 'but with a war on, we have been granted emergency powers, and if necessary, the farm will be requisitioned.'

'I think you should know that he won't take this lying down,' said Janet.

'I know Mr Oliver has volatile nature,' said Mr Telford, 'and for that reason we'll be taking his guns. Please don't worry yourself on our account, Mrs Oliver. You and your team have done a capital job here. I only wish you would reconsider your decision.'

Gilbert Oliver was one of three prisoners being released. He washed and shaved for the last time and walked through unlocked doors into the discharge room. Here, he changed back into his civilian clothes and waited to be signed out. Everything he'd had with him on the first day of his incarceration was tipped out of a box and checked against a list the prison officer had fixed to his clipboard. Gilbert accepted and signed for everything without a word. He desperately wanted to get out of here, but he had enough sense to realize that one defiant move might mean delay. His wallet contained £2 5s. 6d. He'd forgotten why he had so much cash on him when he was brought into prison, but he was glad to have it.

With a bit of luck, he would catch a train straight back to Angmering and be at the farm by early afternoon.

Once he'd reached the safety of the outside world, he turned and gave the prison officer two fingers before heading for the station. He arrived back in Angmering at a quarter past one and made his way through the village on foot.

As he reached the Lamb Inn, Bert Cummings hailed him. Gilbert had never liked the man much, but the offer of a pint to 'wet your whistle and celebrate your homecoming' was too good to resist. Once inside, several villagers greeted him with surprise.

'Thought you was in for six months,' someone said.

'I was.'

'Then by my reckoning, you should have got out next month,' said the landlord with a chuckle. 'What did you do, break out of jail?'

'They take into consideration the time already served,' said Gilbert, reaching for his pint. He took a long gulp and carried the glass to his usual place by the fireside. He didn't notice the rest of the regulars giving each other nervous glances.

'You'll notice a big change when you get back,' said Bert. 'Those women of yours have worked wonders.'

Gilbert kept his eyes on his pint.

'I reckon they made a packet on selling the spuds alone,' another voice piped up.

'They deserved every penny,' said someone else. 'I've never seen women work so bloody hard.'

410

There was a rumble of agreement, but still Gilbert said nothing.

'Course, the man from the Ministry,' Bert went on, 'what's 'is name . . . ?'

'Mr Telford,' said the landlord.

'Mr Telford,' Bert continued. 'He's been advising them and 'e's more than happy. Shame they won't be there to greet you.'

'Who won't be there?' said Gilbert, looking up for the first time.

'They've all gone to Florrie's place to clean it up afore she moves in.'

'Florrie?' said Gilbert, feeling slightly foolish that everybody knew more about his business than he did.

'Young Shirley and Tom's mother,' said Bert.

Gilbert's eyes narrowed slightly. 'They're still here, then?'

'Not for long,' said the landlord. 'Although you'd be daft not to hang on to them. From what I hear, it's that Shirley who's worked wonders. You'd never believe she's only sixteen.'

'Bright girl,' said someone standing by the dartboard.

Gilbert downed the rest of his pint and got to his feet.

'Another?' asked Bert, but Gilbert shook his head and left.

Nobody spoke for several minutes, and then Bert picked up his cap. 'Ungrateful sod,' he said, staring at the door.

'You should have told him about Reuben, Bert,' one of the regulars called.

'Oh bugger,' said Bert. 'I forgot. Well, I ain't chasing after 'im.'

'He'll find out soon enough,' said the other man.

'Happen he already knows,' said the regular.

'He didn't look too happy, did he?' the landlord observed and, glancing up at the clock, he rang the bell and called, 'Time gentlemen, please.'

As he left the Lamb, Gilbert congratulated himself that he'd kept calm. Shoving his hands deep into his pockets, he headed along Water Lane. His thoughts were angry. If he'd had a bit a sense, he'd have got rid of that Shirley right away. The dimwit was useful. He was strong and he'd do as he was told, but his sister – she always did have too much to say for herself. Made a packet, had they? Well, he'd soon remind them that it was *his* farm, *his* produce and *his* money. Good job they were moving on. Good riddance. But they wouldn't be taking anything with them. And as for Mr Telford, he'd enjoy seeing him off. He wouldn't be daft enough to get out the gun again, but it was about time everybody knew the land was his and nobody was going to dictate what he should do with it.

The place seemed deserted when he walked in. He called out, but there was no answer. His first thought was to check his hidden places. He stared up at the mantrap on the wall, now transformed into Hitler's bum with a dartboard in the central position. It didn't amuse him. Instead, he could feel the panic in his mouth. If they'd been mucking about with the trap, had they found the tin?

Snatching the dartboard and the voluminous pants down, he pushed the lever forward and then up. He knew it was difficult to work out how to get the thing down, but once released, the whole contraption was fairly easy to get off the wall. The trick was forward and up when everything about it said to push down and along. The worry was, had they worked it out?

Now that the footplate was out of the way, the wall safe was obvious. He took the key from its hiding place on a bunch of others and unlocked the door. To his immense relief, it was all still there: the money, the deeds to the farm, everything. Next came the dresser. He pulled it from the wall and pressed the spring-loaded catch. The secret drawer flew open, but it was empty. Gilbert let out a cry of rage and thumped his fist down, making the cups rattle. Thieves and robbers, the lot of them. 'That was my money,' he shouted aloud. 'Mine. You had no bloody right.'

He turned and legged it upstairs. When he burst into his bedroom, his rage knew no bounds. *She* had moved her stuff in here! He was faced with *her* cot, *her* clothes, *her* shoes. It even smelled of her. He flung himself around the room emptying drawers and cupboards, piling every-thing and anything into a heap on the floor. Finally, he pushed the bed to one side to lift one of the floorboards. He always kept his piss-pot on it to deter thieves. There was no pot there now. He prised up the board, getting a splinter in his thumb for his trouble. Once it was up, he rummaged around inside the hole. They were still there, his trophies: Stephen's cap, Elizabeth's handbag and Reuben's keys. He should have got rid of them ages ago, but he liked the power it gave him knowing they were there. Alive, they'd all thought he was stupid. They thought he didn't know what they were up to, but he knew all right. They'd thought he was weak, but he was the strong one, not they. Stephen had told him he needed help. He'd even suggested seeing some doctor who dealt with nutcases, and when Gilbert had got angry, he'd seemed surprised. 'Only trying to help,' he'd said.

When his brother had been trampled to death by the cows, it was an accident. He had to admit he'd pushed Stephen, and when he was down, he could see that all the shouting and waving his arms about was spooking the stupid cows even more, but he'd never intended for Stephen to die. That made it an accident, didn't it?

Reuben had been shifty for ages. He'd seen him sniffing around Elizabeth, whispering things in her ear and patting her arm. It didn't take much to work out what was going on. Of course, when he'd confronted the man, he'd denied it, but then he would, wouldn't he? Gilbert had never felt such rage before. After he'd done it, he was disgusted to find that he was salivating and his chest hurt to breathe, but he'd pushed the body all the way into the culvert. The space was so small it had nearly killed him to do it, but he'd managed to get Reuben halfway along at least. He'd kept the keys, first as a trophy, but then later on they served to remind him

414

that he really had done it. Reuben was never found. Nobody even missed the man. Everybody just assumed that he'd moved on to pastures new.

As for Elizabeth, he'd made plans for her, but then he'd caught the stupid bitch walking out with her suitcase. He'd pleaded with her not to leave him, playing the heartbroken husband, but she was having none of it, so they'd rowed and he'd threatened her.

'If anything happens to me,' she'd told him, 'I've left something behind and everyone will know it was you.'

It had taken some doing, but eventually she said she'd stay and he'd promised to be a good husband. The only trouble was, she didn't mean it. A couple of hours later, he'd spotted her racing down the lane towards the pond. He'd caught her easily enough and pulled her into the water. She couldn't swim, he knew that, so once she was out of her depth, it was easy. She'd screamed and flapped about, and he'd panicked when he'd caught sight of some people walking by. They stopped to look, so he'd shouted for help. It had the desired effect. They all thought he was trying to save her. She was still when they dragged her out. His heart was in his mouth when they tried to revive her, but thankfully, it was too late. While they were struggling to bring her back, he just had time to kick her handbag into the bushes and then he'd played the distraught spouse. He was better at it than James flipping Mason. He'd made a pretty good job at the funeral as well. Nice touch that, flinging himself over the coffin and begging them to bury him with her. The only fly in the ointment was the timing. According to the insurance policy, Elizabeth had died three weeks too early for him to make a claim, and suicide (he had to make it look like that to avoid suspicion falling on himself) rendered the policy null and void anyway. He'd been gutted. All the lovely plans he had made for the money had come to nothing.

'If anything happens to me, I've left something behind . . .'

He stared at the handbag again. He'd tipped it out and gone through everything. He'd come back to the house and searched her room high and low. Time and again he told himself she'd been making it up, but there was always that niggling doubt in his mind.

As revenge on the insurance company when they wouldn't pay up, he planned the same demise for Janet. He hadn't worked out how to do it yet – push her under a train, maybe – but he'd do it right this time. This policy would pay out in full if she died after they'd been married for a year, so all he had to do was hold on to her for a few short months just to make it look good. He'd had a go at the brat shortly after she was born, but that nosy Shirley had almost caught him.

Dropping the handbag back in the hole, he headed for Elizabeth's room. One more search, he told himself . . . you never know. As he opened the door, he felt another explosion of anger. She had moved in. Shirley. The minute his back was turned, she'd helped herself to his dead wife's room. Damn, damn, damn. Had she found whatever it was Elizabeth had hidden?

He treated Shirley's things with the same contempt

that he'd shown for Janet's. Everything was tossed on the floor. He even made a sweep of her dressing table with his arm, sending everything crashing and smashing onto the floor. Bloody women. They would not get the better of him. Indeed they would not!

Back downstairs, he carried the mantrap outside and covered it. Returning to the kitchen, he moved a brick at the back of the cooking range. Putting his arm deep inside, he drew out an old army handgun.

# CHAPTER 34

Tom and Vince had spent the day working in the bottom field. The remains of the harvest had been ploughed back into the soil in preparation for spring. Once the stable manure had been worked in, the frosts and the winter weather would do their work. Darby and Joan worked steadily, and for the first time, Tom had done the whole field on his own. Vince was close by, working to clear silted ditches and cutting the occasional deep furrow to draw excess water away at the edge of the field. The hedge had been trimmed as well. They returned to Oliver's Farm tired but content that it was a job well done. Stopping at the barn, Vince unhitched the plough and pushed it inside under cover, while Tom took Darby and Joan on to the stables.

'Give them some oats as a treat, Tom,' Vince called. 'They've worked well today.'

Vince was a tidy worker and always cleaned his tools before leaving them. He was rubbing a rag along a blade when he became aware that he wasn't alone. Whose shadow was that? He thought he heard breathing.

Someone was creeping about the barn. He began to rise to his feet, saying, 'Who's there?'

There was a sudden movement to the left of him and he half turned to see a man with a long piece of wood in his hand. He didn't see the blow coming. He only had time to say, 'What the devil—' before everything went black.

In the stable, Tom had put Darby and Joan in their respective stalls. He measured out the oats like Seth had taught him and gave both animals their treat. He put a blanket over Joan's back while he got the brushes out to groom Darby. Tom loved this time. He would talk softly to the horses with a freedom he found difficult to master with humans. They snorted contentedly and crunched their oats, but then Darby began to look around nervously. Tom talked soothingly, but the horse became more agitated. In her stall, Joan was restless.

When Tom came out of the stall to calm her, he got the shock of his life. 'Mr Oliver!' he cried.

Gilbert was standing in the doorway. 'Yes, that's right,' he said, but his voice was menacing rather than friendly. Darby tugged on his rein, which was loosely wound round the rail in his stall, and snorted.

'We thought you were coming home next month,' said Tom, avoiding Gilbert's eye. Mr Oliver came towards him and Tom backed away. It was only then that he saw the piece of wood in Mr Oliver's hand and panicked. 'I haven't done anything wrong,' he said anxiously. 'I've given them the oats like Vince said, and I was going to rub them down, that's all.'

Mr Oliver kept coming. Tom's foot knocked against a bucket of water and it fell over. 'Now look what you've done, stupid,' said Gilbert.

Terrified, Tom backed up some more and fell over something else right behind him. He heard Mr Oliver laugh as he went over, but then he hit his head on the post that divided the stalls.

As Janet walked into the farmyard, it was eerily quiet. She wondered vaguely if Tom and Vince were still in the fields. If they were, they'd made an awfully long day of it.

She felt dusty, hot and tired but contented. She, Shirley and Florrie had spent the day at Florrie's new home. They'd cleaned it from top to bottom, and then right on time, Len's furniture had arrived from his old place in London. They'd overseen its arrival, and by the time it was all in, Florrie had a nice little place. She'd wanted them to stay for fish and chips, but Janet had been anxious to get back to Lucy. Shirley said she'd prefer to go back as well because she still had packing to do. Florrie had been happy to stay in the cottage on her own, so the two girls had come home together.

As they'd sat on the bus, Janet had said, 'I haven't had a bath in yonks. Let's both have one when we get in. I don't mind going second.'

'What about Tom?' said Shirley.

'We'll get fish and chips from the village for everyone,' said Janet, 'and then we'll send him to the pub with Vince. Oh! I forgot. He's only sixteen.'

Shirley laughed. 'Vince will look after him. He'll love sitting outside with a lemonade and a bag of crisps. And I'll go second in the bath.'

'We'll toss for it,' said Janet.

It sounded like a wonderful idea. By the time they got off the bus, the plan was that Shirley would wait until the chip shop opened, at five-thirty, and bring their supper straight up to the farm, while Janet would go ahead and put some water in the copper to heat up ready for their bath. They'd eat supper, and while Janet put Lucy to bed, Shirley could get the tin bath down and fill it.

After calling in to pick up Lucy from Granny Roberts's place, Janet wheeled the pram towards the farmhouse, but nobody was about. Lucy sat up and her mother tickled her chest, making her giggle. 'Where have they gone?' she said in a sing-song voice, making a game of it. 'Where's Tom? And where's Uncle Vince?'

She pushed the pram inside and picked up her daughter. 'Come on, sweetheart. Let's get you ready for bed.' As she walked into the kitchen, she was suddenly confronted by the mess. Drawers had been tipped out and things moved about. The wall was bare. Something wasn't right and then she realized the mantrap was gone and an open safe on the wall gaped at her. Janet took in her breath. Burglars? They'd been robbed.

Then a voice behind her said, 'Hello, Janet,' and her heart nearly stopped.

\* \* \*

421

There was a small queue outside the fish-and-chip shop, which grew by the minute. It was very popular. Some said they were the best fish and chips for miles around. Shirley was tired and not in the mood for chatting, but in a small village like Angmering, it was inevitable that someone would speak to her. People were interested to know how her mother was getting on and delighted that she was staying in the area, even if it was in a village four and a half miles away. They asked her about her teacher training, although Shirley wasn't sure if she shouldn't put that on hold for a while. The terrible bombing in London hadn't abated, and Hitler's planes had dropped countless bombs for ten consecutive nights already. London wasn't the only city to suffer. Plymouth and Southampton had taken a pounding as well.

She ordered her fish and chips, and waited while Monica coated them with salt and vinegar. The newspaper parcel was warm under her arm and she held it close to her body to try and keep them hot while she hurried home.

'I bet it was quite a surprise seeing Mr Oliver back home,' said Vi Cummings as they passed in the doorway.

'Beg pardon?' said Shirley.

'My Bert said he bought him a pint in the Lamb at lunchtime,' said Vi.

'But he doesn't get out until October,' Shirley blurted out.

'Well, that's what my Bert said,' Vi insisted.

'Next, please,' said Monica, and Vi moved up to the counter.

Shirley hurried on. She felt stunned. Surely Vi had made a mistake. October 22nd, that's what they'd worked out. She counted on her fingers again. Yes, that was right, October 22nd. She was breathless by the time she turned into Dappers Lane and becoming increasingly worried. What if Mr Oliver was back home? Janet would have an awful shock.

Tom opened his eyes. He felt a bit sick, and his head hurt. It hurt a lot. He reached up and touched his forehead. There was an egg-sized lump right at the front on the left. He could feel the panic rising. He was hurt. What was he going to do? His eyes were all funny too. He couldn't see properly. Was he going to die? He didn't want to die. Where was he? As he tried to sit up, he heard Darby snort and remembered that he was in the stables. He tried to move his leg, but it was stuck somehow. He looked down and saw that it was encased in something. It looked vaguely familiar, but he couldn't understand what it was. He tried to move his leg and whatever it was clanked. Darby didn't like the noise, but Tom tried desperately to shake the thing off. Darby's eyes grew wild and he made every effort to pull away from the rein that tethered him. He whinnied and snorted, stamping his feet. When his hoof came into contact with the metal, they both panicked, Darby rearing up and Tom screaming at the top of his voice, 'Shirley, I don't like it! Shirley, I'm stuck!'

She heard her brother screaming as she came along the lane. Dear God, what on earth was happening? She'd reached the gate when she saw Mr Oliver come out of the house holding a revolver. Against every instinct she had, Shirley ducked down by the gatepost, her feet in the ditch.

When Mr Oliver went into the stable, she held her breath. What should she do? Was he going to shoot Tom?

'Keep this up,' she heard Mr Oliver yell, 'and I'll put a bullet between your eyes right now, dummy.'

Tom stopped shouting, and a few minutes later, Shirley saw Mr Oliver come out of the stables. He looked around for a second or two and then went back into the house.

Shirley's heart was in her mouth as she ran across the open yard towards the stables. The horses were agitated and she could hear Tom crying. Quietly she hurried beside the wall and slipped inside. He looked up and she put her finger on her lips to warn him not to say anything, but he was too upset.

'Get me out, Shirl,' he boomed. 'I don't like it.'

'Shh, shh,' she cautioned as she came to him.

'I want to get up,' he cried.

She pressed her hand over his mouth. 'Shh, shh, Tom,' she whispered. 'Tom, listen to me. Don't keep shouting. You don't want him to come back, do you?'

Her brother shook his head.

'Then we must be quiet. Understand?' She took her hand away from his mouth.

'But I—' he began again.

'Don't shout,' she said. 'I'll get you out as soon as I can, but I can't do it if you keep shouting.'

She was right beside him with her arm round his shoulder. He put his head on her chest and she was suddenly conscious that she smelled strongly of vinegar. The fish and chips were somewhere by the hedge, where she'd dropped them.

'My head hurts, Shirl,' he whimpered.

'You've got a bit of a bump,' she said, trying to make light of the huge swelling on his forehead, 'but it's going to be all right.'

'It's swollen,' he said.

'When we get indoors, we'll put some butter on it and make it better.'

Now that she was next to him, she could see his predicament. His left leg was encased in the mantrap. She ran her fingers over it; there was no apparent way to get it off, but then of course there wouldn't be. The Victorian poacher would have had to wait until the gamekeeper came with the key to release him. Tom was stuck in this thing until Mr Oliver produced the key.

Her brother had quietened down now. 'He came back, Shirl. Mr Oliver, he came back.'

'I know,' said Shirley, 'and I've got to get help.'

'Don't leave me, Shirl,' said Tom, becoming anxious again. 'Take me with you.'

'I want to, Tom, but I have to go and get the key. I

425

can't get it off without the key. You do understand, don't you?'

Tom nodded. 'You should get it now.'

'Yes,' said Shirley. 'That's just what I thought. It doesn't hurt you, does it? I know you can't move, but nothing's digging in, is it?'

'I don't like it, Shirl.'

'I know, but I want you to stay quiet,' she said. 'All that shouting was upsetting Darby and Joan, wasn't it?'

He nodded miserably. She stood to her feet and looked around. 'Where's Vince?'

Tom shrugged his shoulders.

'I'm going now,' said Shirley, 'but I'll be back as soon as possible.'

Tom snatched at her hand.

'You keep talking to Darby and Joan,' said Shirley. 'You know how to make them calm.'

As if on cue, the horses snorted in their stalls. Shirley stood in the shadow by the stable door. Somehow, she had to alert somebody and get help. The farm was off the beaten track, so there was no alternative but to make a run for it. God only knew what had happened to Vince, and she dreaded to think what Mr Oliver was doing to Janet. The house seemed quiet enough, but the upstairs window was wide open, and someone was throwing her things out. Her nightdress and petticoat were draped over the drainpipe, and a pair of her knickers had caught on a roof tile. Everything else was in a heap on the ground below. Whatever had she done to the man to make him hate her so much?

She could feel her cheeks moistening with silent tears, but she brushed them angrily away. There was no time to dwell on personal feelings. It would take too long to run for help. Somehow or other, she had to get into the barn and grab her bike.

# CHAPTER 35

As soon as Gilbert left the kitchen, Janet looked around
desperately for a means of escape. She was tied to the
arms of the chair, and her legs were tied as well. Lucy
still sat in her pram, her eyes wide open with unshed
tears. Every now and then, her body gave a little shudder. She sucked the middle two fingers of her right hand
while she twiddled her hair with her left. It was something she always did when she was looking for comfort.

'It's all right, darling,' said Janet as the door slammed.
'Mummy's here.'

The little girl's chin quivered and Janet's heart
lurched. Every part of her wanted to hold her daughter,
but first she had to find a way to free herself.

She managed to bump the chair along the flagstone
floor towards the cutlery drawer, but what was the use?
With both arms pinioned, even if she could get hold of
a knife, it wasn't physically possible to manoeuvre it in
such a way as to cut her bonds. When Gilbert returned,
he shouted again and dragged her chair back to its
original position. The noise upset Lucy and she cried
bitterly.

'Shut that kid up,' he snarled as Lucy cried again. He pulled a chair from under the table and sat down. Then turning to Lucy, he shouted, 'Shut the hell up, will you? You're driving me mad.'

It seemed to Janet that her best option was to try and calm him down. 'If you stop yelling, she'll stop crying,' she said.

He turned to her, his eyes blazing.

'She's only little. You're scaring her, that's all,' said Janet, her voice softening.

Gilbert put his head in his hands. 'This is all your fault,' he said. 'None of this would have happened if it hadn't been for you.'

All her fault? How could it be her fault? He'd come charging in here and smashed up everything and now he was trying to blame her. The man was beyond reason, out of control. Indignation stung her, but Janet forced herself not to retaliate. If she and Lucy were to survive this ordeal, she was going to have to think very carefully before she spoke. She might be physically helpless and tied to a chair, but she was still in every sense of the expression fighting for her life.

'What do you want, Gil?' she said quietly. 'Just tell me and I'll give it to you.'

'I want that witch out of here, for a start,' he spat.

'Who? Shirley? You should have said. Well, she's going soon. She's starting her teacher training.'

He scraped the chair back and stood up. 'Then I'll help her pack, shall I?'

He went upstairs, and a couple of seconds later, Janet

saw something white float past the window, then Shirley's cardigan and her shoes. Several other items of clothing followed, including Shirley's petticoat and her underwear. Gilbert reappeared. 'That's got her sorted,' he said triumphantly.

'Would you like a cup of tea, Gil?' said Janet. 'You look all done in. If you untie me, I'll make a fresh pot.' She could tell he was tempted. Don't push it, she told herself. She shrugged. 'It was just a thought.'

Shirley made it to the barn, but as she grabbed the handlebars of her bike, she heard a low moan. For a second, she froze, but when it happened again, she turned slowly. 'Vince? Is that you?'

She heard a rustle and put down the bike. She found him in the big toolbox, where he'd fallen. He seemed dazed, and there was an ugly and bloody wound on the left side of his cheek. She helped him out and somehow or other managed to get him to the straw, where she laid him down. He was shivering, and although his eyes were open, he didn't seem to know what was going on.

'Who did this to you? Was it Mr Oliver?' He didn't seem to comprehend her questions, and besides, moving him had aggravated the wound on his face and made it bleed. She only had her handkerchief to offer to stem the flow of blood. The gash was going to need a lot of stitches to put it right, which made it all the more imperative that she get help.

Once he was stretched out on the straw, she looked

430

around for something to cover him. The only things to hand were some empty sacks. She unfolded a couple and put them over his shaking body. She wondered about fetching him a drink, but the tap was outside the back door and far too risky.

'I'm going to get help, Vince,' she told him. 'Try to rest and I'll be back as soon as I can.'

She mounted the bike, and with her heart pounding like the clappers, Shirley rode out of the barn. She turned her head anxiously towards the house. So far, so good. It all looked quiet. No sign of Mr Oliver, but then someone grabbed the handlebars of the bike and she came to an abrupt halt.

'Oh no, you don't,' he hissed.

Shirley wobbled furiously and fell off, the bike falling on top of her. She didn't need to see who it was. She recognized his voice instantly. She was trying to scramble away as he picked up the bike and tossed it to one side. Mr Oliver grabbed her foot and Shirley screamed. He was dragging her along the ground. The gravel tore at the flesh on her other leg and her elbows as she tried to stand up. She kicked out, but it was hopeless. A shadow appeared in the doorway of the barn and Vince aimed a blow on Mr Oliver's back with a hoe. He dropped her foot and it gave Shirley the chance to get to her feet. She heard a cry of pain behind her and guessed that Vince had paid dearly for his intervention.

Shirley aimed for the bike, but as she mounted it, Mr Oliver grabbed the back wheel. She stumbled off and found herself inside the stable door, with Mr Oliver hard on her heels. Her breath was coming in short, panicky gasps, and the fear made her feel sick. She felt as if her chest would explode, but all she wanted was to get as far away from him as possible.

Tom began calling her name. She could sense the fear in his voice too. Then she fell again. The horses were to her right, agitated and terrified. They whinnied and snorted, spinning their hoofs in the stall and jerking their heads away from the restraining reins. Mr Oliver bent to grab her foot again, but as he did so, Darby leaned on his front legs and kicked out with his back legs. There was a loud crack as the full force of his hoof came into contact with Mr Oliver's head. He spun away with a scream, holding his face.

Shirley recovered herself quickly. 'Tom, it's all right,' she said, glancing over at Mr Oliver writhing in pain on the straw. There was a good chance he wouldn't recover quickly from that blow, but she didn't want to take any chances. 'I'm going to get help and then I'll unlock that thing.'

Mr Oliver hadn't got up, but she could see his face was already grotesquely swollen. Shirley grabbed her bike and rode away like a bat out of hell. Reaching the gate, which way should she turn? There was a telephone box in the centre of the village near the fish-and-chip shop, but there was also one on the corner of Swillage Lane and Long Furlong. All things considered, she decided to go for that one. As she rode past Patching Pond, she suddenly understood why Elizabeth had gone

432

there the day she died. She wasn't collecting holly for Christmas wreaths. She was running for her life. In the same way that she was, Elizabeth was on her way to the phone box for help.

# *E*PILOGUE

## *December 1940*

Shirley and Janet were on their way into the village. They had decided to walk together, although once they reached Angmering, they would go their separate ways.

Janet needed to order some pink paraffin from the hardware shop, and Shirley was on her way into Worthing on the bus to do some last-minute Christmas shopping.

Lucy was all wrapped up and sitting upright in her pram enjoying the ride. It had taken her a while to recover from the ordeal of that day three months ago. For some time afterwards, every time Janet sat in the chair with arms, she would cry and suck her fingers. It took a while to work out why she became upset, and after that her mother made sure she used one of the other chairs. Although Gilbert hadn't physically touched Lucy that day, clearly his aggressive behaviour had made its mark and she remembered her mother's distress.

'She looks lovely in that pixie hat,' Shirley remarked.

'When I started knitting it,' said Janet, 'it looked

enormous, but now that it's made, I can see I'll be lucky if it lasts the winter. You're growing up too fast,' she told her daughter as she tickled her to make her laugh. Lucy chuckled, showing off her two brand-new bottom teeth; then she clapped her hands and said, 'Da-da-da.'

'Such a lot has happened in her first year,' Shirley said sagely.

Janet nodded. 'Not all of it was bad. I'm glad you're still here and that, in the end, I didn't have to leave the farm.'

They fell silent, each lost in her own thoughts. Shirley was remembering the sickening crunch as Darby's hoof made contact with Mr Oliver's face in the stable. She dreaded to think what he had planned for her that day, but there was no doubt that Darby had saved her from God knows what. She had flown like the wind on her bike to get to the telephone box, where she had dialled '999' for the first time in her life. Shirley explained what had happened as quickly as she could, before dashing back. Her first thought had been to find the key and release Tom from that awful contraption, but when she'd burst into the kitchen, she'd found Lucy scream-ing in terror and Janet on the floor, still tied to the chair. She'd been trying to get to her distraught child when the leg of the chair had struck an uneven flagstone and had toppled over. She wasn't so much hurt as cross with herself for making a bad situation a lot worse. It took Shirley a second or two to get Janet upright, and only a few minutes to hack away at the ropes. As soon as

Janet's arms were free, Shirley put Lucy onto her lap while she tackled the ropes on her legs.

The key for the mantrap was next on the list. They took the large bunch from the hook, hoping against hope that it would be one of them. A quick look in the barn found Vince had recovered fairly well after being violently pushed when he'd tried to help Shirley, but the cut on his cheek looked nasty. Janet, still cuddling Lucy, helped him back to the farm, while Shirley headed for the stables. She found Darby standing over Tom, nuzzling him and nibbling at his hair. He was much calmer, although still anxious to be freed. Mr Oliver lay on the straw, moaning with pain.

The police and St John Ambulance wasted no time in getting to the farm, but despite their very best efforts, Gilbert Oliver didn't survive. They got him to hospital within an hour of the call, but by then the swelling on his face was seriously restricting his breathing. He died shortly after being admitted.

Janet was remembering happier times, like when Mr Telford asked her to reconsider her decision to leave the farm. He had pointed out that as Gilbert's wife, she'd inherit everything anyway and that there was no reason to be afraid any more. It had been a complete about-turn, but one she welcomed with open arms.

When they'd found Gilbert's trophies, their worst suspicions had been confirmed. The one mercy was that nobody had to face the ordeal of a court appearance, and the fact that Gilbert had gone to meet his Maker thanks to an animal he hadn't treated very well seemed to be plain justice.

Mr Telford had promised to be on hand should she need advice, but with Shirley staying on, and with Vince and Seth remaining on the farm, Janet felt confident that she would manage to make a go of it.

'Oh, Shirley, I almost forgot,' Janet said suddenly. 'There's a letter for you.' She had tucked it under Lucy's bedding, meaning to give it to Shirley straight away.

Shirley tore the envelope open as they walked. 'It's from Mum,' she said. 'She says she would love to spend Christmas with us.'

'Oh good,' said Janet. 'Sounds like we've got a full house. Is Len coming too?'

'Apparently not,' said Shirley, 'but he's got a bit of leave coming up in January when Auntie Doreen and Popeye get married.'

'An excuse for another party,' Janet grinned. 'Is your mother well?'

'Very,' said Shirley. The cottage in Goring had been just what Florrie needed. She'd made a cosy home and had already found a new lease of life working the grounds. She had chickens and a few ducks, which meant she had plenty of eggs, and she had great plans for planting in the new year. She also sold paper roses to a couple of shops. One was a funeral parlour, where they used them on wreaths, and the other was a florist's, which used them for bouquets and bridal decorations.

One of the nicest things was that Ruth had come to stay with Florrie for a few days. It gave them time to get to know each other, and her mother had enjoyed being with her baby sister. Together, they had laid a few ghosts.

Len had been home a couple of times, and although Florrie hadn't actually received any money yet, apparently the government was going to pay her up to £500 for the loss of her home and business, with the promise that after the war, she could apply for more. Florrie and Len had decided that when the compensation came through, they would make an offer to buy the cottage, an offer that, hopefully, couldn't be refused.

As for Shirley herself, Janet had persuaded her to write down the story of the Birthday Thief and right now it was with a publisher in London. She was quietly confident that one day, despite the shortage of paper, she would hand a copy of the book to Tom. After all, it was telling and retelling it to her brother that had helped her to perfect it.

They reached the village and Shirley crossed the road for the bus stop. She was only just in time. The bus rumbled in almost straight away. Having manoeuvred the pram so that Lucy could see her go, Janet crouched down with her daughter and they waved to Shirley as she left. Janet knew she was so lucky to have such a good friend. Because farming was a reserved occupation, Shirley could stay on as long as she liked. She was still too young to join the WAAF, the Wrens or the ATS, so she was happy to remain. Janet knew that if the war was still going in 1943, which everybody said could never happen, Shirley might join up, but she'd cross that bridge when she came to it. The terrible bombing in London had gone on for fifty-seven consecutive nights, and thousands of people had been killed and many more injured. It had even reached closer to home, when the town hall in Worthing had been bombed, although thankfully with no loss of life. The upshot of it was that the resolve of the British people had been hardened rather than weakened, as Hitler had hoped.

Just as the bus trundled along Station Road and out of sight, a small group of Canadian soldiers came running down the hill. Janet was suddenly transfixed.

'Have we missed it?' one of them called. She recognized him as Clay, the soldier who had taken a shine to Shirley at the dances some months ago. She was glad Shirley wasn't here.

'I'm afraid you have,' said Janet, trying not to stare but aware that her heartbeat was quickening.

'It's Jane, isn't it?' said Clay.

'Janet,' she corrected, barely glancing in his direction.

Clay looked at his watch. 'What time is the next one?'

'In an hour,' said Janet and another soldier in unison. Janet's mouth had gone dry. The other soldier stared hard.

Clay was annoyed. 'An hour!' he complained.

'You forget,' said the newcomer, turning his attention to him, 'they do things differently round here.'

'Let's go to the pub, then,' said one of the others.

'That doesn't open until midday,' said Janet.

'Oh hell,' said Clay. 'This damned country is like living in the Land of Nod.' He turned towards the grocery shop. 'I need some cigarettes.'

Two of his companions followed him. The other man remained, his eyes locked onto Janet's face.

'Hey,' Clay called. 'You coming?'

'In a minute,' said the soldier.

'Then let me introduce you,' said Clay from the other side of the street. 'Peter, this is Janet. Janet, Peter.'

Janet's heart was thumping, and Peter hadn't stopped grinning at her ever since Clay had said her name.

When Clay and his friends went into the shop, he turned to Janet. 'I heard you got married.'

'I'm a widow now.' Her face was flaming.

'I'm sorry.'

'What on earth are you doing here?' she breathed.

'When the war started,' he said, 'it made me question my loyalties. I couldn't turn my back on the old place. I had to come over and help.'

'It must seem strange to be back in England.'

'It is a bit weird,' he agreed, 'but nice.'

'How do you like Canada?'

Peter's face lit up. 'Oh, it's a great place,' he enthused. 'Great country, great opportunities . . .' He faltered. 'But it doesn't feel like home.'

As if on cue, Lucy clapped her hands and Peter smiled down at her. 'Pretty kid. She's got your eyes.'

Janet said nothing. He looked back at Lucy and an odd expression filtered across his face. He turned his head towards her mother. 'She's . . .' he began. 'You don't mean to say she's . . . ?'

'Oh, let me introduce you,' she said, mimicking Clay. 'Peter, this is Lucy. Lucy, this nice man is your daddy.'

441

# ACKNOWLEDGEMENTS

This book is dedicated to the late Barrie Arthur Stainer, a lovely, lovely man. His wit, wisdom and sense of fun are woven throughout this story. We shared the same mother and only found each other in 2013. Our time together as brother and sister was all too short but I want to thank his two sons, Brian and David, and their families, for making me welcome. I also give a special mention to his dear friend Margaret Bengtsson who, together with Barrie, left me with some precious memories of days out, parties and holidays, all seasoned with a lot of laughter.

I should also like to thank my agent Juliet Burton and my editor Caroline Hogg and the team at Pan Macmillan. Without you I'd still be locked in the broom cupboard and wishing . . .

# Blue Moon

## *by* PAM WEAVER

Worthing, 1933: Ruby Bateman works at the prestigious Warnes Hotel on Worthing seafront. She enjoys her job and the camaraderie with the girls at the hotel, but she also loves a day off . . .

On an outing to the Sussex Downs, Ruby meets handsome photographer Jim Searle and instantly falls for him. The only cloud to overshadow her otherwise perfect trip is the dark mood of her father when she returns home. It's the first of many clouds to loom threateningly over the hardworking Bateman family.

When a tragic accident shakes each family member to the very core, Ruby's older brother Percy turns to the Black Shirts – a group who have recently started making trouble in the town – for support. But when unrest escalates to violence, will he see right from wrong?

Ruby dreams of a life outside of the seaside town with Jim, but it falls to her to hold the Batemans together. However, a long-buried family secret may just undo all her hard work.

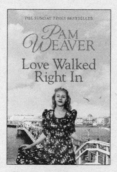

# Love Walked Right In

*by* PAM WEAVER

Worthing, 1937: Ruby and Jim Searle run a guest house in Worthing, but the newly-weds have had a rocky start to their marriage. Their troubles are only set to get worse when Jim starts to unravel a dark secret from his past.

The guest house is in high demand, and Ruby is asked to take in two German schoolboys on a cultural exchange. She agrees, but when they arrive they seem more like grown men and their activities are far from innocent. The Germans' arrival is followed by that of two Jewish refugees, and Ruby does as much as she can to help these young girls whilst they're in her care.

As the country gears up for war, Ruby throws herself into war work as a distraction from her troubles at home. But revelations from Jim's childhood continue to surface, with devastating consequences. And when war is declared, Ruby's life is changed forever . . .

FOR MORE ON

# PAM WEAVER

sign up to receive our

## SAGA NEWSLETTER

Packed with features, competitions, authors'
and readers' letters and news of exclusive events,
it's a must-read for every Pam Weaver fan!

Simply fill in your details below and tick to confirm that you would
like to receive saga-related news and promotions and return to us at
**Pan Macmillan, Saga Newsletter, 20 New Wharf Road, London N1 9RR.**

NAME

ADDRESS

POSTCODE

EMAIL

☐ *I would like to receive saga-related news and promotions (please tick)*

*You can unsubscribe at any time in writing or through our website where you can also
see our privacy policy which explains how we will store and use your data.*